Reviewers have praised Margaret Thomson Davis for the extraordinary realism of her novels set in 19th and 20th century Glasgow.

In *Rag Woman, Rich Woman*, her first novel since *Light and Dark*, she has excelled herself. Inspired by the lives of her own parents, the story follows a tangled web of relationships between people living in the poorest area of Glasgow between the wars. At the centre of it, and dominating the lives of two women, is the mysterious fanatical character of Matthew Drummond, visionary and politician, a working man with unusual charisma.

Margaret Thomson Davis has lived in Glasgow since the age of three, apart from a period of evacuation during the war. She is the author of some two hundred short stories as well as of ten novels.

Also by Margaret Thomson Davis

LIGHT AND DARK
THE PRINCE AND THE TOBACCO LORDS
ROOTS OF BONDAGE
SCORPION IN THE FIRE

and published by Corgi Books

RAG WOMAN, RICH WOMAN

Margaret Thomson Davis

CORGI BOOKS

The poem 'Initiation' by William McIlvanney is reprinted by kind
permisssion of John Farquharson, Ltd. Copyright © 1970 by William
McIlvanney.

RAG WOMAN, RICH WOMAN

A CORGI BOOK   0 552 13321 3
Originally published in Great Britain by
Century Hutchinson Ltd.

PRINTING HISTORY
Century Hutchinson edition published 1987
Corgi edition published 1988

This book is set in 10/11 Paladium

Corgi Books are published by Transworld Publishers Ltd., 61-63
Uxbridge Road, Ealing, London W5 5SA, in Australia by Transworld
Publishers (Australia) Pty. Ltd., 15-23 Helles Avenue, Moorebank,
NSW 2170, and in New Zealand by Transworld Publishers (N.Z.)
Ltd., Cnr. Moselle and Waipareira Avenues, Henderson, Auckland.

Printed and bound in Great Britain by
Cox & Wyman Ltd, Reading

I would like to thank everyone who was kind enough to help me with my research but I feel special mention must be made to the following who gave most generously of their time. My dear friend Jack House, the doyen of Scottish journalism, Lord Taylor of Gryfe, Monty Moss of Moss Bros., railwayman John Brady, and last but not least, Jim Wilson and Willie MacLean who entertained me so often and so well with their reminiscences.

*This book is dedicated to the
loving memory of my father
SAMUEL THOMSON*

First, a confession: I did not know him well
Not well enough to teach you how to know
The quiet persistence of his love, to tell
The padding desperation of his heart,
Having no syllables adequate to cage
The just ferocity of muzzled rage.

He bled. I saw him bleed. And that is all.
Must I confess I had not understood?
His anguish came to me in stunned recall.
Not till the very ebbing of his blood
Had carried custom with it, did I stand
Emptied of action, trying to understand.

What right have I, failing to grasp alive
The spilling measure of a man, to touch him dead?
There should be a teller of his story who could give
Pores to the words he uses. There is none.
For me there's only one thing can be said
By way of reference: I am his son.

(From 'Initiation'
by William McIlvanney.)

CHAPTER ONE

'Don't be ridiculous,' Victoria said as she sauntered through the rain, umbrella held high. 'How could anyone have a baby without being married?'

Her friend Rory's knowledge — at least on the details of the subject — was somewhat vague. Nevertheless, she had absorbed a certainty on general principles. 'I'm telling you, you *can*!'

Victoria's eyes flicked heavenwards. 'Honestly!' she said as if communicating with a higher and more intelligible being than Rory.

Rory felt temper simmering to the surface, 'You can so!'

'You can *not*.'

'You can so!'

'*How* can you?'

Rory hesitated, positive that she was right but angrily at a loss to justify her belief.

'See!' Victoria cried in triumph. 'You don't know!' Despite the triumph her words trailed a thread of annoyance. Such an admittedly stupid and ridiculous claim was nevertheless disturbing, though Rory of course tended to be a disturbing kind of person. They walked in silence for a few minutes.

To the stranger, on that Sunday afternoon in January 1919, Rory McElpy's and Victoria Buchanan's home town of Glasgow might have seemed depressing, even ominous, with its tenement walls black with rain and windows darkly glittering. But to the two girls parading along Springburn Road looking for boyfriends, the city street was cosy with familiarity. To them the rain was a sparkling mirror for their reflections, an excuse to place their feet with extra daintiness thus drawing attention to their new shoes. They were glad, however, when the downpour stopped and they could fold their umbrellas and use them as elegant walking sticks. They were not the only ones of course: Springburn Road was awash with young women surreptitiously eyeing 'the talent' and young men in impudent swaggering groups.

Not that Victoria and Rory did anything to encourage admirers. Indeed, Rory often wondered why Victoria agreed to join in the parade each Sunday. Victoria had a very high opinion of herself and the man who would suit her would have to be special, not one of your common-garden railway workers. These were the men who swarmed about the Springburn streets from the locomotive works or from the railway itself. Springburn was a railway place with — in the short space of half a mile — two company works, two private builders, a station and a main-line cable-worked incline. Many times both Victoria and Rory had admired one of the North British Railways stud of bronze-green locomotives or the blue from St Rollox as they trundled down Springburn Road bound for Finnieston docks and some far-flung railway on the other side of the world. But so far the men who made these giant locomotives and even the engineers who worked them had proved too 'rough and ready' and not 'special' enough for Victoria. At the moment she was holding her dark head high and her brown eyes were withering any young men who had the temerity to whistle or chirp admiration in her direction. Yet she had spent even more time than Rory getting ready for their Sunday parade, brushing her hair and rolling on her best silk stockings. She also enjoyed a good giggle as soon as they were safely past any admirers.

Once they had managed to become serious again, Rory said, 'I wish you wouldn't put them off like that. We'll never get anyone at this rate.'

Victoria rolled her eyes and gave one of her shoulders

a supercilious twitch. 'We want something better than *that*, surely!'

Rory's pride prevented her from continuing to protest in case Victoria detected the urgency of her need. It was bad enough having red hair and freckles, but to lose the respect of someone like Victoria would be absolutely unbearable. There was nothing else for it — despite the craving in her heart, mind and body for almost anything in trousers, her choice of man had to live up to the standards which she and Victoria had so often and so earnestly discussed.

'What about Emma Anderson?' Rory burst out in unexpected glee.

'What about her?'

'You remember? She disappeared for months and then came back all weepy. It was common knowledge that she'd had a baby at her aunty's up North and then had it adopted.'

Victoria brushed this aside. 'Huh, rumours! I never pay any attention to *them*!'

'It wasn't a rumour. That blonde-haired woman who works in the Princes pay-box has a sister up north and her sister—'

'Sadie Telford in the Princes Picture House? She tells more fantastic stories than they do on the screen.'

'But her sister really does live up north.'

'Well, all I can say is — if Emma Anderson did have a baby, she must have been secretly married to a soldier who was killed at Ypres or Flanders or somewhere, and her mother — who was against the marriage in the first place — forced her to give the baby away.'

Rory's face creased up in exasperation. Even if she had been able to prove her case, she knew there was no way that Victoria would concede defeat. Although she admired her friend's strong character and apparently unassailable self-confidence (not to mention her fanciful imagination), it could be infuriating at times.

'If my mother saw me now,' Victoria suddenly announced, 'she'd murder me!'

The idea of Mrs Buchanan murdering anyone made Rory giggle and restored her good humour. Mrs Buchanan was only half the size of her husband and sons, and soft and round like a butterball with a voice to match. Funnily enough, though, she seemed to rule the roost, whereas her own mother often got hoarse with screaming and cursing in her efforts to get things done and nobody paid a blind bit of notice. It was impossible to imagine Mrs Buchanan bawling her head off. Her voice was as quiet and soothing as a prayer and she looked the gentlest of women with her tiny metal rings of spectacles slipping to the edge of her nose and her hands folded softly on her lap. She was small and cuddly and had brown eyes like Victoria's, though the pride in Victoria's eyes gave them a certain coolness which distanced her from everyone.

Mrs Buchanan wore a decent black coat — and not just on Sundays but during the week as well.

Like most women in Springburn, Rory's own mother wore a shawl. Annie McElpy was a tall, angular woman with pendulous breasts and red hair faded to a sandy colour and twisted on top of her head. Indoors she was never seen without her long apron made of sacking tied round her waist. Out of doors, she wrapped her tartan shawl tightly over her head and round her body. Out of doors, too, she was seldom seen without a huge bundle on her back. Helped by Isa, her fourteen-year-old daughter, she collected old clothes or rags from posh areas like Bishopbriggs and then at the weekend sold them at Paddy's Market.

If there happened to be any shoes in the bundle to fit any of the McElpy brood, they had first claim. Although if Annie was particularly hard-up and there was no food in the house, or perhaps the rent was due, the shoes had to be sold like everything else in the bundle. The young ones went barefoot and ragged for most of the time unless charity clad — that meant getting things from the Parish.

Rory had gone barefoot herself in the past and thinking of that was almost as painful as the memory of wearing

14

the Parish clothes. It didn't seem to worry her three younger sisters or the boys — at least, not the twin boys who were only eight. Or the nine- and ten-year-olds, Duncan and Col. They all rejoiced in their clumpy Parish boots and called them 'sliders'; in them, they could slide in the snow and ice to their hearts' content, whereas bare feet spoiled the fun. The older boys — Benny and Joe at eleven and twelve — were, she suspected, more embarrassed and resentful at being dressed for all to see in the ugly flag of charity. They tugged and scratched incessantly at the necks of their jaggy jerseys and bitterly complained about the hacks which the coarse material of the trousers caused at the backs of their knees. They took a fiendish delight in pouncing on Rory when she was outside and tormenting her by their leech-like presence, knowing how their Parish clothes and boots embarrassed her and made her cheeks burn with shame.

Her father made her feel equally ashamed; five-foot nothing in his boots and flat cap, he was known by the legal authorities as 'a recidivist'. He was more commonly known, however, as 'Scrap' McElpy and when he was not getting into fights, he was beating a path between Barlinnie Prison and the room and kitchen flat in Cowlairs Road. He had never done a stroke of work in his life. Or, at least, not in Rory's lifetime. Victoria's father, on the other hand — a tall, handsome man with a stylish moustache that slightly curled up at each end — was respectably employed in Hyde Park Locomotive Works.

However, despite her disadvantages as compared with her friend, Rory had pulled herself up by her bootstrings and now at seventeen was working beside the ladylike Victoria in the Co-op grocers. The Co-op had an excellent reputation; no one in Springburn could beat their steak pies and trifles for weddings, or their boiled ham and tomatoes for funerals. Victoria often boasted that no place in the whole of Glasgow could compete with the Co-op 'cuisine' — to use one of her posh words — although it had to be admitted that neither Rory nor Victoria knew much about any place outside the Springburn district. In fact, Rory still regarded Springburn Cross, from which Cowlairs Road branched off to the left, as the centre of the universe. It was only recently that they had begun the exciting adventure of travelling in the tram-car into the centre of Glasgow to have dancing lessons at McEwan's Dance Studios in Sauchiehall Street. But the city centre was alien territory, with its ornate Victorian buildings and big-windowed shops boasting stiff pink-faced dummies in expensive clothes.

They had heard it said that one big Sauchiehall Street shop called Copland and Lye had a Palm Court Orchestra in their restaurant. They had once hovered in front of Copland and Lye's window and then sidled up to the door, trying to pluck up courage to go in. But the sight of some well-dressed West-endy-looking women flouncing in and out with their smartly angled hats and high fur collars withered away what little courage the girls had managed to clutch around them. Rory had a nightmare thought about suddenly being confronted by a jeering Benny or Joe, scratching at their necks and wiping their noses on the sleeves of their jerseys. Her heart palpitated so wildly at the idea that it was as much as she could do not to take to her heels. Victoria gave the lead, however, and they both managed to walk away with dignity. It was only after they had boarded a tram-car and were safely on their way back to Springburn that they relaxed and enjoyed a giggle at their temerity in having approached such a posh place. They agreed it had been an absolute scream and picked over every move of their brave adventure, reliving the excitement of it all the way back to the Balgray and Victoria's house where they usually had 'high tea'. Victoria's house was not actually on the Balgray, at the top of which lived all the Springburn toffs like ministers and doctors and lawyers. Right at the very top there was even a mansion which looked like a castle; it was called 'The Towers' and in it lived Alexander Forbes-Cunningham, who owned the mine and had shares in the railway and everything else in

16

Springburn as far as they knew. Victoria's tenement house was *almost* on the Balgray, however — just at the bit of Springburn Road which forked off to what was known locally as the low road to the left and the Balgray to the right. Victoria's house was a room and kitchen like Rory's own home in Cowlairs Road, yet it was different in so many ways. For a start, Victoria's house had a scullery as well. It was really special not to have a sink or a coal-bunker in the kitchen. In Victoria's house the range always looked as if it had been newly black-leaded and the edges of the fender polished with steel wool. You could see your face in the fender. Of course, Victoria complained that it was not so nice when you were actually doing the black-leading and polishing. It was a constant source of bitterness to her that she had so many duties, yet her four strapping brothers were not expected to do a thing. Despite this indisputable fact, Rory secretly believed that Victoria was spoiled. Perhaps this was because the Buchanan family had lost three daughters in the cholera outbreak and more recently a son in tragic circumstances a couple of months previously only minutes before the war ended.

Victoria even had a piano and had been having music lessons (paid for by her brothers) for over a year now.

'Sometimes I wonder why we bother,' Rory said now, gazing around as a tram-car clanged along the iron rails which scored a wet-sparkled road. 'It's just the same old crowd!'

The 'same old crowd' were huddling and shuffling together at the draughty corner of Wellfield Street and the hill called 'The Avenue'.

Like Rome, Glasgow was surrounded by hills and Springburn lay on the side of a particularly high one. Indeed, the flagpole in Springburn Park was the highest point in Glasgow. There was no way you could get to the Park without a steep climb and this ruled out all but the fit. Vehicles could, with hair-raising, breath-holding jerks and pauses, struggle up Wellfield Street at Montgomerie Street, but the Balgray still defied any kind of public

17

transport. The electric tram-cars coming from the centre of Glasgow made their whining, grinding journey up the steep gradient of Springburn Road until the tramlines ended at the foot of the Balgray.

There was an immediate bevy of whistles and appreciative chirps as Rory and Victoria passed the Wellfield Street corner on their way to Victoria's 'house' — as every flat or dwelling-place, no matter how small, was called in Glasgow. But the whistles and cat-calls were more cheeky than hopeful. The young men, all on the dole since the end of the war, knew in their hearts that such beauties as Rory McElpy and Victoria Buchanan, both with good jobs in the Co-op and both with big ideas, were not for them. It would be men in brimmed hats and collars and ties they would be looking for, not flat caps and mufflers.

That both girls had enjoyed the attention they received was visible in their pink cheeks and self-conscious dignity as they glided past, but Victoria said, 'What a nerve!'

'I know,' Rory agreed, fighting to stifle the longing she felt. She was as proud as Victoria, but Victoria's pride blossomed from supreme self-confidence whereas hers sprang from confusions. It was a cheeky cover-up, a cocky denial of sins and weaknesses that secretly worried her. If she had been a Catholic, she would never have been out of the confession box.

'Maybe we'll meet somebody at the railway dance this week,' she said, trying to sound nonchalant.

Victoria shrugged. 'It depends if there's anybody special there. The last railway dance was a bit rough.'

Rory made no comment. Victoria's ideas of 'rough' always startled her. Not only that — they also served to remind her never to allow her friend over the door in Cowlairs Road, in case she got to know Rory's father. Her father was just too awful for words. He had let her down from the moment he had drunkenly forgotten she was a girl when registering her birth and called her Rory. There was no telling what he'd do when he was drunk — he'd steal anything for a start. That was another of her night-

18

mares; she could imagine Victoria visiting the house in Cowlairs Road and having her purse stolen, or her coat and hat or anything else she had left lying unattended. Often Rory would wake up trembling and sweating in the night after such terrible visions.

As they approached the part of Springburn Road where Victoria lived, the 'Leerie' was lighting the street lamps with his pole that had a light on the end of it. Each time the pole went up and poked open the glass flap of the lamp, there was a tinkling click and then a pool of grey-green light fell down.

He lit the gas-jets in the tunnel-like entrances or 'closes' to the tenements, thus sending shadows quivering and making dark mysterious caverns of back 'dunnies'.

At the close-mouth, Victoria said, 'I'll see you in the morning, then?' Then she lifted a gloved hand as a farewell gesture before turning and being swallowed into the shadows. Tonight there could be no going into Victoria's house for high tea, because Victoria's Granny Buchanan was on a visit from Edinburgh.

Cowlairs Road was back the way they had just come — at the other end of Springburn — and Rory crossed the road and began retracing her steps. She could imagine the rest of Victoria's evening: no rough-and-tumble of snottery-nosed boys; no curses bawled to and fro; no desperate physical struggles between mother and father. Only peace, quiet and a place to sit down.

Victoria's house could be so quiet that you could hear the tick-tock of the clock. Rory had never heard a clock tick anywhere else and it always mesmerized her — as did the gentle rhythm of Mrs Buchanan's rocking-chair by the fire.

Suddenly she was startled from her reverie by the bump of a hard body against hers.

'I'm terribly sorry, Miss!' Hands gripped her arms. 'Did I hurt you?'

Rory flung a coquettish glance upwards and was immediately more shaken than ever. She had never seen such a handsome man. A bit too pale-faced and thin perhaps, although there was hard strength in his hands and face. But it was his eyes that startled her; in behind their surface anxiety, burned something dark and powerful.

'No, I'm all right.' She made a fuss of brushing herself down. 'It served me right for daydreaming and not looking where I was going.'

Anyone else, she knew, would have come back with, 'Oh? And what were you dreaming about, eh?' Or something even cheekier.

She was disappointed when the man touched his cap and without another word moved away from her. She stood watching him for a few minutes, oblivious of the Sunday strollers, only seeing his tall figure weaving rapidly along. Even after she turned and continued on her way, his eyes still haunted her.

Now, *he* was special, she thought.

CHAPTER TWO

'Granny,' Mrs Buchanan addressed her mother-in-law. 'Do you remember the Fultons?'

Granny Buchanan dabbed some crumbs from the corner of her mouth with a white lace-edged hanky. She was a genteel Edinburgh-reared woman of superior talents; she had, for instance, worked the lace round the hanky herself.

'Were they the ones who went out to Africa as missionaries?'

'Yes, an awful good-living couple. Very religious. They were never blessed with children, but they always used to say that God meant them to be free to go and preach His word to the heathen continent.' Mrs Buchanan peered over her spectacles at Victoria, who had been pouring the tea and not making a very good job of it. 'Be careful, dear, you're splashing it into the saucers.'

Granny Buchanan eyed Victoria more severely. She was a severe looking woman with her hair pulled tightly back and screwed into a bun, and her black clothes were pungent with mothballs. 'Keep your back straight. Haven't I always told you?'

'She's usually as straight as a die,' Mrs Buchanan said. 'What's wrong, dear, aren't you feeling well? You seem to have gone a bit pale.'

Victoria forced herself to push back her shoulders and bring a bright smile to her face. 'No, mother, I'm perfectly all right. I was just dreaming.'

In actual fact, the name Fulton and the connecting word missionary had suddenly enveloped her in the mists of a

21

nightmare. Sipping her tea and absently rolling a nibble of sponge cake around inside her mouth, she struggled to see through the mist and find some logical understanding of the terror that the associated words never failed to trigger off.

She could have been about three or four years of age; she wasn't sure. She wasn't sure about anything in the nightmare. However, she had worked out that it might have happened at the time when her sisters were ill with the cholera, which could have been why her mother sent her to stay with the Fultons. She had had no idea why at the time. Looking back, she could neither see nor feel anything about the details of leaving home or arriving at the Fultons' house. She just saw herself in a gloomy place where everything seemed dark brown or black. The fire was suffocating with dross and feebly smoking. There was a glass case from which stuffed birds glared at her with evil, glittering eyes. But worse, much worse were the eyes of the man.

Her mouth went dry and she had to take a mouthful of tea to wash down the sponge cake. She wanted to know why she was so afraid. Gradually, over the years of her growing-up, she had gained a little more courage. From not associating her terror with anything at all — or with everything — she had forced her mind to dwell on it and try to remember. Crouching fearfully from her thoughts, only peeping apprehensively at them from the corner of her mind's eye, she had nevertheless drawn up the nightmare mist and made harder and harder efforts to see and feel through it.

First, the word 'Fulton' had taken shape and the icy shiver it brought sent her immediately retreating to safety. The next time the word 'missionary' had surfaced and with the shivers came innocent confusion. There was something not right, something which upset her whole childish concept of life. She couldn't understand; she experienced again total vulnerability and helplessness. It was as if something like the ground under one's feet — something on which one had learned to walk and by which one had been made to feel secure — had suddenly disappeared. Was it simply because, separated from her mother and everyone she loved and trusted, she had found herself in a strange place with strangers? She might have thought so, were it not for the man's eyes. They stared at her, his face close up yet indistinguishable except for the eyes . . . down through all the years of her life, freezing her very soul with terror. At seventeen years of age, of course, she tried to be sensible and tell herself, 'All right, you had an unhappy, even frightening experience as a child, but you're a grown-up young woman and you've nothing to be afraid of now.'

However, she could never quite convince herself; she could not even bring herself to question her mother about the Fultons and when and why and for how long she had been sent to them.

'They're home for a visit and to remind people of the constant need for money to further their good works among the poor savages,' Mrs Buchanan was saying.

'They're going back, then?' As she spoke, Granny Buchanan made a gesture towards Victoria and then her tea-cup to convey the message that she wished more tea.

'Oh yes, a more conscientious and Christian couple I've yet to meet,' Mrs Buchanan said. 'It does the heart good to know that the preaching of the word is being done by such good souls. We included them in our prayers at the Women's Guild meeting.'

He was sitting on one of the fender stools, Victoria remembered, and she was standing naked in a zinc bath. The bath was right up against his legs . . . his face was very close to hers.

The woman had left the room; she remembered seeing the back of her disappear through the doorway. She remembered too the instinct that something was wrong, that there was something to fear. The mists gathered again and she could not see or feel any more. Another different picture came to her now — she was crouching back in a dark room in a strange hole-in-the-wall bed.

She was clutching the blankets up to her face, covering her mouth. She was freezing in terror, but still she could not remember why.

'Excuse me.' Victoria rose politely from the table and went through to the scullery. There she splashed her face with cold water, gulped down some of the icy liquid, breathed deeply and determinedly thought of the film that she and Rory had seen recently. It was called 'The Path of Happiness,' a romantic tale of a young woman who had been brought up in the woods and harsh realities of life had been unknown to her . . .

'Bring some more milk through, dear,' Mrs Buchanan called.

'Yes, mother.'

The film had been so romantic and she and Rory had loved it. At times, however, Rory tended to spoil things by being a bit sceptical and, as she put it, 'down to earth'. Of course, the trouble with Rory was that she had no imagination. You had to be artistic to appreciate things of the imagination and Rory was not a bit artistic — not like Victoria, who could already play 'The Rustle of Spring' on the piano.

'Can I give you a tune, Granny?' she asked the older woman now.

'You know my favourites,' Granny Buchanan said.

Victoria went through to the front room, leaving both the kitchen and the room doors open. There wasn't a fire lit in the room, so she knew her Granny and her mother would stay by the fire in the kitchen. They liked the background of her playing and singing, however, and could hear without any problem. Victoria was not shy in using the loud pedal, and she had a well-developed chest which was conducive to a powerful rendering of any song and in any circumstances. She had sung over the chatter and chinkle of tea-cups at the Church Women's Guild and had braved the bedlam of Band of Hope meetings. Nothing abashed her in this area of her life — indeed, her aggressive self-confidence in her talent

24

overpowered and silenced even the most unruly audience.

She launched with gusto into 'The Lord's My Shepherd', then 'Abide With Me' without waiting to be asked for an encore. She could hear both Granny Buchanan and her mother singing along with her in the kitchen. Her mother had a sweet singing voice which floated smoothly and gently in the air, while Granny's had a bit of a quaver in it. Then came another of their favourites, 'The Old Rustic Bridge by the Mill'.

Victoria felt better after performing, and not only because she enjoyed the praise and applause; she took that as her due. It was the sheer enjoyment of the music and the ability to express herself through it that lifted her spirits and transported her on to a higher plane.

She had forgotten all about the missionary Fultons by the time she returned to the kitchen. As she cleared the table and washed the dishes, she sang happily to herself one of her own favourites:

I'm forever blowing bubbles, pretty bubbles in the air.
They fly so high, nearly reach the sky,
Then like my dreams, they fade and die.
Fortune's always hiding, I've looked everywhere;
I'm forever blowing bubbles, pretty bubbles in the
    air . . .

CHAPTER THREE

'I don't care who's nicked your fuckin' kirby-grips,' Annie McElpy bawled in exasperation. 'Just shut up and get out my road. I'm trying to make the tea!'

The black iron kettle was boiling over and hissing water into the fire and now the hunk of bread on the end of the toasting fork which Annie had been holding had burned and was filling the kitchen with an acrid smell.

'If it's not my kirby-grips or my hairpins, it's my stockings or my good blouse!' Rory had never been closer to tears. She was determined to look her very best at the railway dance and could not possibly do so without an ample supply of kirby-grips and hairpins to tame her fiery brush of hair. 'It was bad enough when Jessie and May stole my things, but now Alice and Norma are at it. It's just too much!'

One of the reasons that made it too much was the fact that the twins Alice and Norma, being only thirteen, had nothing worth taking from either need or revenge. The older set of twins — fifteen-year-olds Jessie and Mary — were earning something as skivvies in one of the big houses up the Balgray Hill and could buy 'kirbies' and stockings and blouses worth borrowing. 'Borrowing' was how Rory preferred to put it when she purloined things from her sisters.

Jessie and Mary, however, 'lived in' at the big house and so could keep their belongings in the safety of the attic bedroom they shared. They only joined the fray at Cowlairs Road on their occasional time off.

Fourteen-year-old Isa, the sister in between the two sets

26

of twins, had a bad chest and was always so weak and breathless she couldn't hold down a job. It took her all her time to trail round with Annie and help her with the rags. Then she sat with her at Paddy's Market, looking like a broken doll, waiting for people to buy stuff so that there would be enough money to buy something for the tea. Isa did not have enough strength to sit up straight; she just kept miserably clutching her shawl under her chin like a grey-faced old woman.

Of course, every day both Annie and Isa were bent forward under the weight of their bundles, either in the process of collecting or of later taking some of the rags to the 'steamie' to wash them. If they were clean and pressed, they would fetch a better price.

Unlike Victoria's place, they had no wash-house in their back court — not that it would have been any use if they had. Scrap McElpy would never have gone down at five or six o'clock in the morning to fill the boiler with water and clean out and light the boiler fire. All he was good for, it seemed, was fathering children — especially in pairs. Apart from the two sets of girls and one set of boys (eight-year-olds Geddes and Mungo) there had been twins who had died, making fourteen births in all.

'And you don't care,' Rory accused Annie. 'My hair could fall out for all you care and you're supposed to be my mother.'

'I am your mother, worse luck.' Annie kicked the dog, Henry, out of her way, ignoring his howls and barks. Henry was fat like a haggis, with a rough brown coat and short stumpy legs; he always over-dramatized everything. She spread the charred slice of bread with margarine, cut another slice, stabbed it with the fork and went back to sit with knees splayed wide in front of the fire and hold the bread against the bars. The fire was completely obliterated on top by a large cauldron of soup which was cooking for the next day's dinner. Dinner, according to the skivvy twins, was at night in the big house. In every normal house, however, it was at twelve noon when the hooter went and

27

Springburn was black with hungry men surging from all the works and hurrying home for their soup or sausages or tripe or mince and potatoes. After work, for the McElpy family at least, it was bread and jam or condensed milk, and tea so black and thick the spoon could almost stand in it unaided. Annie kept the tea-pot constantly stewing on the hob; it helped keep her strength up, she said.

'Mothers are supposed to care,' Rory insisted. She often felt that everything was all her mother's fault and this did not exactly endear her to Annie who, as well as being bothered with 'the bile' as she called it, had 'a bit of a chest' and so felt an affinity with the weak and ailing Isa.

'I'll care you in a minute. I'll take my hand off your face!'

'Typical!' Rory sneered and was only saved from a blow about the head by the fact that she was faster and more nimble-footed than her mother. Also Annie tripped over Mungo, who had been crawling along the floor playing trains with an empty Brasso tin. He got the back of her hand instead and his indignant howls of protest were immediately joined by a howling Henry. The racket forced Rory from the kitchen in helpless defeat. It was a miracle she ever managed to get to a dance or anything or all; it was impossible to hear herself think. There was never any room to dress, far less do her hair, even when she could find her blouse or her kirby-grips.

'You're far too young to have your hair up, anyway,' her mother bawled after her. 'And don't tell me Victoria has hers up. I'm sick to death of Victoria!'

Joe, Benny and Col burst in the front door just as Rory was going through the dark shoebox of a lobby with its walls bulging with coats, jackets, shawls and shopping bags.

'Keep out the room,' she warned. 'I'm getting ready.'

They immediately began bouncing and jostling about. 'Rory's going to the railway dance,' they sang, 'to try to catch a railway man.'

She punched them out of her way but only succeeded in increasing their hilarity and making them jink about, preventing her from getting through the room door. She knew it would be fatal to burst into tears.

'Wee shits!' she spat at them. 'Just wait till you want to get ready to go out with a girl!'

The mere idea doubled them up. Girls were cissies, only good for tormenting . . . although it had been rumoured that since Joe had started as a knocker-up on the railway, he had been seen standing in the back close quite pally-looking with Sadie Ferguson, the coalman's daughter.

Rory was saved by her mother shouting, 'Your tea's on the table!'

Always hungry, the boys obeyed the call with riotous cheers and a wild stampede into the kitchen. Their tackety boots thumped and sparked like thunder and lightning on the linoleum floor and gave Rory a headache.

'Rorys, the tea's ready,' Annie called again.

'I'm doing my hair.'

'Did you hear that?' Her mother no doubt was addressing Isa. 'Lady Muck's doing her hair!' The voice was raised again. 'If you don't come this minute, I'll be through there and drag you out by the fuckin' hair!'

Rory hesitated, but knew it was no use. She had been dragged by the hair before and knew only too well what it felt like, so now she trailed through and crushed in at the crowded table. Isa and Annie were having theirs on the fender stools — one on each side of the range, getting a heat — but so small was the kitchen that they were still within touching distance of those sitting at the table.

'Is your chest bad, hen?' Annie enquired after Isa had recovered from a bout of coughing.

Isa nodded. She was skinny like her mother, but more hollow-chested and grey-skinned. Her hair hung in mousy straggles over her face with not a hint of the McElpy red. 'January's always my bad month.'

'Aye,' her mother agreed. 'Bloody snow and ice!'

'And fog.'

29

'Aye. Drink your hot tea, hen. It'll put some strength into you.'

'Is it foggy just now?' Rory queried anxiously. It was not that she was worried about not seeing her way to the dance. The Co-op hall was round in Angus Street, which was just the next one along from Cowlairs Road; she could find her way there blindfolded. It was the ever-pervading filth she worried about. Fog dirtied clothes and skin and blackened nostrils. It was even worse than the dust that seeped out the coal-bunker and crept over everything in the kitchen.

'It's coming down along with the snow,' Isa said, large-eyed and always glad to be the harbinger of doom.

She succeeded in depressing Rory, although shafts of excitement about going to the dance kept lightening her load.

Joe said, with a mouth bulging with Co-op bread, 'Rory was asking me about one of our firemen.'

'I was not!' Rory snapped. 'I only remarked that a man bumped into me and he was wearing railway uniform. I wish I'd never told you now.'

'A big handsome chap, she said, with black hair and eyes that shone out of his head.'

The whole family enjoyed a burst of hilarity.

'I never did.' Rory assumed a shocked expression to cover her blushes. 'You're a rotten wee liar.'

'Honest, Ma!'

'How do you mean?' Her mother paused between slurps of tea. 'Eyes that shone out of his head?'

'Nothing.'

'Don't you nothing me!'

'I just thought he was quite good-looking, that's all.'

'Aye, well. Good looks won't pay the rent and feed the weans.'

Neither do broken-nosed wee bachles like the one you married, Rory wanted to say, but did not dare. Especially at the moment, while her father was spending one of his sojourns in Barlinnie.

It had a been a stupid mistake asking Joe, but she had not been able to resist the temptation. Springburn was like a village and most people knew most people. Every district in Glasgow was like that, she had heard: villages living unto themselves, with their own boundaries and seldom anyone venturing over them. Joe being a knocker-up meant he would know a lot of railwaymen she had reckoned, and rightly so. He had immediately known who she meant.

'I bet that's Matthew Drummond,' he had said. 'A tall fella with a white face and thick black hair. He's a queer bloke.'

'How do you mean?' She had wanted to know, but Joe refused to say until bribed with a silver threepenny-bit.

'A loner, that's what they call him. He never wants knocking-up; he doesn't pal up with anyone. Even his driver says he hardly speaks to him.'

'What family has he?'

'A wee brother, I think. A wee fella younger than our twins — that's the only one anybody I spoke to had seen him with. A right loner, he is.'

Rory thought Matthew Drummond sounded mysterious and exciting and she had handed over another hard-earned threepenny-bit to encourage Joe to find out if the mysterious Matthew Drummond ever went to railway dances. He had discovered that Drummond had attended McEwan's ballroom dancing classes; he must have finished before she and Victoria had started their lessons. Joe also found out he was on early shift this week, so the chances of him attending tonight's dance in the Co-op hall were good. She prayed that he would be there.

She wore her only dress, a navy-blue taffeta with a large pale blue sash low on the waistline. The garment was her pride and joy and she kept it carefully wrapped in an old sheet to protect it from any smells from the pail in the room cupboard. The pail served as a toilet during the night, or when it was too cold to go out to the lavatory on the outside landing, or if someone else was using the lavatory. (This lavatory was shared by two other large families on the same landing.)

After tea, she did the best she could with her hair. Then after successfully pleading that it was Alice's and Norma's turn to do the dishes, she escaped from the crowded kitchen with its suffocating, eye-nipping smell of burned bread (not to mention the onions in the soup). Outside on the landing, she desperately flapped her clothes about in case any of the mingled smells still clung to her.

The stairs were strangely quiet after the noisy daytime bustle. During the day the common entry for the inhabitants of the block of houses, the close and stairs, was a busy thoroughfare for delivery and other traffic. The postman brought letters that everyone got to know about before they reached the person to whom they were addressed. Message boys puffed up the stairs with baskets on their heads. Tinkers came selling clothes-pegs and begging for bread and jam to help feed the pale-faced children they carried in their shawls. Brown-faced shifty-eyed gypsies offered to tell your fortune if you crossed their palms with silver. Milk boys clattered and whistled, with long-handled milk-cans swinging over each arm.

Now, by the puttering grey light of the gas-lamps, the stairs looked comparatively peaceful, although sounds came echoing from behind closed doors — ebbing and flowing, never ceasing. Even very late at night there would be quick passing shadows and echoing footsteps and the sounds of courting couples earnestly whispering in the dark back closes.

Rory went pattering down the stairs and out of the close. It had stopped snowing, but her shoes were squelchy with water before she reached Angus Street. She didn't care as long as her hair was all right.

Victoria was supposed to meet her inside the door, but instead she found Victoria's brother, Willie, who delivered the message that his sister had a sore throat and a bit of a temperature and her mother wouldn't let her come out. Rory felt a rush of sympathy at the outrage. She knew how disappointed and absolutely furious Victoria would be at missing the dance — even more so at perhaps missing a sight of Matthew Drummond. Victoria being her best friend, Rory had of course confided all about him.

At the same time she felt secretly relieved. Victoria was a good-looking girl and there would be enough competition at the dance tonight without her.

She hurried inside, her heart floating light as thistledown, all eager and unsuspecting.

CHAPTER FOUR

Drummond had mixed feelings about going to the dance. Deep down, he wanted to go with the same intensity with which he wanted to own a motor-bike and a gramophone. However, he had responsibilities which made such self-indulgences very difficult if not impossible.

What he earned was needed to feed and clothe the family. There wasn't much he could do about the derelict bothy where they had been forced to live since his father lost his job in the pit. The pathetic attempts his mother had made to turn it into a home before she died did not do much either . . . The inadequate sticks of furniture . . . the too-small pieces of linoleum, the too-small curtains, the oil-lamp that didn't give enough light, the oil-stove that heated the place like a candle. It was hardly surprising that he called in to the pub as often as he could, to warm his gut with a few drinks before having to face the desolation of the place. Somehow it encapsulated the spirit of his mother. She had been such a strange withdrawn woman. He had adored her, but no matter what he had done in an effort to please or impress her — from presenting her with a posy of wild flowers when only six to running away to fight in the war when sixteen — he had never managed to elicit any real warmth from her. She had never been unkind. Nor had she ever been loving. Indeed, often he caught her staring at him as if he were a stranger she didn't like very much. She didn't even seem affectionate towards his father. The private world in which she existed on her own seemed sufficient for her. She had cooked and served and cleaned and responded

34

pleasantly when spoken to, but there was always a high fence around her, an invisible notice which read: 'Do not touch.' Often he had longed to touch her. His admiration for her knew no bounds; she was the quiet, strong, stabilizing centre of his world. His father, although a hard and honest worker and a man of some intelligence, had never had her backbone, her unswerving strength of character. After losing his job his spirit visibly crumbled. Hers never did.

She was capable of love, for she had loved his young brother Jamie. Indeed, the only time he had ever detected the weakness of fear in her eyes was on the night she died. But her fear was not for herself, only about what would happen to Jamie.

'You'll look after him, Matthew, promise me?' She never called him anything but the cool 'Matthew'. As often as not, she never called him anything at all.

'I promise.' He had dared to take her hands in his then; he didn't think she had noticed, for her eyes were distraught with images of Jamie being left without her care and protection.

'For my sake,' she had pleaded.

'I promise,' he said again.

She had taken a deep firm breath, as if making one last effort to retain her dignity and her hold on life. But death claimed her. It had only been days before he had got his first firing turn on one of the North British Railway's engines. Her life might have been easier if she had lived long enough for him to bring home a fireman's pay. He would have made the grade of fireman earlier, had it not been for his under-age service at the front. Sometimes he thanked God for his father's pit accident; it had made his mother tell the authorities about his age and proceedings were started to track him down. The experiences of the trenches still haunted him. However, he knew the reason his mother had had him brought home was not to save him from the horrors of war. His wage packet was needed. He was only too glad to come to the rescue; there was the occasional lapse when he had spent a few shillings at Tucks the bookies, but it had only been in the hope of winning more money to give to her. At least he had not been as bad as his father, who had more than once used the money with which he'd been sent to buy paraffin or food to buy drink for himself instead.

Once when he had come in drunk, Drummond had dragged him outside and punched him unconscious. Later his mother had quietly tended his father's cuts and bruises and then turned to him and said, with what Drummond could only regard as complete disdain bordering on hatred, 'Don't you ever behave like that again.'

'Me? Behave like . . .' He had been speechless; she was beyond him. If he lived to be a hundred, he would never understand her.

Sometimes he would go to the pub to try to blur the memory of his mother. At other times he would sit and pick over every incident of his life with her in cold, clear sobriety. Had his time in the Army had the opposite effect from what he'd intended? But she had been estranged from him long before that. Then what was it he had said or done which had made it impossible for her to feel for him as she had for Jamie? He could think of a thousand reasons . . . And he could think of none.

Now all he could do was try to keep his promise to her and watch over Jamie to the best of his ability.

'He's sleeping.' His father's voice, husky with the accumulation of years of pit dust, scraped through his thoughts. 'Away you go to your dance; Jamie'll be all right.'

'If he wakens up . . .'

'He won't. Anyway, it's time you were getting yourself a click and doing some winchin' instead of worrying about your wee brother.' His father picked up a book, adjusted his spectacles and peered through the inadequate light. 'Away you go and enjoy yourself.'

It was a long trek from the back road down to Spring-burn and the snow was lying thick as a Christmas card.

36

He was wearing his railway boots, his patent dancing pumps stowed safely in the deep pocket of his railway coat. It had been difficult enough to buy a suit for himself; a coat had been out of the question. Such was his determination to keep Jamie out of Parish clothes that he had bought him a whole new outfit for starting school. Real smart, he'd looked, and proud as punch. Somehow, he had had a look of his mother about him that day.

Drummond trudged past the mortuary of Stobhill Hospital and then the perimeter of the hospital, the high railings of which joined those of Springburn Park. Trees hissed in the shadows as snow slithered off bare branches. It looked forbidding, a place seething with ghosts. Only during the day was it welcoming. Jamie loved to fish for tadpoles there, or to play on the swings. Often they played football together. It was dangerous underfoot and several times he almost fell, but there was no avoiding a steep hill on the way down to Springburn Road. The countryside looked foreign and uncharted land under its smooth snowy mantle, fields like newly laundered sheets billowing all around. Further down, the Springburn tenements crushed together like a Dickensian picture and jaundiced spots of gaslight picked out Springburn Road. Then the railway, like a giant skein of wool spread out wider to accommodate the Eastfield shed at one end and the Cowlairs Station and Cowlairs Works at the other. An extra loop of the skein stretched under Springburn Road and emerged at Springburn Station and Hyde Park Works. He could hear the occasional shriek of an engine. Yet how still and quiet it was under the low navy-blue sky! His boots sounded thunderous crunching across the snow. Then, as he came nearer and the ground dipped steeper, he picked up the muffled clang of a tram-car. Already wee Jamie and his father and the old bothy up the mortuary road seemed not just a few miles distant but far away in another world.

As he turned into Angus Street and approached the

37

Co-op halls, he began to feel conspicuous in his railway coat. Later on he didn't feel so bad in his patent shoes and his suit, which although wearing thin was made of good quality material and well-pressed. He was particular about his appearance and he had a good shock of hair which he kept clean and well-brushed. However, his face was too pale and although the exercises that he practised had hardened his body, he could still do with putting on a bit of weight.

In a way he wished he had never come. It was only creating more temptations to grapple with. He had always had to struggle with himself to gain control over his lusts and unhealthy indulgences and all too often he had not succeeded in doing so.

When he was barely sixteen he had visited brothels with some other soldiers on the way up to the front and later on the return journey. It was at that time he had also acquired a liking for alcohol.

At first he had been shifty-eyed when he returned home, fearing that somehow his mother would see what he had done. She had a penetrating stare which seemed to search out the bad things rather than the good. His devotion to her, his desperate efforts to improve himself had all passed unnoticed. Sometimes he felt angry, then anger raged inside him and turned to hatred. He hated the government and David Lloyd George; he hated the war and all the stupid waste of life; he hated the conditions that decent people like his mother were forced to live in. But he never hated her . . . she remained for ever cool and mysterious, untouched and untouchable at the centre of his mind.

The tinny sound of a piano and a fiddle was reverberating from the hall, accompanied by the slide and shuffle of feet. He looked around as soon as he entered and saw a few couples briskly dancing. Some girls lined the opposite wall, sitting on chairs with both feet tidily placed on the floor. All were neat and clean and some had coloured ribbons in their hair. It was the hair which made him notice the girl he had bumped into on the low road the other day — it was thick and fiery red and sported a green ribbon. The ribbon matched her eyes. He became aware that she was smiling across at him — now there was an invitation, he thought, if ever he saw one.

CHAPTER FIVE

Rory could not believe her ears. While Matthew Drummond was leading her expertly in the dance with a walk first, then seven wee trots and a long scooshy glide, he was upbraiding her about the war. And not only in prose but in verse:

> O . . . If you could hear, at every jolt the blood
> Come gargling from the froth-corrupted lungs,
> Obscene as cancer, bitter as the cud of vile,
> Incurable sores on innocent tongues, —
> My friend, you would not tell with such high zest
> To children ardent for some desperate glory,
> The old lie: *Dulce et decorum est pro patria mori.*

She had never heard anything so horrible. 'All I said was,' she managed somewhat breathlessly, 'did you do your bit during the war?'

'I did my bit.' His mouth curled sarcastically round the word. 'In the same stinking rat-infested trenches as Wilfred Owen, the man who wrote that poem. After I came back to work on the railway I had to wear a badge — we all had to — saying "Railway Service", to prevent people like you spitting on us or presenting us with stupid white feathers.'

'I've never done anything like that,' she protested indignantly. It was all so different from what she had experienced before. Usually boys pulled her leg about her red hair or told her what a great dancer she was, or discussed the latest episode of the dramatic serial showing in the Princes.

40

'The philosophy behind your remark is the same and it's expressed in the same kind of cliché'd jingoism.'

'I was just trying to make conversation. It was a joke.'

'Oh, yes,' he agreed with much bitterness. 'The war was a joke all right. An obscene joke. Working men duped into fighting and killing another!'

She was beginning to feel harassed. 'I just don't understand you.'

'Do you go to church?' The dance finished and handsome though he undoubtedly was, with his thick hair and the wild flame in his eyes, she almost wished he would go away and leave her alone.

'Yes.'

'The last time I went to church was while the war was still on. The keynote of the minister's address was, "*Morituri te salutant*".'

She screwed up her face in exasperation, 'I wish you'd talk plain English!'

'Those who are about to die salute you.'

'Oh yes?'

The piano was tinkling out 'Rock-a-by your baby with a Dixie melody' and the fiddler was cheerily scraping an accompaniment.

'May I have this dance?' he enquired with such charming politeness that she had acquiesced and was swinging into his arms before she realized what was happening. She had a sudden, almost uncontrollable urge to giggle.

'The minister spoke of the trumpet call of duty,' he continued, 'And how men died content. They died content!' His voice raised incredulously. 'I hope he dies in agony and burns in hellfire!'

'The minister?' she gasped.

'Yes, the minister!'

She was so shocked that she became confused over the timing of the dance steps. Her feet stumbled and fumbled. 'Oops! Sorry.'

The firm pressure of his hand on her back guided her back to coordination without comment. Eventually she felt

41

she had to say something to dissociate herself from the wicked way he had talked about a man of God.

'The minister would just feel he was speaking in a good cause.'

'Oh, indeed. *Indeed*.' The bitter sarcasm returned. 'The church has always made sure it acted in a good cause. Politicians also make sure that they have one when they are about to wage their wars.'

'Well, if they do act in a good cause — then I don't see why you're so angry with them.'

'It's only their *professed* motives that are credible and these are the motives that ordinary people fight for. They fight to save their countries and to protect their homes. They fight not knowing that war is a device by which they are duped into furthering the schemes of scoundrels.'

'The government, you mean?' He really was unbelievable.

'The governing classes, yes.'

She was glad when the dance ended; before he could corner her into yet another, she escaped with the excuse that she had to go to the 'Ladies' to powder her nose.

There were quite a few girls flapping puffs at the mirror and a sickly-sweet smell of Carnation powder thickened the air.

The girl next to her giggled and gave her a nudge. 'Terrible, isn't he?'

'Matthew Drummond?'

'Who else? It's such a waste, isn't it? He looks so marvellous but my God, what a bore! He's so serious I think his face would crack if he smiled.'

'Surely he can't talk like that all the time?'

'Listen — I've gone out with him and all I got was politics, politics, politics. I stood him up the second time and served him right. He's always getting stood up. I know at least two girls who did the same thing. But does he twig? Not a bit. When he doesn't talk serious, he just doesn't talk. It's as if he didn't know how to.'

Maybe he doesn't, Rory thought, and suddenly she felt sorry for him. The chatter in the room receded and her reflection faded. Matthew Drummond's pale intense face gazed from the mirror. It was then it occurred to her that he looked a very lonely and unhappy man.

When she returned to the hall he was standing against the opposite wall slightly apart from the other men. The others were guffawing and talking to one another in the normal swaggering noisy kind of way young men had. Matthew Drummond looked as if a painful suit of armour encased him. Immediately he caught sight of her he began moving stiffly in her direction. She had not the heart to turn him down, especially when his manners were so impeccably polite, although she found even them somewhat strange and embarrassing. One thing she did appreciate, however — he was a very good dancer.

'I'm sorry if I upset you,' he said.

'Upset me?'

'With my criticism of the establishment.'

She thought he meant the Co-op hall and was trying to remember what he had said about it when he continued. 'But it is very dangerous just to accept authoritarian views without question. You thought, didn't you, that so-called responsible, educated civilized people . . .'

'Oh, the government,' she said, remembering.

The pianist and fiddler were putting their heart and soul into, 'I'll be your sweetheart, if you will be mine'. Everyone was singing . . . except them.

'Do you know,' he said, 'the chief differences between civilized governments and savages?'

Rory longed to sing along with everyone else. She sighed and shook her head.

'The civilized government feels the necessity to invent moral justifications for the gratification of greed or aggression, whereas the savage indulges in these things without hypocrisy.'

She wondered what Victoria would have made of all this and it was then she felt a little warning signal. Victoria might have been impressed. Victoria had always said she could only respect and have anything to do with a man

43

who was cleverer than herself; she also wanted somebody 'special' somebody 'different'. Matthew Drummond was certainly different and suddenly Rory felt possessive. Victoria had everything; a respectable home, sleek black hair, a piano. She wasn't going to have Matthew Drummond! He was hers if she played her cards right and that, her female instincts told her, was easy.

Gazing up into the dark flashing eyes as seriously as she could, she said, 'Surely governments go to war to make the world safe for democracy?'

His whole face lit up. 'That's one of their *professed* motives. Another is to preserve the rights of small nations, or uphold the integrity of treaties, or to protect the fatherland, or to defend the virtue of their women. Their *real* motives are composed mostly of fear and pride — fear of the superior force of other nations which is felt equally by those who are the objects of it, and pride which refuses to make concessions from fear of lowering natural prestige. And as I said, there's the greed.'

Everybody was singing '. . . all my life, I'll be your Valentine . . .'

'Men grow rich during wars, and they know they will. It's not and never has been something unforeseen — nor, I believe, unintended.'

'Fancy!' she said.

Only the idea of what Victoria would think of him kept her going. She was sure Victoria would be fascinated and that certainly made her last out until he took her home.

But never had she been so thankful that she only lived a few yards down the road.

She didn't take him upstairs, of course. The danger of some of her family giving her a showing-up was never far from her mind. They stood in the darkness of the draughty back close while he explained that because man was a moral being it was necessary to appeal to his higher

44

instincts, to inspire his idealism before he would agree to murder for you.

The icy wind was blowing up the legs of her drawers and making her shiver.

'You're getting chilled standing here in the cold. I'm very sorry for being so thoughtless. Allow me to escort you up to your door.'

'No, it's all right,' she said, suddenly feeling sorry for herself to the point of tears. 'I'll just run up myself. Good night.'

He followed her in some agitation, 'May I have the pleasure of seeing you again?'

'Och, I don't know,' she tutted to herself in harassment.

'Please. I've enjoyed your company so much.'

'Oh, all right.'

'We could go for a walk in the park tomorrow?'

'No, on Sundays I see my friend.'

'Next Friday, then? We could go to the Princes. There's a Charlie Chaplin on.'

Charlie Chaplin did the trick; she liked a good laugh. 'All right.'

'I'll call for you.'

'No, I'll meet you at the Princes,' she said hastily and the time was arranged and she was flying up to the second-floor flat more to keep herself warm than from excitement.

All the same, once she was cosily burrowed in the room bed beside Alice and Norma, she did begin to feel excited. But her excitement was at the thought of telling Victoria all about this evening and her next meeting with Matthew Drummond, rather than about the actual meeting itself.

Rory remained awake and thinking long after her twin sisters were open-mouthed with sleep and her four brothers in the other 'hole-in-the-wall' bed were loudly snoring. Isa slept in a truckle-bed that pulled out from underneath her parents's bed in the kitchen; she had always to be near the fire to keep warm.

The snow had turned to sleet now and was wildly scraping at the window. She had a sudden vision of Matthew Drummond's lanky figure hunched in his railway coat trudging the lonely road back to where he said he lived. Somewhere up the hill and round the back road. And she felt sorry for him again . . .

CHAPTER SIX

Mrs Buchanan peeked over her spectacles and smiled when Victoria showed Rory in. As usual, Rory was amazed at the peace of the place. Of course, Victoria's father and four older brothers were out, so that helped. But even when they were all in the atmosphere was jolly and happy, never a ripple of acrimony. The clock tick-tocked in her head like drops of opium.

'Will I light the mantle now?' Victoria asked.

'If you like, dear,' her mother beamed.

The gas-mantle above the range popped, then hissed out quivering light from its fierce, orange centre.

'There!' Victoria replaced the wax taper. 'That's better.'

'Och, I was enjoying the firelight fine,' Mrs Buchanan assured her daughter, then gazed round at Rory. 'You'll be ready for your tea, Rory?'

'I'm starving', Rory agreed enthusiastically and then, catching the hint of sniffiness in Victoria's eyes, added, 'Although of course I know it's not ladylike to say so.'

'Tuts,' Mrs Buchanan soothed. 'If you're hungry there's no shame in saying so when you're asked.'

Rory helped Victoria to fold off the bottle-green plush table-cover with its tasselled fringe while Fluffy, the Persian cat, perched on the arm of Mrs Buchanan's chair and watched Rory with a mixture of disdain and suspicion.

The clock beat its lazy tattoo while she and Victoria smoothed on an embroidered tea-cloth over the scrubbed table. Unable to contain herself any longer, Rory burst out, 'I had a great time at the dance last night.'

47

'You might at least ask me how my throat is!' Victoria was obviously still smarting at the injustice of being kept in.

'Gosh, I'm sorry, I forgot.'

'Oh, thanks very much — and you're supposed to be my best friend.'

'Now, Victoria.' Her mother's quiet voice carried a reprimand. 'I'm sure Rory was very sorry that you couldn't manage to come to the dance.'

'Oh yes, I was,' Rory agreed. 'Honestly, Victoria! And I could see you were all right today. But it was only polite to ask and I just forgot my manners, that was all. You know me!'

'Well . . .' Victoria relented as she sailed like a queen back and forth between the table and sideboard with cutlery, cups, saucers and tea-plates. 'What was it like then?'

Rory's eyes widened with excitement. 'I got a click!'

'You didn't!' Victoria gasped. 'Was there somebody special there?'

'I'm going to the pictures with him on Friday.'

'I hope he's a respectable man.' Mrs Buchanan's voice was edged with anxiety. 'Does your mother know his family? You've got to be so careful with strange men.'

'Mother!' Victoria groaned. 'You're not going to go on again about bad men, are you? Goodness, to hear you talk you'd think they were all monsters. After all, father and the boys are men.'

'There are good men and bad men, Victoria. Aye, and monsters of men!'

Rory's eyes met Victoria's and they had to put their hands over their mouths to suppress their giggles. Mrs Buchanan was always going on about men and the dangers of 'human nature' and how men couldn't help themselves — whatever that meant. She and Victoria thought Mrs Buchanan was an absolute scream when she went on like this.

'Oh, you can smile,' she peered at them over the metal

rims of her glasses. 'You're young and innocent, and that's as it should be. But it's my duty as a mother to warn you and try to protect you.'

This Mrs Buchanan had been successfully doing for some time now, much to the girls' chagrin. One of Victoria's brothers had always been designated to meet them from the dance and see first that Rory was safely home, and then Victoria. As Victoria said, 'We'll never get a boyfriend at this rate.'

Indeed, neither Rory nor Victoria had ever been out alone with a boy. They had been on Sunday School trips with crowds of boys and girls and at Bible Class socials. There had been Saturday night 'bursts', where boys and girls had had a laugh together. The Saturday night bursts were concerts where amateur performers sang, danced, told jokes or played an instrument. Then you got your tea and a bag of buns. The name 'bursts' came from the fact that after you had eaten your buns, you blew up your bag and burst it.

'You don't know about human nature,' Mrs Buchanan said, 'and how men can succumb to it.'

'Mother!' Victoria groaned.

'Take my advice and be very careful, Rory.'

'Oh yes, Mrs Buchanan, I will.' She didn't dare to meet Victoria's eyes. It was not until later when they were both in the scullery washing the dishes that they managed to enjoy a good laugh and the freedom to talk.

'What does he do?' Victoria asked.

'He's a railway fireman.'

'A railwayman?' Victoria sounded disappointed. 'I thought you said he was something special.'

'So he is.'

'But we always talked about collar-and-tie men. Somebody from a shop or an office or even a schoolteacher.' Victoria had nerve enough to aim for a schoolteacher.

'He is special. I bet he's cleverer than any schoolteacher.'

'Don't be ridiculous! How can you be cleverer than a schoolteacher?'

'Honestly, he is. *And* he's handsome. He's even more handsome than Rudolf Valentino.'

'Och, away!'

'Honestly! He's tall and he's got lovely thick black hair and lustrous dark eyes, *and* he's a marvellous dancer.'

'Och, away!'

'Honestly!'

'Fancy, the very night I wasn't there.'

'I wish you had been.'

This was not of course true, because Rory feared that if Victoria had been there with her ebony swathe of hair, her queenly carriage and face blessedly free of freckles, Rory herself would not have stood a chance.

'Tell me all about it. What did you talk about?'

'He quoted poetry to me.'

'Poetry? Gosh, that's really romantic.'

'I know.' Rory flushed with pleasure.

Victoria looked very impressed. She was a great reader and knew everything by Annie S. Swan and Ethel M. Dell. Rory struggled to keep up with her, but she never had any peace to concentrate on books in Cowlairs Road; she was lucky if she got the chance to skim through *Poppy's Paper*. She had a quick and eager intelligence, however, and was grateful for Victoria's willingness to act as a kind of *Readers' Digest* and verbally summarize stories. She had learned a lot from Victoria.

'What poem was it?'

'Oh, don't ask me! I was nearly *swooning* with excitement.'

Victoria let out a squeal of laughter and her mother's voice drifted through like a puff of warm air; 'Mind the dishes, dear.'

Rory could just imagine her half-asleep on the rocking-chair, or calmly knitting a pair of socks.

'Then he asked you out?' Victoria prompted.

'Uh-huh.'

'Well, go on then. What did he say?'

'He's terribly polite. I've never heard anybody so polite.'

50

'*We're* polite.'

'No, not like us.'

'How do you mean?'

Rory hesitated. It was difficult to explain the stilted formality of his behaviour when he was not talking politics. It didn't seem natural; in fact, it was embarrassing.

'Like he's reading out of a book,' she announced triumphantly, half to herself. 'Yes, that's what it was like.'

'Gosh,' Victoria tittered. 'He sounds a bit odd.'

Rory immediately bristled. 'He's tall, dark and handsome and a marvellous dancer. Call that odd if you like!'

'I just wondered. Anyway, I wish I'd been there.'

Rory relaxed again. 'I wish you had, too.'

'Fancy a railwayman being like that. It just goes to show.'

'I know.'

Victoria lowered her voice. 'What did your mother say about you going to the pictures with him?'

Rory dropped her voice to the same conspiratorial tone. 'I didn't tell her.'

'Gosh!'

As if she would care, Rory thought with secret bitterness. Her mother was always glad to get rid of her, or for that matter any of the family. 'You're always under my feet,' she'd accuse. 'Why don't you all get to hell out of here and give me some peace?' All except Isa of course.

'What she doesn't know won't do her any harm!'

'Gosh!' Victoria repeated.

Rory basked in Victoria's admiration. It was not often the shoe was on this foot. 'Anyway, I don't care. I'm seventeen and old enough to do what I like.'

They attended to the dishes in silence after this statement, both knowing it had gone over the score.

At last, Victoria said knowledgeably but kindly, 'Right enough, it is the law in Scotland that you're considered an adult at sixteen. I mean, you can get legally married at that age.'

51

'Can you?' The sudden vision of being married and having a room and kitchen all to herself (and a husband of course) was delightful.

'Oh yes.' Victoria pulled the plug out of the sink and watched the scummy water swirl away. 'I'd love to be married and have babies, wouldn't you?'

'Uh-huh.' Rory was not at all sure about the babies. She had a different vision of babies from Victoria. Victoria talked of cherubs and cooed over angelic creatures cleanly swathed and bonneted and smelling of talcum powder. Her own view of infants had been spoiled by the twins, Geddes and Mungo, who constantly stank of pee or shit and even as infants had snottery noses.

'Would you like to marry Matthew Drummond?'

Rory's face brightened as the idea of opportunity actually being within her grasp. 'I wouldn't mind.'

'Can I be your bridesmaid?'

'Of course. You're my best friend.'

'Gosh! Isn't it exciting!' They clung to each other wide-eyed and squealing.

'Mind the dishes, dear,' Mrs Buchanan repeated patiently.

CHAPTER SEVEN

The fever heat from the stove and the uproar of the bothy card-game filled the hut, but Drummond was oblivious of either. Ostensibly he was reading *The Art of Expression and Principles of Discourse*, but his mind kept wandering to the proposed meeting with Rory McElpy. His stomach tightened at the prospect of her not turning up. He had no idea why he was singularly unsuccessful in normal social contacts, and it deeply concerned him. He had tried everything, but everything had failed to make him the kind of person who mixed freely and was accepted as 'one of the lads'. Although at least he was treated with respect by men — partly, he suspected, because of his study of ju-jitsu and self-defence. And he had also been asked to speak on several occasions at Union meetings and on one occasion had successfully chaired a meeting of the local Labour Party.

Jim Faulkner, the branch secretary, had said, 'You're an exceptionally bright lad, Drummond. You'll go far.'

No, it was not his standing with men that worried him. It was his standing with girls. He wanted to go out with decent girls and he had disciplined himself to behave impeccably towards them. Yet no matter how courteous and attentive and generous he was — he always got balcony seats at the pictures — he never seemed to make a favourable and certainly not a lasting impression on them. He had to keep resorting to furtive journeys to the town and silent couplings with prostitutes, which afterwards left him not only ashamed but more lonely and unfulfilled than ever. Sometimes he wondered if respectable girls had some sort of instinct or intuition which told them he had been with prostitutes, and if that was why they avoided him like the plague.

Drummond wanted a normal life. He wanted to direct his sexual fevers into the safe and respectable channel of marriage. He wanted to have a decent house in which he could give Jamie a proper upbringing and his father some comfort in his old age. That is, if his father lasted into old age; he was forty-five now and looked sixty-five. The accident had caused him to have such headaches that he often found it impossible to read and this shattered him more than the pain itself. His father had always set great store by reading.

It was easy to get angry with him when he resorted to the opiate of drink, but at the same time he felt even more angry on his father's behalf. It was the mine-owner he really hated and longed to thrash, not his father. His father had worked hard and conscientiously despite pain, even previous to the accident — pain of coughing caused by the pit dust, pain of rheumatism as a result of labouring so much in filthy water-logged conditions underground. Yet he had received no compensation, no consideration, no respect. He had been thrown aside like some useless stick. Drummond wished the mine-owner could die the same slow death as his father and then afterwards live in a hell fired by his own coal. Some of his most vivid memories of his childhood had been helping his mother to fill the zinc bath with hot water once she had set it ready in front of the fire. Then when Father came home, it was all steaming full and ready for him. It always amazed him as a young lad to see how black his father was all over; the whites of his eyes were all that relieved the total darkness and only vigorous scrubbing finally removed the quasi-subcutaneous grime. But he and his mother had always to be most careful with Father's back, which sometimes was too tender even to touch. So much of his day had been spent bending and crawling, with his back constantly hitting the planks placed crossways at the top of the low tunnel. Sometimes his whole spine was a string of scabs. The scabs formed by these collisions kept getting knocked off by more blows, and he and his mother had to try to dab father's back clean and put some iodine on the wounds.

He would be for ever grateful to his father for not allowing him to go down the pit. 'The lad's not going down the pit,' he had once overheard him shout angrily at his mother. 'I won't have it. I won't have you visiting the "sins of the father" on him. He's done nothing to deserve it!'

Even now he did not understand exactly what his father had meant. As for his mother's true attitude, he didn't dare think about that. He only thanked his lucky stars (as well as his father) that instead of grovelling down in the bowels of the earth, he had ended up on the railway. He loved his job; it was so full of variety, movement, interest and excitement. What a thrill it was to feel the power of a giant steam engine, to pit one's wits and strength against it and to master it. That's what the fireman and the driver did between them; yet they never lost their respect, admiration and affection for their engine. Each engine seemed to have a life and personality of its own. He revelled in his work and felt genuinely sorry for his father and men like him who had to live their lives trapped under the earth. They deserved far more wages and consideration than any other workers, he thought.

There was no comparison, in his opinion, between crawling along on one's belly in the cold and damp underground and standing on the footplate of an engine as it flew through the countryside, a joyous song in every sound it made.

Suddenly a shout from the gaffer jerked him out of his reverie. 'Drummond, a firing turn for you!'

He responded with alacrity. The more firing turns he could get, the better. It took hundreds of firing turns to reach 'passed fireman' status and he was nearly there. Once he was a 'passed' fireman, he could then start to get driver's turns and eventually become a registered driver.

Drummond wondered what driver he would be doing his turn with as he left the brightly-lit chrysalis of the bothy and found himself in the smoky blackness of the yard, a grey shroud of snow covering the ground. With the help of his hand-lamp he made for the lye and the engines the gaffer had instructed him to fire.

The crisp air whisked down his throat like an ice-pick after the suffocating heat of the bothy and made him feel unexpectedly light-headed and happy. His feet made creaking sounds as he walked and his hand-lamp arced across the coarse-grained leather of his boots and the legs of his dungarees and wobbled a yellow circle in front of him.

The yard seemed quieter, yet each clank or creak or whistle cut through the air, clean and sharp as a knife. Reaching the engine, he held his lamp high and admired the mirror-polish of the dark green giant. Once up on the footplate, he savoured the warm gleam of copper pipes and brass fittings and the wonderful aroma of steam, hot oil and the quiet gentle noise of a large steam-engine at rest. What better job could there be in the world than this?

The driver turned out to be Pincher McCabe, a tall man with a gloomy loose-skinned face like a bloodhound. He had a habit of speaking even less than Drummond himself, but was well-known for his peculiar sign-language on the footplate.

Waving his right forefinger in the air meant, 'Turn the injector if there's enough water in the boiler.' A thumb and finger held up in the air a few inches apart meant, 'Open the door a bit wider,' and this sign was given when he decided the engine was emitting too much smoke after a fire-up.

He was a master of the silent look of reproof — but even without a look, when Pincher McCabe stood up and brushed his overalls down with flicks of a cloth, you knew that there was too much dust blowing about and it was time you dampened down the footplate.

Unlike the other firemen, Drummond didn't mind having McCabe for a 'mate'. In fact, he felt much more at ease with him than any of the other more affable and chatty drivers. With Pincher he could get on with his own work and enjoy it without having to worry about making conversation.

Soon he had the fire made up and the coal broken up and stacked on the tender. Then, before doing anything further, he looked over the side to see where Pincher was. He was up front oiling the front couplings and Matthew shouted to him to let him know that he was going to wash off the boiler front and footplate and check both injectors. He had learned at the Mutual Improvement Classes that a good fireman always checks where his mate is before using injectors in order to avoid blasting him in the face with boiling water.

At last they were ready to move. The signal came off with a bang. The fire was burning through merrily. He had a glass full of water in the boiler, and pressure was just on the point of blowing off at the safety valve at 200 lbs.

Shovel in coal, swing round, coal into fire-box, swing round . . . He began to sweat, but he was happy pushing himself to his limits, his face and neck bright orange in the glow and fast becoming soot-streaked. His wrists and shoulders felt as if they were being wrenched apart, but he gritted his teeth and ignored the strain and even when he wasn't shovelling coal kept himself conscientiously alert — watching for signals, sweeping the cab floor and watching the coal.

After operating the injector, he always looked down at the overflow pipe below the cab to ensure water was not running to waste. In the darkness, the water shimmered in the glow from the ashpan.

He felt so light-headed and happy that he forgot all about the red-haired Miss McElpy. Here he was away in a world of his own, a world where women didn't matter and had no place. A world where he was stretching himself, challenging himself as he lashed the coal into the white-hot fire and the tender bounced in disunity with the engine and the engine itself was like a ball of fire hurtling through the darkness.

It was only after his shift was over and he was faced with returning to the comfortless hovel that made a mockery of the word 'home' that his heart sank. He decided to go into the pub and have a few drinks; he needed something to wash the dirt from his throat and alleviate the parched feeling caused by the heat from the firebox. On his way he saw the pathetic remnants of a young man who looked about the same age as himself, propped on a piece of cardboard in a shop doorway. The man had no legs. There but for the grace of God . . . he thought with a shudder, dropping a coin in the man's cap and sharing the other's shame that it should be so. The number of disabled ex-servicemen begging in the street never failed to shock him. They were like flotsam washed against walls and into gutters, where they sat or stood with cap in hand or with trays slung in front of them displaying boxes of matches or shoelaces for sale. Only the other day he had seen a line of men trickle along the gutter carrying sandwich boards. They were all dressed in what had once been respectable suits and trilby hats, and all were suffering one disability or another. The man leading the line had lost an eye; his board proclaimed:

> Association of Ex-Civil Servants
> A Land Fit for Heroes?
> No Work
> No Money
> No Food
> Is this a fitting War Memorial?

The pub was a warm brown cave of a place and Drummond plunged gratefully into it. Several railwaymen gave him a nod of recognition without interrupting the flow of their conversation.

Fireman Davie Curran was saying, 'But how could we have stopped it, man?'

Big Jock McPherson from Cowlairs shed replied, 'A general strike, of course.'

'What?' Curran made an incredulous face.

'I'm telling you, Davie — if the whole force of the Labour movement and the trade unions and the Co-operative movement had got together to organize the opposition of the working classes, the carnage would never have happened.'

'The trouble with that idea,' Driver Willy Reed ventured, 'is getting international action on similar lines.'

'People in different countries can be mobilized for war. Why can't they be mobilized for peace?'

'I'll tell you why, McPherson,' Curran said. 'A man obeys the call to fight because of patriotism. Every man has a love of his own country and feels a need to defend it against aggression.'

'There's no such thing as defensive or aggressive wars under capitalism. Wars are caused by rivalries of capitalist power struggling for the domination of world market.'

'You try telling that,' — Curran stabbed the stem of his pipe in McPherson's direction to give emphasis to his words — 'to a crowd of Huns pillaging your house and raping your wife!'

Anger fired the big driver's already florid cheeks. 'For Christ's sake, Davie, can you not at least keep the argument above the level of fear propaganda? I'm talking about historical facts. Capitalist wars are fought for profit, for new empires, for places where they can obtain cheaper raw material and labour supplies.'

'I'm talking historical facts as well. Men fight for freedom. They fight in order to make a better world for themselves and their families.'

'Oh, aye. Like we have now! The whole country's seething with unrest and disabled men. And no wonder. The cost of living's still rising. There's shortages of food and housing except at profiteers' prices. Oh aye, I know what our men fought for.'

A man who was crushing past the group carrying refills of beer to friends across the room leaned towards McPherson. 'I hope you got a few white feathers.'

Curran immediately spoke up in McPherson's defence, despite the fact that he had been angry with him. 'Mind your own bloody business!'

'Oh?' the man sneered. 'You another one, then? Afraid to fight, were you? I've seen conchies like you shot!'

'I'll fight all right,' McPherson shouted across at the man, who was now moving away holding the tray of beer protectively high in front of him. 'I'll fight to defeat my real enemy and my enemies aren't abroad. They're right here in this country, growing fat on the profits from the munitions factories and the mines and the mills and the banks and the railroads they own.'

Drummond felt like shaking McPherson by the hand. It never failed to fill him with bitterness when he saw luxurious mansions like that of Forbes-Cunningham, the man who owned the pit down which his father had slaved. The Forbes-Cunningham family had even got their pound of flesh from his mother; her sweated labour as maid-of-all-work in that castle of a place before she had married his father had earned her a mere pittance.

Now his mother was in her grave, worn out before her time by the hard life she had had, and his father was liable to suffer the same fate. Yet Forbes-Cunningham and his family prospered and grew fat and were regular church-goers and so-called pillars of the community. Smug greedy bastards, he thought. They would do nothing for the working classes except suck the life's blood from them.

The only people who would look after working men like his father or the soldiers coming back desperate for jobs, were other working men. This was the fight McPherson had spoken about, and the fight was on.

Men were being driven to exasperation by wage cuts as well as unemployment and the unions had decided to call for a strike. There had been a meeting on the eleventh and the claims decided on were simply no reduction in wages, and a forty-hour week. This was a gesture of self-sacrifice on the part of the workers — many of whom, like himself, were working overtime — to help the workless.

At the meeting the strike was scheduled for 27 January and Emmanuel Shinwell, chairman of the Glasgow Trades Council, stressed, 'This movement for a forty-hour week is not revolutionary in character. Nor is it inspired by the legitimate desire for more leisure. It is attributable solely and entirely to the fear of possible unemployment in the near future and the desire of workers generally to make room for the demobilized servicemen.'

Drummond felt warmed and energized now, and not only by the drink but by the positive realization that something was going to be done to help people like the begging soldier outside.

Leaving the pub, he turned up his collar and plunged his hands deep into his pockets as he set off on his lonely march up the hill.

CHAPTER EIGHT

'Hold still, you dirty wee devils!' Annie McElpy cracked the twins' heads together to give emphasis to her words. They were getting their ginger hair tooth-combed for nits and both were kneeling on the floor with heads bent over the piece of brown paper spread on their mother's lap. Every now and again Annie would examine the paper, let out a shout of 'There's one!' and pounce on the unfortunate louse in its scamper to escape.

'Got you!' she would cry in triumph before pinching it to death between finger and nail.

Rory winced, remembering how a few years earlier she had been forced to succumb to the same rough scalp-scraping as Geddes and Mungo were now undergoing — although they endured nothing without lusty protest, which always started Henry the dog barking hysterically. The twins writhed and wriggled and the dog, a born mimic, squeezed its rough-haired body between them and received the same cuff on the ear as they did.

'Wee middens, the lot of you,' Annie said. 'You torment the life out of me, so you do.'

Just then her husband appeared in the kitchen, fresh from a stretch in prison for stealing lead off a church roof.

'My God, as if I hadn't enough live to deal with!' she greeted him, not uncheerily.

'Now Annie, you know you're thrilled to bits at seeing me!'

He could hardly make himself heard for the dog's mad barking of delight. Henry was in the habit of accompanying Scrap to the pub and being treated to several half-pints of Guinness until, like his master, he was barely able to stagger home.

'Aye, all right.' Scrap turned his attention to Henry at last. 'Calm down, will you?' He caught the heavily bouncing animal and gave its neck a rough rub. 'We'll go out for a drink later on, the pair of us, and make up for lost time — don't worry.'

Scrap McElpy had been referred to pityingly as 'a poor scrap' when he was an infant. The name had acquired a different meaning as he grew older and became involved in one scrap after another.

The children laughed with excitement . . . all, that is, except Rory.

'Hello, Da,' was as much as she could manage, and with barely a glance at the undersized figure in the big flat cap and threadbare, baggy trousers.

With a great flourish, Scrap produced a bag of sweeties. He did everything with a flourish as if he were ten feet tall instead of only five. A howl of delight went up from the six boys, Alice and Norma. Even Isa let out a nasal sound which could have expressed pain but was meant to show pleasure. And of course Henry bounced about like a ball and nearly barked himself hoarse. Scrap went swaggering around not just doling out sweets, but making the children guess which hand he had them in before forcing them to struggle in hilarious exasperation to prise the sweeties from him.

The kitchen was absolute bedlam and Annie kept getting the brown paper knocked off her knee. 'This fuckin' linoleum will be moving now,' she accused Scrap. 'The only time I get any peace is when you're behind bars!'

'I knew you missed me, hen.' Scrap tried to give her a cuddle, but Annie was much bigger than him and flicked him aside with no more effort than was needed to rid herself of Geddes or Mungo.

'Wee shit!' she said, but without malice.

'Ma, I'm away for my bath,' Rory told her.

'All right, hen.'

Friday night was bath night for everybody but the younger ones, who had theirs in the zinc bath in front of the fire. Her mother and Isa 'had a wee wipe down' afterwards, also in front of the fire. Rory, however, went to the public baths. Tonight it was particularly important that she should be perfection from skin to coat, because tonight she was going out on her own with a boy.

Matthew Drummond's boring conversation about politics had completely faded from her mind and she was left only with the impression of an incredibly handsome and clever young man. Really 'superior', as Victoria would say.

She flew along Springburn Road en route to the baths, silently praying that she would not bump into Drummond while she was still dirty and wearing her shabby working blouse. In a brown paper parcel under her arm she clutched her clean underwear, a pair of white lawn combinations with broad threaded ribbons and broderie anglaise decorating the borders, a petticoat trimmed with a flounce that hung just above ankle level and a pair of ivory silk stockings. She would have to wear her black working skirt, but in the parcel was a smart shirt of white jap. Back at home was her pride and joy, a black velvet sailor hat with a soft crown and trimmed with a fancy jet pin. If she tucked and pinned her hair up firmly inside the hat, that hid most of its red monstrosity. She hated her ginger frizz almost as much as she hated her freckles.

Victoria always said, 'I don't know why you make such a fuss about your freckles. You've only got a sprinkling and I think they suit you.'

It was easy enough for Victoria to talk, with her smooth raven hair and creamy skin. However, she generously admitted, 'You have much neater features than me, Rory. I have too firm a jawline for a girl and my nose is too big.'

'It is not,' Rory hastened to comfort her. 'You have classical features, really classical!'

Neither of them was sure what that meant, but both felt it to be something 'superior'.

Rory now handed over her money to the girl at the pay-box in the Corporation baths and got her ticket. It always surprised her how cold the place was, seeing it contained so much piping hot water. The corridor was dark, with a deep throaty echo, and it smelled as if she was walking under the earth. She sat for a time on the wooden bench waiting her turn, her feet getting steadily colder. Eventually the woman attendant, wearing wellington boots, led her slowly to another corridor with doors behind which splashing sounds could be heard. Water ran along a shallow channel in the corridor's stone floor, but the whole floor — indeed the whole place — was damp. Dampness dripped from the ceiling and glistened on the walls.

The woman stopped at an open door. 'In here,' she said and they both entered the vacant cubicle which held a giant bath with a greasy tidemark above the waterline and a lump of cracked white soap like a piece of ancient cheese sitting on its ledge. In front of the bath lay a grated wooden board and there was also a scrubbing brush, but no chair or anywhere to put clothes or belongings. There were no taps either; only projecting pieces of metal which had to be turned on by the attendants. The result of this could be a bath agonizingly too hot or too cold. 'Hurry up!' the woman said. 'There's more than you wanting a bath tonight.'

After the attendant had clumped away, Rory tried to remove the dirty tidemark on the bath, but without much success. Leaving her parcel and her dirty clothes on the wooden board, she got into the bath and was fortunate on this occasion to have it at the right temperature for a luxurious hot soak. Only the pressure of time forced her to surface and brave the icy draughts to dry herself, standing in the bath in case she dripped on to her clean clothes. Shivering, she dressed as rapidly as possible, then hurried back home through the lamp-lit streets.

She got in just in time to hear her mother shout, 'Jo, get the bath out!'

'Och, Ma!' A wail of protest went up, but the zinc bath

65

was dragged out from under the kitchen bed. Everyone knew there could be no reprieve. Their Ma had not time during the week to check if they had even washed their faces and hands, but on Friday nights she insisted on a thorough scrub in the bath. She believed she had certain standards and virtuously defended them. 'What do you think we are?' she would ask. 'Tinkers?' The best that could be done was to argue and fight about who was to go first. First in the bath was the lucky one, for he or she got washed in the cleanest and hottest water. After that, each had to settle for water that became dirtier and colder and was only occasionally topped up with a dribble from the kettle.

After all of them were finished, faces shining and red hair darkly plastered to their skulls, Annie liked to rinse a few clothes through in the bath. As she always said, 'It took half the day to heat that water and a hell of a clutter of pots on that range. I can't afford to waste a drop.'

Scrap had finished his tea and settled down to study the *Racing News* by the light of the hissing gas-mantle. He had kept his oversize pancake of a cap on, as he always did in the house; it added to his aura of impermanence.

'I wonder what the cuddies have been up to while I've been away?'

'One thing you can be sure of,' Annie said, pouring herself a cup and sawing herself a big chunk of bread — she seldom drank or ate until the others were finished. 'The bookie will have missed you.'

'Aye, you're right, hen,' Scrap agreed. He was the most good-humoured of men when he was sober.

Rory went through to the room and, standing on her tip-toes, struggled to put on her hat at the mirror above the mantelpiece. The gas-mantle never seemed so bright in the room and the background of jeers, insults and mocking shrieks of laughter from the crowded hole-in-the-wall beds did not help much either.

'Shut your silly wee faces,' she yelled, getting harassed — but more with the errant strands of hair than with her young brothers and sisters.

66

At last she was ready. 'Cheerio!' she called as she stuck her head round the kitchen door.

'Cheerio, hen,' her mother and father called in unison.

Mrs Gilhooly was on her hands and knees washing the stairs, slapping a wet cloth cheerfully around. 'Watch you don't slip and break your neck, hen! I don't know why we bother about the stairs in the winter. We're daft, sure we are!' Her mountain of fat wobbled with laughter. 'Is this you away out?'

Gingerly holding up her skirts, Rory picked her way carefully past Mrs Gilhooly. 'To the Princes.'

'With your black-headed pal?'

'I'll have to run,' Rory said and made her escape down the rest of the stairs.

The snow was turning to slush and she hoped it wasn't making dirty splashes on her stockings and petticoat. Walking as if on eggs, she rounded Springburn Road on to Gourlay Street and approached the Princes Picture House. Drummond was standing waiting outside and at the sight of him she suddenly knew that he was *the* man for her. It wasn't just his looks — although his eyes alone were arresting enough to class him as exceptionally good-looking — but it was something else which suddenly endeared him to her. She didn't know what it was.

'Hello,' she greeted him, quite cocky despite her wobbly legs and heartbeat.

He raised his cap. 'How are you, Miss McElpy?'

'Fine, and you can call me Rory.'

'Thank you.' He ushered her politely in front of him through the doors of the Princes. 'It's an unusual name — for a girl, at least.'

'Yes, isn't it?' She had no intention of revealing exactly how she had come by it.

He bought balcony tickets and they sat in the front row, a move about which she had mixed feelings. It was nice to be so well-treated and also to get a good view. At the same time, she suspected she was missing out on something by not being in the back row.

She enjoyed the film, however, and the bag of black striped balls they shared between them.

Afterwards he walked her round to her close and seemed pleased and proud that she linked her arm through his. In the back close they stood talking and he told her all about a meeting he had attended the other night. One of the speakers had been Mr Forbes-Cunningham from 'The Towers'. He owned the pit Matthew's father had worked in.

'Do you know what he had the nerve to make the theme of his talk?'

Rory had no idea.

'That war was morally beneficial. He alleged that it braced nations from being slack and pleasure-loving and ushered in a return of the old-time virtues of courage, endurance and simplicity. Could you beat it?'

She could not.

'The man was completely out of date, not to mention out of touch with reality. War in his view was a purge, cleansing the community. He ended by quoting the Bishop of London: "War brings out all that is best in our men." Do you know what I shouted out?'

She did not.

' "Like their entrails? When their stomachs are ripped up by a shell?" '

Rory could well imagine him shouting out such a thing, his pale face flushed with passion and his eyes flashing with temper.

'I've seen it happen,' he said. 'He hasn't!'

'Ooh,' Rory made a face, but he didn't seem to notice.

'In fact, of course, war provides an outlet for all the worst elements in a man's nature. It gives the go-ahead for cupidity and greed. It gives a charter for petty tyranny. It glorifies cruelty. Profiteers grow fat on the power, prominence and wealth the war has brought them. They grow old and they say, "Pacifism is an outrage on the dignity of man; it could deny him his only majestic quality, the knowledge how to die." Could you credit it?'

She could not.

'The fact is that in war the dying is done by the young and the surviving done by the old. No doubt it is this fact which produces the conviction of war's majestic quality in middle-aged businessmen and church dignitaries.'

'Well, it's all over now,' she said in an attempt to soothe him.

'Ah, but for how long?' he asked bitterly. 'For how long?'

His words struck a chord in her mind. 'It's awful cold standing here,' she said.

'Oh, I'm terribly sorry.' He grasped her hands in his and rubbed them conscientiously. 'Is that better?'

She nodded, speechless.

'I hope you're enjoying our evening together nevertheless?'

Again she nodded.

'Dare I hope for the pleasure of another meeting? Perhaps we could have tea in town. In a restaurant,' he added, as if she might not fully understand the grandness of the suggestion.

She did and felt excited and delighted. She had never in her life before had tea, or anything else for that matter, in a restaurant.

'Oh, that would be grand.' She could hardly wait to tell Victoria.

'Excellent,' he said and they arranged it.

He was still holding her hands when he bid her good night and he gave them a little squeeze before releasing them.

It was then that, overcome with gratitude and joy, she bounced on to her tip-toes and planted a quick kiss on his mouth before flying away upstairs.

CHAPTER NINE

Drummond had never been in a restaurant either and both he and Rory had to work hard at not appearing intimidated by the elegant surroundings of the Room-de-Luxe in Miss Cranston's Tea-room in Sauchiehall Street. They didn't talk much during the high tea of fried haddock, chips, a plate of bread and butter and a pot of tea. They were too stiff and self-conscious. However Drummond did manage to tell her about how he was going on strike on Monday, but that it would not last long.

Mr Shinwell had been to the Lord Provost of Glasgow and asked him to get in touch with the Minister of Labour, with a request that the government should intervene in order to reach a settlement. The Provost had forwarded an enquiry and it had been arranged that a deputation headed by Mr Shinwell would return for a reply on Friday the thirty-first, a week today.

'We all have high hopes,' Drummond said, 'that the reply will contain a promise of intervention which in turn will mean negotiation and honourable settlement of our claims. There's going to be a big turn-out to await the news in front of the City Chambers. It has, in fact, the prospect of being something of a gala day. I wish you could come.'

'I wish I could,' Rory agreed politely after she had swallowed a piece of haddock and washed it down with some tea.

'There're going to be pipe bands and brass bands. I'm taking my father and my young brother, Jamie. They'll enjoy it . . . especially Jamie. He appreciates music; he's a very sensitive and intelligent child.'

70

They nibbled at their bread and butter in silence for a few minutes, their backs stiff against the high-backed wooden chairs, their eyes surreptitiously wandering. They had never seen anything like the queer-shaped elongated chairs, the glass doors and wall panels decorated with coloured pieces of glass in the shape of what looked like flowers and fruit.

'I read somewhere,' Drummond announced, 'that the decoration of this tea-room was inspired by a Rossetti poem beginning, "Oh ye, all ye that walk in Willow wood!" '

'Really?'

Rory had to keep taking sips of tea, her throat was so tight and dry. The other patrons seemed very relaxed and at home. Men sported Sunday-looking suits and gold watch-chains and had trilby or bowler hats. Drummond was the only one who wore a cloth cap; immediately on entering the room he removed it from his head and stuffed it into his pocket. Rory was too preoccupied with the deficiencies of her own appearance to share the misery of Drummond's cap; the other women had furs high at their throats and also in the form of luxurious hats and muffs. She felt she was sticking out like a sore thumb in her plain black coat and shabby sailor hat. Too often, she realized now, had it been rolled around the floor by Geddes or Mungo or tossed between them in some game or other. She wouldn't have been a bit surprised if one of the waitresses had ordered her and Drummond to leave.

She was glad to finish the meal and return outside — although it was an experience which was to grow in bravado and overflow with delights by the time she got together with Victoria.

Outside the streets were slushy and difficult to negotiate and Drummond offered his arm for support in case she slipped. They strolled for a time in pleasurable silence, enjoying the city sights and sounds. Despite the weather there was a fairy-land look to the place with its gas-lamps strung out like winking diamonds against a dark velvet

71

sky. Unlike the Springburn streets where 'shawlies' by far outnumbered women wearing coats, here well-dressed women were in the majority. Only when they reached Argyle Street and the River Clyde did poorer folk and beggars begin to overflow from across the other side of the river, from places like the Gorbals. But in Argyle Street there were also sparkling well-fitted windows and plenty of noise and bustle. The motor vehicles made more noise, if not more dust, than the horse traffic — although all the lorries and vans had steel-shod wheels, were drawn by steel-shod horses and made a terrible rattling and clattering on the cobbles. The tram-cars of course added their roaring and clanging to the background; it was all very stimulating and exciting.

Then suddenly Rory felt Drummond stiffen. 'What's wrong?' she asked, gazing curiously up at him.

'It's bad enough to see women and children begging, but it's even worse to see ex-soldiers — some blinded, some minus limbs — cap in hand at street corners. Surely this is a scandalous way for this country to treat its own loyal subjects?'

'Right enough,' she agreed.

'Absolutely scandalous.'

'Is that what your strike's about?'

'I told you.'

'Oh yes,' she said hastily. 'The union wants less work hours so that the soldiers can get some.'

'No one else is going to help them. Employers are reducing wages in every industry. Profits at any price, that's their motto. Wartime profiteers are becoming peace profiteers; they're holding a starving world to ransom.' Rory felt the tremble of fury and distress go through him and with such proximity she became part of it.

She squeezed his arm in comfort. His talk had taken on a dramatic quality for her. As Victoria Buchanan had opened up to her a new world of relative comfort and gentility, so now Matthew Drummond opened up a world of heightened perceptions, dramatic loyalties and a sense of injustice wider and more important than someone nicking her kirbygrips.

Remembering something she had heard or read, she now repeated it with a suitable toss of her head. 'A land fit for heroes, they said.'

For the first time she felt a wave of warmth rush from him towards her.

'So they did. So they did! And it's just been another of their lies, hasn't it?'

They boarded a tram-car and settled in one of the seats as it rocked and clanged away up towards Springburn. It was still quite early in the evening and she wondered what they were going to do now. She suspected he had not enough money to go dancing or to the pictures.

The high tea must have cost him at least three shillings. If she had had a nice house and a respectable family like Victoria's she would have invited him to come home with her. But she hadn't, so it was out of the question.

'A cruel lie!' she said. 'All these poor soldiers begging in the street. Who would have thought it?'

He kept a hold of her arm as if it was the two of them against all the cruel liars of the world. 'It'll be the same with their "War to end all wars". It'll start all over again.'

'Oh no,' she groaned.

'Oh yes. It'll be the capitalist struggle for markets in peace-time with tariffs, quotas, devaluation of currency, the forcing down of the living standards of the working classes, trade pacts and so on. Then as the crisis deepens and the struggle for new markets intensifies, war will break out and the slaughter of millions of working men will begin again.'

'It doesn't bear thinking about.'

'I know,' he agreed.

This time it was he who gave her arm a comforting squeeze. They sat in silence for a time, the tram-car gently rocking them to and fro. At last Rory said, as they neared Springburn, 'There seemed an awful lot of soldiers milling about the town. Did you notice? I mean in khaki.

Not ex-servicemen or disabled. Are there always so many?'

'I don't know. Maybe there's a big contingent back from France and based at Maryhill Barracks awaiting demobilization.'

'I thought I saw tanks as well.'

'Tanks?' It was the first time she had heard him laugh. 'Never!'

'Honestly!' But she laughed along with him, only too glad that they were able to share something else.

When they alighted at Springburn Cross he hesitated at the entrance to Cowlairs Road. 'Perhaps we could go to a café and have a glass of ginger or a plain ice-cream?' His face had a strained, anxious expression as if fearful she might go berserk and order a Knickerbocker Glory.

'Well, just one small one. After that lovely big tea, it's just greed.'

He visibly relaxed. 'Some people eat like that and live like that all the time!'

'Fancy!'

'It's wicked, isn't it?'

Rory hesitated. She had a secret feeling that she wouldn't mind having a fur hat and muff and eating high teas all the time.

'I mean, while other people are starving. I've known people die of malnutrition, haven't you?'

'I'm not sure,' she admitted honestly. She had known people die of a lot of things, but had never actually heard that word mentioned.

'They just don't have the strength to survive. My mother died of malnutrition,' he said bitterly. 'The doctor said the operation was successful. She just didn't have the strength to survive, her body was so ill-nourished.'

'That's terrible.'

'I try to see that Jamie has enough nourishment. He's delicate-looking like her. Nice-looking like her, too.'

'You must be very fond of him.'

His face lit up. 'Oh, I am. Proud of him, too. He's a great wee chap. You've no idea how clever he is for his age.'

In fact, she had a good idea; she would not have been in the least surprised to hear that the child talked knowledgeably about politics.

'He's still in the baby class at school and already the teacher says he'll go far. She says he's got an unusually quick mind. He's far ahead of any of the other pupils and she asked if I'd agree to him being put forward a couple of classes.'

'Did you say yes?'

'Not yet. I'm trying to decide what would be best for Jamie. On the one hand, he might get bored with the baby class if I left him there. On the other hand, he might get frustrated and over-anxious if he was pushed too far ahead. I just want him to be happy.'

'Maybe only one class up would be the best?'

He smiled down at her, a wonderful smile that softened his dark eyes. It melted her gut and knocked her heart off its regular beat. They were in 'the Tally's' by this time, as the Italian-owned ice-cream shop was called. Here, despite its marble counter, mirror-lined wall and marble-topped tables, neither she nor Drummond was intimidated. This was Springburn, their territory.

'I'm so glad I've met you, Rory,' he said.

'I'm so glad I've met you, Matty,' she replied, still chirpy despite the havoc inside her.

CHAPTER TEN

'The Room-de-Luxe in Miss Cranston's Tea-room!' Victoria echoed. 'Oh, my! What a thrill!'

'I know,' said Rory. 'It wasn't just posh. It was real artistic and unusual. You would have loved it.'

'Didn't you feel nervous?'

'Not a bit. He's so confident, you see. Quiet but strong.'

Victoria sighed appreciatively. 'The strong, silent type!'

'And romantic as well. Oh Victoria, you should see his smile! It makes me go all . . .' Rory rolled her eyes and clutched at her chest before both girls folded up against each other in a paroxysm of giggles.

After Victoria had recovered a little, she asked daringly, 'Did he kiss you?'

'I'm not telling you.'

'Best friends are supposed to tell each other absolutely everything.'

'They are not.'

'They are so.'

'Well . . .'

'Oh, go on,' Victoria encouraged with a nudge.

'He kissed my hand.'

'He didn't.'

'He did.'

'Oh, my, how romantic!'

'I know.'

They both sighed, their eyes glazing dreamily . . .

Rudolf Valentino was kissing Victoria's hand, his dark romantic gaze speaking volumes without his uttering a word. He had often looked at her like that and lightly touched her hair and kissed her hand. On the few occasions when he did talk, he told her how beautiful and absolutely adorable she was and how he would gladly die for her. Sometimes some bad men would kidnap her and Rudolf Valentino would come galloping along on a white (sometimes black) horse, snatch her to safety from the villain's arms and gallop away with her. Rudolf Valentino was a strong silent man, but unfortunately she had never come across anyone in Springburn who even vaguely resembled him. On the other hand she sometimes felt — secretly, very secretly — glad about that. To her, there was a strange mystique about men, all men, that made her secretly — very secretly — afraid. She did not know why. Unknown fears fluttered over her consciousness like black butterflies, almost beautiful in their delicacy.

She had more substantial apprehensions about men too, particularly in connection with the married state. She wanted to get married one day. Indeed, Victoria was determined not to end up like so many of the older generation of women she knew. In the family there was always one who became an old maid, a spinster. She always shuddered at the mere mention of the word. Women like that were destined as far as she could see to being mere skivvies, doing everyone else's dirty work, devoting their lives to nursing some relative or other and never getting a word of thanks or appreciation. An old maid was either a figure of fun or a figure of pity, or both. That was not for Victoria. She was going to be married and run a home of her own, be queen of her castle, have lovely babies which everyone would envy and admire.

The trouble — in thinking about marriage — was her apprehension about having to live with a man. It seemed such an incredible, impossible situation. She didn't know how to cope with it. Rudolf Valentino never *lived* with her. She would never dream of taking her clothes off in front of him. This in fact was one of the great problems about the married state that worried her. How did one get to bed in a modest manner? And once in bed, how did one retain that modesty?

There were other seemingly insurmountable difficulties. What about one's monthly illness? Her mother had been so stern in her exhortations about keeping this illness secret that Victoria felt furtive and ashamed. It was a dirty, smelly business and she wasn't surprised that her mother didn't want anyone to know about it. How though, did one keep the secret from the man to whom one was married and with whom one shared not only a house but a bed? The problems, and the frustrations of not knowing how to cope with them, made Victoria feel resentful and angry when she thought of them, so she tried not to think of them.

'Are you seeing him again?' she asked Rory.

'Yes, on Saturday after work.'

'Oh, good, we can all go to the railway dance! I'm dying to meet him.'

'No, we're going to the pictures.'

'You don't want me to meet him!' Victoria accused. 'Is there something about him you're ashamed of?'

'Of course not.'

'You're blushing!' Victoria pointed a triumphant finger. 'There's something wrong you know about. Something embarrassing, is it?'

'For goodness' sake, Victoria, you always make such a drama of everything. Give your imagination a rest for a change. There's nothing wrong; we just want to go to the pictures, that's all.'

Victoria couldn't help feeling a bit depressed and she tried to cheer herself up by clinging to the idea of some sort of mystery surrounding Matthew Drummond. Different intriguing possibilities beckoned her, but her spirits kept sinking and scuttling the bright ideas before they had taken proper shape in her mind. The fact was that she missed Rory when she went out with Matthew Drummond, and she would especially miss her on Saturday; she and Rory always went out together on Saturdays. It suddenly occurred to her that she had always taken Rory's friendship for granted up to now. This wasn't surprising really; after all, they had known each other since they were young children. Rory had had the appearance of a particularly rough and common child in her Parish clothes and, as often as not, bare feet even in winter. Very soon, however, Victoria had discovered her true worth.

Victoria had always been very gentle and ladylike in her neat dresses protected by a white starched pinafore. One day some rough boys had knocked her down in the school corridor and tried to steal her satchel. Rory had been nearby and had come punching and kicking and scratching at the boys, using such bad language that Victoria stopped crying in surprise and horror. Nevertheless, she had been grateful to her protector and decided it was her duty to do something about her. In the first place — that is, after she had recovered and shared her bar of Nestlé's Milk chocolate with Rory — she had informed her that it was not nice to use bad words. Rory had been touchingly keen to better herself and very soon Victoria had taken her not only to her heart, but also to her home.

'Poor wee thing!' her mother had tutted at the wretched poverty of Rory's appearance. 'If I can get a wee bit extra wool, I'll maybe knit her a pair of stockings. A pity she doesn't take the same size of shoes as you, dear. You've got that extra pair Granny Buchanan bought you.'

Victoria must have betrayed a look of relief at not needing to part with her Sunday shoes, because her mother added the gentle reprimand of, 'You've only one pair of feet, Victoria!'

Mrs Buchanan had knitted the stockings for Rory and found a pair of shoes for her; a neighbour's daughter had died and the shoes which had belonged to the dead child fitted Rory not too badly once they had been stuffed at the toes with pieces of newspaper. Rory had been so proud of that first pair of stockings and shoes. And once she had been advised to give her face a more thorough wash and make more determined efforts to dampen down her wild

79

beacon of hair, she became a bit more presentable to be seen with. They had both hated the Parish clothes and many a wistful conversation they had had as children in which they spun dreams of the beautiful clothes Rory would suddenly fall heir to. For instance, Victoria had invented a rich uncle for Rory who would die and leave her a shopful of clothes to choose from. In reality, what happened was that Rory's mother eventually managed to get her some second-hand things.

What a difference it made to Rory's appearance to be rid of the coarse Parish garments. Her manners had already improved, of course; she had been very quick to learn good behaviour and Victoria was genuinely proud of her. They went arm-in-arm to school; they played together, whispered together, shared their sweets and everything else they possessed. They were inseparable as children and Victoria had taken it for granted that they would be inseparable still.

Thoughts of Saturday evening without Rory kept creeping over her, stirring up tiny ripples of panic. She hated to be alone; it was as if she didn't want to know herself. Although she had been accused of being vain and her father often teased her about this.

She believed that if her father and mother or even any of her brothers were going to be home at Saturday, she would have felt all right — at least, then she would not miss Rory quite so much. As it was, her mother was going to visit a sick friend, her father was on late shift and the boys always went their own ways. She supposed she had been so used to jolly company all her life that she just didn't know how to do without it.

Rory was good fun . . .

'Go to the pictures, then,' Victoria said now. 'I don't care!' And she retreated into one of her far-away, absent-minded looks.

CHAPTER ELEVEN

'Ta-ra-ra-boom-te-ay!' Jamie sang at the top of his voice and stamped along between his brother and his father pretending that he was beating a big drum, his mop of curls bouncing up and down. Eyes huge and shiny, cheeks unnaturally flushed, he was agog with excitement.

'Are you all right, Jamie?' Drummond asked.

'This is great, Matty.'

'Do you want to see the band?'

'Yes, please.'

Drummond hoisted the little boy up to sit on his shoulders. 'That better?'

'There's a big flag, Matty.'

'That's the railway union's banner. Can you see the big drum as well?'

'Oooh!'

Jamie bounced up and down, causing Drummond's cap to jerk forward over his eyes. Laughing, he adjusted it. It did his heart good to see Jamie so happy; he only wished his mother could see him too.

His father was beginning to wheeze and cough.

'Do you think you'll manage it, father?' Drummond asked. 'It'll be no shame to you if you drop out, you know.'

'We've not that far to go now. Another five minutes and we'll be at the Square. I'll be all right, son.'

But he didn't sound all right and it took him all his time to speak. Drummond slowed his pace to accommodate the older man. It pained him to see how bent and breathless his father had become; he remembered him tall and proud, with a body like a rock. Now even his face was creased with uncertainty and his eyes often held the surprised helpless look of a child who does not understand why life is hurting it.

The band was belting out 'All the nice girls love a sailor — all the nice girls love a tar.' Drummond did a little dance in time with the music, jauntily weaving back and forth and making Jamie screech with hysterical enjoyment.

George Square was packed solid with people, all with their backs to the magnificent building of the City Chambers. This was because the speakers were on the plinth of one of the monuments. As a result of the crush of attention towards the plinth, the City Chambers end was the only part of the Square that the Springburn column could squeeze into. As they did so, Drummond noticed several rows of policemen fronting the building. Further back and blocking a street at the side, he was interested to see a deep crush of mounted police and thought he caught a glimpse of khaki behind them. Once he had reached the other side of the building, he saw the same picture. It reminded him of what he had read about the cohorts of the Roman legions drawn up for battle.

'Look, Jamie,' he said. 'Look at all the policemen on the big horses.'

'I see them, Matty. I see them,' Jamie yelled. 'And there's soldiers too!'

His father smiled and shook his head. 'They must think we're going to storm the City Chambers and lynch the Lord Provost. Who's that going in with Shinwell, Matt?'

Drummond, who had been trying to listen to Willy Gallacher speaking from the plinth, turned to see. 'I'm not sure. There's supposed to be eleven in the deputation, but I only know Davie Kirkwood.'

'Aye, a fine man, Davie. That's them away in, anyway, I hope they don't take too long.'

'Are you sure you're all right, father?'

'Well, son, I wouldn't say no to a wee dram.'

The words were hardly out of his mouth when,

unexpectedly, there was a shout from the ranks of the policemen fronting the building.

'Truncheons out! Walk, trot, charge!'

For a few minutes there was a stunned silence, punctuated by the methodic crashing of police boots as they raced towards the shocked strikers and their families. As the blue wave crested against the packed crowd, all hell broke loose. A tremendous screaming suddenly burst the silence, sending flocks of startled pigeons skywards.

Rain had swept across the city the night before, churning up a sea of mud — and now men, women and children were sent sprawling on to it.

Drummond's only thought was to get Jamie safely away from the struggling crowd and the rise and fall of police truncheons. The crowd around him was thickening and solidifying as they were crushed into the far end of George Square.

'Father!' Drummond shouted. 'Over here!' He could see his father's face, ashen and breathless, fighting to get nearer. Jamie had started to scream in terror and Drummond fought to keep a grip of his legs while trying to stand his ground until his father reached him. But the relentless line of blue was pressing ever harder. Then to his horror, Drummond saw his father hurled to the ground and before he could fight his way towards him, the older man had been trampled underfoot by muddy boots. Then just as suddenly and even more horrifyingly, Jamie was knocked from his shoulders and disappeared under the jungle of running legs. Drummond was like a mad bull struggling frantically to get to the child. Wildly he punched people out of his way and managed to grab Jamie, muddy and limp like a broken doll, and clutch him up into his arms.

The crowd swirled wildly about, seeking release, and into this maelstrom an ill-advised tram-car driver brought his vehicle from a side street, blocking the only avenue of escape and causing more panic.

Now the air became ponderous with the slow clump-

clump of the mounted police moving forward, the cadence building up as the horses broke into a trot and the crescendo as they galloped forward en masse. Long truncheons crashed down indiscriminately on the backs of heads and blood mixed with mud on faces and necks and torn clothing.

Some people sought refuge in the General Post Office on the south side of the Square. But most were driven against the buildings on the west side and, trapped there, had no alternative but to turn and face their attackers.

The mood changed from shock and panic and the pendulum swung to hate and anger as men fought to protect their families. Crazy with grief and with nowhere else to go, Drummond surged with the others back towards the surprised police, still clutching the unconscious Jamie.

The bedlam soon reached the quiet of the council corridor of the City Chambers, where the deputation waited for a Lord Provost who had no intention of seeing them. On hearing the noise, one of the deputation rushed to look out of a window and discovered to his horror that a battle was raging. This brought the whole deputation running from the building. Davie Kirkwood was at the head and he reached the middle of the roadway just as Willie Gallacher — who had been left in charge of the demonstration — was being dragged along the ground with blood pouring from his head. Kirkwood raised his hands in a gesture of protest when a police sergeant, approaching him from the rear, brought down his baton with such terrific force that Kirkwood fell on his face unconscious.

Drummond found himself thrust into the front line, struggling over the bodies of the fallen. He saw Kirkwood go down and heard someone shout, 'Look what that fuckin' bastard's done to Davie!' Someone else fought like a madman in an attempt to get to Kirkwood as word about his fate flew through the crowd.

Mass rage became furnace hot and in face of it the police lines faltered and took a few hesitant steps backwards. A uniformed figure in front of Drummond held a baton wet

84

and sticky with blood. Drummond lashed one fist forward to connect with a sickly crunch on the policeman's face, smearing the nose across its broad countenance.

Across the Square strikers had commandeered a van stacked high with boxes of aerated waters. It was jammed across North Frederick Street, which rose on a high gradient from the north-east corner of George Square. With the utmost rapidity the boxes were being piled up on their sides across the street, the necks of the bottles ready to the hands of those manning this impromptu barricade.

Waves of foot and mounted police kept trying to rush the barricade, but were driven back in disorder every time. The main body of the strikers closed in on the police across the Square until all the foot police were forced into the municipal building and the mounted police retreated back down each side of it.

Only then did Drummond manage to get Jamie out of the nightmare. He ran with him down on to Argyle Street — not knowing where to go for help and knowing at the same time that his brother, like his father, was beyond help.

CHAPTER TWELVE

The first Rory heard about the riot in George Square was when her mother said, 'You watch yourself going into the town m'lady!'

'I'm not going into the town.' She had just got in from her morning's work and all she wanted was her dinner.

'You were there last week.'

'Well?' She crushed in at the table between Alice and Norma. 'Look at the mess they've made, Ma. Honestly, it's like eating with animals at the zoo.'

The girls and the boys sniggered and when the boys began making monkey noises and scratching under their armpits, the girls spluttered with laughter, spitting out bits of potato despite trying to contain them with their hands.

'Och, Ma, look at them!'

'You could have been killed,' her mother said in a matter-of-fact way before telling the boys to stop their bloody nonsense.

'Killed?' Rory screwed up her face. 'Ma, for goodness' sake, I'm old enough to cross the road without getting myself knocked down. Anyway, you never worried about me getting knocked down before.'

'What a thing to say! Did you hear that, Scrap? What did you expect me to do with a dozen of you, all steps and stairs — take all your hands going across the road? What do you think I am, a bloody octopus?'

Rory cast her eyes heavenwards in exasperation. 'I don't know what this is all about.'

Scrap was reading the morning paper. His cap, huge in proportion to his small gritty face, was pulled well down over his brow. 'By Christ, it must have been a right rammy. I wish I'd been there!'

'Oh, you would!' Annie said. 'Trust you!'

'What are you talking about?' Rory repeated.

Scrap said, 'Have you not heard?'

'Heard what? I've been working hard all morning.'

'There was a riot in George Square. So it says here.'

Annie wiped her nose on her apron. 'Lexy McKay was telling me that her man said soldiers and tanks had been brought in, and barbed wire, and they're all round the town today.'

'A riot?' Rory said. Apprehension had brought her heart up to her ears like a big drum.

Scrap shoved his nose closer to the paper. 'The Riot Act was read, it says.'

'Fighting, you mean?'

'A lot of folk were hurt,' Scrap said.

'And some killed,' Annie added, then noticing Rory's chalk-white face, 'What's the matter with you?'

'My fella was going.'

'I never knew you had a fella,' Annie said with interest. 'Is it anybody we know?'

Rory shook her head and the boys started to chant mockingly, 'Rory's got a fella!' But not for long — the back of Annie's hand soon silenced them.

'It's time you lot were away back to school.'

'It's Saturday, Ma,' they protested.

'Out to play, then. Go on! Or do you want another clout on the ear?' Threateningly she lunged forward with hand raised and, nearly knocking the chairs over, the boys beat a hasty retreat outside.

'You as well,' Annie jerked a thumb at the girls.

With groans at the unfairness of life they too, with the exception of Isa, made their exit.

'He works on the railway,' Rory said after they had gone. 'Matthew Drummond's his name. Oh, Ma!' She began to tremble. 'I hope he's all right. I'm supposed to meet him tonight after work. What if he doesn't turn up?'

'Can you not run to his house now and find out?'

'It's away round the back road.'

'You mean up Stobhill?'

'Yes.'

'If he doesn't turn up, you'd better go and see what's happened to the poor soul. I'll come with you.'

'I'll come as well, hen,' her father offered.

Annie rolled her eyes. 'On a Saturday night? We'd have to drag you out the pub first.' She turned to Isa, who had been lethargically picking at her mince and potatoes. She was a slow eater and each small mouthful seemed an effort of will to lift from her plate, to chew and then swallow. 'I'd let you go, hen, but I'm frightened you take one of your chests. It's a long, hard climb up that back road.'

'Nobody needs to come,' Rory protested. 'I can go by myself.'

'If he's been hurt, what could you do for him?' her mother scoffed. 'You're bloody useless without a pen in your hand.'

'If he's been killed,' Isa said, 'you'll have to identify the body in the mortuary.'

'Oh, Ma!'

Scrap turned to another page of his paper, tossing some words in Isa's direction as he did so: 'That's my wee ray of sunshine!'

'You watch it,' Annie warned him, 'or it'll be your body up in the mortuary.'

'I don't know how I'm going to face my work,' Rory said.

'You'll just go through that door,' Annie said. 'Go down the stairs, out the close and turn left.'

'But, Ma . . .'

'You're not too big to feel my hand across your ear. You'll go to your work the same as Isa and me. Afterwards, if need be, I'll pal you up to your fella's place and do what I can for him.'

Rory didn't know whether to feel better or worse. As she told Victoria later, that afternoon was the most awful in her whole life. The suspense was sickening; at the same time, she knew in her bones that something had happened and he would not come.

'Why didn't you want to ask me to pal you up to his place?' Victoria looked quite huffed. 'Anyone would think you were determined I shouldn't meet Matthew Drummond.'

They were sitting on their high stools behind the long mahogany counter which ran along one side of the Co-op store. The customers put their 'store' books in a slotted box on the counter, then each was taken out in turn, the customer's name called and their order written down inside the book. The book was then taken over to the opposite side and when their names were duly called at that counter, the order was made up by the serving grocers.

If people were in a hurry, it was an agony of irritation if they were served by Big Sam. His full-moon face, white walrus moustache, plum-pudding body and huge white apron made a stately unruffled progress to and fro.

'A bloody tortoise could serve me quicker,' customers often shouted at him in exasperation. But nothing caused a ripple in Big Sam's excruciatingly slow dignity as he sailed back and forth behind the counter. Young Eddy, on the other hand, seemed to think he was on an ice-rink and wearing skates. He kept taking great breenges and slides to pounce on a packet of tea or sugar and come hurtling back again to practically throw it at you in his reckless haste. If butter was marked in your book, he attacked it with his two wooden spades and smacked and battered it about until the customer would call over to him, 'You make me tired just looking at you, son.' And then to her neighbour, 'I don't know where he gets all his energy, do you?'

'MacIlroy!' Rory shouted.

'Right, hen.' Mrs MacIlroy manoeuvred her wobbly jelly of a body to the front of the crush. 'A quarter stone of potatoes.'

Rory's pen scraped over the page while at the same time she said to Victoria, 'I wish I had waited and asked you. But it was such a shock at the time. I still don't know what to think or do.'

'What's up, hen?' Mrs MacIlroy enquired sympathetically. 'It's not Isa, I hope?'

'No, it's my fella. I'm sick with worry.'

'A two-pound jar of apple jelly. How? What's the matter with him?'

Victoria fished in the box and called out, 'Mrs Strachan! It's that carry-on in the town. Rory's young man was going, last she heard.'

Mrs Strachan gasped. 'Oh, is that not terrible! A packet of washing-soda and a box of Beechams Pills. I heard the police had their batons out and were clouting folks senseless. There was blood running down the streets, so there was. A packet of Abdines as well, hen.'

Other women were tightening their shawls and trying to squeeze nearer to hear what was going on. When one child, hopping in a frenzy of impatience, cried, 'Hurry up, Missus!' the nearest adult to him gave him a quick clip on the ear. All mothers united in their treatment of impertinence from the young; whether the offender was one of their own brood or someone else's did not matter in the slightest.

Rory went on automatically writing orders in each book and then in the ledger. All the 'messages', as shopping was called, were on credit and marked in the customer's book. No money changed hands until pay-day, when perhaps a pound or whatever sum could be afforded would be paid in towards the week's shopping. She didn't mind gossiping with the customers. This was an accepted habit in the Co-op, where every customer's name and address was on her book and so she was known by name to the assistants. Although it did get a bit wearing on this occasion, having to repeat the details of her worry to every new wave of women who reached the counter.

The Co-op was a place of constant movement. People moved to 'the desk' (as the mahogany counter was known) when their names were called. Then they moved across the sawdust-covered floor to the grocery counter and waited there. Then, served at last, they staggered out long-armed with filled shopping-bags. To get to the door, though, they had to look out for the 'message boys' barging to and fro with baskets balanced on their heads piled high with 'delivery orders'; or the 'van men' who tottered in under loads of steaming bread.

Rory felt that the day and its constant movement would never end, although despite all her worry and suspense there had been an element of secret enjoyment at being the centre of such attention and drama. Eventually, however, out of the back shop appeared the 'sawdust boy' who dampened down the dust with a bottle of water, swept up the dirty sawdust with a long-handled stiff broom, then from an old tin biscuit box sprinkled fresh sawdust all around ready for the next working day.

He was always tutted at by the customers, who were forced to disperse from an enjoyable gossip and jump out of the way of first the splashes from his water bottle, and then the long wide sweeps of his brush.

'I could just die!' Rory told Victoria. 'Little did I think there would ever be any danger of my mother going with me to Matthew Drummond's house!'

Victoria said, 'I hope you find him alive and well.'

'Oh, Victoria . . .'

'And that everything turns out all right' — a wounded expression still clung to Victoria's face — 'for your sake.'

CHAPTER THIRTEEN

She waited at the close . . . and waited and waited and still didn't know what to do. Eventually Annie came downstairs and dragged her back up to the house. After a family conference, during which she was ignored, it was decided by Scrap that they needed a man's protection if they were going away up that lonely road in the dark.

Annie remarked to Isa, 'He thinks everybody's a bloody robber and toe-rag like himself!'

He conceded that he might be — as he put it — 'a wee bit under the weather', it being a Saturday night; so he designated the eldest boy, Joe, for the job. After all, at twelve years of age he was every bit as big as his father.

Joe willingly agreed to be the escort. In the first place he had nothing else to do; all his pals had gone to the pictures, but he had no pocket money left for this treat after having splashed out on a bar of Fry's Chocolate Cream and two giant caramels called Buttermilk Dainties. The trek up to the back road on a dark winter's night as a protector of his mother and sister had an adventurous ring to it — especially when the end of it promised so much dramatic uncertainty.

Before they set off, Annie had tried to make Rory wear Isa's shawl. 'It's far too cold to go tramping away up there in that thin coat. The wind'll cut right through you.'

Rory almost became hysterical in her refusal. Her mother wearing a shawl was bad enough!

'Silly wee midden,' Annie muttered with a shake of her head as they set off.

In a way, of course, Rory envied her mother the all-enveloping warmth of a shawl. Annie's heavy wool tartan was draped right over her head, clutched under her chin and wrapped snugly all around her body. Rory, in her tammy and loose coat — long though it was — found it let in all the draughts. Her teeth were chattering before they had left Springburn Road and turned on to Wellfield Street. By the time they were breasting the Wellfield hill the wind was blowing apace and she had to hang on to her hat. She wasn't as bad as Joe, of course, who had neither hat nor coat. He kept hopping about like a demented rabbit, thumping his arms across his chest and trying to shrink as far as he could inside his grey Parish jacket. The jacket, a leftover from his schooldays, was too short in the arms and only buttoned with a struggle.

After they had topped the Wellfield hill and were cutting across the fields to Stobhill the wind, freed from any inhibiting buildings, raced wildly about. It was as much as they could do to keep their feet. More than once they had to stop because it was snatching Annie's breath away. Once she got it back she said, 'You and your fuckin' fellas!' They had to keep their heads down to battle against some of the gusts and, mixed with Rory's dread of finding that Drummond had been killed or injured, and the horror of having to present to him her be-shawled mother and bedraggled brother, were feelings of thankfulness that they were with her.

They had to sit on a low wall for a few seconds before braving the last leg of the trek up the Stobhill and round by the back of the hospital.

It had always been a local joke that in Springburn there were six stages of man. Not as in *As You Like It* they were taught in school, where Shakespeare said there were seven. In Springburn there was first of all Stobhill, where you were born (although most folks in fact were born at home); Petershill, when you became interested in football; Springburn Hill, the church where you were married. Balgray Hill was where you went if you were well-off;

Barnhill — being the poorhouse — was where you went if you weren't. Sighthill was the Cemetery and everybody, rich or poor, ended up there. Tonight she couldn't appreciate the joke.

They could see now silhouetted dark against the moonlit sky the backs of the hospital buildings — these were quite a distance from the rough tree-lined track known as the back road. The mortuary building was nearer, however, and across from it stood a solitary stone hovel.

'Poor bugger,' Annie said. 'I bet he hasn't even any gas in there.'

There was no track leading to the stone building and they had to squelch through mud up to their ankles.

'See *you*!' Annie said. 'You'll be the bloody death of me yet!'

Then, before Rory could stop her she battered a fist on the door. Rory went light-headed with panic; the whole episode was suddenly nightmarish in a new way. What if Drummond was perfectly all right and just hadn't wanted to see her again? In her distress and confusion, this thought had never occurred to her until now.

'Oh, Ma, come away.' She tugged at her mother's shawl. 'It doesn't matter. I just want to go back home.'

'What are you blethering about? After dragging us away up here?'

Just then the door opened and by the light of the swaying lantern he held, Rory hardly recognized Drummond. He looked dirty and unshaven and shockingly ill. Then she smelled whisky and realized that he was also drunk.

'Rory was worried about what might have happened to you at that carry-on in the town yesterday,' Annie said, pushing her way in. 'Is that all the light you have, son?'

'I think there's some candles and matches in the sideboard drawer.' His voice was dull and slurred and he allowed Annie to take the lantern from him and go over to the sideboard.

Rory was horrified not at her mother but at the state of the place. By the light of the lantern and the candles which Annie was planting around, she could see that apart from the sideboard, two beds and some wooden chairs crammed into what was obviously just a bothy, there was nothing else. There wasn't even any linoleum covering the rough stone floor. The only thing on the walls was an unhealthy-looking mould.

'Now tell us what happened, son. We're here to help if we can,' Annie offered.

'My father . . .' He stopped, as if struggling to pull the words up from a strangulated throat, '. . . and my brother . . .'

'Now, you're going to be all right, son,' Annie said. 'Don't you worry. I'll make you a nice cup of tea.'

She found the kettle and looked around for a tap. 'Here, Joe,' she said, 'take this kettle and fill it outside.'

'Eh?'

'You heard me.'

'Whereabouts outside?'

Annie breenged forward, hand raised. 'Do you want a cuff on the ear?'

Joe ran outside and was back in a flash with a full kettle and an excited announcement that there was a place at the back where you worked a handle up and down and water gushed out. In no time Annie was putting a steaming cup of strong sweet liquid between Drummond's palms.

'Get that down you, son. It's better than all your whisky for putting a bit of strength in you, I always say.'

There was a thick layer of dust over everything and the beds were crumpled heaps of far-from-clean-looking blankets. There were no sheets or pillowcases covering the striped ticking. Again Rory felt shocked; even in Cowlairs Road they had pillowcases. She couldn't understand it; she had thought he was so superior and had taken it for granted that there must have been a new and posh house built on the back road since she had last been there. After all, she'd never been round this way for years. The mortuary had

95

never made it an attractive road to wander along. She was speechless.

The tea certainly seemed to help Drummond and he struggled to regain some sort of dignity. 'You're very kind. Thank you for coming.'

'What happened?' Rory managed.

'You'll upset the poor lad again, you silly wee midden,' Annie chastised her. Then she added apologetically to Drummond, 'She never has had any sense, her.'

'The police killed them,' Drummond said, with some of the fire and bitterness returning to his face and voice.

'Oh,' Annie gasped, 'is that not fuckin' terrible?'

Rory winced, but Drummond did not seem to notice her mother's coarse language.

'They killed them,' he repeated.

'Drink up the rest of your tea, son,' Annie said. 'Then you'll come back home and stay the night with us.'

'Ma!' Rory wailed. Was there to be no end to the day's horrors?

'Shut your silly face,' her mother said.

The next thing Rory knew, they were all outside and braving the storm, a tight little group clinging to each other, clothes wildly flapping and swirling as they struggled down the steep hill towards Springburn.

CHAPTER FOURTEEN

'She *didn't!*' Victoria's eyes stretched enormous. No one could appreciate the drama of a situation like Victoria. 'And he actually stayed at your place overnight? In Cowlairs Road?' she added, as if that made everything even more incredible.

'What's wrong with Cowlairs Road?' Rory demanded defensively, as if she didn't know.

'Nothing . . . nothing.' Victoria soothed.

'If you'd seen *his* place!'

'I thought you said he was posh?'

'No, I didn't.'

'You did.'

'I didn't.'

'You definitely said he was different and special.'

Rory's expression retreated inwards and she said thoughfully, 'Somehow, despite that place, I still feel he is.'

'What like was it?'

'My mother had to light candles.'

'There were no gas-mantles?'

'There wasn't even any water!'

'Gosh!'

'Or sheets or pillowcases on the bed.'

'Oh, Rory!' Victoria seemed to mentally draw her skirts about her as if to avoid contamination.

Mrs Buchanan was gently rocking in her chair by the fire and leisurely knitting. She sighed and shook her head as she turned the knitting round to start another row. 'If there isn't a woman in the house to look after things, that's what happens. And now the poor lad's lost his father and brother.'

'No wonder things get neglected.' Victoria was quick to take up a long-running grudge, 'when right from the start boys aren't expected to do a hand's turn. It's always girls who are made to do everything. I've even to clean their boots,' she added indignantly to Rory, with a jerk of her head in the direction of the front room where her father and brothers could be heard still arguing about the football match of the previous afternoon. In Rory's house nobody cleaned boots, their own or anybody else's, so she had been spared this outrage.

Victoria's mother said placidly, 'Men are the bread-winners, dear.'

Victoria's head was tilted up in its proud angry posture. 'Anyone would think I didn't work for a living! And they always get any meat that's going as well.'

'Men have to keep up their strength,' her mother said.

'Honestly!' Victoria flung her gaze heavenwards. 'You just don't make sense, mother. One minute you're talking about men as if they're monsters. The next you're trying to justify why they get pampered and spoiled from cradle to grave.'

'Now, now,' her mother murmured absently as she counted stitches along her knitting needle.

Victoria switched her attention back to Rory. 'So it was a right dirty hovel. Well, you needn't have worried about him staying the night at your place, then.'

Rory bristled. 'How do you mean?'

'You and your mother were doing him a big favour.' Suddenly Victoria giggled. 'Gosh! Where did he sleep? Where did you sleep?'

Mrs Buchanan stopped knitting for a moment to peer disapprovingly over her specs. 'Victoria!'

'I was just asking. After all, there's fourteen people in that room and kitchen.'

'There is not,' Rory protested. 'Jessie and Mary are in service.'

'Twelve, then. I'm just curious, that's all. Where did your mother put him?'

'A hurly bed in the kitchen. We've got two; they're kept under the kitchen bed and one gets pulled out when Jessie and Mary get a night off. Isa sleeps in the other, but last night she went in beside my Ma and Da.'

'Is he still at your house, then?'

'No.' Rory hesitated. 'He's . . . a bit strange. He must have left really early before any of us were up.'

'You mean without even saying thanks or cheerio?'

Helplessly Rory shrugged and Victoria suggested, 'Maybe he had to go on early shift at his work.'

'Work?' Mrs Buchanan tutted. 'On a Sunday? Surely not. The Lord said that the Sabbath has to be a day of rest.'

'Yes, mother,' Victoria groaned. She regarded her mother as terribly quaint and old-fashioned. For instance, her mother believed that to buy Sunday papers was going against God's will and forbade the offending articles to come into the house. Nothing her father and brothers could say would convince Mrs Buchanan that they had not been printed on a Sunday. For the sake of their mother's peace of mind, the family had therefore to buy the papers in secret and read them in secret behind the closed door of the front room.

'Are you seeing him again? Are you going to the pictures with him another day?' Victoria asked.

Rory avoided her eyes. 'I don't know. I told you, he disappeared early this morning.'

'Victoria,' her mother said patiently, 'the poor soul will have more important things to think about than going to the pictures. There will be the funeral to arrange. Tell your mother, Rory, that if she's putting round a sheet to help the lad pay for a decent funeral, I'll put in as much as I can.'

'Thanks, Mrs Buchanan. I believe Ma did talk about doing something.'

'It says in the good book that we should help one

99

another, dear. "Love thy neighbour as thyself", it says. Your mother's a good Christian woman.'

Rory was thankful that Mrs Buchanan had never met her mother. She didn't believe Victoria's mother would be fit enough to stand the shock; there seemed such a fragile unreality about her. Sometimes there seemed the same quality about Victoria, despite her strong-boned handsome features. It was as if they lived in a completely different world from the McElpys. Putting round the sheet to help with a burial, however, was a common enough practice.

'A man especially,' Mrs Buchanan went on, 'needs help at a time like this.'

Victoria looked as if she was struggling to swallow words to prevent them from bursting forth and shocking her mother.

'You haven't told Rory,' her mother reminded her, 'about the nice man you've met.'

'He works in a bank,' Victoria said, slightly mollified. 'Archie, his name is. He wears a collar and tie. He's a bit overweight, but he's very superior.'

'How did you meet him?' Rory tried to sound interested and impressed.

'Our Davie's saving up to get married and he met him at the bank. Archie asked Dave for an introduction to me and Dave brought him here.'

'Fancy!'

'A very nice man,' Mrs Buchanan repeated.

Later in the scullery, doing the tea dishes with Rory, Victoria gasped, 'Wouldn't it make you sick?'

'What?' Rory was at sixes and sevens in her mind with thoughts of Drummond.

'The way men get pandered to. You would think times had changed since the suffragettes and the war and women doing all sorts of jobs. But not a bit of it!'

'Of course,' Rory said uncertainly, 'they are the bread-winners once they get married. Or at least they're supposed to be,' she added, remembering her father.

'What do you think *we'll* be doing after we get married?' Victoria demanded. Rory was stumped, so Victoria answered herself. 'We'll be doing housework, cleaning and cooking and washing and things like that. It's not fair!'

Rory couldn't see what was unfair about it. It seemed to her a very fair, indeed enviable set-up. To have a decent man work hard to pay for a roof over one's head and all the necessities of life, in return for which a woman kept the house clean and cooked the food, was just fine as far as she was concerned. To be able to give up her job in the Co-op and be safely established as mistress in a wee home of her own had always been her dream (if one discounted childish dreams of being a tap-dancer or waking up one morning with beautiful blonde hair and minus her freckles). However, at the moment she did not feel fit to incur Victoria's wrath and hold her own in a long-drawn-out argument. Victoria could be like a determined terrier; she never completely relinquished a bone of contention, but kept going back to it and digging it up.

'I can't help feeling sorry for him,' she said, absently drying a piece of Mrs Buchanan's Sunday china.

'Matthew Drummond?'

Rory nodded.

'Right enough,' Victoria conceded, remembering the drama of the occasion, 'to be caught up in a riot — a riot!' She shivered. 'And see your father and brother killed. Trampled to death! Ugh!'

'He said the police killed them.'

'I suppose he feels he has to blame somebody. But they were trampled to death, it said so in all the papers. Do you think you should have anything more to do with him, Rory? Maybe you've made a lucky escape.'

Rory gasped in exasperation. 'Escape from what? George Square? He did ask me to go, right enough, but . . .'

'You see what I mean.'

'But even if I had been there . . .'

'You could have been trampled to death. Just think

101

of it!' Victoria clutched her chest. 'In the middle of that heaving mass, and you trip and fall or somebody pushes you and before you know it thousands of feet . . .'

'Victoria! I feel bad enough as it is. Anyway, the riot wasn't Matthew Drummond's fault. I can't hold that against him and I'm not going to.'

'There's no need to fly off the handle. I'm only thinking of what's best for you. Some people just have a knack of getting into trouble. I wondered if Matthew Drummond was like that, that's all. An awful lot of awful things seem to have happened to him already.'

'That's why I feel sorry for him.'

'Of course, we all feel sorry for him. Anybody would feel sorry for him.' She sounded as if she had cut herself short out of consideration for Rory. Unspoken infuriating words hung between them until Rory burst out, 'Well?'

'Well, what?'

'I can go out with him if I like.'

'I never said you couldn't. He just doesn't seem such a good catch somehow — not when you think of it. Especially now that we know he comes from such a dirty hovel. After all, we always vowed we'd never even *look* at anyone unless they were really special.'

Rory could see Victoria's point. It occurred to her that at some time her mother had been faced with a choice and her mother had condemned herself to a life (if you could call it a life) chained to a man who would neither work nor want. And the house in Cowlairs Road, some might think — Victoria for instance — was little better than a dirty hovel. She had never before thought about what her mother's life might have been if she had not chosen her father. Or about what her mother once might have looked like. Had that gaunt, sallow face once been plump and pretty? Had the faded scrape of hair once been thick and vitally red like her own? Comparing herself with her mother was not only disturbing, but frightening.

'I never said I was going to go out with him,' she said to Victoria. 'I only said that I could go out with him if I liked.'

'That's what I *told* you,' Victoria exclaimed triumphantly, but with a hint of exasperation, as if Rory never understood anything that was said.

CHAPTER FIFTEEN

At first Drummond waited for Rory in the doorway of
the Co-op grocers. However so many women, wide with
shopping bags, were jostling him to get past that he was
forced to move further along the street and stand at her
close. He longed for a double whisky, but had no money
until pay-day. He found himself thanking God (although
he no longer believed in Him) that he had managed to keep
up the payments to the Friendly Society; this had not fully
covered the cost of the burial, but what Mrs Elpy collected
had made up the rest and even paid for a wreath. It had
been an added agony to have to accept the money; like
his mother before him, he had a horror of charity. Despite
this, he did recognize the woman's kindness and was
grateful for what she had done.

It just seemed so unfair that people had to be worried
even about getting a decent burial. It had been a nightmare
of his mother's that she, or any of them, would end up
in a pauper's communal grave; this was the last insult to
their dignity, their pride, their worth as human beings. She
would have done without anything and everything (and
did) in order to keep up the payments to the Friendly
Society. What had people like his mother ever done to
deserve such constant anxiety even to the grave? That's
what he wanted to know. She had worked hard all her
life and so had his father. He daren't think of Jamie;
he felt himself hanging together by a thread . . . one
thought of Jamie would break the thread and he could
crumble to pieces. Only anger strengthened him and he
allowed it to throb through his blood and flame up to

his head. His mother had never been angry or bitter. Nor had his father. That had been their trouble, their weakness. He used to rail at the unfairness of their poverty and deprivation compared with the opulence and comfort of a man like Forbes-Cunningham who made his money from their labours and others like them. But his mother had simply said, 'He has his place and we have ours.'

His father had sighed, 'It doesn't do any good to get yourself all wrought-up like that, lad. You only harm yourself.'

'What's needed here,' he had raged at them, 'is what's happened in Russia. Men like Forbes-Cunningham have been shot.'

'Don't talk like that,' his mother said coldly.

'I know how you feel, son,' his father had been insistent, 'but this *isn't* Russia. They had it a lot worse than us. We've got the unions, the Labour Party, the ballot box. Fight through them — that's the best way for us.'

All right, he would fight through them; he vowed this to himself as he stood tensing his body against the wind which kept whipping round the corner of Cowlairs Road. For the rest of his life he would fight through them. He'd never forget what bastards like Forbes-Cunningham had done to his mother and father. He refused to comply with his parents' acceptance — or at least, his mother's acceptance — of the status quo. As far as he was concerned, Forbes-Cunningham's place was in hell.

Since the day of the terrible happenings in George Square, Drummond had moved about for the most part in a confused dream. His concentration, like his emotions, came and went leaving him bewildered and in a daze. Sometimes the sharp edges of life blurred so much that nothing seemed to matter any more.

For instance, he had only a vague recollection of sleeping in Rory's house and of waking early and seeing in the ghostly half-light Mrs McElpy poking the embers of the fire into life, in order to heat the kettle and make a cup of tea. Two humps in the bedclothes of the kitchen bed he had understood to be a sleeping Mr McElpy and his daughter, Isa. The kitchen had been cold, but airless; the smell of sweat and sour beer lay thick and heavy on the cluttered room.

'A wee cup of tea, son?' Mrs McElpy had whispered hoarsely. She hadn't her teeth in and was clutching her shawl over her flannelette nightgown.

'Thank you. As soon as I drink it, I'll go.'

'No hurry son. No hurry. One more laddie in the house makes no difference to me.'

But it had been impossible for him to face the ordeal of making conversation with the rest of the family and he had made his escape. The next few days were a confusion of strange impressions and new tasks culminating in the burial in Sighthill Cemetery. Mrs McElpy had asked him to stay in Cowlairs Road that night too, but he had declined. He always found mixing with people an ordeal, although he could get up at a public meeting and say his piece with every appearance of cool self-confidence. Previous to these occasions, however, he always spent many hours carefully perfecting what he needed to say.

Work, as usual, had proved a blessing. He wielded his shovel like a creature demented back and forth from the tender to the fire-box, feet astride, swinging his body from left to right.

Into a tunnel, plunging into darkness, shooting out sparks, making a curtain of fire streak past the windows of carriages rattling with the din, a strange, wild world was created that suited his mood — so much so that sudden emergence from the tunnel into daylight came as a shock. But still in the wildness of his grief he responded acutely to the ring of the shovel on the fire-door, the injector's soft song, the slight turn of the safety valve with a full head of steam, the heat and the smell. The crescendo of noise from the engine echoing back from the stillness of the trees and banks played on his taut nerves like music. Whizzing along with telegraph poles looking like a fine tooth-comb, the miles flying from under the whirring wheels, the hot ashes bouncing from the ash-pan and careering in all directions were the tears inside him that he never shed. He was part of the steam locomotive. It was a reflection of himself. It was his world. The other world where strange things happened no longer seemed real. It could not be true that in his native Glasgow barbed wire had been strung around the streets, machine-gun nests manned by steel-helmeted troops and tanks placed at strategic points. It could not be true that a crowd of people, pursuing their legal rights in approaching the Lord Provost to seek his good offices on their behalf, had been charged at and attacked by police.

Alone in the stone bothy in the isolation of the back road, however, he remembered what had happened in George Square all too vividly. He experienced the first wave of helplessness and the sense of injustice which had engulfed the crowd. He felt anger. He felt outrage. For the first time in his life, he felt real identification with class. He was one of the workers whose only protection and salvation was to stand firm together, to help one another.

Thinking of these things made passionate dedication burn in him once more. Yet when he saw Rory approaching and she linked arms with him and he felt her warm soft body close to his, he was in sudden danger of crumbling again and found it impossible to speak.

'Where will we go?' she asked.

Helplessly he shook his head.

'I'll come home with you if you like.' He nodded.

After that he just let her voice ripple past him. She didn't seem to mind his not taking any part in the conversation. She told him about her best friend, Victoria, and what a really nice house Victoria lived in. Victoria's house was in the close and so it was nearest to a lavatory. Victoria's family only had to share the lavatory with one other family — not like in Cowlairs Road, where if you lived upstairs the lavatory was on the landing one flight down and shared by at least two other families.

Victoria had a back green with lovely soft grass, not a concrete back court like Cowlairs Road. And Victoria's back green had a wash-house and tidy middens — not like in Cowlairs Road, where the middens overflowed all over the back court. And her mother had to take her washing to the Corporation 'steamie'. Victoria had a piano and could play tunes on it.

They reached the back road and Rory began giving little squeals and lifting her feet and skirts in protest against the mud. Without thinking, Drummond lifted her and carried her over the worst part on the way to the house. Reaching it, he kicked open the door and then kicked it shut again behind him. It was only then that he became aware of Rory's soft fleshy thigh warm against one of his hands and her breast touching the other through her blouse and skirt and thin coat. Suddenly, all the emotion which had been fighting inside him for release found a new focus.

Still holding her, he kissed her hard on the mouth. At first she struggled in surprise. His mouth moved over her face and neck, devouring her with increasing wildness. He could not control the hungry attack on her, even though he saw the flutter of fear widening her eyes.

Groaning with need, he collapsed down on to the bed with her, his hands joining his mouth now in their abandoned explorations. Soon he felt her begin to respond to him and she started giving little distracted cries that were not born of fear.

They rolled over and over on the bed and then bumped down on to the floor and she was as abandoned as he was. Until at last they were exhausted and still . . . then Drummond thought and felt nothing.

CHAPTER SIXTEEN

If only she could tell Victoria! Rory longed to share this joyous discovery with someone, but she had become increasingly afraid even to let Victoria meet Matthew; her friend was so beautiful that Matthew would be bound to prefer her. She kept telling herself not to be stupid, yet her apprehension was so keen that it was like a pain. At the same time she was deliriously happy, she couldn't hide that. She sang to herself all the time, even at work. There was a new bounce to her walk, a swing to her hips, a sparkle in her eyes. She had found her femininity and was rejoicing in it.

But Rory knew instinctively that the underlying reason for her bliss and fulfilment must remain a secret. The uninitiated Victoria would not understand. Like everyone else, she would be scandalized. They would all condemn her because she was not yet married to Matthew.

So this was what it was all about? Life. Love. Marriage. Having babies. And having a nice home of one's own. What more could anybody want? Marrying Matthew Drummond and living with him for the rest of her days in a room and kitchen in a decent street in Springburn was all she asked out of life. She felt it was a bonus to have as her man somebody clever who read serious books. And who had such a striking appearance.

'Tall, dark and handsome!' she boasted to Victoria. 'You saw him, didn't you?'

'I only caught a glimpse of him that day he waited for a minute or two outside the shop.'

'You must at least have seen how tall he was?'

109

'Has he asked you to marry him yet?'

'Give him a chance!' She laughed. 'I've only been walking out with him for a few weeks.'

She felt certain it was only a matter of time. When two people made love in such an intimate manner they *had* to get married, hadn't they? There could be no other way about it. They belonged to each other. She possessed him and he possessed her. It was only a case of saving up and finding a place of their own in which to live. That was after Drummond had had time to get over the loss of his father and brother, of course.

Victoria said, 'It wouldn't be decent, right enough, for anything to happen so soon after his bereavement.'

'Yes, I know,' Rory agreed. 'So we've just got an understanding.'

They had in fact never spoken about their relationship or their future, but for Rory there was no need. Her understanding was perfect; she felt so much at ease with him now that she could take him home with her and not give it a thought — although it was always a terrible struggle to get him to come. She could even give him a ticking-off.

'For goodness' sake, Matty, stop going on so much about politics. You bore everybody silly. Why don't you talk about the dancing? Or the pictures, or football, like any normal person?'

He did sometimes talk about football with her father. Indeed, Scrap was the only one apart from herself who seemed perfectly at ease with him — not seeming to notice Matthew Drummond's lack of Glasgwegian accent and his polite, almost English speech. Sometimes the football talk became quite heated and voices were raised. This was partly because they had to shout to be heard above the rabble of the children. More than once, however, she had been surprised and secretly thrilled at the way Drummond had lost his temper. He never cursed and swore like her father. On the contrary his voice became unnaturally low as he pushed his face aggressively forward, eyes murderous and mouth mean.

Her mother had remarked, 'You'd better watch that one, m'lady! He's got a hell of a temper. That one's capable of committing bloody murder.'

There had been occasions when he had lost his temper with her. And other times when she didn't know what he was feeling or thinking — like the time he had tried to make her read the awfullest big book she had ever seen. God knows where he got it; it was about political philosophy. She had laughed in his face.

'Me, plough through that? Don't be daft!'

He said she ought to improve her mind and that there was more to life than the foxtrot and Rudolf Valentino.

That was the time when she gave him a wee hint. 'Don't worry, once I settle down in a nice wee place of my own, I won't care about such things any more.'

'What will you care about?' he had asked.

She had glanced up at him coquettishly and replied, 'My man, of course.'

'Nothing else?'

'My house, my family. What else should I care about?'

Mouth twisting, he had looked away and said no more. He was a strange moody man. He wasn't like anyone else she knew and despite his moodiness, his stiff way of talking and his temper — and despite even where he lived at present — she was proud of him. She loved to boast about him to Victoria — although it was an agony not to be able to pour out everything about the new world of experience she had discovered.

She did go so far as to tell how they kissed and cuddled and she and Victoria giggled and sighed, and sighed and giggled about such daring and romantic behaviour.

If only Victoria knew, Rory kept thinking. If only she *knew*! She longed to babble out: 'I nearly go mad with excitement. Even undressing is exciting now. I was terribly shy. Well, you can imagine! But I think I've got enough brass neck for anything now. I take all my clothes off and I lie on his bed not caring about anything except the pleasure of being with him and having him touch me. It's

111

wonderful feeling that it doesn't matter any more about my awful red hair. I just lie there with it frizzing out all over the pillow. I don't even care about my freckles or that bush of orange-red hair between my legs. Yes, *orange* red. Isn't that awful? But it doesn't matter any more, because he loves me.'

She didn't care about Matthew's faults either. She didn't care about his pale skin and the dark hollows that came under his eyes when he had been on night-shift and hadn't had enough sleep. She didn't care about his body being too thin. He had good broad shoulders and she would soon fatten him up all over once they were married and she could feed him with lots of porridge and potatoes.

Nothing mattered because she loved him. He hadn't actually said that he loved her — not in so many words, that is. He was so painfully shy, that was his trouble — not shy with acting, but shy with words. Although funnily enough he loved words, especially in books. She had to laugh at him because he kept trying to educate her. About how to prevent babies, she didn't mind; that was useful to know in their present situation. But all the other stuff? Who needed it?

'I'll have you know,' she told him good-humouredly, 'I was second top of my class at school. Victoria was first; she was the only one who could ever beat me.'

'Learning doesn't just stop when you leave school.'

'It did for me,' she laughed. 'I had enough of all that swotting and sweating. It was absolute murder at home trying to do homework or read a book in the middle of all that rabble.'

'I can appreciate that. But you would have peace and quiet to read here with me.'

This she did tell Victoria. 'Honestly, he's an absolute scream! Fancy him thinking we should both just sit reading together on our time off. Especially some of the books he has, like *Social Environment and Moral Progress* and *An Introduction to Logic* and *Marvels of the Universe*.'

112

She and Victoria fell about and hung on to each other with hilarity at the mere idea. The only marvel of the universe, so far as Rory was concerned — and certainly the only one she was interested in — was him.

'You'd be better to buy sheets and pillowcases with your wages and better food to fatten you up, instead of wasting all your money on so many books,' she chided him.

That had been one of the times he had lost his temper. 'You stupid girl! How can money spent on improving one's mind and broadening one's horizons be wasted!'

'Don't you call me stupid!' she had cheeked back at him, her own temper beginning to flare. 'I learn what I want to learn and that means what's going to be of use to me. And I know what's going to be of use to me better than you.'

'Everything is of use, as you put it, in terms of—'

'Oh, stop talking shit! You're more like a walking bloody book than a man.'

He had leaned forward then, his eyes like cauldrons and his mouth ugly. 'And you're more like something that's crawled out the gutter than a woman!'

She had been so shocked and hurt that she let fly at his face. He flinched at the blow and for a second she thought she had gone too far and he was going to fell her. But the flame quickly died in his eyes and he turned away, saying in polite even tones, 'I'm sorry.'

She forgave him immediately. Nothing he ever said or did could stop her loving him.

'What's it like being in love?' Victoria asked and for the life of her she couldn't give an adequate answer. It was life transformed. It was life worth living — warm, passionate, unselfish, sacrificial. It was never feeling alone.

'It's really *special*,' she assured her friend.

'Maybe I'll fall in love with Archie,' Victoria said hopefully. Archie, as it had turned out, was a good singer and by this time she had played an accompaniment to him on the piano at several occasions like the Bible Class social and the Tennis Club party. Archie was a member of the

Tennis Club, which impressed Victoria enormously. When she was invited to give a solo performance at anything — like the Church Women's Guild, to which her mother belonged — Archie came and turned the pages of her music.

Victoria was proud of Archie and she and Rory vied with each other in boasting about their boyfriends. Often Rory wondered if, like herself, Victoria was having passionate sessions of love-making. She doubted it. Archie's broad open face had none of Matthew Drummond's strange brooding intensity about it. She couldn't imagine Archie rolling about the floor with no clothes on. Come to think of it, she couldn't imagine Victoria ever doing such a thing either — even within the respectability of marriage. Victoria and Archie were very well suited, as indeed were she and Matthew Drummond. It was funny how everything had worked out so perfectly.

At the Band of Hope social, Archie sang and Victoria played, 'Ah, sweet mystery of life, at last I've found you . . .'

And the words echoed gratefully in Rory's heart.

CHAPTER SEVENTEEN

After his shift Drummond went straight to the Co-op hall to attend the Union meeting. Instead of just paying his dues and then leaving, like the rest of the younger men, he took a seat. For one thing, it was warm in the hall. A moist, sweaty heat was generated by male bodies and the high temperature of the radiators was helping to dry out their wet overalls and shirts.

The treasurer was positioned at a small table near the door for the convenience of members who did not choose to remain. At another table at the front sat the chairman, the secretary and the minute secretary.

Drummond could not understand why anyone would choose not to remain. Wasn't the Union the most important thing in any working man's life? The Union was their only hope of protecting themselves and ensuring that they had decent pay and conditions.

The chairman, Mr Ted Bellamy, had a military bearing — an uncanny resemblance in fact to Lord Kitchener, moustache and all. However, brother Bellamy's suit was crumpled, shabby, ill-fitting and made of a coarse grey material. When he crossed his legs under the table, Drummond noticed a large hole in the sole of his boots.

'Brother McColl,' brother Bellamy announced, 'will now read the minutes of the last meeting.'

The minute secretary bounced smartly to his feet. He was wearing his railway guard's uniform and despite his bounce his face was drawn and tired as if he too had just come off a long shift. As usual he had been meticulously conscientious in his preparation of the minutes, although

115

he had to hesitate and peer at his papers several times because of the poor light. There seemed to be something wrong with the pressure of the gas-mantles. Some of the men found this the most boring part of the meeting; there was shuffling of boots and coughing and the noise of those paying their dues at the back lost some of its restraint and grew louder. Drummond glared murderously round at them before leaning forward on the bench seat so as not to miss a word.

Brother McColl was now saying that it had been moved by brother Drummond that a letter should be sent to the Company, in regard to firemen who had previously failed in their eyesight being placed as shed enginemen's mates.

Drummond experienced a deep thrill at hearing his name and his words being recorded in such a manner. He had written them down and scored them out and rewritten them many times, and before getting to his feet and uttering them at the last meeting he had practised doing so at home on his own over and over again. It had been worth it. The battle with and victory over his shyness had given him intense satisfaction. Once on his feet, in fact, he felt far less shy addressing the public meeting than he would have done speaking on a one-to-one basis with any of the individual men. Indeed, he had felt a surge of positive, almost aggressive confidence.

When the time came for him to speak on the motion about the problem of lack of support for the Union from some workers, he addressed the audience in a clear voice ringing with authority — so much so that the noise in the hall began respectfully to fade. The time had passed when his mates had mimicked his polite accent and literary way of talking. They no longer sniggered behind his back or formed an aggressive dislike of him because he was different and didn't join them for a drink or for any social reason. They had come to recognize that he was clever, and his cleverness was being devoted to their interests. They thought of him as 'a rum one' and 'a loner', but when

116

they saw him drinking by himself at the end of the bar they just gave him a friendly nod and perhaps a cheerful, 'Aye, Mat!' and let him be.

'Mr Chairman,' he said, 'the failures of a union are those who give it up. The test of a successful association is its continuance. Sustenance and security are urgently important to us all . . .'

He was aware that the brothers, especially those at the table, were watching him and listening to him with interest and it gave him added pleasure and confidence as he developed point after point.

'. . . those who fail and fall away because they do not keep in touch with the means which keep fellowship and belief in the Union alive. They do not attend the branch meetings. Yet there the business of well-doing is done - business of importance to us all. There the practical sympathy and brotherhood of unionism is shown . . .'

He paused at one point to a burst of enthusiastic clapping. '. . . What we must remember is that without organization we can do nothing. With it we can do all things. If we want to make the principle of democracy successful, we must not leave questions of government to others. We must not only believe but act. We must use the machinery which association puts in our hands; it is the mightiest lever by which the world can be up-lifted. These are my reasons, Mr Chairman, for proposing the motion.'

As he sat down there was stamping of feet as well as clapping. He felt embarrassed and lowered his eyes to stare at the scuffed wooden floor. After the meeting was over, he was glad to make his exit and chose a pub further up Springburn Road rather than the one he knew most of the other railwaymen would make a bee-line for.

Drummond had much to think about and it was not all about the Union.

The question of Rory had been worrying him a lot recently and it was only fair to her that he should make a decision and make it soon. They both enjoyed sexual intercourse, but there was more to life and partnership with a woman than carnal lust. He was fond of Rory and had no desire to hurt her, and because of that he felt he must not encourage her to think in terms of a permanent association if that was not what he intended. There had been a time, at the very beginning, when he might have thought in terms of one day having a more serious relationship with her. Various considerations had come in the way of this, however, and now he was beginning to believe that Rory was not *the* one for him. One day, he wanted to get married and have a decent place in which to live. He hated the bothy and resented the necessity of living there; already he had made enquiries about respectable lodgings in Springburn. He dreamed too of one day having a house with tasteful furniture, which would be a setting conducive to a refined and intellectual style of life.

He would have a gramophone, of course, and a record collection of the world's best music. A bookcase would be essential. However, he couldn't see Rory fitting in to this style of life. He must have a partner who could discuss serious topics and subjects like music and literature with him — someone of sensitivity and concern who would plan with him the best way to bring up children and other important matters which would affect their future as individuals and as a family. He wanted someone who was dedicated like himself to making the most of one's potential and opportunities. Self-improvement had become a way of life to him and it seemed to be the only intelligent way to conduct one's life. It also gave him pleasure and satisfaction. Even more important, he believed that the extent to which he was successful in improving his own capabilities would be the extent to which he would be able to help the situation of his fellow working men.

Rory had seemed interested in this way of life at first, but he saw now that he had expected too much of her. How could she be the type of woman he wanted when she came from such a home? He was not thinking of Cowlairs Road in terms of appearance or anything in the material sense; his own home, after all, was even poorer materially, than hers. In his home, however — poor though it had always been, first in the tiny hovel in the miners' row and then in the bothy — there had always been books. Books had been treated with the respect they deserved and valued for the ideas in them and what they could do to develop and enrich the mind. One of his earliest memories of his mother was of her quiet detached figure sitting by the fire with a book on her lap. He remembered too how his father had gone without a much needed coat, a shirt and getting his boots mended in order to make the extravagant purchases of *Great Pictures by Great Painters* (two volumes, twenty-eight shillings), *Famous Paintings* (twenty-eight shillings) and Dante's *Inferno* (twenty-one shillings).

When he thought of his father's good mind and his valiant efforts at the beginning to improve himself and to help his family, Drummond could have wept he felt such pain. Despite even the terrible working conditions his father endured and the long exhausting hours, he still found time and energy to read and made every effort to encourage his son to do the same. Every time he thought of his father, bile rose in his throat against the man and the class who had been responsible for his misery and finally his death.

Rory's father cared about nothing except football, gambling, drink and theft. There was no sense of right and wrong taught to any member of the McElpy family. Indeed, Scrap McElpy was in the habit of relating every *contratemps* with the police for the general entertainment and hilarity of anyone who happened to be listening. The more outrageous his exploits, the funnier he made them sound and the more his audience seemed to appreciate him. No doubt the children would soon follow in his footsteps. Jessie and Mary were empty-headed silly creatures; only fear and a gorgon of a mistress would prevent them, he guessed, from stealing from her. Rory, so far as he could gather from what she said about her friend Victoria and family, had been saved at least from crime by getting into better company at an impressionable age. But those cheeky devils of boys — he felt certain, and with genuine sadness — were well on their way on the downward path. He spoke to them when he could because he had a soft spot for children and the McElpy youngsters always seemed glad to see him. He gave them a halfpenny each at every encounter, of course; no doubt this increased his popularity with them.

As for the fat, flea-ridden, foul-farting Henry, words failed him. McElpy was being unspeakably cruel to the poor animal, feeding it so much Guinness. Yet there could be no doubt that the man was as genuinely attached to the animal as he was capable of being to any man, woman of beast. Everyone knew poor Henry. Only the other day he had been found lying drunk and unconscious in the street, and the local bobby had carried him home to Cowlairs Road where McElpy was lying equally unconscious. On that occasion, Henry had not managed to stagger all the way with his master.

Mrs McElpy could be kind and it was pathetic that she looked so pleased when he paid her any normal little courtesy. He had once presented her with a bunch of wild flowers gathered in the field behind the bothy, carefully wrapping them in paper so that no one would see him carrying them down the road. When Mrs McElpy had unwrapped his parcel a flush of pleasure had sprung to her sallow, leathery skin and for a moment he thought he detected the woman she once was or might have become, as she held the flowers close to her face. The illusion was quickly shattered, however, when the family started to make a fool of the situation.

'Haw, Ma's got a fella! Ma's got a fella!'

'Hey, Rory, your eye's put out now, hen.'

'Put one behind your ear, Ma, and give us a dance.'

'Shut your fuckin' mouths!' Mrs McElpy had yelled

120

eventually. 'Or I'll stuff the flowers down your fuckin' throats!'

He had a terrible premonition that one day Rory could become like that. Surely he was entitled to something better out of life?

The more he thought of the future, the more firmly his mind was made up. And of course now that he had decided, the only honourable — the only fair, the only logical — course of action to take was to inform Rory. Despite her inadequacies, she had a certain degree of native intelligence and would, he felt sure, appreciate the logicality of the situation.

CHAPTER EIGHTEEN

The set-in-the-wall bed was as deep and as dark as a pit. Rory's nose sticking out above the blankets felt like a splinter of ice, but the rest of her radiated warmth inside the tunnel of bedclothes.

Curled beside her, Alice and Norma were still puttering and snorting in sleep when the quarter-to-eight hooter sounded. Rory could imagine all the streets, especially around Springburn Cross, a seething mass of men. She could hear the crunch and clatter of hundreds of boots on the cobbles. Nobody in Springburn needed an alarm clock — not with the Calais, Cowlairs and Hyde Park calling their work-force out with such loud, enthusiastic blasts.

Springburn was a railway place, depending for its very existence on railways and their equipment. Men either built locomotives, or worked on the railway like Matthew; and each and every one of them talked, breathed, ate and slept railways. When Matthew was not talking about the Union or the Labour Party or the state of the country, he was telling her about the different firing turns he had done and how each steam locomotive had a personality of its own.

Rory had been lying daydreaming about meeting Matthew later that evening and the quarter-to hooter brought her jumping from the bed on to the cold linoleum. She shivered rapidly into her clothes and raced through to the kitchen sink; there she splashed her face with icy water from the swan's-neck tap before groping for a towel and rubbing it over her frozen cheeks. The sink was at the window and despite the darkness she could see a 'midgie-raker' hopefully seeking something of value in the overflowing and rat-infested dustbins. He was holding up a lantern and weak waves of light kept washing over his shabby coat tied in the middle with a piece of string, and his wan unshaven face.

Her mother always said, 'I don't know what the poor bastards expect to find in our middens. If there was anything worth having, I'd be down there myself!'

Often, if it was during the day, Annie would wrap a couple of slices of bread and jam or dripping in newspaper and fling it out of the window for him. 'Hey, Jimmy,' she'd bawl, 'here's a wee piece for you, son!'

Sometimes if one of these or any other unfortunates came to the back court to rake the 'midgies' or sing and dance for pennies, Annie or one of the other neighbours would shout him up for a bowl of soup if they had any. It was quite common in any Springburn close to have to side-step an ancient bearded tramp sitting on the stairs slurping hot soup. Or a young hollow-cheeked ex-soldier.

The Co-op being so near, it only took Rory seconds to get to her work and so she was able to stuff a piece of bread and margarine into her mouth and gulp over some tea before the seven-minutes-to horn went. That gave her time to tug a comb through her hair, stick in some restraining kirbygrips, fling on her coat, race away down the stairs and be at the shop at the first blast of the eight o'clock hooter.

The sawdust boy and the grocery assistants were already there, and she caught a glimpse of Victoria coming sailing down Springburn Road wearing a red knitted tammy and long matching scarf. One of the men unlocked the door.

'Ooh!' Victoria shivered when she arrived. 'Coming into this shop on a winter's morning is like stepping inside an iceberg.'

'Cheer up,' Rory said. 'It'll soon be spring!'

'When a young man's fancy . . .' Victoria gave her a knowing look.

'Eh?'

'Shakespeare.'

'Oh. Do you still remember all that?'

'Mmm. Quite a lot of it. Are you seeing Matthew tonight?'

It was as if the mention of his name had switched on a warm beacon inside Rory's face. Her eyes glowed with it and her features melted with it. She sighed, 'Yes, we're going to "the Tally's" first and then up to his place.'

'On your own, you mean?' Victoria looked both intrigued and shocked. 'Will there be nobody else in the house?'

Rory nearly said scoffingly that she had been alone with Matthew in his house many times before. And what about it? She controlled herself in time, however.

'There will be no need to worry, I'm sure,' she informed Victoria primly, proudly. 'My Matthew is a perfect gentleman.'

'I suppose it is a bit ridiculous always having to have a chaperone,' Victoria said. 'My mother's so old-fashioned and I'm never alone with Archie more than a minute. Even when we stand talking in the back close after we've been to the pictures, father opens the door and calls me in, but I know it's been mother who's told him to.'

Both girls perched themselves behind the mahogany counter on their high stools, took up their pens and opened their ink-wells. Customers had begun to bustle in.

'Hello Vicky, hello Rory. How are you today, girls?'

'Fine, thanks,' the girls chorused automatically.

Victoria was still shivering as she reached in the box for the first book. 'Mrs McKay?'

'Here I am, hen. A quarter-stone of potatoes. Did you hear wee Jennie McPhail was getting married?'

'No!' Victoria gasped. 'Her with the cross-eyes and bandy legs?'

'The very one. Could you beat it?'

One of the other customers piped up, 'Her intended's blind, is he?'

Every customer's bosom bounced with laughter and Victoria and Rory giggled.

124

'Gordon!' Rory yelled.

'Maybe wee Jennie's fella's blind, hen,' Mrs Gordon said good-humouredly, 'but I'm not deaf! Two pounds of sugar. A packet of Oxo cubes and a plain loaf.'

The sawdust boy had now become the 'potato boy' and in the back shop, enveloped in his heavy apron, he had taken up his stance beside the potato bunker. The sliding door at the front of the bunker was opened and potatoes were spilling out with an earthy smell, ready to be scooped up with the potato boy's shovel and banged on to the scales. The boy always whistled piercingly and could be heard even above the cosy babble of customers now rising to a crescendo in the shop.

However, the racket did nothing to prevent Rory from thinking about Matthew. Not only did her mind often dwell on the delights of making love with him, she also enjoyed detailed imaginings about what their children would look like and how she would dress them and play with them. She planned what style of furniture they would have in their house and what kind of table-covers and china. Everything had to be really nice so that she could entertain Victoria there. Life held so much to look forward to and she felt the luckiest girl in the world.

Drummond was on time as usual.

'Well?' She cocked her head cheekily at him and his pale serious face gazed down at her in puzzlement. She tutted with impatience.

'My new hat! Don't you like it? I saved up and bought it in the Co-op sale.'

The hat was her pride and joy and this was the first time she had worn it outside. It had a feather stuck in the front and Victoria had clasped her hands in prayerful admiration when Rory posed with it on behind the counter. All the women customers had loudly sung its praises too:

'Oh, here, isn't that lovely?'

'That makes you look a real toff, hen.'

'Oh my, that's really smart, so it is!'

'Oh, yes,' Drummond now said absently. 'Do you still want to go to "the Tally's", or would you rather go straight up the back road?'

She laughed. 'You can hardly wait, can you?' She seized his arm. 'Well, you'll just have to because I'm starving for a plate of hot peas and vinegar.'

'Very well.'

She didn't pay any attention to how quiet Matthew was as they walked along Springburn Road, because he often allowed her to chatter away to her heart's content without interrupting. She didn't need to pay particular attention to anything. She felt good; he belonged to her; she belonged to him. Everything was as it should be as she swaggered proudly along with him in her beautiful new hat. She kept preening herself and touching her hat as if to make sure it was still there, especially once they had settled at one of the marble-topped tables in the café.

She dived into her plate of hot peas and vinegar with gusto and enjoyment, while he ate his with the same serious, measured concentration that he gave to everything.

'It was a marvellous bargain,' Rory mumbled with her mouth full. 'Fancy! Half-price!'

'I beg your pardon?'

Rory thought for a hundredth time what an absolute scream he was. 'My *hat*, of course!'

'Oh, yes.'

'Sometimes I think you don't listen to a word I say.'

'I do. Tonight, however, I have a more important matter on my mind.'

Her eyes widened with anticipation and gratitude. She had known he would get around to putting his feelings into words eventually. Knowing him, though, he had to wait until he had the right words.

'Something to do with me?' she asked coyly.

'Yes.'

'Well?'

'I will discuss the matter with you later.'

'What's wrong with here and now?'

'I don't think this is the proper place.'

'Why not?'

He sighed. 'Rory, why can't you take my word for it? What I have to say to you must be said to you in private.'

'There's nobody here just now except us,' Rory pointed out.

He was getting annoyed; his jaw tightened and his dark eyes lowered as if to conceal the intensity of his emotion. It always gave her a thrill when he looked like this.

'Well?' she insisted, but still he did not respond.

She patted her hat, imagining how terribly attractive it must look. 'I'm not coming with you to your place tonight, then. So there!'

When she saw how uncertain this made him look, she laughed, 'Go on. Spit it out! Don't be shy.'

He took a deep breath. 'Very well. We have been seeing rather a lot of each other and I therefore felt it was time that we discussed our relationship and decided what form, if any, it was to take in the future. My personal feelings are as follows — I value your friendship, but do not see the relationship leading towards matrimony. I thought it only fair to make this perfectly clear to you.'

For a few seconds the half-smile of expectancy still clung to her face. It was as if she was waiting for him to say, 'No. I'm only joking! What I really want to say is . . .'

But he said nothing and she struggled out of her daze like someone in danger of drowning. 'You bastard!'

'Keep your voice down!'

'Keep my voice down? Why should I keep my voice down, you bastard!'

'Rory!'

'Oh,' she sneered. 'Shocking you, am I?'

He looked more embarrassed than shocked. He also looked as if he was the one being hard-done-by.

'You requested me to state what was on my mind

127

and I've done so. You are behaving in an unreasonable manner.'

'*I'm* behaving . . . *I'm* behaving . . .' she screeched incredulously.

'Keep your voice down,' he commanded once more. 'You're making of fool of yourself.'

'I've made a bloody fool of myself all right. When I think of all the times up at your place . . .'

'Be quiet! Antonio's looking over at us.'

'I don't care who's looking at us!'

'Behave yourself.'

'Ashamed of me, are you? You that's such a well-behaved gentleman?'

His dark eyes were glaring hatred at her now and she could have wept in the face of it. The world had all turned upside down and she was floundering in fear.

'Have you no self-control?' he asked.

She marvelled at the quietness of his voice when his eyes were so terrible. 'You're a scream!' she laughed hysterically. 'You really are! *You* have the nerve to talk to me about self-control? You that jumped all over me every chance you got . . .'

He pushed his face towards her. 'Now that I've found out what you're really like, I wouldn't touch you with the proverbial barge-pole. You're as common as dirt and I only wish to God I'd never touched you in the first place!'

Rory stumbled gawkily to her feet and ran outside. Recklessly, breathlessly she flew along Springburn Road, oblivious of heads turning. All she wanted was to run faster than her thoughts. It was urgent that she should escape the memory of Drummond's fingers stroking her hair, the reassurance of his arms around her, his mouth's tender caress over her skin, the deep penetration of his penis. But the memories came rushing over her senses despite her heedless pace and with them came all her hopes and dreams; her wedding day, her own room and kitchen, having Drummond's children . . . In her blind flight she bumped into several people and only became aware of

128

doing so when, in one collision at the corner of Cowlairs Road, her hat was knocked off. Before she could gather her scattered wits it had bounced on to the road and under a horse's hooves. When she did manage to retrieve it, it was unrecognizable — a broken feather, a crumpled rag and all covered in shit. It was too much and she ran up her close howling and crying, still clutching the hat.

Her father opened the door in answer to the wild battering of her fist. 'What the hell . . .' he began belligerently, but seeing it was Rory and having her suddenly catapult herself into his arms, he was knocked speechless — but only for a couple of seconds. 'Who's done this to you, hen?' His belligerence acquired the form of a self-righteous crusade. 'Tell your Da and he'll sort it out!'

'Matty said I was as common as dirt!' Rory sobbed brokenly.

Having led Rory into the kitchen, her father held up his fist and shook it as he addressed the rest of the family. 'Did you hear that? The bastard! He's going to have this to reckon with!'

'Matty's not going to marry me, Ma,' Rory wailed. 'And look what he's done to my hat!'

'Your good hat!' Annie gasped in sympathy. 'That hat was worth twenty shillings!'

'Twenty shillings?' her husband echoed incredulously. Twenty shillings represented several pints of Guinness and packets of fags and Scrap McElpy's outrage knew no bounds.

'I'll murder the bastard,' he yelled. 'I'll swing for him!'

CHAPTER NINETEEN

'No, Da, don't go, please!'

Rory was not at that moment thinking of Drummond's safety. So acute was her bitterness and distress that she wished he had never existed in the first place. There was no need to worry about him, anyway; everyone knew that. It was Scrap McElpy who was at risk.

The cry was taken up by all the young McElpys, who were not without imagination and a sense of drama. Confusing visions of their father being beaten to a pulp and also hanged by the neck for murder loudened their voices in fear. They followed close behind him into the dark shoe-box of a lobby, where he rummaged amongst the pile of clothes and other assorted articles for his jacket and muffler.

Annie pushed her way through the knot of children. She had retained a certain fondness for her husband through all their vicissitudes and she also had a horror of hospitals. The mere smell of them withered her spirit.

'Don't be a fuckin' fool!' she shouted above the din. 'I'll murder you if you end up in that hospital!'

'I don't care what size he is,' Scrap said as he made for the outside door. 'I'm going to flatten him.'

They crowded after him down the stairs, all shouting loudly in agitation and protest. Doors opened and neighbours joined in the mêlée.

'What's wrong, Annie?'

'The stupid bugger's going to get into a fight.'

They didn't need to ask who 'the stupid bugger' was. Shawls were hastily grabbed and flung round heads and shoulders before joining in the wave of humanity rushing round the corner on to the Springburn Road.

'Scrap, will you come here?' Annie bawled breathlessly. 'See when I get my hands on you . . .'

'Da! Och, Da!' The youngest ones were crying now in open-mouthed, snottery-nosed abandon.

Drummond heard the commotion just as he was passing the corner of Wellfield Street, but at first he couldn't see where it was coming from.

After Rory had left, he had apologized to Antonio for the disturbance there.

'Ach,' the big Italian shrugged. 'Women!'

Springburn Road was busy when he had emerged from the café. It was Friday evening. Men had got their pay packets and women had met their men at the works gates or at the railway and collected their housekeeping money. Many of them were queuing at the pawnshops to retrieve the breadwinner's weekend clothes which had been pawned on the Monday. Others, young and old, male and female, were strolling along enjoying a breath of fresh air and looking forward to a wee treat, perhaps a night at the pictures or hot peas or something sweet from 'the Tally's' . . . or a couple of drinks at the pub.

Most women, old and young, were wrapped in shawls of a material that originally had been tartan but had gone muddy grey with age, constant wear and doubling for a blanket at night. But there were some who were more respectably dressed in long coats and wide-brimmed hats; they, more often than not, were draped on the arm of a man in a trilby or bowler hat and probably lived up the Balgray Hill.

Lamps flickered feebly down the long road, making figures visible but not faces. Drummond hesitated beside one of the dimly-lit tunnels of closes, wondering how he should spend the rest of the evening. He felt shaken, but more from astonishment than distress, at Rory's

131

unexpected behaviour. He thought he would never understand women, but at least he was thankful that he had found out what she was like before it was too late.

The close stank of cats and urine from outside lavatories, and a draught from its dank depths flapped his trousers and nipped his ankles. He wasn't wearing a coat and the misery of the icy air began to seep through to his bones. He turned up the collar of his jacket and tugged his cap further down over his brow. The best thing to do, he supposed, was to go to the pub for a warming drink; the pub was better than going back home. He thanked God that he'd be moving to digs in Springburn Road next week; his window would overlook Sighthill Cemetery, which some might say was not the best of views, but he didn't care. Anything was better than the comfortless bothy. It was not that he minded being on his own . . . but for one thing he wasn't. Rats were becoming an increasing problem and even more important than trying to protect his food from their insidious destruction was protecting his precious books.

Shoulders hunched against the cold, he began walking along the road and had just reached the Wellfield corner when he became aware of the noise. The other pedestrians opened up a space in the pavement and suddenly that space was filled with screaming and wailing McElpys.

He groaned inside. As if he hadn't had enough with one McElpy for one night!

Scrap was at the head of the mob. 'Right, you dirty big leek. You're not dealing with a poor wee lassie now. Put up your dukes. Come on, it's a square do.'

'Go away,' Drummond said in disgust.

'No, I will not go away. You did the dirty on my lassie and you're going to pay for it. Put up your dukes and take your punishment like a man.'

'Allow me to pass,' Drummond insisted. He noticed Rory then, her face scarlet, her hands tugging in agitation at her father's jacket.

'Come on, it's a fair fight.' Ignoring his daughter, Scrap

began dancing about with his arms hugged close against his body and his fists raised.

'Don't be a fool, man,' Drummond said. 'How can it be a fair fight? I'm nearly half your age and double your height.'

'You big jessie, I could demolish two of you no bother. Frightened you'll get your good looks spoiled, eh?'

'I'm not afraid of you, Mr McElpy.'

'Prove it then!' McElpy's dance increased in vigour. 'Come on, I dare you to. Come on!'

Drummond was in an agony of embarrassment, but he knew that the only way to silence the man and resolve the dreadful situation as quickly as possible was to give him the satisfaction of some sort of a fight. He would just have to try to make it as fair as possible. He began peeling off his jacket, wondering exactly how he could accomplish the difficult feat of fair play in the circumstances. Then just at the point when his arms were pinioned by his half-shed jacket, he saw McElpy — quick as a ferret — jerk an iron bar from under his jacket and the scene exploded. Drummond's jaw dropped open and he remembered no more.

Screams of horror vied with the clamour of a passing tramcar. The tram slowed down and everyone inside strained nearer to the windows trying not to miss anything. Only a few on the top deck, however, managed to peer successfully through the darkness and the crowd and see the prone figure of the young man with blood spurting from his hair and making a scarlet mask of his face.

Annie got her hands on her husband at last and dragged him away. Somebody else would attend to Matthew Drummond, she knew, but Scrap McElpy was her responsibility — worse luck.

'Stupid wee bugger!' she bawled all the way back home. 'Now see what you've done. This'll mean another stretch for you and I hope they put you away for good this time. A lot you care for your wife and family! You've always been the same!'

Once shut in the comparative safety of their room and kitchen, Annie poured out a medicinal whisky for herself, Isa and Rory. Rory was in such a shattered state that she could hardly hold the glass. Even later — after Mrs Gilhooly came to report that she and another woman had gone with Matthew in the ambulance and the Casualty department had put in a few stitches and said there was no need to worry because a head wound always bled a lot — she felt no better. She did not know *how* she felt. One minute she was hating Drummond; the next minute she was dying inside with anguish at the loss of him. Then too there was the shame and humiliation of the intimacies she had allowed. Had he loved her as she thought he had, it would have been all right. But now terrible thoughts preyed on her mercilessly. If he had looked on her with cold unloving eyes, he had seen not a glorious head of vibrant curls but a red frizz. He had seen not a delicious bulge between her legs covered in passionate warmth, only an orange fuzz. And she had freckles not only on her face, but some on her arms and legs as well. *And* there was that mole on her bum! Sick with shame and self-loathing, she felt like battering her head against the wall. She wanted to crawl into the darkness under the kitchen bed and hide there for ever. She wished she could have another ten whiskies.

Next day Rory felt even worse when she remembered the public spectacle of the fight and how the shame of her rejection would be common knowledge. The weakness of having a day off work, however, was not allowed.

'Who do you think you are?' her mother demanded indignantly. 'Lady Muck? One lazy good-for-nothing sod in the house is bad enough. You get away to your work, m'lady, and none of your nonsense.'

It was just as she had dreaded and everyone knew. Victoria was waiting at the Co-op door when Rory arrived for work. 'Our Dave told me about what happened in Springburn Road last night. What a terrible carry-on!' Her face screwed up as if delicately disapproving of a bad smell.

Rory flushed. 'It wasn't my fault. I'm not responsible for my father's actions.'

'I suppose he was trying to protect your honour,' Victoria conceded.

'He didn't need to bother. I can look after myself.'

A sympathetic look filtered into Victoria's eyes despite their strained appearance. 'Has Matthew Drummond found another girl? Is that what happened?'

Rory shrugged. 'I've no idea. He's so odd. Of course, our Joe warned me right from the start.'

'What about?'

Rory gave another nonchalant hitch of her shoulders. 'About him being a loner — that sort of thing. Serves me right for not paying any attention to Joe!' She tried to laugh, but failed miserably. 'I wouldn't mind, but it's the time I've wasted.'

'You're young,' Victoria said, trying to sound comforting like her mother. 'You've plenty of time to meet somebody else.'

Rory raised her eyebrows as if surprised at her friend's concern. 'I'm not in the least worried.'

All the same, as they settled side by side on their high stools and prepared themselves for the usual influx of customers, it was obvious that Rory was rigid with worry.

The first customer to appear was Mrs McCrae, a walking stick of a woman with a head perpetually bent forward to catch any nuances of gossip.

'You'll be terribly worried in case your Da's killed him, hen. A packet of pipe-clay, five Woodbines and a tin of Zebra polish.'

'He's perfectly all right,' Rory flung at her, as if she didn't for the life of her know what all the fuss was about. 'Anything else?'

'Half a pound of butter and half a pound of cheese. He gave you the heave, did he, hen?'

'Mind your own damned business! Anything else?'

'Just a pound of sausages. I know how you must feel,

135

hen. It's a bloody shame. Men are right bastards, sure they are!'

'Oh, not all of them,' Victoria corrected. 'My Archie is a perfect gentleman. He wants to marry me, of course, but I don't know if I will. I'm not sure if he's Mr Right.'

Blindly, Rory dug into the box for the next book. She would surely die before the day was out, but she was damned if she was going to burst into tears in front of Victoria.

'Gilhooly!' she bawled to hide the crack in her voice. Then, glaring over at the big Irishwoman as if challenging her to say one wrong word, she tossed her head and asked, 'Well?'

CHAPTER TWENTY

Annie blamed Rory for the bad turn Isa took with her chest. 'If it hadn't been for your carry-on, Isa wouldn't have got all excited and rushed out without her shawl. Our Isa wouldn't be in the hospital now, if it wasn't for you!'

'Oh, that's right,' Rory said bitterly, 'Blame me.'

'I am blaming you.'

'No one ever thinks of how I feel.'

'You had your hat and coat on. You know fine our Isa's got a bad chest.'

'Isa's chest was the last thing I was thinking about at that moment.'

'Selfish madam!'

'I was in a state, Ma.'

'You've always been the same. *You* had to work in the Co-op!'

'What's me working in the Co-op got to do with it?'

'You were far too stuck-up to help me with the rags. Our Isa should never have had to trail around the streets with her chest.' Annie poured herself another medicinal whisky. She had just come from the hospital and was much in need of it.

'Isa wasn't any good at school,' said Rory.

Her mother's eyes widened with astonishment. 'Oh, is that not fuckin' terrible? Our Isa's at death's door and she's calling her for everything.'

'I am not. All I'm saying is that Isa couldn't get a job in the Co-op because she was too slow at writing.'

'Huh,' Annie confided around the room. 'She's slow now. She'll be telling us our Isa's half-witted next.'

Nobody was paying the slightest attention. The girls were chattering between themselves as they washed and dried the dishes, while the younger boys were wrestling on the floor and the older ones were playing marbles. Scrap McElpy and Henry had gone out to put a line on at the bookies.

Rory's face set with stubbornness. 'It's not my fault she had to go round with you.'

'Aye, well,' Annie nodded at her in some satisfaction. 'If Isa's not fit to help with the rags after she comes out, you'll have to.'

'*Me*?' Rory screeched. 'Go round collecting rags?'

'Ah-ha!' her mother cried out in triumph. 'See what I mean?'

Rory was too shaken to continue the conversation. 'I'm away out,' she said.

'Have you got another fella?'

'I don't want another fella. I'm finished with men.'

'Oh, aye?' Her mother cast her a sideways sarcastic glance. 'That'll be the day!'

'I'm going to see Victoria.'

She went through to the front room first to put on her hat and coat and check her appearance in the wardrobe mirror. She checked her appearance a lot nowadays; it had become a source of constant anxiety to her. She had only a dusting of freckles over the bridge of her nose and they were always much fainter in winter. Now, however, she seemed to see nothing else on her face. She had decided that green eyes were an added torment which a cruel God had dished out to her. Her hair, of course, was too awful for words, and she felt like weeping every time she looked at it. She kept trying to darken it down with oil, but the oil was beginning to ruin not only the bottle-green beret that Victoria's mother had knitted for her at Christmas, but also her best hat.

She hated her figure too, and refused to be comforted by Victoria's assurance that it was fashionable to have no bust. She realized, of course, that Victoria, as usual, was not bothering about accuracy. She *did* have a bust, firm as a couple of apples; it was just that she had acquired a dislike of them just as much as every other part of herself.

'You have a nice little figure,' Victoria assured her. 'A bit on the skinny side, but that's becoming all the rage. I'm going to buy myself one of these bust flatteners.'

It was all very well for Victoria to talk safe in her queenly voluptuousness. If Victoria tied herself up and pinioned herself in a straitjacket, she would still look supremely relaxed and superior. Victoria had been a great comfort all the same. She had given up several meetings with Archie to be with Rory.

'What are friends for?' she had explained. 'Men are all right, but give me my girl-friends any time.'

Rory was touched, although she had assured Victoria that there was no need to worry about her because she was perfectly all right. Losing Matthew Drummond, she kept repeating, had not bothered her in the slightest. In truth, it had been a painful blow to her pride as well as her heart. She was glad of Victoria's company and the way their relationship was cemented by adversity. They went along Springburn Road arm-in-arm, with Victoria gripping her firmly as if determined to protect her against Drummond, or any man, should he have the nerve to make a move in her direction.

Often they sat whispering together in Victoria's house and Victoria confided how Archie was all right and how her mother 'just doted' on him, '. . . but he's beginning to irritate me something awful.'

Now Rory stuffed the red hair into the green beret, buttoned up her coat and left the house without even shouting 'Cheerio!' She was thoroughly fed up with how her mother kept going on about Isa. It had been bad enough to visit Isa in the hospital; first of all she had had to put up with her mother's moaning and groaning on the way, and then with Isa's once they got there. She had been sorry for her sister when she'd been gasping for breath so much that she had to be carted off. And she had been shocked into silence when she had seen how fragile and childish Isa looked in the hospital bed. All eyes and whine really, and hardly a ripple on the smooth white coverlet. But what could she do about Isa's chest? It had always been bad and getting worse. She was bound to end up in the hospital sometime; it wasn't Rory's fault.

In a strange secret way, having seen Isa in the hospital had — afterwards, at least — made her feel good. There had always been a tough bit about her and as she left the ailing antiseptic atmosphere, she enjoyed a conscious surge of positive health and vitality. For a few seconds, revelling in it, she felt happy. Then she remembered the desolation of being without Drummond again. The trouble was, it was not simply an emotional desolation — it was physical as well. Her body cried out for his caresses and her need was more than an ache. It amounted to actual pain. This physical need began to obsess her and more and more often she thought of being made love to. She would wake in the morning in a hot sweat and damp between her legs after erotic dreams. Her icy splashings at the kitchen tap gave only a temporary respite. During the day, sitting on her high stool and with her pen diligently scratching, her mind would wander down libidinous paths and she would find herself blushing and fearful in case Victoria or any of the customers had read her mind. She still loved Matthew Drummond — that is, she had feelings for him which were apart from sex. She loved the dark half-glowering, half-shy looks he often gave. She loved his tall and dignified posture, even when he was wearing his dirty dungarees and railway cap and his face was streaked with soot and engine grease. She loved his polite, careful way of talking. She loved his intelligent mind.

Rory knew she wasn't good enough for him; she had always known it. But she loved him just the same.

The emotional pain of her love was one thing. The sexual pain was another. The pain of her love remained tied up with memories of Drummond. The sexual pain began to wander among faceless people and then it flitted secretly in her mind from one real person to another. She would look at Eddy, the energetic grocer, and begin weaving him into her lascivious daydreams. Tam, the baker — swaggering in with the long board of steaming bread balanced on his cap — would suddenly be transformed into a panting lover. Even Big Jack the coalman, arriving when she was at home for her dinner, would immediately stimulate her sexual imagination. She would gaze appreciatively at black bulging muscles as he heaved the sack of coal into the kitchen bunker; she would sense the raw energy in the coal-streaked face, wallow in the maleness of the hairy chest revealed by his open shirt and succumb gratefully to his healthy lust. He remained blissfully innocent of any such occurrence, of course, and went away whistling and clattering noisily back down the stairs. She began to look at men in the street with the same hungry eyes and, had convention allowed it, would have whistled and cat-called and chirped appreciatively at those she especially fancied. Being a woman, she could not do this and so was even more frustrated.

Nothing assuaged the frustration. No pleasure took its place.

She met Victoria at the Wellfield corner and went round with her, arm-in-arm, to the Wellfield Picture House in Wellfield Street. Usually they went to the new Princes Picture House in Gourlay Street; it had been opened about five years now, but they still thought of it as new. The Princes was better class and did not have the rough element of the Wellfield. Tonight, however, they couldn't afford the Princes. Payment for entry to the Wellfield could be made with a few jam-jars and many times the girls had paid by this method when they were still at school and not earning any money. Now, however, they at least had enough cash for entry to the stalls. The gas-lights were turned up when they went into the hall and all its dusty brown shabbiness was revealed. There was the tear and the frayed bits of the curtain and the holes in the linoleum. There was the sea of sweet papers and other debris which had not been swept up after the earlier performance.

The lady who played the piano was settling herself at the front. Soon the lights dimmed and the seediness of the surroundings was forgotten. The piano lady trilled the keys, then she slid into a romantic melody to match the story unfolding on the screen. It was called *Love Levels All* and sometimes, at the very romantic bits, she became quite carried away. So did Rory. Afterwards, while they were waiting for the amateur turns to fill the interval between the two parts of the programme, Victoria sighed, 'I wish we could meet somebody romantic like that, don't you? Somebody who could sweep us off our feet.'

Rory nodded and her chest heaved with a sigh. The film had increased her desperate longing and she released some of her pent-up emotions by loudly booing the girl with some front teeth missing who was now on the stage trying to sing. The girl was also being pelted with screwed-up caramel papers. After that there was a sing-song in which everyone joined with choruses of 'Rock-a-bye your baby with a Dixie melody' and 'Little Sir Echo'. Then a young man juggled balls with great panache for a few minutes before losing the place — to the great hilarity of the audience — and having to chase the balls all over the stage. At last it was time for the next feature film, which turned out to be even more romantic than the first with Rudolf Valentino at his most darkly passionate. Afterwards Victoria and Rory sighed over him all the way to the Wellfield corner, where they parted, Victoria sailing dreamily away to the right in the direction of the Balgray and Rory hurrying tensely in the opposite direction towards Cowlairs Road.

She was thinking that if she didn't get a man soon she would go mad, or explode. Then she saw Matthew Drummond coming towards her and all the sensations of physical intimacy he had introduced her to flared into urgent life. She was one long tremble from head to foot as he came nearer; then just as he was within touching distance he raised his cap, said a polite 'Good evening' and passed on.

Rory could hardly believe it. Had she had enough strength in her legs, she would have run after him; she would have punched him and kicked him; she would have called him all the rotten bastards of the day. But her legs, her whole body were melting like a failed jelly. Only the desperation of her grief and anger gave her enough strength to carry herself home.

CHAPTER TWENTY-ONE

Drummond felt pleased that he had managed to behave in a civilized fashion in bidding Rory a polite good evening. She had acted like a fishwife and her father had lived up to his reputation for criminal violence. He, on the other hand, had behaved like a gentleman throughout the whole sorry affair. He had not pressed charges against Scrap McElpy and he had not held any grudge against Rory.

He went to the baths in Kay Street feeling good. The pond was housed in the same building as the baths and he usually went for a swim once a week, as well as to have his weekly wash.

The pool area was noisy with sounds that echoed ghost-like off the glass roof, sounds of splashing and laughter and shouting and the hysterical cheeping of the birds who lived on the army of cockroaches and beetles that scuttled about in the dampness.

Drummond swam three lengths and felt cleansed, relaxed and strengthened. He was proud of the way his once skinny body had become hardened and muscular. Only a few years ago, it had been thought that he would not be strong enough for railway work. The first hurdle he had had to get across was the foreman; tall and solid as a tree-trunk, he was a man who brought a lot of dignity and pride to the job. He had looked Drummond up and down with disdain when he first applied and told him to 'go away home and eat some more porridge'. Through his sheer dogged persistence and mania for engines, he had persuaded the man to give him a chance to show his mettle and in the end the foreman had agreed. So after running around in the dark early hours knocking up the drivers, he had worked through the stages of greasing and cleaning. Then came his first firing turns on one of the toughest assignments anyone could be given: firing an N.B. 'pug'. This saddle-back pilot engine had no cab whatsoever. Rain, sleet, wind or snow, it never stopped shunting and to be exposed to such weather ten hours a day needed some stamina. You needed, in fact, to be made of iron and certainly his driver of that period had been. Dougal was built like a rock, with a craggy face creased against the elements and the flying bits of fire which caused so many eye injuries on the footplate. Dougal had done his firing for drivers who started their careers way back in the first days of the Glasgow and Edinburgh Railway in 1842. He thought of and worked with engines in the traditional way of those whom the master of their craft, George Stephenson himself, had trained. Driving and firing of railway locomotives was something to be approached with measured reverence and rigid ceremonial; there were proper procedures and Dougal carried them out with unhurried and orderly efficiency.

He showed Drummond how to shape the mouth of a squat N.B. firing shovel with hammer and cold chisel, until it became a tool to conjure with. He taught him how to cut a gauge-glass to size with a file and make it as steam-tight as a bottle, with cotton wick and the skin of the packing he used on the slide valve rods. Every day a job had to be done and done to perfection.

'Never depend on fitters to dry-nurse you,' he had advised.

Drummond regarded him as an artist in handling his engine and from him he had also learned the knack of split-second timing which is the secret of all good shunting.

Now he was getting turns with different drivers, all marvellous characters in their own right and all devoted to their engines. At present he was firing to Harry McAlpine, who seemed able to turn his engine into a flying horse, especially round bends, while all the time nonchalantly chewing tobacco. The old familiar quiver of mechanical muscles which preceded the start of every steam engine was intensifed to an impatient straining at the bit and then an excited champing.

After his swim, Drummond walked briskly back along Springburn Road, taking deep invigorating breaths as advised in his book on *How to Develop the Physique*. At the same time, his usual caution clung to him, warning him to avoid anything that might draw attention to himself. He had to pass Cowlairs Road on the way to his lodgings and it reminded him of Rory again. He was glad to be free of the embarrassment of her, yet he missed her at times with a desperate physical longing. He had to keep struggling to fully occupy himself in mind and body and he worked until he was exhausted to stifle his lustful feelings. Then he read his books, took studious notes and prepared material for the Union, to keep his mind from straying on to other more painful subjects. If he thought of his family, for instance, he became bitter as well as melancholy. He dare not think of his mother and her stoic endurance and red workworn hands . . . or his father coughing his guts up . . . or Jamie, who once held such bright promise.

The Union and, lately, the Independent Labour Party as well, took up practically all his spare time. Both organizations gave purpose and meaning to his life; they were the means by which he could fight the injustices perpetuated on working people like his father and mother. But he would have voted Socialist for no other reason than because Forbes-Cunningham was a Conservative. Big, fat Forbes-Cunningham with his luxuriant moustache and warm fur-lined coat and shiny top-hat, often seen in Springburn and much hated despite the respectful touching of caps as his new limousine honked past, frightening all the horse traffic. Drummond never touched his cap; his hatred went too deep. To him, Forbes-Cunningham was the symbol of all that was wrong in the world. Forbes-Cunningham was not just one of those who got rich off the backs of the poor; he got rich from the war as well. He had invested money in armaments and no one knew how much profit he had managed to salt away from that. Rumour had it that his castle up the Balgray near that end of the park was palatial and stuffed with priceless antiques. Forbes-Cunningham's wife had a retinue of over two dozen servants — no empty-eyed endurance, no red workworn hands for her. Forbes-Cunningham's son, Edgar, had gone to University; he would have every chance in life and everything he wanted. Often he was to be seen careering down Springburn Road on a motor-bike, with a white silk scarf and leather helmet. The apple of his father's eye, Edgar was, so they said. Pity he hadn't been killed in the war — or disabled — or shell-shocked like so many poor bastards. Thousands upon thousands of them! The flower of British manhood made to suffer agonies and the indignity of a death in mud, among rubbish and rats. Young men of no more than eighteen or twenty who ought to have been joking and laughing with their mates at work, or cheering themselves hoarse at football matches, or courting their sweethearts — he had heard them crying for their mammies, armless, legless and dying.

And all for what? So that the greedy Forbes-Cunninghams in every country could have their way. People like him were the ones that working men should fight, never each other. Drummond vowed for the hundredth time to devote his life to such a fight. There always had to be that kind of struggle. People talked about freedom as if it was a blessing which was bestowed just by living in Britain — but had it not been fought for by working people every hard and bitter step of the way?

Right from the 'Tolpuddle Martyrs' (indeed long before them), the government, the landowners, the church, the employers, the law, the rich and the powerful had done everything to crush freedom of any kind for the poor. All down through the ages, the greed, the selfishness, the cruelty of these people were sickening. They did not deserve to live and he hated them. Rory had never appreciated the strength of his feelings, unable to understand how he could have any passion other than a sexual one. He could never have expected any support or encouragement from her in his fight for freedom and justice. What he needed was a more socially conscious woman, someone with whom he could hold an intelligent and wide-ranging conversation. They seemed few and far between, however; maybe he was going to the wrong places. The occasional railway dance was not enough. The trouble was he had stopped going to church — how could he go when he had lost his faith in God? Yet he had to face the fact that most social events had some church connection. He was still struggling with this dilemma, for he must go to just such a serious venue if he wanted to meet a serious-minded woman. And he did, desperately. It was strange, for he enjoyed — indeed preferred — his own company and was perfectly content to sit alone reading his books, to swim alone or walk alone on his off-duty hours. Yet there were times when he experienced deep loneliness.

Tonight had become one of these times, triggered off by passing Cowlairs Road. For a mad second or two, he nearly turned up at the McElpy close on the pretext of asking how Isa was. He had heard that she was very ill in hospital. But the madness passed and he continued with his burden of loneliness to his lodgings further along Springburn Road opposite the cemetery.

Mrs Abigail Kipp, his landlady, had a religious fervour in disproportion to her size. A tiny sharp-faced creature, her faith knew no bounds. Her late husband had played the trumpet in the Salvation Army band and she continued in the same tradition. Not that she could play the trumpet, but he had seen her at the Wellfield corner knocking hell out of a tambourine! Of course he had slunk past, pretending he had seen nothing. Her attempts to 'save' him and drag him into the activities of the Salvation Army was an ever-present horror. The way she chattered to God around the house did nothing to help his conversation either — nor did the fact that she was mean: mean with food, mean with light, mean with coal. The only thing she was not mean with was what she called 'God's pure air'. Already there was a wordless battle going on between them — at least wordless on his side. Every time he went out, she opened the window in his room. Every time he returned, he closed it again. He was all for fresh air, but not in the form of a winter gale blowing inside the house. Sometimes he thought she must be mad.

She didn't seem to mind a bit standing in a circle with the other Salvationists at draughty street corners, even in driving rain and snow, singing at the top of her voice and banging her tambourine. She even looked as if she enjoyed marching with them all around Springburn, with every child in the place skipping and giggling after them as if they were a bunch of pied pipers.

'You should join the Sally Ann,' she kept telling him, 'and make a friend of Jesus.'

He just smiled and escaped as quickly as possible into his room. Spartan though it was — with nothing but bare linoleum, an empty grate, one narrow bed, a small folding table and a chair — at least he had privacy.

Still, he would have to join something soon if he was to meet a young lady of the type he required.

CHAPTER TWENTY-TWO

'Sure, why not?' Rory tossed her head and put on what she hoped was a nonchalant, sophisticated expression. She had gone with Victoria to the railway dance and now she and Sid Ford were dancing the last waltz together. To let Sid take her home meant getting rid of Victoria's brother Tommy, who had been instructed by Victoria's mother to see both girls safely home. Over Sid's shoulder she could see Tommy enjoying himself with a long-haired girl in a brown cord cloth dress, embroidered in yellow to match the yellow clasp in her hair. Tommy would not prove too much trouble. Victoria was floating gracefully around with a tall man with startlingly fair hair; she liked tall men.

'Nobody can look distinguished and special if they're small,' Victoria always said.

Later in the cloakroom, it was all arranged. Tommy would see his girl home. Sid would see Rory home. The fair-haired man would escort Victoria. And they would all lie, if necessary, to Mrs Buchanan.

Victoria said, 'Hasn't George got fantastic hair? That's his name — George Anderson. He's a top-link driver and he's been all over the place — even to England!'

What could she say about Sid? Sid with the low brow and broad jaw like a gorilla? She didn't even like him. But he had muscular arms and broad warm hands which when they touched her, sent her blood hot and fast round her veins.

She had hoped, of course, that Matthew Drummond would have been at the dance — though she didn't know why, because most of the time she hated him. Yet still she kept hoping against hope that it would not be true that they had parted for good. The deepest part of herself could not accept it, refused to believe it. It simply could not be . . . she wanted him so much.

But Matthew Drummond had not come and Sid Ford kept dragging her up on to the floor. He was a cleaner at Eastfield, along the low road past where Victoria lived. Drummond worked at Eastfield as well and later when walking home with Sid she couldn't resist asking — very casually of course — if he knew him.

Sid laughed. 'Oh, aye, we've all seen you walking up the back road with Drummond!'

Rory blushed in confusion. Did that mean everyone knew what she and Matthew Drummond had been doing? 'Everyone should mind their own damned business!' she snapped.

Sid laughed again. He seemed to guffaw or grin at everything and this began to irritate her intensely. He gave her bum a pinch and said, 'Good at the old slap and tickle, was he?'

She knocked his hand away, but the touch of it on her thigh had switched on the heat again. 'None of your damned business, I said.'

He put a gorilla arm round her waist as soon as they entered the close in Cowlairs Road. 'I bet I'm better,' he grinned. 'Come on through to the back close and I'll show you!'

'Leave off!' She struggled, but half-heartedly, and then as his probing fingers began to tickle her she giggled and squealed.

'Come on!' Giggling and struggling along with her, he manoeuvred her deep into the shadows. Then he gave a hoarse half-laugh, half-groan of appreciation when his hands found her breasts. Rory was taken aback at the speed and accuracy of his fumblings. He had knocked her back against the wall and his hands were hard on her naked breasts before she knew what had happened.

'Here, wait a minute,' she tried to protest, but found herself so breathless her voice barely emerged as a weak tremble. The wall was hard and cold against her back and an icy draught was blowing around her ankles and then her legs as Sid hitched up her skirts.

'No, please!'

She felt ashamed and a panic of tears rushed about in her heart, bursting to get out. Yet there was excitement too and around her nerves flew the message: 'Pleasure! Pleasure!'

But it was over so soon and she was appalled and sickened as she watched Sid buttoning up his trousers.

'That was great, hen,' he laughed, 'but this draught's enough to freeze the arse off us. We'd better call it a day — I'll maybe see you again, eh?' And in a few seconds he had gone, whistling and swaggering and rubbing his big hands together.

The sour smell of cats in the close was now mixed with the hot odour of sex. An old newspaper billowed in from the back court and rustled around her ankles. Rory slowly climbed the stairs, bent forward as if holding in the revulsion she felt. She didn't know how she could ever bring herself to look in a mirror again. So strong was her self-loathing that she wanted to fold up and die, but she knew that no such mercy would be meted out to her. Life would go on and she would have to live with disgust of herself.

When she arrived at the house she was taken aback to find everyone awake and up — not only her own family, but Mrs Gilhooly and Mrs Campbell from downstairs fussing about making tea and handing round cups. For a few ridiculous seconds she thought they must all be waiting to tell her what a dirty shit she was.

'Oh, there you are, hen,' Mrs Gilhooly greeted her. 'It's just happened. When we saw the policeman going in the close, we came up right away.'

Rory looked over at her father, who was sitting by the fire rubbing at Henry's ears. 'What have you done this time?' she asked bitterly.

'Me?' He sounded shocked, as if he had never done anything reprehensible in his life. 'What a thing to say to your old Da at a time like this.'

'It's Isa, hen.' Mrs Campbell squeezed Rory's arm. 'She passed away a wee while ago.'

It was not the right time to cope with another grief. The news shook her, but she felt more confused than anything else. 'Where's Ma?' she asked.'

'She's through in the room at the pail.'

'Is she all right?'

'You know your Ma, hen. Tough as old boots!'

Scrap said, 'Isa was her favourite. Poor wee lassie! It's a damned shame, so it is. I wonder if there's any whisky left in Annie's bottle?'

'Aye, here you are!' Annie came into the kitchen carrying the bottle. 'There's enough for a wee dram for all of us. Hello, hen,' she said, noticing Rory.

'Are you all right, Ma?'

'As right as I'll ever be.'

Rory couldn't think what else to say. Her mother said to the younger ones, 'Away through to the room to your bed.'

Tonight they put up no argument. They trailed from the kitchen without a murmur, although afterwards Rory could hear them whispering and talking.

Her mother never wept. Her face was a stiff mask, although she looked tired and the dark crêpy shadows under her eyes had sunk further into hollows. She talked, they all talked about Isa and what a good wee girl she had been as they sat round the fire drinking whisky and then more tea.

Rory kept wishing she could wash between her legs. She felt sticky, and dirty to her very soul. But she couldn't use the sink when everyone was sitting only feet away from it. She dreamed of the public baths and soaking her whole body in hot water and then scrubbing it from top to toe.

'Away you to bed as well, hen,' her mother's voice startled her. 'You've your work to go to in the morning.'

'I don't like leaving you, Ma.'

Mrs Gilhooly patted Rory's hand. 'Mrs Campbell and I are going to stay with her, hen. She'll be all right.'

'Aye. Away you go,' Annie said wearily.

Rory thought it best not to argue. Anyway, what good could she do?

She crept into bed in a daze of misery. It was as if her whole world had crumbled around her and she with it. She rolled herself into a ball trying to keep as far away as possible from the cuddled-together figures of Alice and Norma. It was as if she was afraid of contaminating them. The tiny room and the kitchen were packed with people, yet she was as alone as if she had been on the planet Mars. It was then that the news of Isa suddenly got through to her. Poor Isa, dying by herself in the hospital. Poor frightened wee Isa! She saw her sister in her mind's eye — wrapped in one of Annie's old shawls, the fingers of one hand clutching it under her chin. The other hand hung on to the bundle that was slung over her back and weighed her down into a continuous stooping position. Rory saw the small, wan face and straggles of hair that hung over it and she wept. Isa was only fourteen and what kind of life had she had? They had never been able to afford the medical attention she needed. A doctor was a luxury that none of the McElpys had ever enjoyed. But sometimes Annie managed to get Isa a bottle of Parrishe's Mixture on her Co-op book. Apart from that, Isa had just to resort to kneeling over bowls of steaming water with a towel draped over her head.

The younger ones used to laugh at her doing that and her mother had always slapped them for it. Annie would miss Isa terribly . . . But one thing was for certain. Rory McElpy was not taking Isa McElpy's place collecting rags or hawking them at Paddy's market.

Rory stuffed the blankets tightly against her mouth so that none of her brothers or sisters would hear her broken-hearted sobs. 'Oh Matty,' she kept thinking. 'Oh, Matty!'

CHAPTER TWENTY-THREE

Victoria's face tightened in incredulity and she drew back her head as if trying to avoid the distaste of Rory's words. Yet she echoed them.

'Between your legs?'

'You've seen pregnant women,' Rory said. 'The baby is in her stomach. Well, that's how the seed gets there.'

'But . . . but the way to the stomach is through the mouth. You're daft!'

It gave her momentary release to make this accusation. Rory was being at her most worrying and Victoria was beginning to feel trapped by the acutely distressing nature of what she was saying.

'I am not!'

'You are so.'

'I am *not*.'

'How do you know it's true?'

'Somebody told me.'

'Huh! That awful Sid Ford, I'll bet. What does that ignoramus know? And fancy letting him talk to you about things like that. You're not supposed to talk about your private parts to *anyone*.'

'No, it wasn't him.'

'I don't know what you see in him. Honestly Rory, I don't know what's come over you recently. You're going to get the sack from the Co-op if you're not careful. You've been getting everything mixed up in people's books and you've been adding up the ledger wrong.'

'I read it in a book,' Rory said desperately.

Victoria looked around in an affronted manner as if to

155

say to everyone: 'Did you hear that?' But there was no one in the Buchanan kitchen except themselves. Mrs Buchanan was out at her weekly prayer meeting. Mr Buchanan, being a very social man, was out — unknown to his wife — at the Boundary Bar, having a drink with a crowd of friends. The boys were out either with girl-friends or with their mates.

'Fancy you reading dirty books! I just don't know what's come over you, Rory. I really don't.'

'I'm so worried and upset, Victoria.'

Victoria stared at her friend. Rory didn't look well. Her face looked smaller and paler and the skin beneath her eyes seemed to have gone thinner. A delicate tracery of blue could be seen there. And her eyes were so wide and anxious.

'I'm not surprised,' she said, 'after reading all those awful things.'

'I had to tell you so that you'd understand what's happened and why. I've no one else to turn to. You are my friend, aren't you, Victoria?'

Victoria felt flattered and pleased at being the only one Rory could turn to. 'Of course.'

'Through thick and thin, we always said.'

They had made all sorts of vows when they were children. Once, in trying to be blood-sisters like they had seen in a cowboy and Indian serial in the Wellfield, they had cut their wrists and nearly killed themselves by mistake. Mrs Buchanan had had to tie hankies tightly round their arms and rush them along the road to Doctor Patterson's. It had taken Mrs Buchanan ages to get the bloodstains off her rag rug. And Mrs McElpy had nearly murdered Rory for causing the expense of visiting the doctor.

'Through thick and thin,' Victoria echoed importantly.

'I'm in terrible trouble,' Rory said.

The self-importance crumpled from Victoria's face and was immediately replaced by a mixture by genuine concern and curiosity. 'Are you?'

'It's to do with what I've just been telling you.'

The incredulity returned to Victoria's expression. 'About how the seed for a baby goes up between your legs?'

'Yes.'

'I still don't understand that.'

'You know how there's an opening there?'

Victoria did not. Not only was it never allowed in the Buchanan household to mention one's private parts — it was strictly taboo to look at them as well.

'You mean where the water comes from?'

'No, behind that.'

Victoria looked aghast. 'Not . . .'

'No, there's another place between. It's where our monthlies come from.'

'Oh.' Victoria had forgotten about that.

'When you're going to have a baby, that stops and the blood goes to make the baby instead.'

'Oh,' Victoria repeated.

'Then after nine months or so, the baby comes down that way.'

'Between your legs?'

'Yes.'

Victoria thought it was all too shocking and disgusting for words. Yet babies were so lovely; she was totally confused and couldn't help feeling it was all Rory's fault. 'That's terrible!'

'I know,' Rory agreed. She looked as if she was close to tears and suddenly a dreadful thought struck Victoria. 'You're not . . .' Her voice dropped to a shocked whisper. 'You're not trying to tell me . . .'

Rory nodded.

For a long minute there was a stunned silence, broken only by the leisurely tick-tock of the marble clock.

'Oh, Victoria,' Rory said. 'I'm so upset.'

It seemed such an inadequate thing to say in the circumstances and Victoria looked as if she was about to say, 'Don't be daft' again. But no words came out.

'I didn't want it to happen,' Rory went on. 'He pulled

157

me into the back close that first time he took me home from the dance, remember? I struggled and said no, over and over again, but he was stronger than me and . . .' She gazed at Victoria, who stared back as if transfixed by a snake. '. . . he knocked me against the wall and before I knew what had happened — he'd done it to me. I only went out with him again to tell him that I'd missed my monthly and that he would have to marry me.'

'Oh, Rory?' The thought of Rory being tied for life to such a coarse, horrible creature was an absolute tragedy.

'Then I thought — no, I couldn't and wouldn't marry such a beast. Not even if he went down on his knees and begged me to.'

Victoria avoided Rory's eyes for a second, wanting to spare her from seeing that she had not been fooled. Sid Ford had refused to marry her, that was the truth of it.

'Quite right,' she said. 'You deserve a lot better than him.'

'I asked him what I should do — I mean about the baby. And he said . . . he said to get rid of it!'

Victoria was stunned with horror. 'Get *rid* of it?'

'Oh, it won't be like a real baby yet — not with arms and legs and things. There'll only be a kind of bag with a wee drop of blood in it, that's what Sid said.'

'I still don't see . . .'

'Sid said if I burst that bag it would come away and I'd have nothing to worry about. He said I could do it myself.'

Normally Victoria had a strong healthy stomach, but suddenly she felt queasy. A headache was starting as well, something she never suffered with.

'Oh dear . . .' she said, half helplessly, half in exasperation at herself.

Rory had begun to tremble visibly. 'I'm going to do it.'

'But how?'

'I'll push a sharp knitting needle up.'

Victoria's head drew back again and even her stomach

tightened. Any minute, she thought, I'm going to be sick. 'You can't!' she gasped aloud.

'What else can I do? Think of the disgrace, not to mention the doctor's bills. I don't even know if doctors do such things.'

'Oh, Rory!'

'Will you stay with me, Victoria?'

Victoria struggled with herself.

'Oh please, Victoria!'

'Yes, but . . .'

'Thank you.' Rory was struggling with herself, trying to retain some dignity.

CHAPTER TWENTY-FOUR

They picked a night when all the Buchanans would be out, but decided against doing it in the house in case the rag rug or the linoleum got stained. The wash-house in the back green was a better place — indeed it was the only place. The McElpy room and kitchen were never empty, and there wasn't any wash-house in Cowlairs' back court.

The next day was Mrs Buchanan's turn for the wash-house and she always had the key the evening before. They could lock themselves in with some candles and no one would know.

Sometimes Victoria forgot the awfulness of the whole affair. It seemed at those times an exciting adventure, a secret drama like something at the pictures. Rory was the pathetic waif in dire distress as a result of the wicked machinations of the villain. She, Victoria Buchanan, was the brave heroine who came to the rescue and organized everything so that the wicked villain's evil was thwarted and the poor victim was saved.

Everything went according to plan. Rory arrived looking so pale that her freckles seemed darker. Mrs Buchanan peered over her spectacles at her before going out.

'Are you feeling all right, dear?'

'Yes.'

'You look very pale.'

'It's just that time of the month.'

Mrs Buchanan seemed puzzled at first and then so shocked that she went away without her handbag and had to come back for it. Victoria closed the door after she had finally gone.

'Poor mother,' she told Rory. 'She is *so* old-fashioned.'

'Did you get the wash-house key?'

'Of course. I told you I would, didn't I?'

'Do you think we should go now?'

Victoria hesitated. It was all very well acting the heroine, but this wasn't the pictures. 'If you want,' she said uncertainly.

Rory produced a towel from under her coat. 'I sneaked this out the house so that I could wash and dry myself afterwards.' She replaced it beneath her coat and hugged herself as if she were cold.

'All right, come on, then,' said Victoria. 'Have you got the knitting needle?'

'Oh, I forgot.'

Victoria went over to a drawer and brought out one of the needles from the sock that her mother was knitting.

'Maybe we'd better take a longer one as well,' Rory said. 'I don't know how far up it is.'

Victoria raked about the drawer and produced a long steel needle. Both girls stood silently staring at it for a few seconds. Then Rory grabbed both needles and shoved them under her coat.

'Come on. I don't suppose it'll take a minute.'

'Yes,' Victoria agreed. 'The quicker it's over, the better.'

They left the house like a couple of burglars, peeping out into the shadows of the close first to make sure that no one was there. Victoria felt it was like the pictures again; it was very dramatic tip-toeing out with only the hissing of the gas-lamp in the close and the traffic outside echoing as if it was far away. It was then they realized it was foggy. Fog always muffled sound, making a cocoon of silence like a wall.

They clung to one another as they stepped cautiously out of the back close and felt their way across the back green to the wash-house. 'It's a bit of luck for us that the fog's come down,' Victoria whispered. 'There's no danger now of any of the neighbours seeing us from their back windows.'

She unlocked the wash-house door and then gently locked it again after they were both safely inside.

'Where's the candles and matches?' Rory asked.

'Here in my pocket.'

After a minute or two's fumbling in the pitch blackness, Victoria managed to light one candle and fix it in a bottle on a shelf. Then she lit two candles that were already there; one she positioned on top of the brick boiler. The wash-house was icy-cold and damp and had a lingering smell of the slimy black soap and soda that the women used in their efforts to rid their husbands' railway dungarees of accumulated grease and dirt.

Both girls shivered.

'It's a thought to take off my knickers,' Rory said.

Victoria felt embarrassed. Rory could be rather coarse at times.

'But I suppose I'll have to.' Rory's features creased with anxiety. 'It would be a bit awkward otherwise, wouldn't it?'

Victoria looked away and shrugged. 'Do whatever you have to.' She kept her head turned away and her chin raised as if she was above and detached from any such painful embarrassments as someone taking their knickers off in her presence. It was more than an embarrassment. It made her feel within touching distance of wickedness. Her mother never allowed words like knickers to pass her lips — or the lips of anyone in the family. 'Underthings' was the most usual word used and even then in a discreet undertone accompanied by a slightly warning look as if to say: 'Be careful. Watch your tongue. This is a dangerous area.' When she was much younger, words like 'combies' could be used, but with the same sense of sin. Her father quite often asked where his clean 'drawers' were. This would make her mother 'tut-tut' as she went to fetch them; but because father always said the word in such a cheerful and unselfconscious way, 'drawers' never seemed quite so bad.

'Gosh, maybe I should have put Vaseline on the needle.

It's not going up very easy,' Rory said breathlessly.

Victoria couldn't resist screwing her eyes round to glance in Rory's direction. Her friend was squatting down on the stone floor. Hastily she averted her gaze again.

'Is anything happening yet?' she asked eventually.

Rory's voice came out fainter now, more like a kind of groan. 'No, but I've got it up. Maybe I should stab harder.'

Victoria shuddered. The squeamish feeling was returning, bringing with it waves of weakness. She prayed that she wasn't going to faint. It suddenly seemed unbelievable that she was standing in a cold dark wash-house instead of a warm kitchen. She held the kitchen desperately in her mind's eye: the gas-mantle lending a silver sheen to the green plush table-cover; the fire giving a warm red glow to the steel fender, and the wood of her mother's rocking-chair, and a fainter flicker on the dresser over on the side wall. The soft flames also flickered on the sepia photographs and softened the stiffly posed figures.

Rory was groaning again. Just groaning . . . not saying anything.

'Are you all right?' Victoria queried without turning round, but Rory didn't answer. After a time the groaning began to unnerve Victoria and she forced herself to look. Rory was lying on her side on the floor now.

'Rory, are you all right? Has it come away? Will we go back to the house now?'

The groans were turning to strangled moans as if Rory was screaming through clenched teeth. And she was writhing about.

Victoria felt frightened. 'Rory?'

Rory was grunting, moaning, trying to speak.

Victoria took a couple of uncertain steps towards her. 'What's wrong?' But the only response was another of Rory's teeth-gritting screeches.

'Oh, Rory!' Victoria stood, nursing her hands, wondering what to do. Then before her horrified eyes she saw a dark gush of not just blood, but lumps of what

163

looked like liver swirl around the wash-house floor.

Rory saw it too.

'Victoria!'

'My God!' Victoria's high-pitched squeals joined Rory's. 'Oh, my God! My God!' She had never seen so much blood in all her life. The wash-house floor was covered in it; it came gushing over her shoes with its flotsam of flesh, making her screams of horror vie with Rory's in a mad chorus . . .

Then suddenly Victoria's screaming stopped. She didn't know whether it was because of Rory's terrified face appealing to her for help, or a natural vein of courage surfacing within her, but she managed to strangle her screams into silence, take a deep shuddering breath and start picking her way over to her friend. The towel Rory had brought lay on top of the boiler; she lifted it and then struggled to pull Rory backwards to a dry piece of floor.

'Put this between your legs. It must be all away by now. Here, fasten it round your waist with my belt. And then put your . . . put your drawers back on.'

'Oh, Victoria.' Rory was weeping now and struggling weakly and unsuccessfully with the towel. In acute mental distress Victoria forced herself to help her, shocked as much by the sight of a woman's private parts as by the blood that stained them. But the two fused in her mind in a picture of such horror she could not cope with it. Yet Rory was holding on to her, vulnerable and trusting like a child. She fixed the towel and then after that was done they both clung to each other in the acuteness of their distress.

At last Victoria managed, 'I'll try to move you further back and then get some water to wash your legs. Can you get your stockings off?'

In a shared struggle, Rory was propped up against one of the tubs. 'What about the floor?' she sobbed. 'Oh, Victoria, everybody will know!'

'No, they won't. There's a drain over there and I'll sweep

it all down. I'll pour basins of water on it and sweep it all away down the drain. Don't worry.'

Rory kept gazing at Victoria with large terrified eyes as if everything was beyond her understanding. She looked so pathetic that Victoria put her arms around her and, helplessly, they both wept.

CHAPTER TWENTY-FIVE

Victoria thought how strange it was that she could carry on living her life as if nothing had happened. Her little routines like getting up in the morning and dressing in front of the fire with her bare toes curling into the tufts of her mother's rag rug, for instance. She slept in one of the kitchen set-in-the-wall beds with the curtains closed. Her mother and father slept in the other and the boys shared the beds in the front room. Her father and the boys all left for work earlier than her, so it was safe and private for her to get up and put her clothes on. Even so, her mother had taught her always to dress and undress under the billowing tent of her nightgown — a human body was something that should never be revealed. Now Victoria knew why and it was horrible. Her mother had often boasted with quiet satisfaction, 'I've been married to your father for many a long year and he has never once seen me immodestly uncovered.'

She had always obeyed her mother, although she had often thought she was being old-fashioned and over-anxious. Now she knew better. When she had disobeyed her mother and not allowed Tommy to take her and Rory safely home, the terrible thing had happened. All the horror that Rory suffered was what her mother must have meant when she had warned them about men. Sid Ford had caused it to happen to Rory. The blond-haired driver called George could have made it happen to *her*! She felt sick and ill at the thought. As it was, she had got a fright that night with George Anderson while they had been standing talking in the back close. She had been chatting

166

about a most interesting book she had just read when suddenly he had touched her bosom. Not just touched it, but placed his whole hand — both hands — over it. She had knocked him away immediately, but he tried to grab her again and she had flown away from him to the safety of her door and the key under the mat.

Victoria had gone to bed violently trembling, almost too afraid to take her clothes off even in the dark privacy behind the closed curtains of her bed. Archie had never behaved like that. But, she realized now — *he might have done.* As her mother often said, 'You never know with men — even the nicest of them can fall prey to their own human nature. They can never be trusted.'

She carried on living her life and daily routines continued. Then suddenly the horror of Rory's abortion would become a reality again. It would flood her mind's eye, saturate her brain, paralyze her nervous system. She would stop in the middle of dressing, or eating, or writing a customer's order in a store book. Then she would close her eyes and feel as if she was dying.

Life went on, little routines went on. Yet nothing would ever be the same again.

Rory had struggled into work next day. Her mother was still too preoccupied with her grief about Isa's death to notice how ill she looked; but as Rory said, she would soon have noticed if she had stayed off work. However, it would have been so much better in more ways than one if Rory had stayed home. She had been making mistakes and getting into trouble from the boss more than once during these past few weeks, and she had been warned more than once too. Victoria had tried to keep an eye on her, tried to straighten out her confusion, tried to cover up for her when possible. But in the end it was no use. Poor Rory seemed ill not only in her body but also in her mind.

Eventually, she got her books.

Victoria had gone home with Rory that night to try to soften the blow to Mrs McElpy. Not for Mrs McElpy's sake, but for Rory's. It had proved another nightmare experience which kept returning to haunt her. Rory had seemed too dazed to say anything and so she had announced to Mrs McElpy, 'I'm afraid I have bad news for you, Mrs McElpy. Rory has been sacked from her job.'

Mrs McElpy was peeling potatoes at the sink. She was a tall, angular woman with a scrap of sandy hair unsuccessfully twisted up on top of her head. Now she put down the knife she had been using and dried her hands on her sacking apron; then she strode over and gave Rory such a blow across the face that it made Victoria cry out. The dog started barking and a small man jumped up from the chair by the fire and shouted, 'For Christ's sake, Annie!' Rory just shuddered and didn't make a sound and Victoria put a protective arm around her.

'Mrs McElpy, it wasn't her fault. She hasn't been well.'

'You keep your hoity-toity nose out of this. It's none of your fuckin' business!'

'Now, Annie,' Scrap McElpy repeated. 'For Christ's sake . . .'

Victoria flushed scarlet, but kept her head held high. 'Rory is my best friend and I care about her even if you don't seem to.'

'I'm the one that's to feed the wee messin, not you.' Annie turned on Rory again. 'That does it, m'lady! Don't you think you're going to laze about here while I go out slaving. Isa wasn't too proud to help me and you're not half the girl she was. She was a good girl, was Isa.'

'Annie, there's no use going on about Isa. She's gone,' Mr McElpy said.

'I know our Isa's gone. What I'm saying is, that one there is going to help me with the rags whether she likes it or not.'

'Aye, well,' Mr McElpy subsided back into his chair and the dog stopped barking. 'Fair enough.'

Victoria could feel Rory trembling and knew she was trembling herself. It seemed an absolute miracle to her now that Rory was such a well-mannered person, coming from such a family.

'Rory's had a terrible shock. I think she could be doing with a cup of tea,' Victoria said bravely.

'Oh?' Annie McElpy said. 'And what's stopping her from taking one? There's the pot on the hob.'

'It's all right,' Rory managed at last. 'Sit down, Victoria. I'll pour a cup of tea for us both.'

Annie went back to peeling the potatoes. 'You've only got yourself to blame,' she said to Rory. 'Stupid wee midden! Pour a cup for me as well, hen.'

Victoria stayed as long as she could force herself to put up with the foul language and the foul smell of the place. She guessed one of the worst smells was coming from the dog, a fat ugly-looking creature with a coarse brown coat and a face like a grumpy old man. In fact now that it was lying at Mr McElpy's feet, bewhiskered face down on paws, it seemed to be mumbling and grumbling.

There was certainly a lot to complain about in this house. There were no bed curtains and the valance was stained and crushed and bulged out and up with all the obvious junk that was stuffed under the bed. There were things stuffed under the greasy-looking cushions of the two chairs which sat one on either side of the fire. The fire grate was a disgrace; it looked as if it had never seen a bit of black-lead or steel wool since it had been installed. There were no rugs on the floor, not one. And there were innumerable worn patches on the linoleum. The only good thing was the fire which was well poked-up and blazing.

'Do you fancy a wee piece and jam, hen?' Mrs McElpy asked.

'No, thank you,' Victoria replied.

'How about you, Rory? Will I cut you a slice, hen?'

'No thanks, Ma. I don't feel hungry.'

For days afterwards the foulness of the place depressed Victoria. It mixed with the horror of the abortion and made her feel sick. Indeed, these recent events had turned her life completely upside down. It was becoming more and more difficult to keep to normal and familiar routines all the time. She was unable to stop her mind erupting in turmoil every now and again.

She was still very fond of Rory, of course. There were times, however, when she didn't understand her. For example, Rory had been prepared to take their usual Sunday parade along Springburn Road hardly more than a couple of weeks after the abortion.

'But we couldn't!' Victoria had been horrified.

'Why not?' Rory immediately wanted to know. 'Are you ashamed of me or something?'

'No, it's not that.'

'What, then?'

She couldn't tell Rory of the irrational fears that kept haunting her. Sometimes she felt that if a man just looked at her something bad was bound to happen. She shrugged. 'I should have thought you would have had enough of men by now to last you a lifetime.'

'There must be some decent ones around,' Rory answered.

It wasn't just the secret fear of men, though. Other secret feelings had come to torment Victoria. Rory was having to go out with her mother collecting rags. Certainly she collected in other districts, not Springburn, but the fact remained: Rory McElpy was *a rag woman*. Little did Victoria ever think she would be seen — far less be friends with — *a rag woman*. How could one, even if one wanted to, meet decent boy-friends if one kept such disreputable company? She *did* feel ashamed of Rory and that was the truth of it. At the same time she felt ashamed of feeling ashamed. Rory was still Rory. They still whispered together in the Buchanans' scullery; they still went to the pictures together and shared a bag of caramels, chewing in earnest unison as they concentrated on the film. They still both enjoyed a romantic story, whether it was on the screen or in a book. Victoria still related — with as much feeling and drama as any actress — the contents of books she had read and Rory had not.

And after all, Rory didn't *want* to be a rag-woman. She

tried to keep her spirits up in that cheeky 'why-should-I-care' way she had, struggling valiantly to hold on to some vestiges of pride. Nevertheless, it was perfectly obvious that she was suffering terribly. Rory was ashamed as well.

Victoria felt sorry for her. But still, it was terribly embarrassing knowing her. When they went to church together now, even though Rory was dressed very respectably in well-brushed hat, coat and shoes, it wasn't the same. Victoria felt stiff and self-conscious; even her mouth had a stiffness that made it look hard and bitter. She kept her head held high, but the pain and tension of her embarrassment also showed in her eyes.

It was all a far cry from what she and Rory had planned for each other. They were both going to do something special with their lives. Not for them the humdrum ordinariness of the existence of most Springburn girls. Most girls slaved as skivvies to some hoity-toity women. Then they escaped to marriage — or so they thought — only to slave as skivvies for men. She and Rory had dreamed of better things for each other.

Now where had all their dreams gone?

CHAPTER TWENTY-SIX

'Not bad, eh?' The Hyde Park workman remarked to
Drummond as he casually spat to one side in an attempt
to conceal his pride.

They were standing in the crush of people who had
gathered to watch the latest locomotive emerge from
Hyde Park Works in Vulcan Street, off Springburn Road.
It was destined for the docks and then China or India or
some other far-off land. Springburn was the cornucopia
from which flowed famous classes of locomotive for the
five continents.

The people of Springburn were well-used to the spectacle
of huge out-of-gauge engines moving majestically down
Springburn Road on a long articulated trailer with two
snorting traction engines in charge. The sight never lost
its ability to arouse in everyone a sense of wonder and
admiration, however.

The big gates of Hyde Park swung open at last and
there were appreciative gasps from the crowd as the
gigantic work of art fashioned in shining steel, a thing
of power and beauty, moved forward. North British
Railway officials, policemen, officers of the Glasgow
Corporation all buzzed importantly about. There was
also a representative of the Tramway Department to
make sure that the top of the boiler was sheeted with
rubber and that no accidents happened en route to the
docks. For most of the journey the tram wires would
be only a very few inches above the engine. A man from
the Water Department was also in attendance; it had not
been forgotten that one of these Hyde Park engines had

once sunk down through the road and burst a water main.

A spontaneous cheer went up from people lining the pavements and leaning from open windows as the locomotive made its slow, dignified progress over the cobbles of Vulcan Street, vibrating as it did so every dish on every shelf in the surrounding houses. The traction engines billowing yellow smoke from their copper-capped stacks continued to ease the engine forward and the cavalcade of officials came after it at a brisk walking pace or in vehicles. Round the elbow bend of Springburn Road it went and down the hill past St Rollox and slowly, slowly it trundled under Inchbelly Bridge while everyone held their breath. There seemed no more than one inch at most between the chimney cap and the bottom of the girders.

Drummond turned away feeling two feet taller and inches broader in the chest. One day he would drive an N.B. locomotive. One day he would be a top-link driver, hurtling across the country in an express train — an Edinburgh to London, for instance. It gave him something to look forward to. There were other things too, of course. He had been made branch secretary of the National Union of Railwaymen and was kept busy with Union work during his off-duty hours. Railway men often much older than himself were coming to him with grievances and problems and he was becoming adept at writing letters and arguing on their behalf.

He was also becoming active in the Independent Labour Party, an organization which he found both literate and literary. In the worst slum areas of Glasgow, groups would collect to read a single daily paper and would subscribe to and read *Hansard*. If illiterate, they would listen to the latest speeches in Parliament being read aloud to them. Drummond himself had read to groups of black-faced miners, tired from their shift but eager to listen and learn nevertheless.

As often as he could he went to hear the Orpheus Choir which had been founded by Hugh Roberton, a member of the ILP. He had also attended lectures on music given by the directors of the Moody-Manners Opera Company. A talk by Bernard Shaw had drawn a huge audience and been most intellectually stimulating.

All the meetings were held every Sunday in the main Glasgow theatres and there were usually singers and a choir as well as a speaker. He had even been to Miss Buick's tearooms in Renfrew Street and joined in the debates with other politically conscious young men who met there such as Shinwell, Wheatley, Maxton, Dollan, Campbell Stephens and William Gallacher. But he began to find the debating atmosphere of the tea-rooms too rarefied and theoretical for his taste. In any case he was never easy in convivial company and he eventually withdrew into aloofness.

Nevertheless Drummond's horizons were broadening and it often occurred to him how fortunate it was that he possessed enough sense and good judgement not to choose Rory McElpy as a life-time partner. He could not imagine Rory enjoying the talk by Bernard Shaw. Or even the Orpheus Choir. All the same he had been sorry to hear that she had lost her job. There had been some sniggering and talk about her in the railway bothy. A cleaner called Sid Ford had made crude innuendoes about a shared knowledge of Rory, but he had frozen any conversation with the man by saying, 'I had the honour of being a friend of Miss McElpy.'

He had stopped her in the street once and offered his sincere condolences on the death of her young sister. She had been curiously reluctant to stand and talk. Rory had always been an enthusiastic chatterer; even when she was angry, it was a positive emotion which she put into words in no uncertain manner. Her evasive eyes and obvious impatience to escape from him did not seem in character. Then her mother had come out from a nearby shop, her tall figure draped in a dark shawl. She looked even more gaunt than he remembered her. He had repeated the condolences and she had nodded, made no reference to the sad event but seeming pleased nevertheless that he had

174

spoken of it. All she had said was, 'Rory's helping me with the rags now. I thought she was going to be no fuckin' use at first and we'd all starve. I can't feed our crowd with the few bob I make on my own. Joe's the only one of the boys bringing anything in and that's not enough to buy our gas-mantles, far less feed us. But she's getting the hang of it now.'

'I'm glad,' Drummond said. 'It's so difficult to find work at present. The United States are mass-producing goods in up-to-date factories by means of modern techniques and shipping them across the Atlantic. British manufacturers are responding by cutting their costs, reducing workers' wages or dismissing as many employees as they can. I believe unemployment will soon reach the two million mark.'

'Aye, well, they can always depend on my man to keep their numbers up,' Annie responded.

He didn't know what to say to that, so he just gave an uncomfortable half-smile, tipped his cap to both ladies and bid them good-day.

It was somewhat of a relief to know that Rory had found a way of earning some money. Since hearing of the family's double misfortune, he had been wondering if he should offer them any financial assistance. He felt some responsibility for Rory; they had enjoyed a certain level of intimacy and her mother had been most kind and supportive to him in his hour of need. Now Rory was gainfully employed, it saved him any more worry on that score. It was particularly fortunate that she was working alongside her mother; no doubt her company would be a comfort to Mrs McElpy and it would be more congenial for Rory than being stuck inside a shop all day.

He returned to his lodgings to have his tea and get ready to go to the railway dance. He hadn't been to one for some time and he missed the actual exercise of dancing; he enjoyed the challenge and the rhythm and the mastering of the intricate steps.

Mrs Kipp, his landlady, was talking to God when he

entered the house. 'Wasn't there a lot of sinners came to the benches this week, Lord? All weeping and wailing and served them right, did you not think?'

If people attending the Salvation Army meetings had 'sinned' during the week, they went and sat on the side benches and confessed and asked forgiveness and mercy and everyone else shouted hallelujas for them or something. Drummond had never been to one of these meetings, but he was picking up odd pieces of information from Mrs Kipp.

'Good evening, Mrs Kipp,' he greeted her in passing the kitchen to reach his room.

'God willing, your tea'll be ready in a couple of minutes.'

'Thank you.'

There was a chipped enamel jug of cold water in his room and an equally chipped enamel basin. He stripped off his railway dungarees and greasy shirt and washed as best he could in the basin with a piece of blue-veined soap. Then he changed into his clean semmit, drawers, shirt and suit. The mirror over the fireplace was clouded and brown-stained with rust. It involved much difficulty and peering this way and that before he managed to get his hair brushed to look its best. Then he went through to have his meal.

'I was just saying to God,' — Abigail Kipp's razor face and beady eyes, like the rest of her person, were alive with energy and enthusiasm — 'there's an awful lot of His work to be done in Springburn.'

Drummond looked at the piece of cheese and hunk of bread that was supposed to suffice as his only meal and he cleared his throat.

'Mrs Kipp, I do feel that after a day's work a man needs a more substantial meal. It's not as if I have been home for any dinner.'

'Did you hear that, Lord?' Mrs Kipp darted a look upwards. 'And so many of your poor folk starving in the world! Forgive his selfishness and greed, oh Lord, for my sake.'

'When I don't have dinner in the middle of the day, Mrs

Kipp,' Drummond persisted, 'I must have it later. I am entitled to at least one cooked meal every day.'

'It's not,' Mrs Kipp addressed God again, 'as if I eat any more myself.'

'Your nutritional requirements, Mrs Kipp — as an elderly lady with a small physical frame — are very different from mine. I am over six feet tall and I shovel at least 3 or 4 tons of coal every shift.'

'There's nothing to be ashamed of in honest toil,' Mrs Kipp told him, adding to the ceiling, 'Is there, Lord?'

Sometimes he felt he could strangle the woman. 'In future, Mrs Kipp,' he said firmly, 'I wish a decent cooked meal.'

However, as he ate the bread and cheese there was not much hope in his heart of ever getting a decent meal. Cooking could dirty the range and Mrs Kipp believed that cleanliness was next to godliness. She was never at peace from scrubbing and polishing except when she was out banging her tambourine and shouting her hallelujas. Next to greedy capitalists like Forbes-Cunningham there was no one Drummond hated more than religious enthusiasts.

CHAPTER TWENTY-SEVEN

'Why the hell shouldn't I?' Rory's green eyes sent daggers darting straight at Victoria.

Victoria gazed around as if so astonished that she hardly knew where she was. 'I was only thinking of you. I don't know why you get so worked up. You've always had a quick temper, Rory, but honestly it's getting worse.'

Rory was white around the mouth and her mouth had a hard half-twist, half-tremble to it. 'You never questioned my right to go to the railway dance before,' she accused.

'Sid Ford could be there tomorrow.'

'So, tell him to stay away.'

'Rory!'

'He's the one who should be punished, not me.'

'I only thought you might get upset. You know how ignorant and insensitive Sid Ford is. He might even bring up about you . . . you know . . .'

'No, I don't know!'

'About you being . . . I hardly like to say it, Rory . . . I'm the last one to want to risk offending you.'

'A rag woman?'

'You know what some people are like!'

'I do an honest day's work and that's nothing to be bloody ashamed about.'

Victoria patted her hair and tried to think about something else. 'Of course not,' she said absently.

Rory was boiling inside with rage. She knew perfectly well that Victoria was ashamed of her and she hated her friend all the more because she would have felt the very same herself. Indeed, she did feel the very same. She hated the indignity of having to carry a bundle and insisted on carrying it in her hand like a shopping bag instead of slinging it over her back — although it felt much less heavy that way. She also hated the toffy-nosed women at whose doors she had to beg for old clothes. She hated Paddy's Market, where she had to squat on an upturned orange box in the draughty lane and wait for people to ruffle through the clothes and examine them minutely before trying to knock down the price her mother was asking.

'Whether you like it or not,' Rory said, 'I'm going!'

Victoria gave a big sigh. 'I'm not stopping you.'

But she wished she could. Rory being a rag woman was bad enough, but you couldn't even trust her to be discreet about it. There had always been a perverse bit about her friend and recently it had got worse. She was impudent with it now and always ready to throw down the gauntlet or jump on you with some accusation or other. Rory, in fact, was getting very hard to bear.

They had just been to the pictures and seen *For Husbands Only* about a convent-bred girl who, on being introduced into society, falls in love with a predatory bachelor. Discovering that the bachelor is merely toying with her affections, she marries a slow-witted man out of spite and then proceeds to make the flirtatious bachelor fall head over heals in love with her. It had been a very glossy and amusing production and Victoria decided she would just think about that.

Rory said, 'See you tomorrow night inside the door, then?'

'Fine,' Victoria replied before sailing away.

Rory couldn't sleep for hours that night. Friday nights were sleepless at the best of times, because on Saturdays she had to face the ordeal of Paddy's Market. This time she had the dance to lie and worry about as well. A sickly smell of urine from the pail in the doorless cupboard didn't help . . . nor the persistent scratch-scratch of a mouse in one of the dark corners . . . nor the sad nasal song of a drunk man outside.

She didn't know how she was going to face the dance, but she was determined to brazen it out in the same way she had to employ every day when going round begging for rags and every weekend hawking at the Market.

Alice and Norma were lying very still and snoring loudly and deeply. It always amazed her how quickly they slept. Of course they had recently managed to get jobs as skivvies to Mrs Forbes-Cunningham at 'The Towers', and it was exhausting and heavy work. They had to carry coal buckets up miles of stairs, they said. They had innumerable fires to clean out and attend to; they swore there were so many in fact that they hadn't been able to count them. Alice had got lost looking for one of them on her first day and was eventually discovered crying helplessly in the corridor, coal-pail in hand.

Like the other twins Jessie and Mary, Alice and Norma slept in at their respective 'big house' most nights. As a result, Rory quite often had the bed to herself. Tonight, however, was their night off.

Rory drifted into a nightmare sleep eventually and awoke startled by her mother's bawl from the kitchen. 'Rory, are you going to stay there all day?'

She still insisted on wearing her coat, although it was thinner and shabbier than ever. Nothing would induce her to wrap herself in Isa's old shawl. 'I'll go out in my skirt and blouse without anything over it rather than be seen wearing a shawl,' she told her mother. Although now that the sun shone most days, that would not have been too much of a hardship.

'Your pride, m'lady,' Annie warned, 'will be the death of you yet.'

They were late in reaching the Market much to Annie's annoyance, but she quickly got into her stride. 'Come on, come on!' she shouted, sauntering back and forth behind the trestle table that Rory had set up, jingling coins in one of her big hands. 'Get your bargains while you're young. Turn them over, hen,' she invited a woman who was

180

gazing at the mountain of garments. 'Every one of them dirt-cheap. See that wee dress? It's yours for sixpence. I'm being cruel to myself, but I can't help my generous nature.'

While they were there, Scrap and Henry came squeezing through the crowd calling and barking greetings to the various sellers on either side. The crush was due to the fact that there was barely two or three feet of walking space between the goods spread out for sale on tables and on the ground. In fact most of the merchandise was on the ground being shuffled over and stood on, but nobody seemed to mind.

Paddy's Market was situated in Shipbank Lane, a long narrow area like a crack in a wall. Once you squeezed in, you were flanked on one side by a railway bridge with a line of tunnel-like arches into which hawkers also crowded and on the other side by a high fence. Everywhere was festooned or piled or littered with boiler suits, shawls, scabby furs, christening robes, ladies' dresses . . . The hawkers were not all women. A coolie from one of the ships held out a packet of cigarettes for sale and an old man held out a coat which he obviously had need of himself. Another man squatted beside a battered suitcase containing oddments like razors and bootlaces and button-hooks. Yet another sat on the ground, wearing a long raincoat tied with string; he had a bald dome with a ragged fringe of grey hair and a nose like a cluster of figs. Beside him he had spread brown paper on which he neatly displayed one rusty penknife, one pair of dancing pumps, one headless doll and one glass juice squeezer. Here it was, not so long ago, when Irishmen once stood trying to sell the shirts off their backs in an effort to get a few pennies with which to feed their starving families. But mostly there were rag women with bundles of clothes that they tied up in a sheet and slung over their backs when they were not displaying them on the dusty ground of the market. Rory felt hemmed in and oppressed by the Lane, yet it had a bright bustle and there was a tough resilience about the hawkers that she secretly admired.

Shipbank Lane cut south of the Briggate or Bridge Gate, so called because at one time it led to Glasgow's only bridge across the River Clyde. Now there were the railway bridges towering over it to give extra meaning to its name. The area was a crush of tenements and brick bridges cutting across the streets at all different angles, giving shelter and a cheerful echo to the place.

Scrap McElpy saluted Kath, the rag woman who sat on a box just along from Annie. 'Morning, Kath!'

She nodded in recognition. Kath was like a mountainous Buddha, with knees splayed wide but modestly covered with a bed sheet that looked as if it had been trodden on by innumerable feet — as indeed it had. On the ground in front of her was another sheet on which faded lace curtains and antimacassars, stained table-covers and blankets lay in tangled heaps. In one fist Kath held a mug of steaming tea, in the other a thick hunk of bread; in between masticating, she was shouting, 'Fit for a palace, every one of them! Fit for a palace. See for yourself.'

A worried customer was saying to Annie, 'But are you sure it's her right size?' And Annie was earnestly giving the assurance: 'I'd rather say it wasn't than it was. Do you know what I mean, hen?' The customer didn't look too sure.

'Hello, Da,' Rory greeted her father.

He rubbed his hands enthusiastically together as he swaggered around beside her. 'And how's my bonny wee lassie, eh?'

Before Rory could answer, Annie interrupted, 'No, we can't spare a few bob. We've not got enough yet to buy a loaf, never mind a few potatoes for the dinner.'

Mr McElpy raised his shoulders and spread out his hands in amazement, 'Did I say a word about money? Did I say . . .'

'Away and boil your head,' his wife told him.

'You're a hard woman, Annie. A hard woman.'

'I'm fuckin' soft in the head. I married you, didn't I?'

Rory got up and began pacing about. The sunshine was

182

accentuating the stale smell of old clothes that thickened the air. The sour stench of sweaty bodies was becoming more pungent too and dust being shuffled up by so many feet was hanging in a huge cloud the whole length and breadth of the lane. She longed to escape from the place, but knew she had no chance. Automatically she tidied the clothes on the table, noticing as she did so that there were some genuinely good garments amongst the piles.

Jessie Mason from the stall opposite also noticed when she strolled across for a chat. 'Here, can I borrow that brown coat, Annie? I'll give you it back in the morning. I've my son's wedding tonight and I haven't a decent stitch to my back.'

'Sure, hen,' Annie said. 'Help yourself.'

Annie was generous in this respect, Rory had noticed. Several times she had seen her lend clothes out. There was also a man who did a turn entertaining at weddings and other functions, and he regularly borrowed a suit from Annie's stall for each occasion.

'Where did you get these?' Rory asked her mother after Jessie Mason had returned to her own stall.

Annie glanced at the coats Rory was fingering. 'Some old woman died and her son was clearing out all her stuff. What do you think they're worth?'

She had begun to ask Rory's advice about prices, for her daughter had looked in more shop windows and was more aware of what decent clothes cost than her.

'New, that coat must have cost 3 or 4 guineas.'

'Och, away!' Annie was impressed. 'Fancy anybody having that much money to spend on their backs!'

The coats and dresses which had obviously come from the same opulent source looked out of place amongst the other cheap garments and Rory stood staring at them. Eventually she said, 'Why don't we charge folk for good things like that?'

'But they bring them back next day.'

'We should charge them for the time they've had them.'

'Eh?'

'So much per day. Or so much per twenty-four hours.'

'What an idea!' Annie gave an incredulous burst of laughter.

'What's wrong with it?'

Annie laughed again, but this time with some bewilderment. 'I couldn't do that.'

'*I* could.'

'Take money from friends who just want a wee loan of something for a special occasion?'

'Why not?' Rory stared at her with green eyes becoming feverish.

'God, I believe you would!' her mother said.

'It need not be just the odd friend,' Rory said thoughtfully.

'How do you mean?'

'Something's just occurred to me.'

'Oh, aye. You always were one for the big ideas.'

'You know how Jock McTurk does turns at lots of functions?'

'So?'

'And he always wears that evening suit from our stall.'

'So?'

'He could work that into his act.'

'You've gone off your head. Do you know that?'

'No. I mean it, Ma. He could advertise the fact that we lend out clothes.'

'Stop talking nonsense. We haven't got clothes good enough to lend out.'

'Look at these coats and dresses. Look at the one Jessie Mason's going to wear at her son's wedding.'

'You know as well as I do that that sort of stuff doesn't come our way very often. Some poor soul had died and her son was clearing out her things.'

'It could be a whole new line of business,' Rory said, as if hardly able to believe it herself.

'Oh, aye,' her mother observed sarcastically. 'We could perch another stall on top of this and tell Jock McTurk to spread the word that we have a lending department upstairs.'

'That's it!' Rory exclaimed.

This time her mother laughed heartily and shook her head, calling over to Jessie Mason, 'Would you listen to her?'

'A separate place — that's it!'

'Oh, Ma, if I had a wee shop!'

'Oh, aye, with one suit in it? And a couple of dresses and coats!'

'Oh, Ma . . .'

Maybe it was just a wild dream. Nevertheless she clung to it in a desperate attempt to save her pride and her sanity.

CHAPTER TWENTY-EIGHT

There was a man singing in the back green and Victoria pulled down the kitchen blind so that he could not see her getting dressed in front of the fire. The man was roaring out 'Danny Boy' in that half-throttled way back-court singers had, at the same time as sliding up and down the notes. It could not have been any louder if he had been inside the house. This was one of the disadvantages of living in one of the bottom flats — or 'a house in the close' as it was more commonly known.

She had the house to herself; her parents were away visiting Granny Buchanan, who was even more old-fashioned than her mother. Granny wore a tied-on bonnet with a peak down her forehead. She also favoured a pelisse and never was seen in any colour but black, except for a wee touch of purple on her bonnet. Dave and Tommy were out walking with their young ladies. She didn't know where Willie and Sam were, but she had locked the door so that they could not barge in and see her in her knickers. It was a relief to be able to wear this particular 'underthing'. For too long her mother had insisted she wore combinations of the type she had been encased in winter and summer as a child. They had been a constant torment to her — all tight and sore between her legs — and she had never been able to properly voice her complaint about them. Just one tug in the offending area would elicit a shocked 'Victoria!' from her mother.

'But mother, they're hurting me between the legs . . .' she would begin, only to be silenced with another horrified 'Victoria!' and, 'it's wicked even to speak about . . .' her mother's eyes tentatively flicked in the direction of the place in question before hastily retreating again ' . . . about down there.'

The man had stopped singing outside and she could hear the faint chinkle of pennies being thrown down from upstairs windows. Inside the house there was a noisy scraping from under the bed. Fluffy, the cat, had had kittens again and her mother had put them in the zinc bath so that they wouldn't be running up the bed curtains and getting into all sorts of mischief while she was out. They couldn't escape from the zinc bath; they kept trying, but they just slid back down until, exhausted, they fell asleep in a heap.

The knickers were sheer joy. Victoria furtively stretched and then quivered her thighs, savouring their freedom. Her shot-silk taffeta dress in all different shadings was also a source of great pleasure. She mentally did a skip, hop and jump through to the wardrobe mirror in the front room to admire herself while still keeping her normal dignified gait and posture. She had always believed that conscientious practice in keeping one's head held high and one's back straight made one look really special. Archie once said she carried herself well, and of course he was perfectly right.

As she surveyed herself in the mirror, she was reasonably happy with what she saw. She was not pretty in the sense of being small and delicately boned or having a petite nose or a rosebud mouth; she had more character, more presence than anyone like that. As Archie once said, she was a fine figure of a woman. Archie had been quite besotted with her and sometimes she wished she could have felt the same about him. It would have been so romantic. Somehow, however, despite his collar and tie and his job in the bank, she couldn't. Especially now she knew what you had to allow a man to do so that you could have babies and — almost as bad — how babies were born. It was all terribly rude and dirty and absolutely disgusting. She tried not to think of how frightening it was as well. Often she managed so successfully to blot all such thoughts from her mind that she could quite happily romanticize about boyfriends and excitedly giggle about finding one, exactly as she used to.

It was a warm summer's evening, but she had promised her mother that she would put on her coat in case it might be chilly by the time she emerged from the dance. It was a dark blue coat and with it she wore her scarlet tammy that her mother had knitted in artifical silk yarn. With her blue-black hair and fine dark eyes, she suited scarlet.

Rory met her inside the entrance door of the Co-op building and Victoria couldn't help noticing how shabby she looked; that old black coat of hers was so thin it was more like a dress. She was wearing her green woollen tammy with all her hair tucked up inside it. Recently she had got thinner and her skin had a pale translucent appearance. In a sudden rush of affection and pity, Victoria linked arms with her friend.

'Do you hear what they're playing?' She rolled her eyes at the sounds issuing from the hall upstairs. 'The Lancers! I'm not sorry to be missing that, are you? All that galloping about.'

'I know. It makes me sweat,' Rory said. 'And sweat can ruin a dress under the arms. You can't get nearly as good a price for a dress with sweat stains.'

'Ladies don't sweat,' Victoria corrected. 'Horses sweat, men perspire, ladies *glow*.' Rory giggled as they went into the cloakroom and deposited their coats and tammies.

The piano and fiddle had stopped and there was a noisy clatter of feet and chatter of tongues as people returned to sit or lean against opposite walls. Then as Rory and Victoria emerged from the cloakroom the musicians struck up the new 'I'm Forever Blowing Bubbles.'

'That's more like it,' Victoria said.

'I wish it was the Dixieland Jazz Band playing.'

'No such luck,' Victoria sighed. But she began quietly to sing to herself in time with the music. 'I'm forever blowing bubbles, pretty bubbles in the air . . .'

Someone came over and asked Rory to dance. Victoria hated to be the one left standing; it was so embarrassing.

She invariably stiffened and her face tipped higher. She kept telling herself that the person who had chosen Rory in preference to her must be stupid, and she wouldn't have anyone stupid even if he went down on his bended knees and pleaded with her to dance.

She was busy thinking this when she was suddenly confronted by a tall, striking-looking man with a shock of raven-black hair, a pale face and eyes that gazed at her coolly and politely — but behind the veil of politeness seemed to burn a riveting intensity.

'May I have the pleasure of this dance?' he asked.

Victoria smiled and gave a little inclination of her head to indicate that she agreed to bestow on him this pleasure. Then she allowed him to lead her on to the floor. Once she was in his arms, it was a most peculiar sensation. First of all, she felt as if she was floating. In a way, she wasn't conscious of him at all — at least, not as a separate person. It was as if a lost part of herself had been found and made her complete. She was serenely happy. There was something in that vague faraway place in her mind that might spoil the serenity, but she always ignored that area of her mind.

She became more aware of their separateness when he began to speak. 'You have an excellent singing voice.' She hadn't realized she had been softly singing to herself as they danced.

'Thank you.'

'May I ask your name?'

'Victoria Buchanan.'

'Oh.'

Victoria stiffened. 'You sound disappointed — I can't think why. I have always thought my name had rather a good ring to it.'

'Indeed it has, Miss Buchanan. It was not disappointment you heard but surprise and perhaps a little dismay.'

'Oh? Why surprise and dismay, then?'

'I'm Matthew Drummond.'

If she had been in the habit of using swear words, she would have used one then. But all she said was, 'Oh!'

'I sincerely hope you will not hold it against me, Miss Buchanan?'

The dance ended and saved her the trouble of replying. She managed a vague supercilious kind of smile and returned to where she had been standing, but Rory was nowhere to be seen; she could be very annoying at times. Victoria felt uncertain what the correct behaviour was in such a situation. She always liked to know where she was and with anything to do with Rory, it was very difficult to know. The piano and the fiddle struck up, 'If you were the only girl in the world . . .'

She could see him coming towards her again. He looked so tall and gentlemanly and immaculately groomed that it was hard to believe he could be a railway worker and wear greasy overalls and a railway cap. He looked really special.

This time he sang softly as they danced, 'If you were the only girl in the world and I was the only boy . . . nothing else would matter . . .'

It was wonderfully romantic. His deep, rich voice flowed hypnotically over her, making her close her eyes. They were floating around as one person again and it was most peculiar, but pleasantly so. While they were dancing, she forgot all about Rory. There was a little room off the hall where you could buy a glass of lemonade or a cup of tea and a tea biscuit, and just as the dance finished her partner said, 'Would you care to accompany me next door for refreshments?'

Victoria said, 'Yes,' without thinking. To be with him seemed so right and natural. She sat proud and straight-backed at one of the little card-tables set out with a prettily embroidered tea-cloth, while one of the Co-op waitresses went to fetch the lemonade.

'Rory thinks very highly of you,' Drummond said. 'When she spoke of you, she always gave me the impression of a very beautiful, very intelligent person. I now realize just how accurate that picture was.'

Victoria's mouth primped in an effort to control the pleasure she felt. 'Rory is my best friend,' she said.

'I am sure we both hold her in high esteem.'

'Oh, yes.'

The lemonade arrived, also a plate of biscuits which Drummond politely held towards her.

'Thank you,' she accepted with equal politeness and then proceeded to take a dainty nibble.

'I understand you are an avid reader?' Drummond said.

She gave a little inclination of the head, a regal nod. Having a piece of biscuit in her mouth, she was taking no chances of spoiling a beautiful encounter with a spray of crumbs.

'I wonder if we have any favourite books in common?' he asked. She gave a delicate lift of her shoulders and he went on, 'I recently acquired and have been deeply interested in *The Trial and Death of Socrates*. Have you read it?'

She paused for a moment, her eyes fixed on a point over his right shoulder as if trying to recall if this particular book had been part of her vast stock of reading matter.

'No,' she said eventually, 'I don't believe I have.'

'A fascinating book.'

'A fascinating man.'

'Yes, indeed. If you wish to borrow the book, Miss Buchanan, I would be delighted to oblige you.' Victoria primped her mouth into one of her uncertain smiles and said nothing. 'At the moment I'm reading Atkinson's *The Art of Logical Thinking*, which is all about the laws of reasoning. It goes into the concepts, and reasoning by induction, by theory and hypotheses, deductive reasoning, reasoning by analogies and so on.'

She raised a polite eyebrow. 'Really?' He was a most unusual railwayman. Indeed, it seemed to her that he was a most unusual man. She felt proud to be sitting drinking lemonade and eating tea biscuits with him and talking about things like reasoning by analogy. She gazed around the room, hoping that everyone was watching and listening.

'May I have the honour of walking you home after the dance, Miss Buchanan?'

Her eyes roamed proudly back to him. 'Oh, yes, Mr Drummond.'

191

CHAPTER TWENTY-NINE

First of all a little negotiating had to be done with Victoria's brother Dave, who was supposed to see her home. Matthew Drummond attended to Dave. Then there was Rory. Victoria had only caught the occasional glimpse of her during the evening. She seemed quite carried away with the number of partners eager to dance with her and was flushed and laughing. Victoria tried to signal across the crowded room that she wanted a private word, but Rory was too excited to pay much attention. Eventually Victoria gave up and left without having spoken to her. She was secretly glad, of course. Had she really thought about it — which she didn't — she would have realized that she did not try very hard to get hold of Rory and speak to her. Rory had a very tenuous hold on her mind for the whole evening. Once Victoria left the dance on the arm of the tall dark-eyed Mr Drummond, Rory ceased to exist at all.

They strolled in a leisurely fashion along Springburn Road, while she explained to him that after working hard all day and then doing jobs in the house to help her mother, she preferred to relax with a good novel rather than serious non-fiction books. He understood perfectly.

'It is to your credit, Miss Buchanan, that after attending to so many tasks and duties, you read anything at all.'

He recommended some good authors: Jane Austen for her irony and wit; the Brontës for their passion; Dickens for his stories and social comment. She told him she looked forward to reading the books he suggested, whereupon he said he looked forward to hearing what she thought of them.

They stood in the back close and were so engrossed in

conversation that Victoria even forgot about the smell from the lavatory and that they were actually standing up against its wooden door. With Archie, the smell annoyed and offended her so much she could never quite concentrate on him. They were on first-name terms by this time and Drummond had rather shocked her by revealing atheistic views. She was attempting to point out to him that in his complete turning away from God just because of the attitude of some ministers to the war, he was throwing out the baby with the bath water, so to speak. Then suddenly, just as Matthew was telling her that he took her point, an unexpected voice from behind the lavatory door cried out, 'I'll get bloody pneumonia if you two don't call it a night and let me out!'

Victoria recognized it to be the voice of Mr McTaggart from the other house in the close and she could have dropped dead with humiliation. Drummond looked embarrassed too, but he managed to say quickly that he would like to see her again and she replied with equal haste that if he wanted to see her again he should take earnest care to see to it that he did. Then, before he could even shake hands and bid her good night, she skimmed away into her house, leaving behind her the sounds from the lavatory of an angrily tugged chain and thunderously gushing water.

She could not get into her bed quickly enough and lay behind the closed bed-curtains with eyes tightly shut. That awful vulgar Mr McTaggart from next door! Trust him to spoil everything — she didn't know how she would be able to face Drummond again. The distress to Mr McTaggart's untimely and undignified interruption opened the floodgate to other distress and she remembered why. Even if everything had gone well in the back close, should she, *could* she see Matthew Drummond again? The idea of not seeing him again was impossible to contemplate, and part of her struggled to relegate Rory to that misty area of her mind where reality was swallowed up and disappeared. But Rory would not disappear . . . not that she really wanted her to. Rory was still her best friend and a strong sense of loyalty forced her to consider the position and what it might mean. Rory had been in love with Matthew Drummond. Did she feel the same way about him? It wasn't all that long since they have been walking out together. Yet Rory had gone out with Sid Ford so soon after her parting from Matthew Drummond. Surely that meant she no longer felt the same about him? Surely she wouldn't mind if *she* became friends with him? Somehow Victoria could not convince herself, but she did know beyond all doubt that she couldn't cause Rory the distress which such a relationship would mean if her friend was still in love. She and Rory had been through a lot together and somehow their shared experience bound them as close as Siamese twins. She began to feel remorseful about allowing Matthew Drummond to walk her home, even about dancing with him. The moment she had discovered who he was, she ought to have politely declined his advances in loyalty to Rory.

Her mouth tightened with resolve and she turned her face to the wall.

For the first time in months, Rory felt tolerably happy . . . if one could call an unexpected lightening of spirits happiness.

The idea about renting a shop and hiring out decent clothes — really good quality stuff that most people couldn't afford to buy — had been the first light in the tunnel, but her mother had pooh-poohed the idea to begin with.

'Where would you get this good quality stuff?' Annie wanted to know. 'I told you, that decent stuff belonged to a poor woman who died.'

'People are dying every day,' said Rory.

'Yes I know, but . . . ?'

'They put death notices in the papers.'

Her mother stared at her. 'Do you mean . . .?'

'And the relations are too upset to think properly. If I watched all the papers, if I got in right away and spoke to the next of kin or whoever . . . offered to do them a favour . . .'

'You always were a clever wee shit. Brass-necked as well.' She hesitated thoughtfully. 'You think there would be enough to keep us going? And pay a shop rent?'

'Bound to be.'

'How can you say "bound to be"? Are you planning to go around murdering folk to get the clothes off their backs?'

'Can't you see?'

'You've enough nerve for it,' Annie admitted.

'Hiring, I said. Once we get a stock of clothes, they're always ours. It's just a matter of topping up the stock and keeping a bit of variety going.'

'Hiring? Oh, I don't know, hen. Who would want to pay for borrowing clothes?'

'I've already asked Jock McTurk and Jessie Mason and they have agreed to pay seven and sixpence a night.'

'You'd no fuckin' right. What'll they think of us?'

'I don't care a damm what they think of me.'

'Anyway, one or two folk in the Market's not enough to keep a shop or anything else going.'

'It won't just be them. There are bound to be other people who don't want to buy something new for every special occasion like weddings and funerals and dances. Or who can't afford to. Or people who just want to impress other people and make out they've lots of different clothes.'

Her mother sighed. 'I wish I had your energy, hen.'

Annie had never had quite the same spirit since Isa's death. Sometimes Rory would find her sitting by the fire, hugging her cup of tea, eyes wearily closed. Although if she asked what was the matter, she would be told to mind her own business.

'You don't need my energy,' Rory said. 'I can organize it myself.'

'Oh, aye, and how are you going to manage that?'

'I'd work night and day, Ma. If I could get a wee shop and work for myself, I know I could make it succeed. I'd wash and press the clothes when they need freshening. Everything would be kept perfect, just like new.'

'Is this that pal of yours again? Her and her fancy ideas?'

'No, I've never even mentioned it to Victoria. I thought of it myself.'

'Aye, well you were always a clever wee shit right enough.'

Rory could hardly wait to tell Victoria and rehearsed the scene in her mind before meeting her at the dance. She would choose the perfect moment — probably at the interval when the pianist and fiddler were taking a rest and having a drink of lemonade. Then she'd say, 'Oh, Victoria, you'll never guess! I've had this marvellous idea. I know you'll be as pleased and excited about it as I am . . .' And Victoria would be pleased for her. Victoria wanted her to get out of her present predicament as much as she did herself. Renting a little shop and dealing in better-class goods was definitely a step in the right direction.

Being asked to dance so quickly and so often helped to lighten her spirits as well. It was so unexpected and flattering and it seemed as if every cleaner in the Eastfield shed was competing to have the pleasure of her company. She felt grateful to them for helping her to feel happy again. These past few weeks had been a nightmare, physically and mentally. She had thought she would never stop bleeding; a steady trickle had gone on and on and on and she had to wear a piece of rag tied constantly around herself and resort to all kinds of devious ways to wash the rag without anyone seeing her. Often the only privacy she had to do so was on her knees in front of the lavatory pan in the toilet on the landing. She always pulled the chain several times so that the water in which to wash the piece of cloth would be clean. But still her natural fastidiousness shrank from wearing anything which had been immersed in the cracked, discoloured and smelly lavatory pan. Her mental sufferings were terrible as a result. Then there was the constant fear of being found out, if it wasn't her mother bawling at her when she was locked in the lavatory, it was one of the neighbours.

'How many times do you need to pull that chain? What the bloody hell are doing in there — elephant shit?'

Gradually the bleeding had become less and then one morning she had taken her usual furtive look under the blankets at the cloth and it was unstained. She had flopped her head back on the pillow and cried out loud like a halleluja. 'Oh, thank you, God!'

'Eh?' Alice had mumbled, coming half-awake. 'What did you say?'

'Nothing.' She had felt so relieved she could have hugged Alice and Norma and all the boys still snoring in the other crowded beds.

For the first time in years, it seemed, she felt she could get back to normal and try to find a bit of enjoyment in life. She decided that was what she would to at the dance — indeed, that was what she was doing. Until, that is, she had seen Matthew Drummond dancing with Victoria. They looked made for each other, and there was something about the way they were dancing, the way they were gazing into each other's eyes. That was how Rory had hoped Matthew Drummond would look at her and she longed to run up to him and plead with him to love her. It wasn't fair that he should be looking at Victoria like that. Why should Victoria have everything? What could Victoria give him or do for him that *she* hadn't done? Her distress became a kind of hysteria as she continued dancing with her flatteringly eager partners. She laughed and flaunted them and her popularity as if to say to everyone, 'See! I don't care about Matthew Drummond. See how many other admirers I have. I don't need him! I'm happy as a lark.'

She even allowed a crowd of them to walk her home after the dance. Three or four of them were all pals, they said, and they were all going the same way. They laughed and talked and larked about. Afterwards she could not remember what they had said or what she had said; her mind had been so confused with distress.

However, she did remember the exact point when she became afraid. She had reached her close and was just turning quite cheerily and cheekily to bid them good night when she was jostled inside. The men were still laughing and joking and talking, but she experienced terror as they pushed her into the back close.

'Just a minute,' she said loudly. 'I'm having none of this; I'm going upstairs.'

'Of course you are, hen,' one of them laughed, 'in a minute!'

'A minute each' another chuckled.

'Get out of my way,' her voice betrayed apprehension. 'Let go of me!'

But they paid no attention. Their laughter became dirty. 'Come on! You can't kid us — we know you're no Virgin Mary.'

A pack of animals closed in on her.

'Ma!' she shouted desperately.

Then one of the animals held a big smelly paw over her mouth . . .

CHAPTER THIRTY

Sunday was another Market day. Saturday and Sunday were the two most important days of the week, the days the money was earned. Somehow Rory got through Sunday. She had no choice but to get through it and in doing so, she found strengths in her which she had never thought existed. She struggled to carry an extra large bundle to the Market; she set up the table and sorted out the clothes; she exchanged greetings and gossip with the other hawkers; she haggled with customers over prices; she paced about in front of the table shouting, 'Come on, come on! You can't afford to miss what's here. Genuine bargains. Giveaway prices. This is your lucky day, folks . . . Come on, come on!' She didn't even stop to have something to eat at midday and eventually her mother said, 'For Christ's sake, are you never going to give it a rest? Have you gone off your nut or something? Get a cup of tea inside you; you're getting on my nerves.'

Sometimes she believed she was going off her head. Life was a raging sea which was overwhelming her. At other times she felt full of fight and wanted to kick at everything and everybody — kick out at the whole of her stinking, rotten life.

But all the time, like a horror film unrolling before her unwilling eyes, she saw the faces of the men who had raped her, felt their obscene bodies, smelled them. She had been standing holding the cup of hot tea her mother had forced on her when the crowd of animals had come guffawing up to the table. With one quick movement she sprayed the boiling liquid over their faces and then, while they were

199

howling in shock and pain, she grabbed her mother's cup and repeated the performance.

'You dirty bastards!' she said. 'Don't you ever come near me again!'

After they had disappeared, her mother asked, 'What was that all about?'

'I had my reasons.'

'Aye, well. Don't just stand there — pour us some more tea.'

After that Sunday Rory kept herself obsessively busy. She studied the papers, wrote down the names and addresses of the deceased and trekked for miles around the suburbs pleading for their clothes. Recklessly she told every lie that she thought might serve her purpose. To a grieving daughter she sympathized and said she had known the departed: 'The dear lady was always so kind to me. Many a nice chat we had.' Then she gradually let drop how her own mother was ailing and in need of some decent warm clothing.

'Forgive me for mentioning this, I know how distressing it must be for you. But I'm sure your dear mother would understand. If you want to clear out her things, I would greatly appreciate . . .'

If the 'departed' happened to be a child, she borrowed Annie's wedding ring and pretended she had children of her own and was struggling to keep them warm and decent.

Annie was shocked. Her lack-lustre eyes regarded her daughter in disbelief. 'You're fuckin' terrible! Taking advantage of folks' grief, especially when they've lost a wean.'

'It's a hard life,' Rory said with a shrug. She hadn't a scrap of emotion left over for anybody else at the moment; all she could think of was what might happen to herself as a result of what the animals had done to her. Deep down, she was feverish with terror. At one time she prayed that the bleeding would stop; now she prayed day and night that it would start. She prayed too every time she entered the shadowy close in Cowlairs Road; she prayed for courage, prayed to keep calm as she passed the black hole leading to the rear of the building. Memories of the rape kept leaping out to terrify her and make her feel nauseated. She had not yet told Victoria anything about what happened, although she longed for comfort of a shared anxiety. So far her pride (and her shame) had prevented her. However, she knew if she had to face the terrors of another abortion, Victoria — no matter how shocked and horrified she might be — would face it with her. She knew Victoria and that was why — or at least it was one of the reasons why — she insisted that she felt nothing for Matthew Drummond any more. It was quite obvious that Victoria had fallen for him and that her talk about not seeing him again was just out of loyalty to Rory. It was the least she could do for her friend, in return, to spare her any pangs of guilt.

'Rory, you're not just saying that, are you?' The brown eyes were strained with genuine anxiety. 'I don't want anything to do with him if it means you'd be upset at seeing us together. I mean it. Honestly!'

'I know you do. And I mean what I say too. I swear to God I don't care a twopenny toss about Matty Drummond!'

She tensed herself in expectation of God casting her down for lying in His name. Matthew Drummond was her saving grace and she loved him all the more for it. Had it not been for the times when he had been gentlemanly and respectful to her; had it not been for the tenderness as well as the passion of his love-making; she would have believed that all men were no better than animals. She could have wept for love and need of him, but she realized that it was no use. She knew now that she should never have allowed Matthew Drummond to make love to her. Men no longer respected you enough to make you their wife if you gave in to them before marriage.

God did not strike her down for denying her love and she hurried on to tell Victoria about her idea of charging people for borrowing clothes and making a business of doing it. 'That's more important to me just now than any man,' she assured her friend. 'I'm going to make a go of

201

it, Victoria. I'm going to work like mad to build a successful business.'

Her words had the ring of truth and Victoria was convinced at last. She clasped her hands to her breast, eyes honey-soft. 'Oh, Rory, everything's starting to go right for us now, isn't it? I'm so happy, aren't you?'

They hugged each other and Victoria was so carried away in her mind by the delightful prospect of a relationship with a man she had found so intriguing that it did not occur to her that Rory's eyes were shimmering with tears of anguish, not happiness — that she was trembling with distress, not joy.

At last Victoria had met someone special. He wouldn't always be a railwayman. Already he was establishing himself both in the Union and as a member of the Labour Party. An admirable career could be carved in either, and both were collar-and-tie jobs. He had far too fine a mind to waste the rest of his life doing nothing but shovelling coal or driving dirty engines. He looked the smartest man in the hall in the stiff collar and well-pressed tie he had worn to the dance.

She never doubted for a moment that he would contact her again and of course he did. She received a letter in so neat and perfect a hand that it was a work of art and a wonder just to look at. The contents, however, took her aback and she experienced a slight unease. She had never read anything so flowery before, not even in romantic books. The speed at which she heard from the writer also gave her a twinge; she tended to rush into things herself, but did not like other people rushing her into anything.

Drummond had sat up half the night sweating blood over the letter. At first he had written a brief businesslike halfpage of the type he would have penned for his branch of the Union or the local Labour Party: concise, to the point, not one adjective or adverb in sight. He had torn up several efforts like this and had tried to catharize his emotions first of all by writing in his diary an undisciplined outpouring of an entry which began:

How unexpected was the happening of this big event. I had not the slightest inkling of what was in store for me. Yet how glad I am that it was so. I went to the railway social and dance tonight and my lucky star was shining for me. For we have met, my fate and I. My cruse of grace is full. Oh, what a beauty is my beloved! Beautiful, warm, charmingly mannered and an intelligent conversationalist. Nothing will ever equal the absolute conviction of this moment. My heart's and mind's desire had at last come true. I have made up mind to marry her . . .

Eventually he accepted the fact that this was like all social situations in as far as his awkward nature was concerned; it was fraught and annoying and he knew he was liable not to get it right. Only the conviction that Victoria was the woman for him made him labour at several other versions of the letter to her. After writing it, he copied it neatly into his journal. He kept a journal as well as a diary; the journal was a covered exercise book and he used it for writing critiques of books he had read; recording apt quotations; composing essays on different subjects that interested him and copying letters he had either written or received. In his journal, he wrote at the top of a fresh page. 'My first love letter to my future wife.' Then he laboriously continued.

Dear Victoria, you said that if I really wanted to see you again, I should take earnest care to see to it that I did. I write to you moved by the supreme desire to be granted the privilege of being with you. Cold ink does not seem to me a sufficiently powerful and persuasive medium wherewith to lay at your feet in the most attractive light the offer of my deep sincerity and good intent . . .'

Drummond groaned. He seemed only able to do one thing or the other — short, cold sentences which seemed insulting in the circumstances, or this laboured style which made him look as if he was a sentimental idiot. He decided that to risk making a fool of himself was better than to risk insulting Victoria.

'However much one may eagerly endeavour to melodize every sentence,' he continued, 'however much one may seek to refine and shape one's thoughts before ushering them into the presence of such a desirable example of modern womanhood such as you . . .' He cringed at this point and cupped his hand over his eyes. He didn't even know how to express the fact that he couldn't express his feelings — in a way, he didn't want to. He was a very private person and it was anathema to him to let his emotions ramble loose like this. Only the vision of Victoria kept him desperately trying. He wrote about primrose paths along which he had glimpsed the love gates of his destiny and ended with the hope that this words would 'provide an acceptable cameo of the happy, ambitious impressions which meeting you has made upon me. May I sign myself, with affection, Matthew Drummond.'

In his haste to be finished with the torment of the letter, he had nearly put it in the envelope and sealed it before he remembered the most important item and had to insert it as a postscript. 'Most important of all, I want to meet you next Sunday. It is the only day I can break the bonds of work to come to you. Will you name the time and place? M.D.

Then he strode out to the post-box and got rid of the epistle before he could tear it up again. The moment he had posted it, he knew he could not bear to think of the rejection that it might precipitate. As soon as he returned to his lodgings he shut himself in his room and, ignoring Mrs Kipp's enthusiastic hymn-singing as she flew energetically about the kitchen, he settled down to study Nietzsche. It was usually his happy time, for he enjoyed his own company and the companionship of his books, but tonight he was irritated by the way his mind kept wandering. He was annoyed at having made a bloody fool of himself and part of him resented the situation engendered by meeting Victoria — not by Victoria herself, however, who remained in his mind as a vision of perfect womanhood. He realized it was the vagaries of his own nature which were making him suffer and resent the threat to his privacy and peace of mind that entering into a serious courtship would entail.

A worrying maze, a veritable social jungle lay before him and somehow he would have to negotiate a path through it. He suspected that none of the books he had believed relevant to such a situation, and that he had studied so assiduously, would after all be of much practical help — books like *Woman* by Alexander Walker, in which woman was physiologically considered as to mind, morals and marriage. It was all very disturbing.

He went through to the kitchen for his supper and Mrs Kipp said, 'He's in a black mood tonight, Lord. What he needs is to sit on the bench at the Sally Army. He needs to cleanse that black heart of his.'

He ate the frugal meal in silence. The woman was obviously off her head. She looked as if she had St Vitus' Dance as well; she couldn't sit still a minute but was for ever singing or talking or darting about. He prayed that she wouldn't begin banging her tambourine; she often did so in the house and on more than one occasion he had nearly crashed it over her bird-brain and made a necklace of it. Once when he had been on night-shift and she had started on it, he had jumped out of bed and rushed through naked, shouting at her to stop the bloody racket and let him get some sleep. She had been shocked rigid at seeing him with no clothes on and had never made another sound for the rest of the day. But by the next day she had forgotten.

'A black mood comes from a black heart, doesn't it Lord?'

He went out for a drink and then to bed early, where he had a wet dream which caused him to suffer all the more.

Next day he fiercely concentrated on his work. He was

firing with Fred Strachan, a driver whose state of mind was reflected by the way he wore his cap. When the skip or peak stuck out over his left ear, it meant a cursed mood and he didn't want to talk. If the peak was down over his eyes and the back well pushed up, it indicated that he was in the best of humours. Fortunately on this occasion the skip on Strathan's cap was well tugged round over his ear and his mouth was clamped shut. Drummond was in no mood to respond to jokes or any kind of social chit-chat. All he wanted to do was strain himself to the limit of his endurance heaving coal by the shovelful into the fiery furnace. The only sound he wanted to hear was the shriek of the whistle, the roar as they flashed through stations or the metallic ring of swiftly moving couplings and connecting rods.

Soon he was transported, as always, into a magic world of passions and excitement that was womanless and totally absorbing.

CHAPTER THIRTY-ONE

Dear Matthew, (Victoria dashed off a few words while she
was eating her dinner)

I was pleased to receive your letter, though I didn't
expect to hear from you quite so soon. Now, regarding
your letter, I really don't know whether to be angry or
not, because your expression of thought seems to me
very elaborate indeed. When I read words such as you
wrote, it seems to me sort of unreal. I am not insinuating
that you were writing one thing and thinking another,
but I must always be candid. So you think you would like
to meet me on Sunday? I am going to be candid again.
I would like to see you. I will look out for you somewhere around the foot of the Balgray about 3.30 pm.
                    Yours sincerely
                    Victoria Buchanan

Actually, seeing Matthew Drummond was not all that
important. She wanted to see him, it was true, but there
was no desperate urgency about it. She already enjoyed
herself; she liked her job; she had a busy social life with
always being in demand as a pianist at everything from
Brownie socials to Co-operative funerals. Moreover, she
was happy at home (even with her extra duties as compared
with her brothers.) It was a place indeed of much laughter,
love and happiness; she had never once heard her mother
and father quarrel. Her father ('big Geordie' as he was
known in Springburn) called her mother by the affectionate
term of 'the wee one' rather than 'Martha' most of the time.

Often he would arrive home from work and snatch her up in the air and in that rich, warm voice of his would greet her, 'And how's the wee one today, eh?'

'Geordie!' Mrs Buchanan would gently reprimand him. 'Put me down this instant!' Then when he did, she would allow herself a little smile and shake of the head and say with answering affection. 'You're an awful man!'

Sometimes it was one of the boys who grabbed his mother, tossed her into the air and cried out, 'How's the wee one, then?' More often or not, of the boys it would be the younger Sam or Willie. Dave and Tommy were usually content with a hug or a quick tickle at her plump waist when passing.

'Honestly!' Martha would tut at them. 'What am I going to do with you boys? Behave yourselves this instant!'

'Who are you writing to, dear?' she asked Victoria now. 'Matthew Drummond.'

'A man?' Her mother sounded shocked.

'You remember, mother. He's the one who lost his father and brother in the George Square riot. His mother died not long before that.'

Martha's stern expression collapsed into sympathy. 'Oh, aye. The poor soul!' But Big Geordie asked, 'Was he not going with your red-headed pal?'

Victoria drew herself up in dignity. 'They did know each other slightly for a time, I believe. But that was ages ago.'

'But Victoria,' her mother sounded puzzled. 'Why are you writing to him, dear?'

Victoria waved a dismissive hand. 'Och, he wrote to me the other day, asking if he could see me again. I danced with him at the last railway social.'

Martha peered over the top of her spectacles. 'I think your father and I are entitled to know what you are saying in your letter,' she said.

Her daughter sighed. 'Mother, I am eighteen. My hair's up and I'm a grown woman.'

'There's more to being a grown woman than having your hair up, Victoria.'

208

'Oh, all right,' Victoria said hastily in an attempt to avoid a lecture on human nature and the vagaries of men. 'I'm telling him to meet me at 3.30 pm on Sunday somewhere around the foot of Balgray.'

'You will do no such thing,' her mother said quietly. 'You'll have him call for you here at your home, and you'll introduce him to your father and me so that we can decide what we think of him.'

'Oh, mother!' Victoria wailed. 'Girls don't do that nowadays. Not until they're going seriously with a boy. What will he think?'

'He'll think that you're a respectable girl from a good home whose parents care about her.'

'No, he won't; he'll think quite the opposite. He'll think I'm a brazen hussy who's rushing him. Isn't that right?' she appealed to her brothers, who were enthusiastically wiring into their mince and potatoes. 'Dave, Tommy, Sam, Willie?'

'Well,' Dave said after swallowing a mouthful, 'she's got a point, mother. I would leave it until maybe the next time or the next time again. It's not as if we don't know who he is. And I've met him.'

'What is he like son?' Martha asked. Dave was the most serious and dependable of her male offspring.

He shrugged. 'A decent enough chap, I suppose.'

Martha looked anxious again. 'You don't sound very sure?'

'Yes, I am. It's just that he's different somehow — shy, I suppose.'

'Och, well,' Martha conceded, 'that's no great fault. Poor lad! He's alone in the world too. Bring him in to meet us next time then, dear. Or next again, like Dave says.'

Victoria nodded, then stuffed the letter into the envelope and sealed it. Dave had put her off a bit by saying that Matthew was shy. She didn't want a shy man; somehow the word had connotations of weakness. If she wanted a man at all — and in her more realistic moments, she doubted it — he would at least have to be strong. But this was not the moment to argue about whether Matthew

209

Drummond was a shy man or a strong, mysterious silent type. She had her work to go to and tonight she would have to hurry home for it was Granny Buchanan's eightieth birthday and there was to be a family party. Family parties were great fun. Everyone did a party piece and she accompanied them on the piano — unless it was a recitation, of course. Uncle Hamish always recited 'Tam O'Shanter' or 'Dangerous Dan McGrew'. Father had a lusty singing voice and did justice to songs like 'Two Lovely Black Eyes'; or sometimes, in more sentimental mood, he would sing a duet with Martha of 'John Anderson, My Jo' or 'Love's Old Sweet Song'. On her own, Martha would delight the company with 'The Old Rustic Bridge by the Mill' and 'Just A' wearyin' for You'. Granny Buchanan always sang, 'The Lord's My Shepherd' — she had a very sweet singing voice for an old lady. Then there would be community singing of 'Daisy, Daisy' and 'In the Good Old Summertime . . .'

Sometimes the boys did magic tricks; sometimes they told jokes, but if they did they had to be careful these were of the type that did not in any way offend their mother or Granny Buchanan. Then Aunty Teeny could tap-dance. In fact, the whole family was so talented and so willing and eager to share their talents that Victoria had quite a fight to get a song in as well as accompanying other people. She enjoyed singing almost as much as playing the piano.

The night before, she had helped her mother until the early hours baking scones and sponges. That meant keeping the fire stoked up, because it was the fire that heated the oven. They had both fallen into bed afterwards flushed and exhausted, but happy with the success of their efforts.

Granny Buchanan, who lived in Edinburgh, was staying the night after the party which meant another night's limited sleep for Victoria. Granny had to sleep with her and kept getting up during the night to use the chamberpot. The old lady could just about manage to 'dreep' down from the high bed, but always found it impossible to climb back up again without her granddaughter's help. However, it never occurred to Victoria to mind the struggle to hoist up the frail body and tuck it in each time. She loved her grandmother and it was quite a novelty to have someone to cuddle into. The only person she had ever slept with was Rory. Once Rory had been for tea and had such a cough and temperature that Martha had said, 'You can't go out again in that cold wind with a fever like that, dear. You cuddle into Victoria's bed and I'll give you a nice hot drink. Dave will go and tell your mother that you'll be all right. Victoria and I will take good care of you until you're better.'

And so they had. Victoria enjoyed her nursing duties and later, cuddling in beside Rory and whispering together behind the closed curtains of the bed. When Rory got better and went home, she had missed her terribly. Victoria enjoyed company; she blossomed in it. Victoria had never been shy in her life.

CHAPTER THIRTY-TWO

So he had met her. The first hurdle was over! Drummond
was so relieved that he thanked God that Mrs Kipp was
asleep when he returned and he could retreat to his room
and sit by himself in silence. Normally he cursed the
landlady for being too mean to give him a fire. For once,
however, he was unaware of the damp chilliness of the
place; all he could think of was how the evening had
progressed. Carefully he unrolled it and played it back
scene by scene like a film. It looked as if it had gone well.
He had decided beforehand to make no amorous advances
towards Victoria, feeling it vital to keep a firm rein on his
carnal instincts now that he had embarked upon a serious
enterprise of the heart. Therefore he did not advance
beyond a pleasant give-and-take discussion in a general
way of mutual hopes, desires and beliefs.

Sitting motionless on the edge of his bed in the small,
moonlit room — he had been so preoccupied with his
thoughts — he'd forgotten to light the gas-mantle — he
believed he had not shaped too badly. Victoria, of course,
was such an easy person to get along with. She was an
extremely sensible girl, proficient in homely gifts — she
had told him about how she baked scones and sponges for
her Granny's birthday party. She radiated energy and good
health and as if that wasn't enough, she was beautiful to
look at. He found it such a joy to watch her that there were
times when he lost all self-consciousness of speech and
laughed and talked in a perfectly normal fashion.

He didn't know how long he sat grey-fingered by the
moon before he lit the gas and drew the blind. Then he

212

took out his diary and journal. He could not sleep until he had recorded this important milestone of his life. At the small table by the window, he began writing, 'My first evening out with the woman of my dreams . . .'

From that time onwards, he also began to seriously consider his financial situation. After his second and equally successful evening out with Victoria, when they went to the Princes to see *A Mother's Secret*, he made an inventory of his estate. At the top of his journal, he wrote in capital letters; 'MY ESTATE — 1919.' Then he recorded the fact that he had one pair of boots; one pair of dancing pumps; one dark grey suit; one pair of working trousers; one cap; one working shirt; one dress shirt; one collar; one muffler; one reefer jacket; one railway coat and thirty-nine books. He had no savings — a state that would have to be rectified if he was planning at some future date to marry. The prospect of marriage to Victoria filled him with both joy and despair. He had never found it easy to save and his Post Office Savings Book had gone up and down so fast that it was hardly worth putting the counter assistant to the trouble of marking anything in. By the time he paid Mrs Kipp, the Union and the Friendly Society, there was not all that much left of his wages with which to do anything. He treated himself to a regular dram, of course. That would have to stop. Yet it was such a comfort to slip into the quiet back parlour of the pub with its welcoming fire and small table in the corner where he could sit and read or surreptitiously observe people, eavesdrop on their conversations and later write up his thoughts on the same in his journal. It was good, too, to feel the warmth of the whisky in his belly. Indeed, he felt more at home and comfortable in that warm, private corner of the pub than he had ever done anywhere else. After thawing out for a while and with a second whisky under his belt, life in fact took on a very pleasant aura and he even began to think of himself as quite a fellow.

But now it would all have to stop. He made up his mind to set himself a goal: a hundred pounds by next year, that was what he would aim at. Sometimes, however, he would be overcome by the sinking feeling that Victoria did not share his hopes for the future. What if, when the time came to ask her to marry him, she said 'No?' he was only too well aware that she led a busy, happy life without him. He only saw her once a week at most, which was partly because of his shifts, partly because of lack of money and partly because of Victoria's other engagements. He determined to ask her to become engaged to be married as soon as possible. This depended largely on his success in saving one hundred pounds, so he began keeping a cash-book and detailing in it all his expenses. Each pay-day one page was set out for his 'Credit Account' and the other for his 'Debit Account'. Each week, try as he did, he could never balance them satisfactorily. In desperation, he began heading each week's page with urgent printed reminders to spur him to do better: 'Save Something!' 'Save something *More!*' 'For Victoria's sake — £100!' 'For God's sake — Save *Something!*'

He was helped in a way by being sent to work up north for some weeks in what seemed a no-man's land. So isolated was the place that there were not even any lodgings near the railway, let alone a pub, and he had to live and sleep in a railway hut when he wasn't working. The separation from Victoria was worrying, but he forced himself to trust in the old adage of 'Absence makes the heart grow fonder' and made the most of a touching goodbye. They promised to write to each other every day of the three weeks he would be away, and he left cheered by the warmth of her kisses and her assurances of how badly she would miss him.

In one sense, it was a happy time for Drummond. After each day's work, he sat in his warm railway hut with writing paper, notebooks and reading material in front of him. First he wrote to Victoria. Then he studied the news-papers left for him by one of the drivers and made notes on the political situation in the country. Notes were also carefully made about other items of interest or education, like the item about how lighthouses lured migrating birds to a cruel death. Eventually, before lying down to sleep

214

on the wooden bench which served as a bed, he always stepped outside for a breath of air. The heat from the stove could reach suffocating proportions. Outside, the small hut was encircled by total blackness and swirling rain, so after a few deep breaths he thankfully retreated back inside his oasis of heat and light — happy to return to the companionship of his books. He always read until his eyelids became pleasantly heavy, then he blew out the lantern and drifted into sleep to the soft patter of rain on the roof.

During these three weeks, his off-duty hours in the hut disturbed only by the clanking of a shunting engine or the roar of a passing express, he thought very seriously about all aspects of his future and planned how he must prepare for it.

First of all, there was his personal behaviour with Victoria. During the weeks when they had been going out regularly together, their habit of good-night kissing and cuddling in her back close had been established and this had entailed a build-up of sexual excitements. He suspected, however, that the sexual web she was weaving around him was a delightful game to her, and that she had given not the slightest thought to realities or results.

He must think for her in this matter. A good deal of self-discipline was necessary on his part to keep within the limits of love-making he had set himself. He was determined to do nothing that would make him feel ashamed afterwards. Victoria was a temple of purity that must not be desecrated and he must force himself to continue keeping both their passions under control until their love could be sanctified in marriage.

Many times he sustained himself by remembering the occasion when he had visited Victoria's home. What a blessed revelation that was! Her mother seemed to him everything a mother should be; he adored her on sight and liked to think that her gentle eyes gazed on him with approval. With what homely comforts the house had abounded. There had been a glowing fire and a colourful rug in front of it. How strange, almost sensuous it felt to have a soft rug under one's feet. He had been invited for tea and it delighted him to watch Victoria busy herself by removing the plush table-cover and spreading on a linen cloth which had coloured flowers embroidered in each corner. Back and forth she strode, fetching china from the sideboard and setting it out with such dignity and grace. She was supremely conscious that he was watching her and admiring her — he could see this by the pride in her eyes and the studied perfection of her every movement. He felt relaxed. Mrs Buchanan, calmly knitting a pair of socks, seemed perfectly content during his long silences. Victoria gave the impression of being happy too and sometimes she sang quietly to herself as she worked.

It was a vision of what home life could be like and it nearly brought tears to his eyes. In a way, it was fortunate when her father and brothers arrived. They had been to a football match and were overflowing with energy, enthusiasm and good-humoured banter.

'The wee one' and 'Our wee one' they called Mrs Buchanan. He smiled at their joking and his face lit up with appreciative enjoyment watching and listening to their part in the happy scene. It was only when they addressed remarks to him and tried to draw him in and make him a participant rather than an observer that he experienced discomfort and strain. He tried his best, but he never felt it was good enough. No matter how hard he tried, he could not be gregarious and naturally sociable like Victoria's father and brothers. He was aware that every time he opened his mouth he put some degree of strain on everyone, but was at a loss to know what to do to correct this regrettable fault in himself.

Still, on the whole his visits had gone well and Victoria's family had been good enough to accept him despite his peculiarities. He was intensely grateful for that.

Now his ambitions and hopes for the future had clarified and particularized. Not only did he wish to educate himself to his full potential — not only did he wish to be a top link engine driver — not only did he wish to marry Victoria . . . He longed for a home of his own.

CHAPTER THIRTY-THREE

'You've got a nerve!' Victoria gasped.

'It looks a mess at the moment,' Rory said defensively, 'but just you wait until I've finished cleaning it up!'

'I don't mean that, I mean the size. I didn't realize it was a big double-windowed shop; it's as big as the Co-op!'

Rory flicked her eyes towards a ceiling darkly draped with cobwebs. 'You always exaggerate everything!'

'It's huge!'

'It is not.'

'It is so.'

'The Co-op has two counters.'

'You could have three counters in here!'

Rory bristled. 'Why shouldn't I have a big shop?'

'I was just thinking of all the work.' Victoria's eyes widened dramatically. 'And the *rent*!'

'The first month's paid up.'

'How on earth did you manage that?'

Rory avoided Victoria's incredulous stare. 'Ma had a bit put by.' This she felt Victoria would understand for Mrs Buchanan often spoke of the importance of having 'a bit put by for a rainy day,' but her friend looked so puzzled that she felt obliged to add, 'And I'm not afraid of hard work.'

Victoria seemed to give herself a mental shake in an attempt to jerk to attention. 'I'll help, of course. That's why I've come.' She had already helped by trailing round innumerable streets with Rory to put leaflets through doors advertising the new kind of shop about to open. Indeed, it was through Victoria's influence that a printer friend of

Archie's had produced the leaflets in the first place, and at rock-bottom price.

'Thanks, Victoria. I'm terribly excited, aren't you? Stockwell Street is such a good situation. Just off Argyle Street and a building like this — what could be better?'

It was in fact a somewhat dilapidated, weather-beaten edifice of grey stone. The frontage, however, was over seventy feet long and the building was four storey's high. It had been divided into shops and offices and workrooms; a central hall, with an internal balcony surrounding it, housed a pottery and porcelain warehouse.

'It's certainly better to be in the town rather than in Springburn,' Victoria agreed. 'You'll have the chance of customers from all over the place. And this is a busy part of town as well.'

'It's a good time to get started, too. Christmas and New Year aren't all that far away and there's plenty of dances and functions then. People are bound to need clothes.'

'But why should they borrow instead of buy?'

'Hire,' Rory corrected.

'Hire instead of buy, then?'

'Why not?'

Victoria sighed. 'Well, I certainly hope for your sake that they do.'

'We'd better make a start. It will take ages to get rid of all this dirt.'

'Just a moment,' Victoria said. 'We must protect our hair; I've brought these white squares which Mother makes out of old sheets. They're handy for dusters as well.'

Rory dutifully copied Victoria and covered her hair, firmly tying one of the squares of cotton at the nape of her neck. Then they began by each standing on a chair and, with the awkward help of a brush and a mop, fought through the cobwebs to clean the ceiling.

Soon they were gasping and out of breath with their exertions. They were also so tickled with spiders and webs cascading on top of them that they were reduced to tearful hilarity.

'My God!' Rory managed at last as she wiped her nose and cheek with the back of one hand. 'We must be mad! What are we laughing at? This is dammed hard work — and we've still the floor to do.'

'I know, it's ridiculous.' Victoria climbed down off her chair just in time before being racked by two bouts of sneezes. 'The dust's going up my nose. The whole thing's quite absurd when you think of it.'

They went through to the back shop to fill pails at the sink, then staggered with them to the front area. 'How do you mean, it's absurd?' Rory asked breathlessly.

'I still can't see how you can possibly pay the rent for a place like this. What happens after the first month?'

'I hope I'll be making enough profit by then. And of course Ma will still have her rags and her stall; if need be, we'll run up our store book for a few weeks.'

They worked side by side down on their knees, scrubbing with wide sweeps, wiping up the suds with a cloth, squeezing the cloth over the pail and then wiping again until the floor was as clean and as dry as they could make it. Working their way backwards, they ended up at the back door where they collapsed into a sitting position and, leaning against it and each other, rested their aching bones. The shop looked bigger than ever and depressingly bare.

'Where are you going to put all the clothes?' Victoria, who had never been as physically strong as Rory despite her more voluptuous appearance, was becoming irritated with fatigue.

'That is a bit of a problem,' Rory admitted.

'A bit of a problem?' her friend echoed incredulously. 'You might as well still be in Paddy's Market if you've to heap them all on the floor or on that counter.'

There was silence for a moment and then Rory said, 'Do we know any joiners? All it would need is two upright bits of wood with a long bit joining them at the top to hang coathangers on.'

They thought for another minute and the Victoria said, 'You know that girl our Dave's getting engaged to?'

'Lexy McWhirter?'

'Her brother's a carpenter. Is that the same thing?'

'I think so. Oh, Victoria, do you think you could ask Dave to ask him?'

'I could ask him myself. There's to be a family gathering tomorrow to celebrate the engagement and he'll be there.'

'Do you think he'll do it?'

'I won't know until I ask, will I?'

'Actually, I'd need more than one stand — and quite a few shelves as well. And it would be great if I could get dummies to display some of the garments in the window.'

'I don't think he could make dummies,' Victoria said dubiously and they both found some relief in a weak attack of giggles.

'I've managed to find a lot of men's clothes,' Rory said. 'Gosh, you've never seen such stuff, Victoria; it's been well worth all the trailing about I had to do to get it. Things posh people wear at weddings and balls and all sorts of important events.'

'I hope everything's in good condition and not moving with fleas like Paddy's Market?'

'Oh no, most of it's like new. *Is* new in fact. Men's evening suits, top hats and beautiful boots. My Da and the boys were after some of the boots, but I wouldn't let them touch them. You should see the ladies' clothes as well, all wrapped in sheets with mothballs. They've been hanging in wardrobes never getting worn in case they wore out, I suppose.'

Victoria rolled her eyes. 'That's stupid! If I had good things, I'd wear them and enjoy them every chance I could, wouldn't you?'

Rory hestitated. There was a reckless, careless bit about Victoria that made her feel insecure.

'You wouldn't!' Victoria accused, as if hardly able to believe her own words. 'You'd be a miser if you had the chance.'

'I would not.'

'You would so.'

' would *not*. Money makes money and I have to be careful to conserve everything I've got.'

'You haven't got anything!'

'I have the clothes and they represent money. I must be careful with them; I've worked too damned hard to get them to be anything else.'

Suddenly a man's voice startled both girls. 'You can't be the new merchants, you're too young and pretty!' He smiled, but his eyes made a backcloth of sadness. Rory guessed he might be in his fifties, but looked older; his body sagged forward, as if he couldn't be bothered holding it up.

'I'm the new shopkeeper,' Rory said as she and Victoria struggled to their feet, 'but I'm not open for business yet.'

The man sighed. 'I just came in to say hello. I own the hatter's business next door.'

Victoria tugged off her head-square, tossed her dark head and favoured the man with one of her charming smiles. 'Do take a seat, Mr . . .?'

'Donovan.' He heaved another sigh. 'Miss Winters — she's my assistant — she thought you might be ready for a cup of tea, and I suppose she's curious to meet our new neighbours.'

Despite his smile, Rory had never seen anyone so depressed. His eyes were muddy with despair. 'Thanks,' she said. 'I'm parched.'

'How kind,' Victoria smiled graciously. 'We'll call in as soon as we make ourselves respectable.'

After he had gone, Rory said. 'He was a right cheery Charlie!'

'Very genteel, though.' Victoria undid her apron and tossed it on the counter.

'Mmmm. His clothes were good; his suit was best quality Melton. But it was hanging far too loose on him and it didn't look good. Either he lost weight and can't afford to get his clothes altered to fit, or else he doesn't care how they look.'

'Rory, you're getting absolutely obsessed with clothes.'

'Well, no wonder. I've lost pounds of weight myself with

all the tramping about I've had to do to find decent stuff. Clothes are my business, don't forget, and I'm determined to make them not only my bread and butter but my jam.'

In actual fact, she secretly thanked God that she was thinner rather than fatter. The bleeding had come and the release from tension had been wonderful. She prayed so hard for it to begin, promising God that she would be angelic for ever after if He would only be merciful and grant her this one favour. When her blessed release arrived, she felt like going down on her knees and thanking God in a truly humble fashion; but she couldn't because there was always some other McElpy around and they would have hooted with derisive laughter if they had seen her. So she had to go down on her knees in her mind.

'Come on,' she said cheerfully to Victoria. 'Let's give our faces and hands a wash and comb our hair and then see what kind of place he has next door.'

Freed from the anxiety of becoming pregnant, she had swung from the depths of despair to the heights of optimism. Now she believed the city of Glasgow was her oyster and she could accomplish anything — anything that is, except Matthew Drummond's love. She tried not to think about that and was glad that she was too exhausted each day to have any energy left to think or feel. Only thoughts of the terrible rape in the back close took advantage of her defences and brought shudders of fear as she hurried home each night in the dark. She had taken to washing herself all over at the kitchen sink so frequently, or going to the public baths so often, that Annie said there would be nothing left of her soon and that everyone knew too many baths weakened you. Sometimes when she saw Victoria with Matthew, the pain of his rejection flared up again, but she was beginning to come to terms with that too. After all, he had been a bit of a bastard in the end. He had had everything he wanted from her and then had the nerve to tell her to her face that he wasn't going to marry her. He ought to have married her; it would serve him right if she told Victoria all that he'd done. Then he would get a dose of his own medicine because she would soon tell him where to get off! Sometimes she wondered if she should really confess to Victoria, but her friend boasted so much about how wonderful he was that she just hadn't the heart to disillusion her. Once she had come very near to it, though, when she bumped into both of them in Springburn Road. They had been dressed in their best, Victoria wearing her new brown coat with the touch of fur on the high collar. Her father and brothers had all clubbed together to help her to get it. On her glossy dark head was a real tippy hat, also trimmed with fur. Matthew Drummond's suit was brushed and pressed and he was wearing what looked like a brand-new shirt. His boots were gleaming — Rory had never seen such well-polished boots. He and Victoria had an air about them; they carried themselves with the same dignity and pride.

On her way home from her daily trek and weighted down by the burden of clothes she had collected, Rory was painfully conscious of her own dusty shoes, shabby coat and woollen tammy which was disintegrating into holes. At that moment she hated Victoria and Matthew — hated them so much that she could have said to Victoria right there and then, 'What have you got to be so uppity about? He made love to me a hundred times before he ever set eyes on you!'

But she only exchanged polite words of greeting with them . . .

'Is that us ready then?' Victoria asked now.

'Yes, I've just to lock up. It looks great, doesn't it, Victoria?'

They stood at the door in silence for a minute, surveying the place through the gathering shadow of the winter's afternoon.

'I can see the shop's potential,' Victoria agreed, 'but I daren't think how you're going to manage to run such a business, Rory. It seems a crazy idea.'

'Why crazy?'

'Well, risky then.'

'I've been in risky situations before and survived,' Rory assured her. 'I'll survive this one!'

Victoria didn't realize just how many risks were being taken. She had needed money to pay the first month's rent in advance and in a panic of desperation had allowed her Da to come to the rescue. He had stolen a sack of sugar from the Wellfield grocers and she and her Ma had been up all night making fudge and treacle toffee to use it up before the theft of it was discovered next morning. (If anything was stolen for miles around, they usually checked on Scrap first.) Some of the fudge and toffee was taken out by the boys first thing in the morning, to sell round all the doors in Springburn; the rest was carried by Annie and Rory and hawked further afield. Enough money for the first month's rent and a little capital had been gathered by that means, also by Scrap picking somebody's pocket in the bookies.

What she would do about the second month's rent if she didn't make enough profit to cover it, Rory had no idea. Depending on her Da was far too risky. Anyway, she wanted to succeed on her own.

As she locked the door of the shop, she vowed that she would make a success of it no matter what it cost.

CHAPTER THIRTY-FOUR

Mr Donovan's shop impressed Victoria and she gave Rory a furtive nudge of appreciation as soon as they entered. Rory thought it too dark and old-fashioned and she wasn't surprised that it was not packed with customers. Indeed there were no customers at all. Saturday should have been the busiest day of the week, but the place had the air of a gloomy Sunday. Its church-like appearance was reflected in the dark woodwork of the mahogany panelled walls and the stained-glass tops to the front doors and the door into the back premises.

Rory decided that the decor must be wrong, or the method of conducting business, or both. What was the use of lots of rich wood from floor to ceiling, deep drawers with brass handles and a slate-grey carpet in a hat shop, if you didn't sell any hats?

Then it occurred to her that the shop, like its owner, also had a neglected look. In places the carpet was caked with muddy footprints that no one had bothered to brush off. The shelves, the counter, even the top hats and bowlers on display were grey-filmed with dust.

Rory turned a critical eye on Miss Winters, the frosty-haired bespectacled assistant. She couldn't be much use for a start.

'How do you do?' She came creeping forward to greet them like an undertaker welcoming the family of the bereaved.

'Miss Winters has been with me for thirty years.' Mr Donovan made a sad attempt at a smile. 'She knew my wife.'

'Dear Mrs Donovan,' Miss Winters whispered reverently. 'My wife died six months ago.'

'Oh, I'm sorry,' Rory and Victoria murmured in unison.

By this time, they were in a back cavern ill-lit by a weakly wavering gas-jet. On invitation to be seated, both girls perched straight-backed on wooden chairs after declining to remove either hats, coats or gloves. Miss Winters poured out tea from a silver pot into fine bone china cups; she was obviously a very ladylike person, Victoria later remarked, and far too superior for shop work.

'Nothing seems to have gone right since then,' Mr Donovan continued morosely. 'My health hasn't been good and the business has fallen away. I used to have two young men assistants and a charwoman, but I had to let them go. I don't know what I'd do without Miss Winters.'

'Faithful to the end,' Miss Winters murmured and blinked through pebble-thick glasses as if fighting back tears. They dutifully sipped their tea — all that is, except Mr Donovan who just sat staring through the gloom at his.

Again Rory was reminded of a funeral. The scraggy, bent figure of Miss Winters was encased in a floor-length black dress on which she had pinned a black jet brooch high at her throat.

Eventually Victoria said, 'Haven't you any family, Mr Donovan?'

'Oh, eh?' He seemed to awaken as if from a dream, but reluctantly. 'Yes, a son Donovan. He's living down in London just now.'

Victoria gazed at him in polite puzzlement. 'Donovan?'

'Yes,' he nodded. 'Donovan Donovan! It was my wife's idea. We couldn't think of another name for him; nothing seemed as suitable. My wife used to always say, "He suits the name more than you do." It's a tough sounding name isn't it? And he always looked tough even as a child.' His eyes faded far away. 'I remember my Grandfather. He was an Ulster man. Tough as old boots. I suppose Donovan must take after him.'

'Have you any grandchildren?' Victoria encouraged.

Mr Donovan's mouth twisted into a wry smile. 'I can't imagine Donovan settling down in one place long enough to get married. He's knocked about all over the world. He's a newspaperman.'

Miss Winters leaned confidentially forward, 'Mr Donovan is far too modest to mention this, but his dear son received an award for his courageous work as a war correspondent.'

'Gosh!' Victoria's eyes glazed and Rory could see the romantic images flicking across the screen of her friend's mind.

'Doesn't he want to come home and be of some comfort to you?' she asked abruptly. 'There's plenty of good newspapers in Glasgow he could work on.'

'I told him there was no need. Everything was fine, I told him. I know he's hoping for the chance to go abroad again. He was in Germany for a time as a foreign correspondent after the war.'

Another heavy silence followed until Rory suddenly announced, 'Thanks for the tea. We've got to go now.'

Once out on the street, Victoria said, 'That was awfully rude of you.'

'What did I do?'

'It was the way you did it. Honestly, you're so insensitive at times, Rory.'

'It's because I am sensitive that I couldn't stay in there another minute. It was like being entombed.'

'Nonsense! Did you ever see such lovely china? Fancy having china in a back shop.'

'It was depressing.'

'Well, what do you expect? The poor gentleman has lost his wife and he's weighed down with grief. He probably saw her fade away before his eyes, change from a beautiful rosy-cheeked woman to a gaunt pathetic . . .'

'Victoria, you're away in that picture we saw the other day, *The Last Days of Dolly*.'

'That was really good, wasn't it?' Victoria said, unabashed. 'I really enjoyed that picture.'

They were strolling along the gas-lit Argyle Street now, part of the vast throng of Glasgow citizens free of toil and determined to enjoy themselves. Rory however, had promised to go and help her mother home with whatever rags she had left.

'I'm going to the pictures again tonight,' Victoria said. 'Did I tell you? With Matthew.'

'Oh, yes.' Rory averted her eyes. 'I forgot.'

'And just look at the time.' They both gazed up at the shadowy face of the clock on the Tron Steeple. 'I haven't really time now to go to the market with you, have I?'

'I suppose not,' said Rory.

'If you really need me to go, of course I will.'

'No, you've been a great help already, Victoria. Thanks very much.'

'Oh, you're welcome,' Victoria said grandly. 'After all, what are best friends for?'

They kissed goodbye and Rory stood for a minute to wave to her friend as she swung on to one of the tram-cars which came rocking and clanging along the road.

Eventually, jostled by the crowd and forced to move away, Rory struggled to retrieve the positive feelings she had experienced earlier. But the depressing atmosphere of the hat shop and then the reawakening of her grief over the loss of Matthew weighed heavy on her. Her confidence about her new business venture began to sag. A flutter of fear at the enormity of what she was proposing to do started in her stomach, then lurched up to knock her heartbeat off balance.

She must be mad, she told herself. Her mother was right; she had developed delusions of grandeur. Not that Annie had put it quite so politely, but that was what she meant. Harassed along the lively street by the huge throng of people, she suddenly felt small and helpless. In Paddy's Market, with its raucous good-humoured racket that was so familiar to her, she felt lost.

'Here she is at last!' Annie's voice reverberated through the noise like a trumpet in a string band. 'Where the hell have you been — as if I didn't know!'

'The shop needed a good clean-out,' Rory was forced to yell back, an effort which somehow made her feel better. It seemed to trigger off everything positive and spunky in her nature.

'That one's brains need a good clean-out,' Annie bawled across to Jessie Mason. 'Have you seen the size of the bloody shop she's taken on?'

'You'll all be laughing on the other side of your face when I make my fortune,' Rory shouted. She felt quite cheery as she tossed the rags into a sheet and tied each corner into the centre to make a bundle, then dismantled the trestle table. Annie was drinking a cup of tea to put enough strength into her to get home; she told Rory, 'Make two bundles, hen. I can carry half.'

'No, it's all right, Ma. I can manage.'

Rory slung the bundle over her back. She knew it looked incongruous against her best hat and gloves, but let people think what they liked or say what they liked. Why should she care? Now that she had a shop, she'd show them!

CHAPTER THIRTY-FIVE

Drummond had told Victoria that he had fallen in love
with her from the first time he met her. He had known,
he assured her, from the moment he set eyes on her that
she was the only one for him. Her love, she had told him
in return, had come more slowly but it was deeper as a
result. In truth, sometimes Victoria thought she loved him
and sometimes she didn't. She often wished he wouldn't
spoil a perfectly pleasant, indeed uplifting evening of choir
music at the church hall, or earnest discussion about the
state of the world, by insisting on standing in the back close
and kissing her. It somehow lowered the tone of their social
engagement. Men really were awful in this respect; Archie
had been the very same. She loved Drummond when she
didn't understand him, when he was denying her what she
thought she wanted, when he was being stronger than her.
She loved him, too, for being more clever — although she
would never have admitted to him that she considered him
better than herself in any way whatsoever. She was a
young woman of strong will and used to getting her own
way. It was perhaps the novelty of being thwarted that
appealed to her; not that she found being thwarted at
home, as she sometimes was, in the least appealing.

Only a couple of weeks ago she had told everyone at
work and at the bible class that she had new 'squirrels' —
a fur pull-through, a muff and a little fur hat with red
cherries. She'd be wearing them next Sabbath, she boasted.
When the next Sabbath came she preened herself in front
of her father and mother to show them how smart she was
before leaving for the bible class.

'Aren't all the girls going to be jealous of me!' she had remarked with satisfaction.

Her father had looked at her and said, 'Oh, aye? Well, just you go away through to the room and change into what you wore last week and see if the girls are jealous of that.'

The situation was a dreadfully humiliating one for her, but she knew there was no getting out of it. Her father was a good-natured man but when he put his foot down, that was that and there was no getting the better of him if he didn't want you to. The boys also realized this. If her father thought they were getting too cocky, he would challenge then to some feat of strength like elbow wrestling, or jumping up on the table — or an actual fisticuff fight. They had never accepted the latter challenge; the boys knew their father's physical strength.

'He's got a fist like a sledgehammer,' Dave once said.

With Victoria he was usually more indulgent, but he had his limits and the incident of the 'squirrels' was one.

Drummond was strong, but not only in a physical sense. There was a mysterious something about him which she could never quite fathom and it started to have an almost hypnotic effect on her.

Social occasions began to be flat and uninteresting unless he was there. She persuaded him to come along when she knew he was on a suitable shift, but it was never an easy task; it took all of her womanly wiles and ingenuity, which made him a challenge and all the more intriguing. It was impossible for her to imagine anyone simply not wanting to attend a social engagement because they preferred to be on their own. No one could prefer loneliness to companionship — it did not make sense. It was not so much that she was gregarious, although she did love the company of others; being in the limelight was what she enjoyed. A born performer, she blossomed like a flower in the sun when she had an audience and it was an added pleasure, of course, if Drummond was part of that audience. He came every week to have tea at her house too, and the uneasy acceptance her family gave him added even more spice to her life. She had fiercely defended him when she asked everyone what they thought of him after his first visit.

Her father had scratched his head. 'Like Dave said — decent enough bloke, I suppose, but . . .'

'But what?' Victoria stiffened, ready to take on all comers. 'What's wrong with him?'

'Nothing, dear,' her mother soothed. 'But he's a bit of a showman type, is he not?'

Victoria laughed derisively. Her mother had never seen any kind of show in her life; she'd never even been to the pictures. 'A showman? What on earth do you mean?'

'Remember that's your mother you're talking to,' her father warned. 'And you know fine what she means.'

It was true. She did. Matthew Drummond looked different from the normal everyday Springburn man. With his fine features, glowing dark eyes and longish black hair, he could have passed for an actor, a musician, a writer or some such person.

'Well,' she said with her head in the air, 'I don't care if anyone else likes him or not. *I* like him!'

'I never said I didn't like him, dear,' her mother murmured.

'Well, none of you have acted the same about Matthew as you did about Archie.'

'How could we, dear? Matthew isn't Archie. And now that you mention Archie, dear, I must admit that I still don't see why you stopped going out with him. He was such a nice lad.'

'Mother!' Victoria groaned. The very fact that everyone wanted her to marry Archie was enough to put her right off doing any such thing.

'Ah, well,' her mother sighed. 'As I've said before — you'll maybe go further and fare worse.'

After Drummond's first visit, her father and the boys usually made themselves scarce when they knew he was coming. Not that they had anything against him — they liked him, they assured Victoria — but they just couldn't feel relaxed in his company. 'He's too clever for us, Victoria. He's like a walking encyclopaedia.'

'Just because he's educated himself,' Victoria said in a voice which suggested her brothers had sunk to a new depth.

She was glad she was not like them, that she could appreciate someone who knew a thing or two. She determined in fact to show everyone, Matthew Drummond included, that she knew a thing or two as well. Someone in the church had told her about a study group in town and she persuaded Matthew to join. It turned out to be very exciting and special and Matthew had not only enjoyed it but spoken up in the debates in a way which made her preen with pride. He went a bit over the score in expecting her to read a flow of pamphlets, but she accepted and hastily skimmed over Leonard Woolf on 'Imperialism', Tawney on 'The Acquisitive Society' and Cole on 'Guild Socialism', but while scanning the pamphlets her mind was flitting like a grasshopper on to other things. Concentration had never been her strong point. To concentrate too deeply on one thing for any length of time was too static for her; she had a bright quick-silver mind and enjoyed change and movement — unlike Rory who, once she got an idea into her head or set herself a course of action, was like a bulldog with its head down and something gripped between its teeth. She would never let go.

Despite Victoria's brief skimming she could always, with a bit of luck and a lot of nerve, give Drummond the impression that she had grasped the essentials. Her whole life had taken on a completely new dimension since she had begun to walk out with him. She felt elevated above the normal run of things and the more she felt this, the more highly she regarded Matthew Drummond. It wasn't just his intelligence she admired either; he had a hidden strength and a passion that she only occasionally caught glimpses of, but it intrigued and thrilled her.

She genuinely had missed him when he went up north

to work for a spell. And when she met him again, the impact of his dark eyes had decided her right there and then. If he asked her to marry him — and of course he would in time — she would say 'Yes'.

Forgotten were all her previous worries regarding the practical details of living with a man. She had always had a bit of a Micawber streak and it now came happily to the fore. Everything would turn out all right. She enjoyed lovely romantic dreams of their life together. Sometimes he got mixed up in her imagination with Rudolf Valentino, but that didn't matter. She was happy. It was especially enjoyable showing off her handsome escort at all the functions she attended. As she told Rory, All the girls are as envious as anything! You should just see the way they look at Matthew. I'm sure there isn't one who wouldn't like to be in my shoes.

Then, just as she had expected, one day Matthew Drummond asked her to marry him — or at least, to become engaged to marry one another. He had kissed her hand before slipping a beautiful diamond ring on her finger; he was always surprising and delighting her by doing or saying something different.

He had cashed in his life insurance policy to get the money to buy the ring — something which obviously worried him. He was an awful worrier about the future while she never gave it a thought. After all, it said in the bible, 'Sufficient unto the day is the evil thereof'. That was good enough for her.

She could hardly wait to show everyone the ring. Especially Rory.

CHAPTER THIRTY-SIX

'Wouldn't you prefer to mark the occasion of our engagement by an evening out on our own?' Drummond asked. He had an instinctive dread of the big engagement party that Victoria was planning.

'No, I wouldn't,' Victoria said. 'What have you got against my family?'

'Nothing!' he assured her.

'My friends, then?'

'Not a thing, Victoria. It's just that I would prefer to spend the evening alone with you.'

In point of fact, he had begun to feel that what he wanted was to be alone with himself. Or at least, more often than of late. Much as he loved Victoria, he felt they had been seeing each other too often. His feelings of being overwhelmed by a busy, noisy social whirl plus the strain of keeping his sexual needs in check was making him edgy and irritable. He longed for a bit of peace and quiet. All his life he had needed time to sit by himself and reflect and he had become used to silent unhurried hours of his own company. These were his precious times when he could enjoy reading, studying and writing.

'Och, there'll be plenty of times when we'll be alone after we're married.' Victoria waved aside his objections and he didn't pursue the matter. After all, it was perfectly understandable that Victoria would want a party to celebrate the occasion. It was the custom, especially in the Buchanan family, to celebrate in this way and he determined not to let Victoria down. Yet the thought of being put on display, so to speak, for the benefit of the members of Victoria's family he had still to meet, and of having to converse with an unlimited number of people, made him fervently wish the railway would send him to work in Alaska — at least until it was time for his wedding day.

Rory was also dreading the party. 'You don't want me there,' she said to Victoria. 'It's a family thing.'

'I do so,' Victoria said and gave her a hug to prove it. 'You're my best friend and you're going to be my bridesmaid, aren't you?'

Rory gazed at her in barely disguised horror. 'Oh no, I couldn't.'

'Why not?' Victoria wanted to know.

'Well . . . I . . . I used to go with him, remember?'

'Don't be daft!' Victoria said impatiently. 'What does that matter? You said yourself that he means nothing to you, although I hope you at least like him now for my sake. Oh Rory, I'm so excited and happy!' She gave her friend another hug. 'Of course you'll come to the party and of course you'll be my bridesmaid. Silly!'

Rory had been coping relatively well with her emotions up to that point. She had been helped by the fact that her business venture had made a good start, thanks to her tough and tireless efforts. Far from only having, as her mother prophesied, Jock McTurk and a few regulars from the Market, she already had such a host of customers that she was obliged to take on a young girl assistant called Mamie McFarlane. The profit made also enabled her to pay the next few months' rent and buy two second-hand dummies for the windows (one male and one female) and a long mirror. She had even been able to add to her floating capital.

Shelves and clothes racks had been put in before the shop opened and her stock of clothes neatly folded or hung on them. It had soon occurred to her that it was a bit of luck she had managed to obtain not only garments, but also accessories like boots and shoes and gloves and hats, and even ties, shirts and ladies' blouses. People could completely rig themselves out in her shop for a very modest hiring fee and she daringly placed an advert in the *Glasgow Herald* proclaiming this fact:

> Every customers' manifold needs
> supplied for a very modest lay-out
> of cash at Rory's.

Mamie McFarlane thought it a wonderful advert and she cut it out and stuck it up on the wall in the back shop. Of course Mamie — an orphan scarecrow of fourteen years — was so thankful to get a job and a roof over her head that she thought everything about Rory's was wonderful. She slept in the back shop and made her tea, heated her soup or fried her sausages on the gas-ring there. She opened the shop first thing in the morning to let Rory in and locked it again behind her when Rory left every night.

'You're making a slave of that wee lassie,' Annie accused. 'It's a disgrace, so it is!'

'She's not only happy, Ma, she's grateful. I saved her from the poorhouse or worse.'

'Poor wee soul!' Annie's indignant compassion was not to be denied. 'And there's not a pick of flesh on her bones.'

'I give her food.'

'What food? A half-loaf of bread a week and a few sausages?'

'She's lucky I give her that; she should feed herself off her wages.'

'Huh!' Annie hooted with derision. 'She couldn't feed a flea with what you pay her. You'll take her a bowl of my soup tomorrow, m'lady, and every day I make a potful. *And* you'll take her a piece of my cloutie dumpling every time I make one of them!'

'Och, Ma!'

'Never mind your "Och, Ma". That wee lassie needs something to stick to her ribs.'

The soup and the cloutie dumpling paid off right enough, because it sent Mamie into such a seventh heaven of gratitude that there was no stopping her working. She polished the linoleum with fiendish energy until she could literally see her scarlet perspiring face in it. The counter was rubbed until it gleamed and all the clothes carefully brushed sponged and pressed until they looked like new.

Mamie was not quite so good at attending to customers because she was liable to become too excited, but Rory was confident that she would improve with practice. As for the fiery spots on her face, with any luck they would disappear with age.

Luck, Rory felt, was on their side. Although everything was not plain sailing.

One customer, for instance, had not brought back an evening suit and accessories. She eventually went to the address he'd given — much to Mamie's nervous consternation — and found him there right enough. Quite a posh place in Pollokshields too. But he'd told her to 'fuck off'.

'I'll go now, mister,' she said, 'but I'll be back.'

Mamie had listened to the story of what had happened, and what happened next, with rapt attention and admiration.

Rory had returned shortly afterwards with Joe and Benny who, although still young lads, were now much taller than her and hefty with it. They were also active members of a notorious Springburn gang, despite all her efforts to keep them respectable.

'Now, you shit,' Rory told the man. 'Give me back the clothes you hired and the cost of the extra time you've had them. If you don't, my brothers will change the shape of your face with either their fists or their razors. Take your pick!'

One look at the McElpy brothers with their bull-necks, rough-hewn features and cropped red heads was enough. The man wasted no time in complying with her wishes.

Rory had filled her mind and her time with her work and, like the eager Mamie, would have denied herself

238

everything and anything to help keep it going. Of course she was glad about getting a black dress and coat that happened to fit her, because she knew it would look better from a business point of view if she was plainly but smartly dressed. But soon she decided that because all the other shops in Glasgow had black-dressed assistants, she would be different and dressed herself and Mamie in white Jap blouses and smart black skirts. If it was too cold, they wore stylish jackets.

She still saw Victoria occasionally; her friend insisted they kept in touch. 'Just because a man's courting me doesn't mean that I'm going to neglect or abandon my girl-friend,' Victoria loyally insisted. 'Anyway, you can't talk the same with a man — or have a good giggle. I enjoy your company.'

Rory could see that she meant it and was touched. At the same time, it amazed her that Victoria couldn't see the agony she was suffering on the days when they did get together. It was fine, of course, when Victoria wasn't speaking about Matthew Drummond, but she spoke about him so much. Rory kept telling herself it would pass; she had heard it said that time healed all things and she believed this to be true. There were days and nights when she never gave Matthew Drummond a thought, when her mind was too full of other things. Then Victoria would speak of him and their future life together, would show her the sheets and pillowcases and cushion covers she was gathering for her 'bottom drawer'. Victoria would tell her of the houses she and Matthew were looking at and Rory would long for it all to be happening to her. Somehow, deep down, she had never accepted that it would not, so ingrained in her was the belief that she and Matthew Drummond belonged to each other. Victoria's happy talk of marriage seemed a temporary aberration — it confused her, but it didn't convince her. She still had so much passion in her, such a desperate need to feed its flame.

Being forced to attend the engagement party and worse, the prospect of being a bridesmaid, meant having to unravel confusion and face facts. She didn't know how she could do that.

The evening of the engagement party arrived and Rory steeled herself to go. She was late in arriving and as she stood in the close trying to pluck up courage to knock on the door, she was aware of the babble of voices and hearty laughter filling the house. It seemed so near and yet so far from her. She felt an outsider and would have preferred to remain that way — she had not much in common really with any of the Buchanans.

However, she tucked a strand of hair under her sailor hat before reluctantly rapping at the door. She was startled at the rapidity with which the door was flung open and Victoria — dressed in a froth of printed chiffon in shades of pink — hauled her in.

'I was just passing through the lobby,' she explained. Her eyes stretched huge in a face flushed a far more hectic pink than any shade in her dress. 'Come on in. We're having a great time. Uncle Hector is an absolute scream. He dressed up as a boy scout with big hat, short trousers and all, and did a turn. Oh, I wish you'd seen it! Give me your coat and hat; I'll hang them up here.'

Victoria looked radiant. Everything glowed and fizzled around her as if at any moment she was going to take off like a flying machine and do wild aerobatics.

'I'll comb my hair in the scullery. There's a wee mirror there, isn't there?' Rory said.

'Och, don't be daft, you look grand.' Victoria grabbed her arm and propelled her towards the room door. 'Come away in.'

Rory's desperate protests died on her lips as she found herself plunged into the Buchanans' crowded front room. 'Most of you know my pal, Rory McElpy,' Victoria shouted over the racket. 'But for those who haven't met her, here she is.'

'My word,' Granny Buchanan said, 'Every time I see that red head I can hardly believe it. What a mop!'

Granny Buchanan was very old and liable to say

anything that came into her head. Everyone knew this, including Rory, but that didn't make it any easier to bear. She sat down on one of the jaggy horsehair chairs, trying to smile as if it didn't matter. The gas-mantle flamed raucously and sent orange shadows flickering over the white china dogs perched on either side of the mantelpiece and on the sampler that said in different coloured letters: 'The Lord is my Shepherd'. Everyone was sitting more or less in a circle and they had obviously been taking it in turns to do their party pieces.

'Come on now, Matthew,' Victoria called out. 'It's your turn!'

Rory looked across to where Drummond was sitting and thought she had never seen anyone appear so out of place. He was like someone who had strayed from the pages of a romantic novel. There was a passionate, cultivated air about him which set him apart even from Mr Buchanan, who was a fine figure of a man. Suddenly Rory forgot her own miseries and her heart went out to him; he was obviously in an agony of embarrassment.

'I'm sorry, Victoria.'

She didn't seem to notice his distress. 'Don't be daft! Come on!'

'I cannot do anything.'

'Of course you can!'

'No, I cannot,' he repeated.

'There's no such word as cannot. Give us a wee song!'

'Victoria, please . . .' His head was lowered, his eyes desperately directed at the floor.

'A recitation, then.'

He tried to ignore her. At any moment, Rory thought, he's going to explode.

'Och, don't be so coy, Matthew!' Victoria laughed and everyone except Rory laughed along with her. 'Come on, a wee tap-dance then?'

Suddenly he looked up, eyes blazing. 'Why won't you leave me in peace, damn you!' he shouted. 'You stupid woman!'

241

For a moment there was a stunned silence and then Mrs Buchanan said in her normal gentle voice, 'It's time to get the tea ready. Come on through to the kitchen and give me a wee hand, son. The fire'll need stoking up and the big kettle put on.'

The atmosphere relaxed and began to return to noisy normality as Drummond left the room with Mrs Buchanan — not forgetting, even in his eagerness to escape, to allow her to pass through the door first. Once safely in the quiet kitchen, he said, 'I'm terribly sorry, Mrs Buchanan. I do hope you'll forgive my rudeness.'

She gave him a faint smile. 'Maybe it's Victoria you'll have more need to apologise to, son.'

'I will in due course.'

'Aye, well. The coal's in the bunker through in the scullery.'

Suddenly he bent down and kissed her check, making her flush in surprise and say, 'Tuts, you're an awful laddie!'

Back in the room the party was going full swing and with much hilarity. They were now singing 'Ten Green Bottles' — all, that is, except Victoria and Rory who had withdrawn into a corner in the pretext of setting out the dishes on the gateleg table put up especially for the occasion.

'You shouldn't have kept on at him,' Rory insisted.

'Kept on at him!' Victoria was still pale and wide-eyed with shock. 'All I did was ask him to do a turn the same as everybody else. What's wrong with that?'

'He's not the same as everybody else.'

'He is so.'

'He is not.'

'How is he not?'

Rory's face creased in her anxiety to put her feelings into words. 'He's . . . he's just different, that's all. You'll have to accept it, Victoria; he won't change.'

'Oh, won't he?' Victoria straightened up as if girding her loins for battle. 'We'll see about that!'

CHAPTER THIRTY-SEVEN

Victoria accepted Drummond's apology gracefully but coolly. Indeed she froze under his goodnight kiss, half-turning her face away as if he was insulting her again. That night Drummond couldn't sleep. Next day, the hard physical labour his job entailed plus his desperate anxiety had a shattering effect on him. The trouble was that he could find no excuse for his behaviour. He kept pestering himself with questions. Why couldn't he have just been like any normal person in that room and contributed something to the evening's entertainment? What could have been more harmless and innocent? What gathering could have been more friendly? It had been bad enough to keep churlishly refusing such an innocent request . . . bad enough to shout his refusal. But to call Victoria a stupid woman and in front of all her friends and relations was unforgivable. Worse, it was untrue. Victoria was not stupid. She was a fine, upstanding, intelligent woman. In fact she had everything: beauty, intelligence, domestic talents, artistic talents and a happy, sunny, trusting nature. He was the luckiest man alive to have found such a woman. If anyone was stupid, it was him — to risk losing such a prize. Perhaps he had lost her. When a note came to inform him that she was otherwise engaged and could not see him as previously arranged this coming Saturday, he was plummeted into depression. His books, even his journal afforded scant comfort. He did not know what he would have done had it not been for his work. Even there, although his energies were totally stretched and his mind concentrated to its utmost, he was still aware of an empty, sinking sensation in the pit of his stomach. It reminded him of how he had felt when he was in the trenches and shells were exploding all around him. His life was on the line now just as it had been then.

Saturday was a no-man's land without her. He claimed his corner seat in the pub and spent more money on whisky than he had ever done before. It began to make him feel more optimistic and after decanting himself from the pub, despite the lateness of the hour he swaggered down Springburn Road to Victoria's house and knocked boldly on the door. There was no reply and, still buoyant with good cheer, he determined to march to and fro outside until she returned from wherever she was. He had reached the Wellfield corner and was about to turn and walk back to the Balgray again when he saw Victoria and Rory approaching arm-in-arm. There was something so ridiculous about the situation that he almost laughed. He felt it could only happen to him. Fragmented memories of Rory in bed mixed in his head with the alcohol and his longings for Victoria.

He stood, swaying a little, in the path of the two girls. 'Good evening, ladies.'

'You're drunk!' Victoria accused, the horror in her voice like a hand warding him off.

'If I'd been with you, my love, I would have had no sorrows to drown.'

'Stand aside and let us pass!' Victoria commanded.

Rory touched his arm. 'Are you all right, Matty?'

'Ah, Rory,' he said. 'I believe I owe you an apology as well. I realize now . . .'

'You're just embarrassing us, Matthew Drummond.' Victoria dragged Rory away, calling over her shoulder, 'I'll see you tomorrow. Outside my place at the usual time.' Then after they were out of earshot, she added to Rory, 'Wasn't that awful?'

Rory shrugged. 'I don't suppose there's a man in Springburns who hasn't got drunk at some time or another.'

'Nonsense! There's my father, for one. And my brothers.

244

My father's a member of the Rechabites and the boys and I have all been regular attenders at the Band of Hope. I'm not having any stupid drunken carry-on after we're married, and I shall tell Matthew Drummond that in no uncertain manner when I see him tomorrow.'

And she did. Drummond was glad. For one thing, he was furious with himself at the amount of money he had spent on alcohol — money which ought to have gone into his Post Office Savings Book. He agreed with what Victoria said. If they were going to be married he would need to save every penny he could get, and he'd also need to adapt his behaviour. He wasn't a 'loner' any more; he had a partner, and lots of people who would be related to him by marriage. He would have to change his attitude and be more outgoing and sociable. As it happened, for most of the time before his marriage to Victoria — what with his work on the railway shifts and the overtime he took in order to make extra money — there weren't any more opportunities for big social events. (He had even missed Dave Buchanan's wedding.) His adaptability was therefore never put to the test.

Nor did he give it much thought. The only ripple on his otherwise idyllic engagement was the first opportunity which came up for the house of his dreams. Victoria had heard of the house first because it was Co-op property, a room and kitchen and scullery in a beautiful red sandstone building. He had been on a long run to Newcastle and unable to get to the Co-op to put his name in for it, so Victoria had said she'd better go anyway. With her being a Co-op employee, it meant they would stand a very good chance of getting it, especially if she went right away. Oh, how excited he had been all that day! With every shovel of coal dug out of the tender and heaved into the firebox, he had fashioned some tasteful scheme to make the house beautiful. After work, despite his fatigue he ran all the way to his lodgings, didn't wait to eat the meal Mrs Kipp put on the table for him but after a quick wash and change out of his dungarees off he raced again, only stopping a few streets from Victoria's home to compose himself so as not to appear too childishly eager, too obviously full of rosy thoughts about his house. It took him aback to find the Buchanan household calmly getting on with their supper and their talk about how Granny Buchanan was beginning to wander about the streets and forgetting her name and address and what ought to be done about it. The old lady was apparently refusing to leave her own house in Edinburgh and come to live permanently with the Buchanans.

Invited to join them at the table, he nodded and half-smiled his acceptance to Mrs Buchanan, his attention more urgently on Victoria and the news of whether or not the Co-op had given them the key to their very own house. Victoria met his anxious gaze with serene smiles and queries of, 'Would you like some more bread, Matthew?' or 'Have you tried mother's home-made apple jelly?'

It was well on in the evening before Victoria remembered to even mention the house, and then only after he had managed to get in a question as to what had been the result of her interview.

'Interview?' she had echoed with raised brow. And then, 'Oh, that! I didn't have time to go.'

He was shocked into silence and his mind refused to function for a few seconds. The continuing conversation amongst the Buchanan family lapped about him like a vast sea on which he was no more than a piece of flotsam. He felt lost and unable to understand how Victoria could be so casual about the chance of a house. Depression engulfed him and he was incapable of struggling free of it until he was bidding Victoria good night at her door. Even then, so heavy was his depression that he could hardly be bothered kissing her.

'You're in one of your moods,' she accused. 'You promised me you were going to control this moodiness of yours.'

'I'm just disappointed, I suppose,' he said.

246

'Disappointed?' Her voice rose with incredulity. 'What have you got to be disappointed about?'

'There would be others after the house, no doubt.'

'Och, are you still on about that?' She gave an impatient flick of her hand. 'There will be lots more houses. That's no excuse for sitting through there all evening with a face like fizz.'

He supposed she was right, but it took him a day or two to get over the surprise and confusion of finding that she felt differently about some things from the way he did. Of course it was easy to convince himself that he was the 'different' one, that he was the one at fault, not Victoria. Victoria was so refreshingly normal and there wasn't a soul in Springburn who would say otherwise. But God knows what everyone thought of him!

Victoria regarded him as something of an unknown quantity and, as the wedding drew near, she was beginning to say to Rory things like, 'Gosh sometimes I wonder if I'm doing the right thing!'

'Getting married, you mean?' Rory asked.

Victoria pouted and fingered her lips. 'Sometimes I feel I'm better suited for business. I like being out and meeting the public.'

'Don't you love Matthew?'

There was a worried hesitation and then a hint of uncertainty in her voice when replied, 'Yes, of course.'

'I suppose it's just wedding nerves,' Rory said.

'What is?'

'The way you're feeling.'

'I'm not nervous.'

'You are so.'

'I'm not!'

'You said a minute ago that you didn't know if you were doing the right thing.'

'That doesn't mean to say I'm nervous.'

'Oh, all right, have it your own way.'

Rory was in no mood to argue; she was working herself

into the ground every day partly because the business was deeply obsessing her and partly because she dare not give herself a minute to think of the coming wedding. She had started to trek round to all the tailors in the city and buy up their misfits, or 'pork' as they were known in the trade. These were the suits which for one reason or another customers had never come back to collect. Tailors were glad to get rid of them cheap and they gave her the chance of stocking garments of different sizes. She had found very early on that it was not so much a case of having a variety of different clothes that mattered, but a variety of different sizes. The tailors, sitting cross-legged in their cloth jungles of back rooms, got to know her and were only too glad to see her during the quiet and difficult times. She had also made a point of finding out about wholesale warehouses in order to buy more accessories. In addition, she still kept her eye on the death columns and visited the relatives of the deceased as she had done at the beginning. Only now she offered to buy the wardrobes of the departed instead of conning the grieving relatives out of them. She had to buy from wholesalers too, however, because the demand was becoming so great — and not only to hire but to buy.

Miss Winters had come creeping in one day to inform her that poor Mr Donovan was in such a state of deep depression that he could no longer care about anything. 'So it falls to me, Miss Rory, to be judicious and conscientious in his interests.'

'Oh?' Rory raised a brow. In her opinion, Miss Winters was anything but judicious, conscientious or anything else in Mr Donovan's interests.

'I must therefore, Miss Rory, object to you selling hats in your establishment.'

'You can object if you like, Miss Winters. It won't stop me.'

'But . . . but that is most unethical. Mr Donovan is the hatter in this street.'

Rory shrugged. 'He can stock clothes and gloves and

248

footwear like I do. I don't care. Let the best merchant win!'

'Most unethical,' Miss Winters repeated. 'It will be the ruination of poor Mr Donovan. I shall have to inform his son. His dear son is unaware of his father's unhappy situation. When he finds out that you have been persecuting poor Mr Donovan, he will I'm sure change his plans about going abroad and return to Glasgow instead.' She leaned forward, peering close into Rory's face. 'Then you will be sorry, I can assure you, Miss McElpy.'

'I've nothing to be sorry about. Now you must excuse me, Miss Winters. I'm extremely busy.'

She had told Victoria how busy she was too and had made every excuse to get out of having anything to do with the wedding, but Victoria was adamant that she would have everything to do with it. Of course Drummond had also been working like a slave and because he was not able to see so much of Victoria, she felt all the more urgent need of Rory's company. It had even come to pass that Rory was supplying Victoria's wedding dress. On one of Victoria's many visits to the shop in Stockwell Street she had seen the dress hanging on the rail; it was a new acquisition and Rory had spent bitter-sweet moments fingering the silvery satin and weaving hopeless dreams around it.

She had been doing just that and gazing wistfully at it when Victoria had breezed into the shop. 'Oh, Rory!' she cried out in immediate delight. 'You've got me a dress! Oh, I knew you'd do something wonderful for me — I just knew it!'

She was so excited and her hands trembled so much that Rory had to help her into the garment and button it up for her.

At last they both stood in front of the long mirror surveying the result. The glass reflected the two girls side by side, Rory slightly behind Victoria. Victoria was radiant and elegant in the silver-white gown which complemented her glossy dark hair and eyes. Rory, in contrast, exuded a strong mixture of tragic defiance and a very business-like air in her tailored high-neck blouse and shirt.

'I don't care how much it is,' Victoria declared. 'Mother and father and the boys will help me. I just *must* have it! It's absolutely me. Oh Rory, how clever of you to find it. Of course, nobody knows me and what I'd suit as well as you do!'

'Forget about price,' Rory said. 'Just hire it and give it back to me afterwards. Nobody ever uses a wedding dress again. Wedding outfits are turning out to be my best line in business — I wish I could get more of them.'

'Well, I'll pay your hiring charge.'

Rory shook her head, her mouth twisting a little. 'This will be my treat.'

'Oh, Rory!' Victoria pounced on her to rock her to and fro in an enthusiastic hug. Rory felt enveloped in the delicious smoothness of satin, the fragrance of roses from some previous wedding bouquet and the faint whiff of Co-op toilet soap from Victoria's skin. She closed her eyes, willing herself not to feel anything. What was the use?

'I feel much happier now that I know how I'm going to look,' Victoria said after she had released her. 'Not that I wasn't happy. It's just . . . well, you know how my mother's always gone on about men.'

Rory stopped helping her friend out of the dress and stared at her in surprise. 'Your mother hasn't said anything against Matty, has she?'

Victoria's brown eyes became slightly evasive. 'Well, not exactly. But we don't need her to tell us about men any more, do we?'

'You shouldn't judge every man by the likes of Sid Ford and his crowd.'

Victoria gave a half laugh. 'My mother said men are all the same.'

'Matty's different.'

'So you keep telling me.'

'You ought to know him by now. Don't you think he is?' Rory asked.

'He's a nice man, I'm sure. Yes, he's a perfect gentleman.' Victoria seemed to be trying to reassure herself. 'He's a bit moody and he's got a temper, but he loves me, he really does. He'd do anything for me.'

'I know.'

'Only sometimes I wish . . .'

'Wish what?'

Victoria's eyes acquired their sideways sniffy expression. 'Human nature is so awful — I wish it wasn't.'

'Poor Matty,' Rory thought.

She could see that as far as Victoria was concerned, it was going to be a case of closing her eyes, opening her legs and just thinking of England.

CHAPTER THIRTY-EIGHT

Drummond wrote to Victoria every day, though sometimes he didn't send the letters but just copied them into his journal instead. Often he wrote in bed, because his room was so cold and the covering of blankets his only source of heat. He wrote neatly, his pen moving over the paper with excruciating care. Often he would begin 'My dear girl' or simply 'Dear Victoria'. He always signed the letters 'Yours, Matthew Drummond'. In the letters he wrote in his journal, however, he began 'My wonderful loving wife-to-be' and signed them 'Loving you for ever'. Sometimes he got completely carried away and painted imaginary pictures of Victoria working proudly about their own home. 'And when that imaginary scene becomes, with time's slow passing, a glad reality,' he wrote, 'gone I trust for ever will be bleak mornings like this when the only contact I have with you is this sheet of paper.'

To himself in his journal he recorded: 'I have not very long to wander about free and single now. My wedding day is but two months distant. I wish I could say it is tomorrow. It doesn't seem so long ago since that never-to-be-forgotten night of the railway dance when I proposed to my beautiful Victoria. The proposal was actually made in the early hours of the morning after I'd walked her home. It was cold and we stood together in her close and I found the right words at last. I remember she gazed very seriously up into my eyes, as if searching for something she could trust. The suspense was like a cord tightening round my throat before she eventually said "Yes".'

Married life had often seemed a kind of promised land to him. Now his mind was always bright with pictures of warm fireside scenes and of loving and being loved.

Then came one of the most memorable entries in his journal — and how he enjoyed writing it. It was headed 'Our House' and underneath he wrote, 'We are to get the key of our house this week. Hurrah! A certain warm and cosy abode is henceforth *OURS*. Just fancy me the respectable resident, the worthy taxpayer, the esteemed citizen. From now on the cold winds may howl as much as they like outside. Inside that ever welcoming, oh so well-loved place, everything will be warm and comfortable and happy . . .'

In the cold emptiness of his lodging room, he sometimes fondly imagined that Victoria would be sitting quietly writing in her diary much the same sort of things. He had given her a diary at Christmas, as well as a leather handbag. In fact, the only things Victoria had written in her diary were reminders of shopping she had to do. It was one of her duties to bring home any messages her mother needed from the Co-op. Scribbled willy-nilly across the pages were things like, '2 Plain loaves, a packet of pipe-clay and black-lead polish'.

More recently, however, there were more exotic items: 'White or silver shoes, a fancy garter (with blue on it), white underskirt and drawers'.

She had no time for diaries. Life was getting more and more hectic. Now there was the house to get organized, ready for moving into after the wedding. It had been very thrilling the first time she and Drummond had unlocked the door and walked in. It was the same size and style of house as her mother's and father's, the same style indeed which housed half the folk in Springburn — a small lobby, a room to the front, a kitchen and scullery to the back. To Victoria and Drummond, of course, it was completely different. Right away Victoria said proudly, 'It's really special,' and he wholeheartedly agreed.

In the kitchen, as well as a range and small barred fire

on which to cook, there was a gas-ring that folded down from the side — a very special innovation.

'Have you noticed, Matthew,' Victoria said as they strolled around surveying their domain, 'how even all the floorboards are? Not one wobbles or squeaks.'

'The ceilings look pretty good too,' Drummond commented. 'Hardly a crack anywhere. It's the same with the walls.' They fingered the walls as if hardly able to believe their good fortune.

'Of course,' said Victoria, 'the colour scheme isn't our taste.'

'I thought a Morris paper for the room,' Drummond suggested.

Victoria nibbled at her lip. 'I don't think the Co-op have that kind,' she said doubtfully.

'We'll go into town to purchase it,' Drummond said grandly.

'Oh, Matthew!' She flung her arms around his neck, her excitement and joy suddenly overflowing. It was as if she had at last been given the dolls' house she had always secretly wanted. He held her very tightly and his lips meeting hers seemed to fuse their deep happiness together. So intense was the experience that Victoria began to feel quite faint. Then he firmly released her and said, 'Of course, we'll get the furniture in the Co-op. It'll mean quite a substantial dividend to put in our store book.'

Hand-in-hand, they stood gazing in wonder at the small bare rooms with their set-in-the-wall beds like black caverns (one in each room), the greasy grey ceilings with cobwebbed corners, the walls dark-stained by someone else's furniture. Victoria had never enjoyed herself so much in years. They discussed what superior furnishings they would have. Everything would be in impeccable good taste. Victoria did not go so far as to say so, but she believed that people would come from miles around to admire it. She had lovely pictures of herself entertaining all her friends and relations and nobody telling her what to do or not to do. Here, she would be 'Queen of the

Castle'. She could cook whatever she fancied, arrange the furniture as the notion took her. She could wear what she wanted and do her hair as she liked. She could go in and out without her mother asking, 'Where are you going, dear?' and 'When will you be back?' She could really be grown-up — she would be a married woman.

All the fears which had been niggling at her about losing her freedom by getting married completely disappeared. Everything reversed and she now felt only the irritations and restrictions of being single.

As the wedding day drew near, they concentrated on buying what they needed for their nest. Drummond spent every free moment in the place papering and painting it, or just standing — sometimes with eyes closed, soaking up the atmosphere and the incredible reality of it being the home he was about to share with his beloved wife.

At other times, when he was at work, Victoria came with Rory. They scrubbed the place from end to end and thoroughly cleaned and black-leaded and polished the grate and washed and polished the windows. Rory also agreed that the house was special. After all, most young couples started their married life in a 'single end' as a one-roomed flat was called.

Wedding presents were piling in, nearly all from Victoria's friends and relations, although Drummond was surprised and somewhat embarrassed when presents arrived from Walter Agnew, another fireman, two of the drivers he had worked with and the Local Labour Party. Drummond had certainly done Walter Agnew a favour by successfully fighting (through the Union) his case for compensation after an accident he had been involved in, but the present of a beautiful blue vase with a gold dragon coiled around it astonished and impressed him. He said, and Victoria agreed with him, that the vase — like the painting in the gold frame given by his branch of the Labour Party — was generous to a fault and in extremely good taste.

Rory's present was a beautiful linen supper-cloth with lace edging and lace-edged napkins to match. Not even the

Buchanans had ever possessed anything so posh as napkins, and again the happy couple were impressed and delighted. They suspected that the supper-cloth and napkins were not new. Nothing Rory ever had was new. But the gift looked as if it had never been used and it certainly was beautiful.

Only once did they allow themselves to have an evening out together. The house was all ready, the wedding only a week off, so they decided to celebrate by going to the railway dance. Rory was there too and when another man took Victoria up for a dance, Drummond asked Rory. He was hardly aware of her in his arms, however, being too busy trying to keep his eyes on Victoria, as she swept around the floor. She was wearing a turquoise dress that was all gauzy and floaty and had never looked so beautiful, so ethereal. He had never seen any woman with such a good posture. Even her head was perfectly poised on her perfect white neck. And oh what a noble head, more queenly than any queen! Even though crowds of dancers came between them, even though her attention kept being diverted by the gaiety and pleasure of the dance, back again would come those wide brown eyes to search him out and fasten on him. Never before had he been so sure of her love.

Then came the most important entry in his journal. 'My Wedding Day', he wrote at the top of the page. And then: 'Ah! My Day has come at last. Oh, slow in coming time. The one goal of all the year. The central event of my life. And ere it passes to its treasured close two lives will have, with sacrament and love, been forever joined. Two lives; sweetest hers and undeserving mine . . .'

He had wakened early and the house was quiet. The patchwork bed-mat made from scraps of shirts, dresses and suits belonging to generations of the Kipp family had slid off his knees and hung down on to the floor. He hoisted it up around him, settled his journal on his knee and savoured the intense enjoyment of writing in it. As he gazed around the room he would shortly be leaving before recording a description of it, he saw the faded sepia wall-paper with the damp brown patches; the sepia photographs of generations of the Kipp family in formal pose, the men vying with each other in bewhiskered severity, the women in stiffly corseted black; the chipped water-jug and bowl on the table over at the window; one sparred wooden chair; bare brown linoleum . . . Nothing else. Except of course the bed and the yellowed lace curtains. 'But I must rise,' he wrote, 'for who would lie contentedly abed on a radiant today such as this. A love-crowned, delicious day is before me. So, quickly through to the kitchen for a lodger's last breakfast. And Mrs Kipp can be as mean as she likes in the amount of porridge she serves up. She can even bash away to her heart's content on her tambourine. Nothing or no one can spoil this day for me.'

Later, back in his room again and this time sitting at the table, he wrote, 'It is the afternoon. The event is nearing. There is no nervousness within me, nor qualms of any kind besetting me. I am just seriously and confidently wishing myself forward to the solemn "I will" of the marriage moment . . .'

And later still: 'Now it is seven o'clock. I must begin to dress. The car comes for me in an hour. What a long brushing this suit needs and must get. But I'm going to look well this night, I know it. Thank goodness my tie is giving me fair do this time. It is sitting obedient enough as yet. Twenty minutes to eight. My hat — what a tippy hat — my gloves, my flower, the ring, all are in order under my determined gaze. For nothing must outwit me. A last look in the glass. Better get my hat fixed on. Ah, that will do. My gloves now. Specks of dust have landed on my suit, bringing with them a spark of anger. A moment's sharp brushing and I am myself again. Now, I think that's absolutely all. Yes. And so at last I stand ready, a bridegroom-to-be, waiting for the car.'

He had been pressed by Victoria to ask Walter Agnew to be his best man, and he had refused to contemplate such an embarrassment at first. After all, it was not as if he and

Agnew had been friends. He had often seen him at the Union of course, and in the railway bothy when they'd both been waiting on firing turns; he had even visited his house a couple of times to get all the particulars about the accident from him. But they had never been friends.

'Of course you have,' Victoria insisted. 'And stop calling him Agnew, his name's Walter. Honestly Matthew, I don't know what to make of you. You're so peculiar at times.'

'How about one of your brothers?' he had suggested.

'You don't need one of my brothers; you've got Walter. The best man's supposed to be a friend of the groom, not his prospective brother-in-law.'

She was right. But still it was with agonized resentment that he'd eventually asked Agnew. To his surprise, Agnew had responded to his stilted request with a cheery, 'Aye, of course I'll be your best man, Matt. Glad to be able to help you for a change.'

Now Walter had arrived at Mrs Kipp's to collect him. 'I've brought a bottle,' he announced, producing a bottle of whisky from his hip pocket. 'Have a swig, Matt. It'll steady you up.'

But Drummond refused. When he stepped forward to the altar he wanted his eyes to reflect love, not whisky.

But first there was the happy breathless scuffle through the colourful fountain of confetti and the unexpected crush of neighbours in Springburn Road before he could reach the car. His heart warmed with gratitude towards them and he managed a smile and a wave before leaning back on the softly bouncing cushions of the car and murmuring, 'Well, here goes for my life's best job.'

CHAPTER THIRTY-NINE

Victoria gave a short laugh. 'Anyone would think you were going to my funeral instead of my wedding.'

'You don't look all that cheerful yourself,' Rory said.

Victoria's mouth trembled into a smile. 'I'm all right. Come on, let's check ourselves in the mirror.'

Rory rustled over beside her, her yellow taffeta dress catching the sunshine from the window and becoming like sunshine itself. The two friends stood side by side in silence for a minute or two, Victoria staring at Rory's slim daffodil figure topped by a coronet of tiny green leaves and white flowers. Rory gazed at the white shimmer of Victoria's gown and her veil flowing from a coronet that sat half-way down her forehead. At last Rory said, 'Nothing will be the same after today.'

'I don't see why not. We'll still be the same.'

'That's a damned stupid thing to say. You'll be married to Matty.'

'That won't change me.'

'It will so.'

'It will not.'

'Oh, all right, have it your own way. You usually do.'

'I wish you would relax,' Victoria said.

'You're a fine one to talk about relaxing,' Rory responded.

'I'm perfectly relaxed.'

'You are not.'

'I am so.'

'You're trembling. Look at you!'

'It's just excitement.'

'You can't be both relaxed and excited.'

'Oh, be quiet, Rory. You're supposed to help me, not argue with me.'

Rory turned away from the mirror and went over to the window to lean her brow against the cool glass. 'It's not that I don't want you to be happy,' she said.

'Och, I know you do.' Victoria came flying over beside her, the bouquet she was now clutching swirling the air with heady fragrance. 'Don't worry, Rory. You'll always be my best friend, nothing will ever change that. Oh look, there's the car!'

Sure enough a Co-operative limousine had drawn up outside, much to the excitement of the waiting crowd of people. Then the door burst open and Mr Buchanan strode in, a proud figure with his curled moustache and high stiff collar. He offered his arm to Victoria. 'Come on, then. Don't dilly-dally.'

Victoria had gone so white that Rory thought she was going to change her mind and refuse to budge. But when her father tucked her arm through his, she somehow succeeded in moving forward beside him.

Rory picked up her posy, her face muscles tightening. All she could think was, 'This is goodbye to Matty.' She had never been as much of a dreamer as Victoria. Hard reality was never far from her mind, and the reality of this day was that somehow she would have to get through it. Outside, the waiting crowd cheered lustily. There were shouts of 'Good luck!' and heartfelt cries of 'Oh, doesn't she look a treat!'

The air was thick and multi-coloured with confetti. The two girls choked and coughed with it and had to lower their heads and run for the shadowy interior of the car. Then Mr Buchanan rolled down the window and just as they were moving away he flung out a handful of coppers. They clinked to the ground, to accompanying squeals of delight from all the children in the crowd.

Many times when Rory and Victoria had been children they had taken part in a 'Scramble' — as the pouncing on money thrown from a wedding car was called. Not that

Victoria had ever been very good at this free-for-all; even as a young child she had possessed a certain amount of ladylike dignity. It had always been Rory who had fought her way most successfully through the wild tumble of children and grabbed a share of the pennies rolling about the street.

Victoria was unusually quiet now, leaning back in the corner of the car, lovely but ghost-like, her pale apprehensive face gazing wide-eyed from its nest of white veil.

Her father, normally a cheerful talkative man, seemed for once unable to think of anything to say. The best he could do was to pat his daughter's hand a couple of times and say, 'We'll soon be there, hen.'

Indeed, it only took a matter of minutes to get from the house to the Co-op hall where another joyful crowd — this time made up mostly of Co-op customers — buzzed with excited expectancy as the car came into view. There was more confetti and more shouting now:

'You look lovely, hen!'

'Good luck, Vicky!'

'Och, you're a bonny wee lassie!'

'He's a lucky man, so he is!'

Upstairs inside the building, Drummond was waiting in a side room with his best man. He knew the next car to arrive must be the one carrying the bride and he couldn't resist peering down on the street below. It was a scene he would ever remember. The car drew up and eager hands pulled the door open. He glimpsed a tiny white shoe, a flow of glistening satin, a flutter of flowers, a froth of snowy veil and then the crowd closed in.

'Come on through now,' Walter Agnew urged, plucking at his arm and steering him in the direction of the door and the main hall where all the guests were sitting. The minister was standing ready at a table in front of them.

Someone handed Drummond a slip of paper with the wedding hymn on it and he started to read it to quell a burst of confusion. A soft rustle at his left elbow accentuated this emotion and he succumbed to the temptation

261

to glance round. And there was his love's face, pale and sweet. Everyone was singing now, 'Oh, perfect love . . .' The piece of paper in his hand shook; this was disconcerting and he was fearful of it being noticed. A prayer followed in which their love, their hopes, their marriage were offered up to heaven for blessing.

Soon he heard himself say 'Yes' in a clear voice, then a small 'Yes' echoed at his left. A long white glove was unrolled. He felt Victoria's nervousness and he had to hold her hand very firmly so as to keep it steady in order to get the ring on her finger. Then, as if in a dream, as if everything had gone into slow motion, they kissed as man and wife. Married, he thought. Partnered for life. The custodian of priceless treasure. He was dazed with good fortune.

People were shaking hands with him and Victoria was the centre of a crowd of admiring girl-friends; there was much laughter and chatter among them. Victoria's face had now acquired a rosy colour and there was a look of radiant happiness in her brown eyes that delighted him. Neither he nor Victoria were very hungry for the Co-op supper of steak pie, peas and potatoes. Later, however, they enjoyed the dance. What a strange delight he felt, dancing with his wife. He noted every nuance of feeling as they circled the floor — the soft slipperiness of satin against his hand and through it the pulsating warmth of her body; the glimmer of her raven-black hair in the gas-light; the soft depths of her dark eyes; the skin with the delicate glow and texture and perfume of rose petals.

Drummond knew he had no need to record the impressions of this evening in his journal. He knew he would always be able to look back on his wedding and think of every wonderful detail of it with the same clarity and delight as he did now. Time would never dim this evening. No matter what happens to me in the future, he thought, I can look back and say, 'I was happy then.'

But time flew. It was three o'clock in the morning, the band was playing and everyone was singing:

Three o'clock in the morning, We've danced the
    whole night through;
And daylight soon will be dawning. Just one more
    waltz with you.
That melody so entrancing, seems to be made for
    us two.
I could keep dancing with you forever, Dear, Just
    with You . . .

They were swirling around in a dream of love, until
everybody gathered themselves together and wearily but
happily sang, 'Auld Lang Syne!'
    The car was at the door again and he felt bewildered
with joy. He was going home.

CHAPTER FORTY

Drummond couldn't get the key to turn in the door. The landing was dark and he had to feel for the keyhole. Victoria heard him growl, 'Damn!'

She experienced a nervous kind of loneliness, but managed to gather some dignity around her and say, 'I'm not in the habit of having people swear at me.'

'I'm not swearing at you. I'm swearing at this damned key.'

'You did it again!' she accused.

He visibly struggled with himself as well as with the key. 'I'm sorry, Victoria. I don't know what's gone wrong with this. Ah! There it is. What a relief!'

He pushed open the door. 'Just a minute!' He caught her arm as she was about to sweep past and she turned a pale luminous face towards him, eyebrows raised in polite enquiry.

'It's the custom,' he said, 'for the bridegroom to carry the bride over the threshold!'

Before she could gather her wits together he had swept her up into his arms, entered the dark lobby and kicked the door shut behind him. Her mind told her that she ought to feel thrilled. After all, a mixture of Matthew Drummond and Rudolph Valentino had done this to her many times before. All she felt, however, was apprehension.

'You'll have to light the gas,' she said as he groped his way in the lobby, misjudged the kitchen doorway and bumped her against the wall. 'Put me down!'

'Did you get any matches?' he asked after he had

deposited her on to the floor and they were both fumbling their way into the kitchen.

'Did *you* get any matches?' she retorted.

'You were the one who was to stock up with all the messages, Victoria.' His voice was calm and reasonable, but she took it as an insult.

'How dare you!'

'How dare I what?'

'Try to make out that it is my fault.'

'It's not a case of apportioning blame. Wait here — I'll try in the scullery drawer.'

Victoria heard a thump out in the lobby and an 'Oh, bugger it!' as her husband fell over something. Her heart palpitated. In all the time she had known him, she had never realized that Matthew Drummond indulged in such bad language. She began to shiver and couldn't be certain if it was because of fear or cold.

The kitchen fire was not lit and the amazing thought occurred to her that she would have to light it herself if she wanted it lit. At home, her mother had started the fire every morning so that the kitchen was nice and cosy for all the family getting up.

He returned in a few minutes, a black shadow in the grey room. Her eyes were beginning to get adjusted and she could also see the dark cavern of the bed and the black blobs of furniture.

'No luck!' Drummond said. 'There's no need to worry, however. We'll manage into bed. And it will soon be light.'

Suddenly Victoria longed to be safely back home. She would have done anything to escape. And to think that she had committed herself for life! She was stunned by the tragic awfulness of her situation.

For a second or two they stood staring at the ghostly figures of each other, then Drummond said in a husky voice, 'Do you wish me to help you to take your dress off?'

'Certainly *not*!' she gasped, beginning to tremble again.

After another minute's silence, he said, 'All right. I'll go through to the room and wait until you're in bed.'

After he had disappeared, loudly stumbling and quietly cursing along the lobby again, she tugged herself out of her dress, underskirt, bust bodice, corset and drawers, nearly weeping in her desperate haste. Her nightdress was folded ready under the pillow and breathlessly she pulled it on. The bed was high and she had to make several attempts to hoist herself up on top of it. Again she was harassed with keeping tears at bay in case she might be caught in the undignified position of having one leg up on the bed, one leg down and hands tugging. Eventually she managed it and burrowing deep under the bedclothes, she was aware of the cold crisp feel of new linen and the aroma of the Co-op drapery department. Nothing had the homely smell of sweat or soap. She was aware, too, that at any minute a man would be coming into bed beside her. It didn't feel decent. Just because the minister gave her a bit of paper saying she was married, that didn't make her a different person. The fears and beliefs in certain taboos she had had the day before had not miraculously disappeared. She was still the same Victoria.

During her courtship there had been kissing and cuddling, but she realized now that it had been at best just a novelty, an act, a game spiced with danger. In her heart she had always known she was perfectly safe. How could she be otherwise with her mother's door only yards away from the back close where she and Drummond always stood? Inside that door within calling distance were her six-footer of a father and her equally robust brothers. Now, suddenly, everything was frighteningly real and she was alone and unprotected.

She clutched the bedclothes high up to her chin and tightly closed her eyes when she heard Drummond come into the room. Her body had become as stiff as a steel fender, her legs glued together as all the things Rory told her about what men did came panicking back into her mind.

Drummond slid underneath the bedclothes beside her and her heart began to thud so loud and strong that she could hardly breathe for the pain of it.

'Oh, Victoria,' he said without touching her. 'I love you.'

Stiffly, fearfully, she turned her face towards him and found they were almost nose-to-nose. He had quite a nice nose; it was very straight, not Roman-shaped like hers. She could just make out that he was beginning to need a shave. Round his mouth — quite a nice mouth, it was too; wide but not thick-lipped — and round his chin, shadows darkened. His eyes glowed softly at her and she could see the love in them. That love helped her to relax, but gradually, apprehensively . . . like someone testing the sea with a toe.

'I love you,' he repeated softly, 'now and always.'

It was then that she remembered she loved him too. Perhaps, she thought daringly, it wouldn't hurt to let him have one wee kiss? Closing her eyes, she puckered her lips.

His kiss felt gentle and not unpleasant and when his arms went around her it was just like when they were courting in the back close. Soon, however, his kisses became more urgent and his hands slid inside her nightgown. When she felt the shock of his hot skin against hers, her first instinct was to struggle away. Only his whispered reminder that they were married and it was all right prevented her. She allowed his intimacies with growing apprehension and disgust and tried to stiffen away from him. She cringed in fear when he came on top of her and cried out in bewilderment and pain when he penetrated her. Afterwards, she experienced such a welter of disgust that she felt nauseated. Even the fact that he cuddled her in his arms until he fell asleep did not help. She lay exhausted but wide awake, her mind festering, her body throbbing with pain. Surely it wasn't right of Matthew to give way to his animal instincts so early in their marriage? She knew this sort of shameful behaviour was necessary at some point in order to have babies, but not immediately, not on the very first night of their marriage, surely? Thinking of babies made her remember the horror of Rory's abortion and the agony and terror her friend had suffered. Did that same agony and distress occur when one had a baby? Perhaps it was even worse? After all, a baby was bigger and more solid to come away than just blood and bits of flesh. Victoria felt herself go icy cold and sick with fear. Surely Matthew ought to have at least waited for a decent interval before subjecting her to the risk of such an ordeal.

His arm was still around her and now its hardness under her back had become uncomfortable. It added to her resentment. There he was, sleeping peacefully without a care in the world. How could he! Tears stung her eyes. She felt lonely and confused, resentful and ashamed.

More than anything else, she wished that her marriage had never happened and she could be back home with her mother, safe and comfortable and happy. What made everything a hundred times worse was the fact that she knew her pride would never allow her to admit defeat and return home. She had made her bed and she knew she would have to lie on it. Her resentment against Matthew bubbled up like a fountain, spilling over everything. She hated his arm intruding underneath her back; she hated his deep, self-satisfied breathing; she thought it absolutely disgusting that he hadn't worn either pyjamas or nightshirt. Never before in her life had she heard of anyone doing such a thing. Had he no shame? No sense of decency? Tears burned like acid down her face. It was too awful for words that she had got mixed up with such a man. It was terrible to try and sob quietly and without her body shaking too much in case it wakened him. She would see *him* weep before he'd ever be allowed to see her. No man was going to get the better of Victoria Buchanan! If he thought he had degraded and humiliated her, he was wrong.

But when the next night came and again he came on top of her, she was once more confused and indecisive. Again she cringed in her mind and tried not to move a muscle, like an anxious doe who imagines that complete stillness will protect her. But everything happened exactly as it had the night before and again she was left to lie wide-eyed and shocked.

During the day it was not so bad. Matthew was charming and attentive and so handsome that it gave her a secret thrill every time she stole a look at him. There was also the novelty and delight of her new home to take up her time and attention and the honeymoon treats of a day into town, high tea in Miss Buick's and then to the cinema. The film, however, — *The Price of a Good Time* — although enjoyable was disturbing.

Still, there were other treats like having her church and bible class friends to tea for the first time. Matthew insisted he had an important Union meeting to attend and disappeared before anyone arrived. In her excited preparations for the big event she had not time to argue with him. She made a mental note, however, not to let him get away with dodging any other social occasion in future. It was one thing if he had to go to work. Even a Union or Labour Party meeting might be permissible if it was truly important — that is, in furthering his career prospects.

She suspected, however, that these meetings would have to be carefully monitored in case they would be used simply as an excuse to pander to his unsociable moods.

The tea-party, despite the fact that Matthew had let her down by not being there, was a huge success. She had used the beautiful table-cover and napkins that Rory had given her and of course her rose-patterned wedding china. She had baked jam sponges, Empire biscuits and coconut Madelaines, and made dainty sandwiches cut in crustless triangles. With what pride had she circled the table admiring her work before everyone arrived. With what joy she had welcomed and entertained all her guests.

There were the posh girls from the Co-op office as well as the grocers, and even the very ladylike Miss Collins and Miss Blakely, the Co-op milliner and dressmaker. She had not of course invited any of the girls from the fish-shop, because they were smelly; they would have ruined her good cushions and chairs.

Rory had said at first that she couldn't come, but

Victoria had reminded her in no uncertain terms of what a good friend and support she had been at the important times in Rory's life. 'Now surely the least you can do in return is come to my first tea-party.'

And so Rory had come, looking very pale and drawn.

'You're driving yourself too hard, that's your trouble,' Victoria told her. 'You should relax and enjoy yourself more often.' Sometimes Rory reminded her of her husband — she had that same withdrawn, intense look she sometimes noticed about Matthew.

'Are you happy?' Rory had asked and she replied, 'Of course!' As indeed she was on that day of the tea-party . . .

She wanted to confide in Rory about her secret worries and confusion in bed, but couldn't. In a way, what Rory had said on the day of her wedding was true — 'Everything will be different . . .'

How could she, now an experienced married woman, expect an unmarried girl like Rory to understand the intimate problems of the married state? Unfortunately, it was equally unthinkable to confide in her mother and ask her advice. Mrs Buchanan would shy away in immediate horror at the first mention of anything to do with what happened in bed.

Then one day not long after the tea-party, when Matthew was on late shift and she had arranged to go to the pictures with Rory, an opportunity arose to speak to a more unshockable person. She had called for Rory at Cowlairs Road, but Rory had not yet returned from her shop and Annie McElpy opened the door — as sallow-skinned as ever, her big bony frame wrapped in a brown sacking apron.

'Oh, it's you! Come in, hen. Rory's not back yet, but she shouldn't be long. Do you fancy a cup of tea?'

Victoria nearly refused, for the cups never looked too clean and always were brown-stained with tannin inside. However, instinct told her it would be prudent to accept. For once the house was quiet and empty, at least of people. Apart from the clutter of furniture, the small kitchen was a fetid jungle of wet washing drooping thick and low from the four-barred pulley that dangled from the ceiling.

'Mrs McElpy, I'd like, if I may, to ask your advice,' Victoria burst out suddenly.

'Fire ahead, hen.' Annie slurped at her tea, then wiped her face on a corner of her apron. 'I'll help if I can.'

Victoria stared in an anguish of embarrassment at the older woman; at her gaunt dried-up face and weary eyes.

'I'm very worried about my husband's behaviour,' she began.

'Oh, aye?' Annie took another slurp of tea.

'I'm not sure . . . I wondered . . . I mean, do you think it's . . . it's decent . . .' Victoria flushed, 'or even natural . . .'

'What is, hen?'

Victoria's fiery colour deepened and spilled down her neck. 'Twice in the first week we were married . . . he . . . you know. I mean . . . twice . . . and so soon. To tell you the truth, Mrs McElpy, I'm having a terrible struggle trying to keep him at bay. It's a constant source of worry and distress to me!'

Suddenly Annie laughed. 'My God, hen, if you had my Scrap you'd know all about it! He'd be on top of me twice a day if he got the chance. You go home to your good man tonight and think yourself damned lucky — that's my advice, hen.'

Victoria was shocked. While she was thankful that Matthew was not the wild beast she had thought he was in this respect, at the same time she didn't feel any different. Despite her efforts to reassure herself and remind herself that she loved her husband, disgust, shame and apprehension kept circling around her like a menacing pack of wolves.

CHAPTER FORTY-ONE

Victoria had always thought of herself as a very capable, sensible type of person. There were those — Rory, for one — who might have disagreed with this assessment of her character. But what Victoria thought, Victoria believed. She decided that she simply must keep Matthew's demands on her to a minimum — say once a week at the most, once a fortnight if she could manage it. If she could do this — and she *must* do it — then marriage would be quite a happy state to be in on the whole. It was fun cooking nice meals and having Matthew praise her efforts so enthusiastically; that was one thing about Matthew — he did appreciate all her talents. If was fun too planning what they would still like to do to their house, and the luxuries they dreamed of one day acquiring. She enjoyed talking to Matthew; he could converse on so many different and unusual topics. On the whole, she was extremely proud of him . . . if only his human nature wasn't always so ready to rear it's ugly head. She had to be very careful about that, she had found, indeed for ever on the alert. It could suddenly become a problem at the most unexpected times — like when he got his gramophone. She had never seen a man, or anyone for that matter, appear so happy. Joy shone from his eyes. He had made quite an occasion of the day the gramophone was delivered; he'd brought in ice-cream wafers and a bottle of lemonade and they had made iced drinks and toasted their good fortune at acquiring such a prize. It wasn't new, but in extremely good condition, and they had heard about its potential sale from Rory. Someone she had come across had died and all their effects were being sold off. It was a chest-high rosewood cabinet with a hinged lid and an oval mesh front where the sound came out, and a handle at the side for winding it up.

Matthew bought a record called 'Greensleeves' and he did a slow waltz with her to the haunting refrain. He was so happy that he actually sang while they danced round and round the kitchen:

> Alas my love! ye do me wrong
> To cast me off discourteously.
> And I have loved you so long
> Delighting in your company.
> Greensleeves was all my joy,
> Greensleeves was my delight,
> Greensleeves was my heart of gold,
> And who but Lady Greensleeves.

She had been thoroughly enjoying the event until he began to tighten his hold on her and she recognized the first danger sign — his heavy breathing.

Heart battering in alarm, she had to push him away immediately and make some excuse about needing to do something else. She hurried through to the scullery and left him with his record while she made him a good strong cup of Bovril, hoping that would be sufficient to satisfy his needs. (They'd had the gas ring removed from the kitchen to the scullery and planned one day to have a gas cooker with a gas oven put in the scullery too. 'When my ship comes in,' Victoria said.)

It upset her when their relationship was spoiled in this way. As far as she was concerned, her marriage would be idyllic if it wasn't for the weekly ordeal in bed. Sometimes she managed to employ delaying tactics and make it nearer the fortnightly mark — in fact, she was getting rather clever at this — but it was still an ordeal to continuously be on one's guard against.

Then of course there was the lesser but still annoying

273

business of Matthew's moodiness. His singing of 'Green-sleeves' had returned to her mind later as proof of how he was only being moody and perverse when he refused to perform at parties or any kind of social gathering. For instance, it was not true — as he claimed — that he couldn't sing. His singing of 'Greensleeves' showed that he had a very nice singing voice. His speaking voice, although sometimes stilted and literary in content, was deep and strong yet with a likeable, kindly resonance to it. It was the same with his singing voice.

'You're a very good singer,' she had accused. 'There's absolutely no reason why you shouldn't sing at anybody's party.'

He had not responded verbally and she had taken his silence as acquiescence, an unspoken agreement that there would be no more of his silly nonsense in future. Yet the manner in which he half-turned away his head and the glance that escaped round in her direction should have warned her, she realized afterwards, that the battle was not yet won.

She made a mental note at the time, however, that when she gave her next tea-party she would make sure that it took place during Matthew's early shift week when he would be in. She had promised to have some of her old Co-op customers to tea and was looking forward to them coming. As usual, Matthew was pleased and happy because she was pleased and happy — a trait she found particularly lovable about him — and he helped her to get the room ready by putting the kitchen chairs through and the tea-trolley with the cake-stand on it and the plates of scones and pancakes she had made. She covered it with a tea-cloth to keep off any dust. Not that there was any dust — she'd been dusting and polishing half the day, singing happily as she did so, for she delighted in showing off her lovely home at its very best. It was the only time she was really interested in housework; if no one was coming she caught up with her reading, or made some excuse to get out and around. Matthew happily shared her busy preparations; he even brought in some flowers for her to put in vases and make the room look still nicer, and she rewarded him with a nice kiss and hug for that. Then before the guests arrived they stood hand-in-hand, proudly surveying their domain. It was at times like these that she had no doubts whatsoever of the value of the married state over any other.

Nothing was without its faults and drawbacks, however. And Matthew's faults began to manifest themselves immediately her eager, watchful eyes saw from the front-room window her guests moving en masse along Springburn Road and then disappearing up her close. At that moment she also became aware that Matthew had disappeared into the kitchen; quickly she tracked him down.

'Now look here, Matthew, this is your home as well as mine and your guests as well as mine. It's only natural as well as polite that you should welcome them with me at the front door and then make some attempt to be hospitable and share the entertaining of them.'

The now only-too-familiar scowl had settled on his face. 'Away you go, woman; they'll be knocking at the door in a minute. Just leave me alone. They're not my guests. I don't know any of them, or do I wish to.'

'How dare you have the temerity to suggest that there is something wrong with my friends?' Victoria had become an iceberg of anger.

'I am not suggesting that there is anything wrong with your friends, Victoria. All I'm saying is — leave me in peace to do what I want to do.'

'Oh, you mean to sulk through here by yourself? No, I won't allow you to behave in such a wicked unsocial manner — for your own good if for no one else's!'

'Go away, woman,' he repeated, beginning to look like a trapped animal in danger of going berserk. 'Just go away and leave me alone!'

'No, I will not . . .'

He rose.

The door-bell saved her from any further confrontation,

however, but as she hurried to answer it she flung a parting shot over her shoulder. 'You come through to that room and behave like any other normal sane person, do you hear?'

It amazed Drummond how his wife changed so dramatically the moment she opened the outside door to her guests. The iceberg melted like magic and she was almost singing her welcomes, so warm and enthusiastic was she. There was much laughter too as everyone surged through to the room; then the sounds became muffled as the door shut behind them.

He breathed a sigh of relief and settled down to write in his journal, but no sooner had he relaxed than he heard the room door open and Victoria's voice sing out, 'Come through and meet the ladies, dear!'

His first reaction was to stride through and take her by the throat. When the sweetly singing tones repeated their request, he could do nothing but cringe in an anguish of embarrassment.

'Darling!' she was trilling now. 'The ladies are waiting!'

He had no choice but to struggle to his feet and make a stiff, awkward passage from the kitchen to the front room. His mind was racing in its feverish attempts to grasp at some theme on which to hang words, or some headings to guide him through the jungle of what he was supposed to say. But there was not sufficient time.

Feeling ill to the point of total collapse, he entered the room and faced the barrage of expectant eyes. He took up his stance at the side of the piano and placed one hand on top of it — as much for support as anything else. Then he cleared his throat and said, 'Good evening, ladies. You are most welcome to our abode. I hope you will all enjoy your visit and have a delectable tea.'

With that he escaped from the room as decorously as he could. He had not reached the kitchen when he heard gales of laughter, but he didn't mind that. He didn't mind anything, as long as they left him alone.

Later, however, after the guests had gone, Victoria

did not leave him alone. 'You did that on purpose!' she accused.

'Did what?'

'You know what! You stood there as stiff as a poker instead of being friendly and natural and putting folk at ease. We all felt like clapping when you finished. It was ridiculous. You immediately put a strain on the whole occasion and no one felt comfortable until you went out again.'

'Well,' he said, 'in future you know what to do. Don't ask me to come in.'

'Oh no,' Victoria assured him. 'You're not going to get out of your responsibilities as easily as that. Not when you've got me to reckon with!'

It was strange, Drummond thought, how even when he felt like killing her he could admire her.

CHAPTER FORTY-TWO

Rory recognized the fact that Argyle Street was a great thoroughfare — lined as it was with buildings four storeys in height, basements occupied by shops and upper flats by offices, hotels and dwelling-houses. Its pavements were a moving mass of people and the roadway constantly thronged with tram-cars, carts, cabs and barrows. Argyle Street started with the Tron Steeple, but it was at Stockwell Street that the great thoroughfare really began. Stockwell Street, *her* street, ran straight to the River Clyde and was crossed there by the Victoria Bridge. The bridge was built of white granite and spanned the broad river in five fine arches. She could not have chosen a better place to have her shop than between this grand bridge across the river, and the street that was the heart of Glasgow.

She had already built up a regular clientele who returned again and again to hire outfits. Not only that but because of the excellent situation of the shop, she had quite a brisk passing trade. She and Mamie were hard put to it at times to keep up with it all. Now she had four curtained-off areas with long mirrors for the convenience of customers. Many of her regulars, however, felt no need to try on garments; she had taken a careful note of their measurements and they could depend on her to know what would fit and what would not. Her range of different sizes was now quite considerable. Having very soon discovered that during certain times of the year tailors were so quiet they were almost starving and had no money coming in to them at all, these were the times she chose to make her visits and offer them next-to-nothing for their 'pork'. There were

278

always a number of suits — hanging up in tailoring establishments, either finished or in a 'baste' stage — which customers never came back for, yet the wretched tailors had laid out money on the cloth and having it worked on. Despite the names they called her ('Rory the Robber' was one) and the volubility of their protests, she was a godsend and she knew it.

Recently she had got to know of an excellent cutter who, because of the quiet season, had lost his job in one of the best tailors in Glasgow. She immediately offered him employment.

'You're mad,' her mother said. 'How can you afford to pay a man's wages every week when even a big posh firm can't afford to keep him?'

'They have a lot of employees, Ma. I'll only have him. And I'll make good use of him, don't worry. I'll get my money's worth!'

And so she had. Now, as well as buying tailors' made-up 'pork', she bought their cloth. She had her man — Joshua Cowan — expertly cut the material in the back shop, three suits at a time. Then he delivered the bundles to the bespoke tailors; they kept them under the benches in their workshops and when it was quiet and they hadn't got anything to work on, they brought out their store of ready-cut material and busied themselves with making it up.

The trouble was, the back shop wasn't big enough to serve as a cutting room for Joshua, as living quarters for Mamie and a place to do the cleaning and pressing of clothes and a thousand and one other jobs. She needed to extend her premises. On one side of her was a thriving bookshop; on the other side was the anything but thriving hatter's belonging to Mr Donovan. Rory decided it would be doing Mr Donovan a favour to relieve him of the worry of it.

She began visiting his shop every day to tell him so, while Miss Winters twitched around like a spider on the woodwork. Mr Donovan only sighed and shrugged and sighed again. In order to press her point, Rory began not only to hire out hats but to sell them — and sell them much cheaper than Mr Donovan. This was done by a method which she had begun practising with different lines, whereby she bought direct from the manufacturers and cut out the wholesale middle-man. It meant a lot of travelling about to factories and work-rooms to negotiate personally with hatmakers, glovemakers, shoemakers and shirt-makers. But it was worth it.

However, this increased her stock because she had to buy in fairly large quantities. What with this and more suits being cut by Joshua and made up by the bespoke tailors, and the subsequent increase of business, a rapid expansion of premises was inevitable.

Eventually she wore Mr Donovan down. With a deep, deep sigh he said, 'Oh, why not? I've no longer any heart for it — or anything else for that matter.'

She bought his shop at a low price, but one which she thought was fair in the circumstances. No time was wasted in getting him to sign the papers — nor of course in telling Miss Winters that her services would no longer be required. As Rory said to Victoria, she should have been retired years ago. 'Poor Mr Donovan's son will hear of this and this time he *will* believe me. Mr Donovan cannot hide the truth from him any longer,' Rory mimicked and then added, 'God knows what the old witch has been writing to the son!'

Apart from acquiring Mr Donovan's premises, she was also concentrating on improving her original shop. She believed she had to upgrade the appearance of the establishment in accordance with the quality of her merchandise. After all, the cut of her suits was on a par with Savile Row in London. She knew this not only because Joshua Cowan told her so — not being a man to hide his light under a bushel — but also because she now made a study of the tailors' fashion periodicals.

Indeed there had been one or two people of the calibre of the Forbes-Cunninghams who had actually bought some of her suits. She did not advertise the fact that she sold garments, but when the request was made and a good profit negotiated from the transaction she was satisfied. She had already made several improvements, of course, over and above the fitting areas; with the help of Benny and Joe she painted and papered the whole place in a very tasteful colour scheme copied from a high-class magazine. She had had more wood shelves made, too, having discovered it was better to keep clothes folded rather than hung. For one thing, moths didn't like folded clothes. Benny and Joe had helped her to lay a carpet and she had draped the windows with dark plum velvet.

'You're getting above yourself, m'lady,' her mother warned. 'It would fit you better to put some money into the house to help feed yourself and us. We're eating bread and marg, I owe money on my store book — and *you're* buying carpets!'

'It's an investment, Ma,' Rory tried to explain. 'I have to plough everything I make back into the business. I've got to make it succeed.'

'It *is* fuckin' succeeding,' Annie shouted in exasperation. 'But what's the good of it if we're still worried to death about where our next meal's coming from?'

'If you could just be patient for a wee while longer,' Rory pleaded, 'I'll be able to help out soon.'

'That's what you said last week and the week before. I'm working myself into the ground trailing round collecting rags all week, and standing every weekend at the market trying to make enough to feed us, and you're coming it in that posh place of yours. It's fuckin' ridiculous!'

'Ma, there's this shop next door to mine and I just had to have it. It'll make all the difference to making the business a proper success. Just think of it! I can have both premises knocked into one big establishment.'

'You *are* crazy! You're a bloody miser as well; you're never going to part with a penny.' Annie seemed hardly able to believe her own words. 'Not one penny,' she repeated.

'Ma, it's my big chance.'

281

'You're just the same as your Da,' Annie told her.

'What?' Rory squealed indignantly. 'How can you say such a thing? He's never done a stroke of work in his life, but I'm working night and day to build up a successful business.'

'You both go your own way,' Annie said bitterly. 'You don't give a tinker's cuss for me. Isa was the only one that ever gave me a hand. Our Isa was the only one who didn't put herself first. She was the best of the bunch, was wee Isa, and don't you forget it!'

Fat chance! Rory thought. Her mother was going on about Isa more and more these days — raking her up from the grave and nursing every memory close to her chest. Never a word of appreciation, far less praise, was meted out to *her* for her undeniable business achievements. Miserly she might be at the moment in as much as she only paid the bare minimum into the house (not a penny more than when she worked in the Co-op) and never so much as bought herself or any of the family a bar of chocolate. But if they had any sense, she told herself, they'd see that what she was trying to do — and knew she could do — was worth making some temporary sacrifice for.

Annie would have had apoplexy if she had known the exact amount of money Rory was making and ploughing back into the business. To her it would have seemed a fortune and it was a considerable sum by any standards, but somehow the money as such had no interest to Rory. It was the growth of the business that fascinated and obsessed her . . . the fact that she could do it . . . the sense of achievement. It was not being kicked around any more. A sense of her own worth was growing with the growth of the business and she felt she looked better too. Her hair had been cut to a new short length and she suited it. Her slim figure also appeared at its best in the straight lines of the new frocks and costumes, and she looked equally well in the fashionable long-waisted artificial silk jumpers both crocheted and knitted. She liked to wear green- or gold-coloured jumpers or blouses to complement the colour of her eyes, while rich brown costumes or dresses did the same for her hair.

More than one of her male customers had cast an admiring eye in her direction and she enjoyed their flattering attention, especially when it emanated from a gentleman of some means. Her enjoyment was fleeting, however, and was never any serious competition for the deep satisfaction and pleasure she obtained from business triumphs.

Sometimes Rory was honest enough to admit to herself that deep down she was still smarting from the rejections and insults she had suffered from men in the past. She knew, as she had once said to Victoria, that one shouldn't judge all men by the likes of Sid Ford and his kind. Yet the way he and his gang of friends had debased her by raping her had affected her more than she could explain even to herself. She still had nightmares. She still woke up shuddering and shaking, with cold sweat prickling her skin. She still felt secretly frightened of the dark.

She still hurt, too, when she thought of Matthew or met him with Victoria. Marriage seemed to agree with him. He was still thin-faced, pale and intense, but she noticed he smiled a lot more. It was his smile that could reopen old wounds and twist a knife in her heart. And he smiled at her with what seemed genuine pleasure and affection when she went to visit Victoria.

Victoria had begun to confide in Rory about the harassing difficulties and irritations of her marriage. It appeared that she had to fight tooth and nail to make Matthew stay in and be sociable when she was having visitors — except, that is, when she was having Rory and then she was impatient to get rid of him.

'I thought he was never going to go!' she would say with a roll of her eyes. 'Now we can have peace to have a cup of tea and a nice long chat!'

At first she would listen with a show of interest to the answer to her opening enquiry, 'And how is the shop doing?' But soon a glazed, absent expression would drift over her eyes and Rory suspected that if she had said, 'The shop's been burned down and I've given all the clothes away for nothing!' Victoria would murmur, 'That's great, Rory. I'm so glad for you!'

Victoria only came urgently to attention when it was her turn, and then she launched into her never-ending string of nit-picks about Matthew. Naturally Rory suspected that Victoria's real worry was none of the things she actually complained about.

To give Victoria her due, however, she never spoke in a complaining way about him to anyone else, not even to her mother. Rory had been present when Mrs Buchanan had asked worriedly, 'Are you all right, dear? Does he treat you kindly?'

'Oh, yes, mother,' Victoria had replied with alacrity. 'I'm perfectly happy. Matthew is a wonderful husband.'

Indeed, she was in the habit of boasting about Matthew to all and sundry. He still refused to make an appearance at most of her social gatherings and escaped to the pub or went for one of his many walks up to Springburn Park, where he would sit alone reading a book or writing in his journal.

To her visitors Victoria would lie like a trooper and tell them that Matthew sent his apologies and would love to have been there, but he had to take over some-one's shift because they were ill. Loyalty had always been one of Victoria's strong points. Indeed it surprised Rory that she confided in her about Matthew at all, although she realized it was one thing Victoria letting off steam but quite another if *she* said one word of criticism. Once she made the mistake of saying — in agreement with what Victoria had been complaining about for over an hour — 'Yes, he does have a ter-rible temper. I remember he turned on me a couple of times . . .'

Victoria's back and face had immediately become encased in ice. 'You must have done something terrible to make him turn on you. Matthew is a perfect gentleman . . .'

Then she launched into a eulogy which contradicted everything she had been saying before.

Victoria could be a most contrary woman. As far as her complaints about Matthew were concerned — his moodiness, his temper, his unsociability — she had known about all these things before she married him.

Why don't you just let him be? Rory kept longing to ask. And she kept thinking: *I loved him before you. I loved him with all his faults. Why can't you?* She couldn't bear to see Victoria try to change him.

CHAPTER FORTY-THREE

Drummond tried to suffer what he regarded as Victoria's extreme sociability with good grace. It was certainly easier to bear than her apparent abhorrence of him in bed, but nevertheless it was a terrible thorn in his flesh. His involvement in Union affairs meant not only attending meetings but collecting contributions from the men who did not turn up there. This was all right when he collected their dues at work, or even called at their houses for the money; he could then do what was necessary in a brief and businesslike manner.

If, however, any of the men called at his house to pay their contributions or once he was Branch Secretary to consult him about some complaint or problem, no such brief and businesslike procedure was possible.

Victoria would welcome them like favourite guests and despite his warning scowls, would press them to join her in a cup of tea and a sampling of her home-baked scones. This put him completely off the matter in hand, which often was of great urgency and importance. He had to admit to himself on such occasions that listening to Victoria's tinkling laughter and cheerful rendering on her piano of 'The Rustle of Spring' made him long to wring her neck. At best he rudely interrupted the social proceedings to tell her to go through to the kitchen and leave then alone; she always left immediately and with great dignity. A gulf of embarrassment had then to be overcome — no easy feat, because he suspected the railwaymen enjoyed the diversion of being entertained by his lovely wife and disapproved of the churlish way he treated her. He had tried other ways. He had explained to her that when dealing either with other people's money or with work problems, serious concentration was needed. That was why his work colleagues must be shown into the front room and left alone with him until he showed them out again. She could have as many friends and visitors as she liked, and welcome to them, but she must not interfere with the people who came to see him.

Victoria had laughed and said, 'Don't be daft! How can I let anyone come to my house without giving them a warm welcome and a wee cup of tea? Anyway, they enjoy it.'

He didn't care a damm if she was right or not. He did not want, he would not *allow* her to make a social circus of the work he'd so seriously dedicated himself to doing. Eventually he shouted at her before the arrival of any railwaymen, 'I'm warning you! Don't you dare put your nose round that room door while I'm in there.'

But she had dared, and dared, and dared again. It was as if he had issued a challenge to her and the front room had become a battleground of wills. Victoria, he had discovered, was a very strong-willed woman.

He secretly admired her for it, but his admiration in no way weakened his resolve. Indeed, his fury boiled over into violence after one occasion when two men had been to discuss a most urgent issue and she had mixed in to such an extent that an important point had been forgotten. Drummond had to face the annoyance and embarrassment of following the men back to their respective homes to rectify the omissions.

His fury had burst like a conflagration in his head and he dug his hands into her shoulders and shook her with such violence that she began to stagger and lose consciousness. He could have wept with concern at her temporary weakness and with regret at his unbridled behaviour. His anger forgotten, he nursed her in his arms and soothed her with loving words and passionate kisses. Once she got her breath back, she lectured him — not loudly or angrily, but in that terrible cool distant way which reminded him so much of his mother. There was a far-off secret centre to Victoria that he never seemed able to reach, far less understand, no matter how hard he tried or how loving he was. It had always been like that for him, as far back as he could remember. Every time he lost his temper, Victoria said, 'You ought to be ashamed of yourself!'

And he was. He realized now that he had always had the flames of temper licking around him. In the past, however, he had for the most part been successful in keeping them doused down and contained. It was strange how, with Victoria, the person he loved and cared about most in all the world, this feat seemed so impossible. Hardly a day passed without some flare-up, large or small. Hardly a day passed without him suffering the anguish of regret and self-reproach.

Victoria kept saying, 'You don't know how lucky you are, that's your trouble.'

But he did. He was most acutely and constantly aware (without Victoria and every man in the N.B. Railway reminding him) that he had a wife in a million despite her inadequacies in bed. She was young and inexperienced, but she would learn. She would become more mature and loving in this area of their life, he kept assuring himself desperately. Meantime, he had so much to be thankful for. Not for him one of the legion of young women who 'let themselves go' after marriage and looked like sluts and went slopping down the road to the Co-op in their house slippers and aprons. They neglected their houses as well as their appearance and entertained themselves by what was known locally as 'having a good hing'. That meant leaning from an open window, arms folded on the window-sill, watching the world of Springburn go by.

Victoria was always neat and smart-looking. She carried herself with as much — if not more — queenly dignity as she had always done and she kept their house bright and comfortable. He had noticed that she suffered a tendency to be careless with his things, however. During her cheerful bouts of tidying up she would stuff everything out of sight without a care where she was putting it. This had caused him innumerable panics — and wild eruptions of anger — when he could not find the Union cash-book, or his journal, or the notes he had carefully compiled for the speech he was about to deliver in the Springburn Town Hall.

He could never guarantee now that he would be able to arrive at any meeting in the calm state of mind that was so necessary on these occasions. Miraculously, though, he was always able to give the appearance of calm. He knew it was a weakness to lose control of oneself in an argument and he never lost his temper in public debate. Nominated for election as branch secretary of the Union, it had been a close thing as there had been several committee members at the Union meeting who were trying to put in their own men. The branch also put him on the municipal panel and eventually he had been asked to contest a seat. He felt very honoured at this because it marked the kind of standing and reputation he had among the NUR members of Eastfield.

Recently, unknown to him, Victoria had attended a public meeting in connection with his attempt to win a place on the Parish Council. He had been heckled unmercilessly. The Conservatives, from all over the city it seemed, had turned up en masse to try to put him down. They had not succeeded. In fact he had been elected and was now about to take his place as the first Socialist and youngest member of not only the Council but of the Poor Law Committee. It would mean his not only sitting face to face with local bankers and solicitors, but with Alexander Forbes-Cunningham.

His supporters had congratulated him on the way he had conducted himself at the meetings at which he'd spoken, particularly the last of the campaign when the heckling had been so violent and intense. But as soon as he arrived home Victoria had set upon him. She was coldly furious.

'How dare you!' she said quietly. 'How dare you keep

all your self-control and good temper for strangers? Don't you ever give me the lie that you can't help your temper. You can help it all right.'

He had been exhausted after having done an early shift, overtime and then coped with the unusually large and rowdy meeting. 'I don't know what you're talking about, woman,' he said dismissively.

'Oh, you know all right. You won't fool me any more with your lies. I was at that meeting tonight.'

He groaned and cursed himself. He couldn't bear it when she mixed in with this side of his life. Sometimes he almost agreed with her when she accused him of still being a selfish bachelor at heart; he wanted, he needed, he had to have an area where he could feel private and alone.

'In future,' Victoria informed him with a bitter twist to her mouth and the icy eyes of an enemy and a stranger, 'I'll have your self-control in this house. In future, I won't listen to your excuses or your apologies.'

'Oh, shut up!' he said. He was so exhausted he didn't even care about the distance she put between them in bed. Most times he cared very much about the way she punished him by her withdrawal of love. But not that night.

He learned later that he had compounded his crimes of the evening by keeping her awake half the night by selfishly snoring. He began to have the sinking feeling that their relationship was on such a dangerous downward path that no effort of his to save it could work. Even making secret lists of his faults as reminders in his struggle to overcome them proved useless. It worked temporarily and to some extent; they had tender reconciliations and sometimes they laughed together at his peccadilloes and the situations they caused. Nothing changed the course of their lives to any meaningful extent, however — until, that is, Victoria became pregnant. Then their moments of tenderness increased and there were times — especially in the later stages of her pregnancy — when Victoria acquired moments of such appealing helplessness that his adoration of her knew no bounds.

He worried about leaving her so often because of his long shifts and his Union and now his Council work — knowing she was the kind of person who never liked to be alone at any time. He decided to have a private talk with Rory and plead with her to come and stay with them for the last couple of weeks of the pregnancy, so that she could be near Victoria to comfort and help her at the birth. Of course, there would also be a midwife and a doctor in attendance. Even so, he was worried sick. Victoria was not nearly as strong as she looked.

He chose the day when he was attending a Council meeting to visit Rory and went to the shop because that was where she mostly was from early morning until night-time. The meeting had gone on longer than he'd expected and it was quite late by the time he made his way towards Stockwell Street. A delicate smir of rain dampened his skin and made him turn up his collar. Not that he minded the rain — he enjoyed walking by himself in any weather. As often as not, he was so deep in thought he never noticed whether it was rain, hail or snow. At the moment, though, emotion had taken over from comtemplation and all he wanted was for Victoria to be safe and well.

Nevertheless, as he trudged towards Rory's place he did take note of the colour of the sky and the way that, against a backcloth of darkness, it was luminously tinged with a stain of iron rust and quickened and shuddered as if from some strange force rising from the city. The force, he knew, was the ever-present sign of Glasgow's furnace cordon.

He loved everything about Glasgow: the furnaces firing the sky, the fanfare of whistles from the boats on the river, the streets trembling with the vibration of machinery, the incessant clang of the riveter's hammer from the shipyards — all the noise, all the energetic boisterous bustle. He savoured it as an onlooker, yet glad of the knowledge that he was part of it.

Rory's shop had gilt letters above it which proclaimed to everyone that it was 'Rory's'. He suddenly felt hesitant about going in and for a minute confusion overcame him. He had the feeling that this couldn't be *his* Rory. The windows were tastefully draped and in one he saw gents' suits which he could never imagine himself being able to afford. They made him feel self-conscious and shabby, despite the fact that he was wearing his Sunday best; he always dressed in his good suit when he attended Council meetings. Eventually he forced himself to enter.

The door pinged loudly and immediately a spotty-faced girl with long mousy hair tightly tied with two white ribbons catapulted towards him.

'Can I help you, sir?'

'May I speak to Miss McElpy, please?'

'What name shall I say, sir?'

'Mr Drummond.'

'Mr Drummond, Mr Drummond,' the girl kept repeating to herself as she flew away into the nether regions, white hair-bows sticking out like wings.

He glanced around. It seemed incredible that this was Rory's place — 'plush' was the word that came to his mind. It had the aura of money about it and was as far from Cowlairs Road or Springburn Road as life on another planet.

'Hello, Matty.' She emerged from a velvet-curtained area pale and proud-looking. But despite her head being held so high she was still 'his' Rory. For one thing, no other woman had ever called him Matty.

He smiled. 'You're looking well.'

'I'm fine. Never been better.'

'I'm glad.'

'I've a bottle of whisky in the back if you'd like a nip. I keep it for special customers.'

He laughed, doubly reassured by the familiar cockiness

in her voice. 'I'm afraid I'm no customer, I couldn't afford to patronize this establishment. Actually, I've come to ask you a favour.'

'Come through anyway,' she invited.

He followed her into a large but cluttered back shop. She moved an ironing-board and a rack of clothes back against some packing cases in order to make a path for him.

'We sponge and press things during the quiet times,' she explained, then added, 'What's the favour?'

Drummond told her of his concern about Victoria and how he would feel so much more easy in his mind if Rory was with her during the last couple of weeks. 'It's my shifts, you see. The chances are I wouldn't be there when she needed me. Please say you'll come, Rory — for Victoria's sake if not mine.'

Rory lit a cigarette in a long holder. Then through a mist of smoke she laughed at him, 'Oh Matty, don't look so shocked! Haven't you ever seen anyone smoke before?'

'Not a woman.'

'Why shouldn't women smoke if they want to?'

'Women have more delicate constitutions. It can't be good for them.'

'You're just old-fashioned. And so serious, Matty. you've always been the same . . . What the hell's that racket out there?' Her face and voice suddenly changed from the softness of wistful affection to steely annoyance as Mamie's excited voice came echoing through like the clamour of half-a-dozen.

'Rory,' Drummond appealed in desperation, 'will you come?'

'What?'

'To be with Victoria.'

'Yes, all right,' she replied, only half her attention on him.

'Oh, I knew you would. I knew you were still my Rory.' Despite the awkwardness of her elegantly held cigarette holder, he pulled her into his arms in an impulsive hug of gratitude.

Just at that moment, to his and Rory's surprise, a man strode into the back shop followed by a loudly protesting Mamie.

'Who the hell are you?' Rory said. 'How dare you come barging in here like this!'

CHAPTER FORTY-FOUR

Rory was embarrassed as well as annoyed — annoyed at
Drummond almost as much as the other man, who introduced himself as Donovan Donovan, the hatter's son.
Trust Matthew to do the socially awkward thing and cause
embarrassment. He had no right to take her in his arms
for any reason at all, or in any place, but especially not
in her business premises where her employees or anybody
else were liable to come in.

Then of course, Matty nearly made things a hundred
times worse by facing up to Donovan, who was half-a-
head taller and heavier built, and ordering him out. Again
she could not help thinking in annoyance that he had no
right. Why should he refer to her as 'my Rory' and act as
if he had some sort of claim on her? Why should he feel
justified in acting on her behalf? She was barely able to
control her irritation and persuade him to leave and allow
her to deal with Donovan.

'I know why he's here,' she explained. 'It's to do with
business, Matty. I can handle it.'

'Are you sure?'

'Yes, of course.'

She had allowed him to give her an affectionate peck
on the cheek, then watched his shy, self-conscious tread
until he disappeared round the corner into Argyle Street.
Then, tugging protective anger around her, she returned
to deal with the man in the back shop.

Rory gave his tanned rocklike features a scathing supercilious look through the cloud of her cigarette smoke. 'So
you're Mr Donovan's son?'

'I am.'

She glanced up at the fawn snap-brim hat that was tilted back to reveal a profusion of brown curls. 'Well, you obviously haven't your father's good manners. For one thing, he would have had the decency to remove his hat.'

'My God!' Donovan shook his head. 'You've the nerve to talk about decency!'

'Why shouldn't I?'

'Because you don't know anything about it.'

Rory took another leisurely puff at her cigarette before speaking. 'I take it you must be mad because I've bought over your father's business?'

'Come now, there's more to it than that.'

'Oh?'

'You ruined him first. Then you browbeat him into practically giving you the place — an old man who was still grieving for his wife.'

'Is this the kind of sentimental rubbish you write in your newspaper?' Rory asked.

His blue eyes narrowed. 'I'm an investigative journalist and I think you need investigating.'

'Your father ruined his own business. I did him a favour by taking it off his hands.'

'I've heard that story before.' Donovan's smile was a gritting of teeth and a deepening of cleft chin as if someone had ground a knuckle into it.

Rory didn't like him; his aggressive maleness triggered off fearful and humiliating memories. She stubbed out her cigarette. 'I'm very busy, Mr Donovan. I must ask you to leave now.'

'Oh, you can drop the "Mister".' He gave her another of his hard smiles. 'This is the beginning of a long-standing relationship.'

'You think so?' Rory raised a sarcastic brow.

'I'm going to stick around for as long as it takes, sweetheart.'

'As what takes? And don't call me sweetheart!'

296

'To show you that you're not going to get away with it.'

'If you're meaning the purchase of your father's shop, that has already been completed.'

'Without living to regret it, sweetheart.'

'Don't call me sweetheart, I said.'

'All right, honey.'

His smile was mocking and his deep-set come-to-bed eyes angered her with the way they seemed to penetrate her most naked sexuality, her most secret needs. Flushing at the impertinent indecency of his eyes, she snapped. 'I have nothing more to say to you, Mr Donovan. Goodbye.'

'I've a lot more to say to you. But it can wait,' he told her. 'Au revoir.'

She couldn't help noticing how different he was from Matty. There was certainly no shyness about that self-confident stride, that easy swagger.

For the rest of the day, despite being busy with customers, the irritant of Donovan gave her no peace. She began to realize that she had manoeuvred herself into a safe siding as far as her personal life was concerned. She grieved over the loss of Matty and used up all her emotional strength trying to stifle the feeling she had had for him. What strength she had left, she concentrated on her business. She could no longer envisage any other man in her life; no other emotional involvement was worth the candle. Men came and went in the shop — even handsome, wealthy men like Edgar Forbes-Cunningham — but they remained as shadows across the surface of her life with no power to get near her and she never gave any of them a second thought. She was glad of the safe place she had backed into. Now that she came to think of it, she'd suffered enough passionate emotions with Matthew and more than enough of physical abuse from other men to last her a lifetime. All that mattered now was the growth of her business. Only in that direction did her emotions, achievements and true happiness lie.

She was honest enough to recognize an awakening of feeling when she experienced it, however. Despite her dislike of him, Donovan had stirred physical longings inside her which she believed she had tamed and rid herself of once and for all. Rory knew such an awakening was not only ridiculous — after all, she'd only been in the man's company for a few minutes — but dangerous. She felt herself floundering back to the foolish vulnerable days of her youth when physical longings were a secret agony, something that feverishly possessed her to the exclusion of everything else.

An undercurrent of fear refused to be hardened away, but she fought to ignore it and plunged determinedly into her work. First she harangued the workmen to get started on the structural alterations to convert the hatter's and her present shop into one large establishment. At the same time, she began negotiations to acquire the first-floor offices which had become vacant. That meant more structural alterations; an opening to be hammered through the hatter's ceiling and a staircase fitted to link the shop with what would soon be the new factory workroom upstairs. Joshua Cowan was looking forward to having a much larger workshop and also the assistant she had promised him. She had discovered when the leases of the other upstairs premises expired and already she was planning to take them over and use them as the cleaning workroom where the clothes would be sponged, 'spotted' and pressed after each hiring.

She had also persuaded her four sisters to give up their skivvying jobs and come to work as cleaners and pressers. Joe and Benny were unemployed and she had no difficulty in getting them to work regularly for her, doing the collecting and delivering instead of the over-worked Joshua. They were more than willing when they saw the new horseless van she had acquired for the purpose, but it was a harder task to get them to dress in respectable dark suits and stiff-collared shirts and keep themselves clean, well-brushed and well-spoken. She had to bully them mercilessly to train them in correct and polite behaviour.

More recently she had been trying to persuade her mother to consider giving up the rag collecting and the stall in Paddy's Market and work in the cleaning and pressing department with the girls.

'You're a bloodsucker, do you know that?' Annie had accused. 'Don't try and kid me that you're doing me any favours! You're roping the whole family in to work for you for next-to-nothing, like poor wee Mamie.'

All the family, that is, except Scrap. He was strictly banned from the premises, something which greatly offended him and which he kept claiming he did not understand.

'Joe and Benny were unemployed and the girls hate skivvying,' she reminded her mother.

'I can see us starving if we all work as slave labour for you. We're practically starving as it is.'

'We eat no less than we ever did — and that's better than a lot of folk, Ma.'

'And worse than a whole lot more! You're the limit, do you know that? There you are, dressed like Lady Muck and off you go every day to a palace of a place covered in carpets and velvet and gold — and here we are without even a rag rug to our names or a net curtain on our windows.'

'A bloody disgrace!' her husband echoed, as if carpets and net curtains had always been his main concern.

'I was thinking we should move,' Rory said. 'There's no point in spending good money on a dump like this.'

'A dump . . .' her mother screeched indignantly. 'The only home you've ever known? And lucky to have had it, m'lady.'

'A bloody disgrace!' Scrap repeated.

'I've seen a house to rent in a nice red-sandstone tenement in Broomfield Road facing the park, Ma. I've already asked the factor about the rent and it's not much more than here — considering, that is, that it has three more rooms.'

'Three? . . . Three? . . . You mean a four-room and

kitchen?' Her mother gaped at her. 'What would we do with a four-room and kitchen? We'd be like peas rattling round in a drum.'

'Ma, there'll be thirteen of us once the girls are at home. You and Da can have one bedroom; the girls can have one between them; the boys can have one as well and I'll have a room to myself. The kitchen is huge and can be converted into a living-room cum dining-room because there's also a decent-sized scullery which could be converted into a kitchen. But the really marvellous thing about the house, Ma, is that it's got a bathroom. A bathroom, would you believe? Just think of the luxury of having a bathroom to ourselves!'

Eventually her mother managed, 'You're getting beyond yourself. I just don't know how you're going to end up.'

'I do,' Rory said. 'I'm going to end up a very successful and very wealthy businesswoman.'

'Would you listen to her?' Annie appealed to Scrap. 'What would you make of it? What would you fuckin' make of it?'

He shook his head, took off his large pancake of a cap and scratched his balding scalp to indicate that it was completely beyond him.

'You'll love the house, Ma,' Rory assured her.

'How am I going to pay the rent of a four-room and kitchen?' Annie scoffed. 'What do you think I am, a magician?'

'I'll pay it,' Rory said.

'Do you hear what I hear?' Annie asked Scrap. 'Did m'lady actually say she was going to pay our rent?'

'About time she paid for something in the house,' Scrap said.

Rory could have reminded her father that he was the one who never paid any money into the house for rent or anything else, not her. But she refrained. She had long since come to terms with what a hopeless case he was; nothing could be gained by arguing with him, accusing him or even pleading with him. One just told him straight and hard

— like she had about coming near the shop: 'If you put a toe inside my shop door on any pretext whatsoever, I'll either get one of my tailors to run you out by the back of the neck or I'll get the local bobby to do it. I know him and he would.'

And Scrap knew her, and she would.

'It'll have to be put in my name of course,' Rory said.

'What?' Scrap rose to his full five feet. 'She's gone over the score now, Annie. The rent book has to be in the name of the man of the house. It's only right.'

'Oh, sit down and shut up, Da!' Rory said. 'You'll start the dog barking.' Indeed Henry was already agitating about and testing his voice with sharp whining yelps.

'Here, you.' It was Annie's turn to rise indignantly to her feet. 'You watch your tongue. He's your Da, don't forget!'

'As if I could.'

'You're asking for my hand across your jaw, m'lady.'

'I'm entitled to a say in things. And I say that because I'm the one who's earning the money and paying everybody, I'm the head of the house. Therefore I'm the one who should have her name on the rent book.'

And so it was eventually arranged despite her parents' opposition.

'I like it here in Cowlairs Road.' Her mother began to sound worried as the plan to move became a reality and the rent book for the new big house was secured. 'I've such gems of neighbours and I'm so near the Co-op.'

Her father showed concern about the distance from the bookies, but was distanced even further by being arrested for attempted house-breaking. His excuse in court on this occasion was, 'We're going to move to that road, your honour, and I was up to do some work in the place and wandered into the wrong close by mistake.'

The fact that he had been 'wandering' in possession of a crow-bar and a jemmy did nothing to help his plea of not guilty.

Rory was glad that he was now out of the way for a

comparatively short time at least, so that she could organize the move with some semblance of efficiency. This was one of the things that helped to divert her thoughts and emotions from her meeting with Donovan.

Until suddenly he exploded into her consciousness again and in a way that could not be ignored.

CHAPTER FORTY-FIVE

The time had come to keep her promise to Matty and go from the shop every day for the last week of Victoria's pregnancy. She had originally promised to go for the last two weeks, but what with all the upheaval with workmen doing overtime trying to keep to her schedule for her alterations, and also the move to Broomfield Road, even Matthew had conceded that she was performing a miracle by coming to stay with Victoria every night for one week.

She had barely moved in when Matty arrived home from a Union meeting ashen-faced. He tossed a newspaper on to the table and said to her, 'Read that.'

The paper was the *Evening Gazette* and it was folded open at a page headed 'The Searcher'. There were several articles, but the main one bore the headline 'The Mad Hatters'. This article was written in humorous yet damning style about Rory and how she had not only succeeded in ruining Mr Donovan, but was hell-bent on ruining the wholesale trade as well. It ran:

A clash of cloches has set the bonnets twirling in the middle of Glasgow. What makes it all the more interesting is that it is a battle of the sexes as well. Opponents are an old-established male hatter and a svelte titian-haired *femme fatale*.

The gentleman hatter is a member of the venerable Trades House of Glasgow. His opponent can be charitably described as a corner-cutter . . .

Rory didn't smile, but she said. 'It's very funny.'

Victoria, who was reading it over her shoulder, wailed, 'It's not funny at all. Oh Rory, even if he hadn't mentioned your name! What a disgrace! Oh dear!'

'Is it true?' Drummond wanted to know.

Rory shrugged. 'It's one way of looking at it, I suppose.'

'You mean you did ruin the man and rob him of his shop?'

'Don't sound so bloody pious and self-righteous!' Rory had never felt so irritated by Drummond. 'What's it to you, anyway? He wasn't in your Union.'

'I thought it only fair to give you a chance to explain,' he said stiffly.

'I don't need to explain anything to you or to try to justify my actions. In the first place, Matty, you know nothing about business.'

'The methods of employers is much the same whether it is in the retail trade or in industry. I'm only too familiar with this sort of business practice, Rory. I'm fighting it all the time.'

'You'd better not take me on, Matty. This man has made a big enough mistake.'

'What are you going to do?' Victoria queried anxiously. 'What can you do? Oh, dear . . .'

'There's no need for you to get upset, Victoria,' Drummond said.

'Oh, don't be daft,' she snapped irritably. 'Rory's my best friend, isn't she?'

'Yes, I know. But in your condition . . .'

'My condition's your fault, not hers.'

Drummond sighed. 'I'm going through to get my overalls on. It's time I was away to my work.'

'Your piece is ready in your piece-box,' Victoria called after him. 'In the scullery.'

After he had gone Victoria said, 'I wonder who this so-called "Searcher" is?'

'I know who he is all right,' Rory told her.

'Who?'

'Donovan. I met his father the other day and he was

304

saying that his son had got a job on the *Gazette*. He was apologizing for Donovan barging in on me. God knows what the old man will think of this!' She jabbed the paper with her cigarette holder.

'He was a very genteel person, right enough,' Victoria said. 'And with such a nice soft Irish voice.'

'His son's not genteel, I can tell you — a right tough-looking character. He talks about me being ruthless, but it's a case of the pot calling the kettle black, if you ask me!'

'Oh Rory, you're not like what he says. I don't believe it.'

Rory lit up a cigarette. She was smoking a lot recently; it helped to calm her nerves. 'The old man had let the business run down. You saw it yourself. I was doing him a favour taking it off his hands. I told the son, but of course he didn't believe me.'

'He's out to get you.' Victoria's eyes widened dramatically. 'He's going to ruin you. And just when you're doing so well.' Suddenly she burst into tears and stood blubbering helplessly like a grounded whale.

Rory put her arms around her. 'Nonsense! You surely know me better than that. No man's going to ruin me.'

'He's trying to, Rory.'

'It's not going to work.'

'What can you do?'

'Just you wait and see!' Rory gave an exaggerated wink and Victoria couldn't help giggling weakly through her tears. Then suddenly she said, 'I'm frightened.'

Rory knew without any explanation that Victoria had changed direction and was now referring to the approaching birth. Despite all her friend's happy chatter over the preceding months about the coming event and her delight in collecting and showing off all the baby clothes she'd bought, knitted or been given, Rory had detected an undercurrent of fear. It was embarrassing to have Victoria admit it, however.

'You'll be all right. Thousands of women have babies — one after the other. Look at your mother! And my mother! They came through it all right.'

Victoria began wringing her hands. 'I can't help remembering . . . it keeps coming back . . . I keep remembering how awful it was for you.'

'Don't be silly, Victoria. It'll be nothing like what happened to me. Sit down and relax; I'll go and make you a cup of tea.'

'But are you sure, Rory? I mean, how do you know?'

'I know I had an abortion. Yours is a perfectly natural pregnancy — think yourself damned lucky.'

'Right enough.' Victoria eased her enormous bulk down on to a chair. 'And I do like babies.'

It was after the cup of tea that the contractions started. 'Now just keep calm,' Rory ordered firmly. 'You are going to be fine.'

But it was a long and difficult night. Victoria paced the floor at first, her lips tightly pressed together, kneading her hands as if they were lumps of dough. Nothing would persuade her to sit or lie down and eventually Rory was pacing with her, or rather half-staggering, as she tried to support her friend's weight. When Drummond returned from his shift in the early hours of the morning, Victoria would not allow him to come near her.

She was quite kind about it at first. 'No, Matthew,' she managed to squeeze out. 'I'll be all right. Just you go through to the room and try not to worry.'

As the labour progressed and Victoria's agony increased, however, she began to sob and shout, 'He did this to me! I'll never forgive him. I'll never let him touch me again.'

Eventually she was screaming the one word, 'Jesus!' It wasn't a curse; Victoria never swore. it was a desperate plea for mercy.

The midwife was impatient and at one point slapped Victoria's legs. 'It's your own fault things are going so bad. Stop clinging on to your pal and do something to help yourself!'

Rory was furious. 'A lot of bloody help you are! As if she wasn't in enough pain. Don't you dare belt her again or you'll get one on the jaw from me!'

'Ladies, ladies,' the doctor appealed. 'Stand back out of my way. I'll have to give her chloroform.'

As a result of the chloroform, Victoria did not see little Jamie being born and he was bathed and swaddled as she lay unconscious. Rory held him in her arms and touched a petal-soft skin and wondered at the miracle of him. He was so like Matty that she started to weep and that was when Victoria's attention began to drift back.

'What are you crying for? It was me who had all the pain.'

'I'm exhausted. I've been up all night.' Suddenly she laughed. 'I'm sounding ridiculous, aren't I? I hardly know what I'm saying. I'm so happy for you, Victoria. He's really beautiful.'

Victoria accepted the baby from Rory and stared at him, eyes brimming with pride and joy. 'He is right enough. Oh, Rory, can you believe it? I've actually managed it. Somehow I never thought I would.'

Still laughing, Rory shook her head. 'When's your mother coming?'

'She's bringing something for our dinner.'

'I could have seen to that.'

'I know, but my mother wants to take her turn. She's going to come in for a few evenings this week. And of course Matthew will be here during the day, so I'll be all right. You can go home now.'

'Thanks very much! As soon as you don't need me, you cast me aside.'

Victoria was immediately alerted with concern. 'Oh no, I didn't mean it like that, Rory. You're very welcome to stay here as long as you like.'

'I know, I was only joking. It's high time I put in an appearance at Broomfield Road. What with being at the shop every day and here every night, they'll be forgetting what I look like. Worse still, if they've read last night's *Gazette*, they won't want to remember.'

'Gosh, I forgot about that.'

'I don't blame you.'

'Let me know what happens, won't you?' Victoria said, but her attention strayed dreamily back to the baby again. Gently she kissed him. 'I promised to call him Jamie after Matthew's brother, did I tell you?'

'Yes. It suits him.'

'Hello, Jamie!' Victoria kissed him again. She looked grey-faced and exhausted, but the lovelight was beautiful in her eyes. 'Hello, my very own wee boy.'

CHAPTER FORTY-SIX

Rory had written an advertisement stating in large print and in no uncertain terms that yes, she had bought the hatter's shop in Stockwell Street and she was proud of the fact, because in no time she was transforming it from a dying concern that nobody patronized into part of a thriving business which not only gave extra people employment but served the best needs of the citizens of Glasgow and at the lowest possible prices.

She took it to the newspaper offices herself rather than send Mamie or one of the boys; she was hiding behind nobody and had nothing to hide. Already she had put up large posters on her shop windows turning round everything Donovan had said in her favour and cocking a snook at him. The poster blazoned out things like 'The corner-cutter who cuts the best suits in Glasgow' and 'The Mad Hatter who sells hats at give-away prices' . . . 'The battle of the sexes — Come inside and meet the one who won'.

The *Citizen* office was in St Vincent Place, which ran off George Square with its prize-winning municipal buildings fronted by noble statues. St Vincent Place was imposing too, with the big Clydesdale Bank building and the head office of the Anchor Line Steamship Company which because of its stark white colour stood out boldly amongst its neighbours. The *Citizen* offices in comparison huddled back, heavily ornate and sleepy-looking, in dark red stone.

Rory clipped lightly up the outside stairs to the front entrance. She was sporting brown shoes with a daringly high heel and a strap buttoning across her ankle; her hair was covered by a brimless cloche with a gold buckle on the front. Her light green and brown checked suit was topped by a brown coat lined with the same dashing check and she allowed it to fly open as she ran up the steps and entered the building.

Once inside she hesitated, not knowing whether to proceed upstairs or enter through a door to a ground-floor room.

'Can I help you?' A fat man in a creased greasy-looking raincoat who had just descended the stairs, tipped his hat.

'I've an advert for the paper,' she said.

'You want to go in there, then.' He indicated the door nearest her. 'Upstairs is editorial and up top for compositors.'

'Thanks.'

The man's eyes took in every detail of her slim, stylish appearance with obvious appreciation. 'It's a pleasure.'

Rory wasted no time in doing what she had come to do. Time was a precious commodity these days, especially when she was having to travel about so much to personally persuade manufacturers to accept her orders of goods and supply them direct to her shop. She was hell-bent now on selling as well as hiring — and selling as wide a variety of goods as possible.

'There's always been a thrawn bit about you,' Annie accused. She and Scrap were 'absolutely affronted' by the 'Searcher' column in the paper and even more so by Rory's 'shameless' reaction to it.

'Aye,' Annie said to Scrap. 'She's a fine one to be telling us how to behave ourselves.'

This remark typified the deeply-felt grudge her parents had against her since she had begun a determined but so far not-too-successful campaign to make them dress better, speak better and generally behave in a more 'respectable' fashion.

Rory was smiling grimly to herself now — wondering what not only her parents but the whole of Glasgow would think of the very large and expensive advert she had just paid for, to be impudently placed on the same page as the 'Searcher' column — when she suddenly bumped into Donovan as he came catapulting from the lift, in as much hurry as she was herself.

'Oh, it's you,' Rory said. 'Watch where you're going.'

Despite the sharpness of her tone, inside the very blood in her veins seemed to have lost its way.

He raised a brow, 'Well, well, and what brings you here? Come to beg for mercy, have you?'

She gave a sarcastic laugh. 'That'll be the day! It would take more of a man than you to get the better of me, I can tell you.'

'Really?' His eyes were hard like chips of slate, yet full of mocking amusement. 'Like the man making love to you in your back shop? A married man is what I'd expect you to go for, of course. It's what you're good at — stealing other people's property.'

'You don't know what you're talking about. Why don't you just mind your own business?'

'Sweetheart, it is my business to ferret out information about people. Matthew Drummond, married to Victoria née Buchanan. A political animal. Brilliant, but Bolshie. Climbing fast in the Union. On practically every committee in the Council . . .'

'Out of my way!' Rory commanded.

The maleness exuding from the loose-limbed well-muscled body in the smart London suit was acutely disturbing and she felt angry at herself for being so disturbed. He stood aside in mock politeness and she swept past him and out of the building.

So intense was her inner confusion that she turned right instead of left and found herself in Buchanan Street with Donovan still at her elbow. 'Not going back to the grindstone? Why don't you join me and the boys in the *Citizen*'s howf for a drink, then?' With a jerk of his head he indicated Cairns' pub on the corner of Buchanan Street and St Vincent Place.

She knew the invitation was an insult for respectable women did not set foot in Glasgow pubs. He might have been away in London for a long time and pubs might be different there, but he knew Glasgow all right.

'I hope your drink chokes you!' she said.

'Oh, charming!'

Rory crossed the road and kept going until she came to West Nile Street. There she gave a surreptitious glance behind her and was relieved to see no sign of a tall broad-shouldered man in a snap-brimmed hat.

Relaxing with relief, she stood for a few minutes watching the trace-lads sitting in the shop doorways with their horses at the kerb in front of them. They were waiting for the single-horse carts which were too heavy-laden to take the steep incline of West Nile Street; then they would hire out their horses to haul them up the hollowed tracks that were there for the easy rolling of cartwheels. The giant Clydesdales were placidly feeding from their nose-bags as they waited and pigeons fluttered around their big shaggy feet to peck up the corn that fell on the ground.

As Rory stood waiting, two of the horses moved away up the hill with a load, sparks flying from their shoes as they struck the cobbles. Glasgow was a place of hills. Hills were everywhere. At night, travelling on top of a tram-car on her way home, they did strange things with the night perspective. They festooned the street-lamps in fantastic coilings, suspended them in mid-air like jugglers' balls, rocketed them up behind tall church spires and showered them to earth again like dropping fireworks in the far distance.

But it wasn't night yet; the city was alive with people and traffic bustling about doing their business. And so should she be. She made her way down to Argyle Street. The buskers were entertaining as usual, clinging to small segments of the pavement outside the picture houses despite the crowds crushing to and fro around them. She passed the wee Egyptian clapper with the ancient pram that housed his equally ancient gramophone dancing energetically on his board. Further on the flower-seller at the corner, warmly wrapped in her tartan plaid was pleading 'Come on, hen, give yourself a treat, penny a bunch.'

Rory didn't feel like working, which was unlike her as she genuinely enjoyed everything about the business. Now there was the time-consuming yet challenging travelling about and meeting the manufacturers. Of course she always insisted on meeting the boss. She was at the moment considering going down to London to speak to a famous shirt manufacturer and try to persuade him to become one of her suppliers. The thought of visiting England — another country — gave her a physical thrill. She thrived on challenges. Life was a challenge, a great adventure. She had made it that way and made it by herself.

Shits of men had made her suffer and tried to ruin her life before, but she had survived and she'd survive this shit of a newspaperman. The strength of her feelings once more confused her — she was violently trembling inside. Yet why should she feel so enraged? Desperately she tried to soothe herself. What was she worrying about, for God's sake? What was there to be so afraid of?

Beyond caring how she shocked the Glasgow populace, she lit a cigarette and gratefully dragged at it as she walked along the street.

CHAPTER FORTY-SEVEN

'Christ, you're a lucky devil!' 'Beer' Baillie growled at Donovan.

The name 'Beer' Baillie was used to distinguish him from 'Milk' Baillie, the other reporter who was notorious for preferring milk to alcohol. He was referring to the fact that Donovan had been allocated the job of showing the famous actress Amelia Manners around the building that afternoon.

The editor's secretary emerged from the editor's office at that moment and said, 'I don't know why anybody would want to see round this place. Look at the disgraceful mess!' She indicated the ankle-deep sea of papers which not only covered the entire floor of the reporters' room but crested high against each desk.

Donovan ripped a sheet from his pad, screwed it into a ball and flicked it amongst the rest. 'It's because I've met her a few times in London,' he said, answering Beer Baillie and ignoring the secretary.

'I suppose you'll be the one picked every time anything like this happens now — just because you're a Fleet Street man?'

'Listen, mate,' Donovan said. 'You're welcome to her; I'm off women at the moment.' Beer Baillie's jeering laughter was joined by all the other men in the room. 'I'm telling you,' Donovan insisted. 'This bloody woman in Stockwell Street has got right up my nostrils.'

'Whassat? What bloody woman?' Crab McKay, the sports reporter, awoke from his alcoholic haze. He always consumed too much whisky at lunch-time and often had

314

to be bodily dragged from Cairns' pub and propped back at his desk to sit out the rest of the afternoon. He also had a weakness for crabs and was in the habit of sending his boy assistant out to White's in Gordon Street to get him one, so that he could sit most of the day while he was awake, chewing at it. In fact he had eaten so many crabs that he'd come to look like one, with his bald pink head and broad pink face.

'Rory McElpy,' Donovan said. 'Damn stupid name for a start.'

'Whassa matter?' Crab blinked blearily across at Donovan. 'Jilt you or something?'

'Go back to sleep, Crab,' said Beer Baillie.

'No, I wanna know about this bloody woman. An' wha' she did to my old pal Donovan.'

'It's what I'd like to do to her,' Donovan told him grimly. More jeering and whistling greeted this remark, but he didn't even smile. 'When I think,' he said, 'of the job that was lined up for me . . .'

'God, yes,' Beer Baillie agreed. 'I remember now. Foreign correspondent in "Gay Paree", wasn't it?'

'Whass this bloody woman got to do with it? Thass what I wanna know.'

'According to my father's assistant, she systematically ruined the old man's business — used every devious and unfair method known and unknown to man. Then eventually she fast-talked him into practically handing it to her on a plate. I had to come up and see for myself and sure enough he's a broken man. It's as if he hasn't anything to live for any more.' Donovan tossed his pencil down on his cluttered desk. 'I felt guilty enough, not being able to attend my mother's funeral. I was over in America and it was impossible to get back in time.'

'Christ, I didn't know that,' Beer Baillie said.

'When I got this pathetic letter from Miss Winters and then saw the state my father was in — and all because of this wretched McElpy woman — I could have killed her. Because of that bitch, I felt I hadn't any choice but to

315

apply for this job. I had to be with the old man to try to give him some support.'

'Thass terrible.' Crab belched loudly. 'Bloody bitch! Should be made to feel sorry.'

'Don't worry,' Donovan assured him. 'She will!'

'Da-a-rling!' A loud voice suddenly trilled across the room. 'Donovan, you wicked man, why weren't you waiting at the front entrance to meet me?'

Not only the voice filled the room, but a heady perfume as well. Donovan swung his chair round, then rose from it grinning a welcome. 'Hello, gorgeous!'

A slim blonde in a white cloche with a huge shocking pink feather pierced across the front of it came weaving an elegant path between the desks towards him, the silk of her cerise-coloured dress flaring lightly out and teasing every man she squeezed past. A V-neck was cut low to beneath her waist, but filled in with a white pleated chiffon front. 'Darling, don't care about me any more?'

'Sure, sure,' Donovan said. 'I'm giving you dinner, aren't I? As soon as the grand tour's over.' He strolled towards her and skilfully deflected her enthusiastic embrace at the same time as leading her from the room, one arm still hooked round her waist. Her feet barely touched the floor.

'That was the reporters' room,' he told her after they had left it. 'Off it we've a few other rooms, one for the city editor — the chap who looks after the stocks and shares — one for the editor and one for his secretary.'

'Darling, you are mean . . .' she pouted.

'I suppose you want to go down in the lift?' he said.

'But I want to see all round the place.'

'Down to the machine room, then back up top to the case room. All shall be revealed, sweetheart.'

'Is that a promise?' she fluttered her lashes up at him.

Laughing, he deposited her in the lift and clanged shut the gates. No sooner had he done so than she tried to cling round his neck and find his lips. Again he disentangled himself. 'I never make love while I'm on duty, sweetheart.'

'Since when?'

'Since I returned to Scotland. They've different priorities up here.'

'You're no different. I adore you.'

'Sure, sure!'

'I know you don't believe me.'

'I believe you're a very good actress, honey. You just don't know when to stop!'

'Darling Donovan, haven't you any idea how attractive you are?'

'The machine room,' he announced as they emerged from the lift at the basement. 'There's no use trying to talk in here; you'll never make yourself heard above the noise. Nor will you hear anyone else. Only the men who work in the place can talk to each other. They've found just the right tone and pitch.'

Noise suddenly battered against them, sucked them in, beat them mercilessly around the head. Amelia screwed up her face and held dainty gloved hands protectively to her ears as she was led briefly around the huge roaring, whirring machinery.

The case room that housed the compositors at the top of the building was as silent as the grave in comparison — only much warmer and friendlier. Indeed, Donovan had been heard to say that the *Citizen* had a very pleasant family atmosphere, was a real dawdle compared with Fleet Street and he wouldn't have minded *choosing* to spend some time here. Any time except now! Often it could be so quiet and easygoing that the editor, so the legend went, had once bought a set of draughts to keep the reporters occupied and out of the pub.

'So, have I got it right, darling?' Amelia fluttered her eyelashes again. 'Reporters go out on a story. Then either 'phone it in or come in to the reporters' room and write it up. It then goes to the sub-editor and the chief sub, then up to the case room, then down to the machine room . . .'

'If I know you, sweetheart, there's method to your madness.'

She blew him a kiss. 'Didn't I tell you? I'm up here to

317

rehearse a play set in a newspaper office. If it has a long run in Glasgow, you'll be seeing a lot more of me, darling.'

As they emerged from the building, she clung to his arm and leaned her cheek against it.

'I thought so,' he said. 'You were just making use of me. Remind me to do the same with you some time.'

'Some time soon, I hope.'

It was when he was laughing at this retort that he noticed Rory McElpy. She was coming in the opposite direction, almost within touching distance.

'Working hard as usual?' she remarked in passing.

'Impudent little bitch!' Donovan said.

'Trouble, darling?'

Donovan's eyes narrowed and glimmered down at Amelia with the kind of sexuality which she often confessed to friends made her feel like begging for it. 'No woman troubles me, sweetheart.'

The next morning Donovan had to take a great deal of good-natured banter from the rest of the *Citizen* reporters about what they guessed he had been up to the night before. He refused, however, to be drawn into giving a detailed report on his evening's activities with Miss Manners. Eventually they gave up trying and settled down to the usual drawing of straws to see who was to attend the North Court — where all the big cases like murder were heard — and who was to be the unlucky man to spend the morning in the South Court where there were just the 'dirty cases'. Only one man needed to go and sit through the 'dirty cases' because they were never reported — cases of homosexuality, lesbianism, sodomy and bestiality. It was all very well being amazed at the apparent respect-ability of an old Scottish farmer who was accused of bestiality, although Donovan for one had long since ceased to be amazed at anything. What was the use of sitting there listening to the gentlemanly-looking farmer explaining that he'd found his sheep with its horns stuck in a fence and been unable to resist her, if you weren't allowed to write

318

it up and put it in the paper? It was because of this irritating inhibition that nobody ever wanted to be the one to attend the South Court. The only reason somebody *had* to attend was in case the Judge dropped dead. (That *could* be written up.) This time it was Beer Baillie's unlucky day.

'Oh, bugger it!' he exclaimed.

'You'll get enough of that this morning, don't worry!' Crab McKay laughed. He was always perfectly sober until lunchtime; unlike Jock McGill, the city editor, who was a constant whisky-drinker.

Donovan said. 'It's a wonder the police courts have any spare time for anybody except Scrap McElpy.'

'It didn't take you long to find out about him,' McGill commented. 'He's small fry, though. And harmless enough. Drunk and disorderly.'

'And theft?'

'Petty. Nothing big. And its only when he's had a few.'

Donovan raised a sarcastic brow. 'That's taken into consideration, is it? That's why he gets such paltry sentences?'

McGill shrugged, then asked, 'You gunning for him as well?'

'Just interested.'

'How's your father?'

Donovan's face hardened with bitterness. 'He worked conscientiously all his life. He built up his business and his reputation on honesty and fair dealing, and what consideration has he got? Tricked and taken advantage of by smart-asses and small-time crooks. He's given up, he's turned his face to the wall. That's how he is.'

McGill avoided Donovan's eyes and turned to Crab who was happily gnawing on a pincer. 'See *you!*' he said. 'You make me sick!'

CHAPTER FORTY-EIGHT

'Miss McElpy, Miss McElpy!' Mamie came running through from the back shop waving the newspaper she had been reading. It was her dinner-time and she enjoyed devouring the news along with her soup. The front shop was very large, incorporated as it was with Mr Donovan's shop area which was now the gentleman's department. A corridor ran along the back regions, off which were several 'back shops'. It still disorientated Mamie and at first she could not see Rory. Joe's burly figure was immediately visible, however, stiff and immaculate in his dark well-cut suit and high collar, he considered himself a manager now and Rory's right-hand man.

He ruled the growing staff at Rory's with much the same brand of toughness as when he had been ruler of the Springburn gang called 'the Burners'. For the customers, he had perfected a sergeant-major type politeness.

Joe had become interested in being in the shop rather than out delivering — this job had now gone to Coll — since getting his eye on one of Rory's regular customers: retired sea-captain McKay and his daughter, Fiona. Captain McKay was reckoned to be worth quite a bit of money. His daughter had dark mischievous eyes and a rosebud mouth, and she wore small fur hats and big fur muffs. Rory was never sure which Joe found more attractive — the daughter's looks or the father's bank balance. Bullet-headed, steely-eyed Joe was as hard as proverbial nails. She could never imagine him being in any way romantic. But he was always quick to see the main chance.

'What's up now?' he rapped impatiently at the excited

assistant. Then lowering his voice, he added, 'I'm warning you — I'll have you out on your ear.'

Mamie was immediately subdued and had turned white-faced to retrace her steps when Rory appeared.

'What was all that racket?'

'I told her,' Joe growled.

'Well, Mamie?'

'It was in the paper, Miss McElpy.' Mamie picked nervously at her spots.

'Don't tell me I'm in another "Searcher" article?'

'No, Miss McElpy. It's Mr Donovan that had the hatter's shop. He's died, Miss McElpy.'

Rory took the paper. 'All right. Now get on with your work.'

'It's my dinner-time, Miss McElpy, but if you want me to . . .'

'Get on with your dinner, then.'

'Yes, Miss McElpy.'

'What do you bet he'll blame you for his old man snuffing it?' Joe flexed his shoulder muscles. 'You ought to have let me do him over long ago.'

'Have you seen the size of him?' Rory asked. 'Anyway, he's causing us enough bad publicity as it is.'

'I could stop his poison pen; I'd leave him without hands. But I suppose you're right about the publicity.'

'I know I am. And you're not going the same way as Da; you're going to behave yourself and get on. Why don't you start courting that Fiona McKay?'

'I have.'

'Good! Well, just concentrate on her and your work and leave me to deal with Donovan.'

Joe shrugged. 'You're the boss.'

Rory went into one of the fitting-rooms, opened the paper and found the death notices. She bit her lip. He had been a nice old man. Well, not old really when you came to think of it — only fifty-eight. She had quite often shared her afternoon tea-time with him — either in her shop or in his. And they'd talked. Admittedly she always used the occasions to get a word in about the advantages of him selling her his shop. But they had talked about other things too. He had told her all about his wife, Maureen, and showed her photographs. He'd also talked about Donovan and was obviously proud of him.

'Maureen and I were born and brought up in Ireland, but things got pretty bad over there. We were practically starving at one point,' he had told her. 'So when we knew she was expecting we managed to get over here, hoping we might be able to make a better life for our child. She doted on that boy. We were always a very close family. Now with her gone as well as Donovan . . .' He gave a long, tired sigh. 'At least Donovan's done well. That's what both Maureen and I always wanted — that Donovan should have a good life.'

'And you certainly succeeded in giving him every chance,' Rory said, struggling as usual to cheer him up.

He shook his head. 'No, Donovan made his own chances. He succeeded without any help from me. He was born and brought up in the Gorbals and he was a man before I managed to make a decent living here. I didn't give him anything.'

Remembering his Gorbals background made Rory understand Donovan's aura of inner toughness despite his relaxed, nonchalant appearance. You had to be tough to survive in the Gorbals.

You had to be tough to survive Cowlairs Road, Springburn as well. Remembering, she also experienced a fellow feeling with Donovan. He wasn't the product of some strange far-off English town; he had Glasgow in his bones, like her. Then it occurred to her that despite his toughness he would be grieving now and perhaps grieving alone. As far as she knew, Mr Donovan had no relations in Glasgow; his wife had been an orphan and he, like Donovan, was an only son.

At first Rory toyed with the idea of going to the *Citizen* offices to speak to him and offer her condolences. But she kept shying away from putting the idea into practice and eventually decided that she would just go to the funeral and pay her respects. It wasn't the custom in Glasgow for women to be at a graveside, but Rory had never been one to pay much heed to accepted conventions and customs.

The funeral was held in the Southern Necropolis which was next to the Cathedral and, like most of Glasgow, was built on a hill. She had been told that it reached a height of over three hundred feet and afforded one of the best views of Glasgow; not of course comparable with the view from Springburn Park.

Rearing up beside the ancient weather-blackened Cathedral, the hill of the Necropolis with its tiers of tombstones was like some macabre wedding cake. Rory entered through the Elizabethan portal on which was sculpted the arms of the City and of the Merchants' House on a double shield. Once through the gates, she crossed the single arched bridge known as 'the Bridge of Sighs' and began to climb the rising ground to where she could see a small huddle of mourners. She recognized a couple of elderly male wholesalers and one or two equally elderly customers who had remained loyal to Mr Donovan. And of course there was the unmistakable figure of the deceased's son. As she drew nearer, she noticed that he was wearing a well-cut navy suit of good quality serge and an immaculate white shirt. His less-than-smart fawn raincoat was slung carelessly over his arm, however, and he was clutching his hat in tight-fisted hands. There was a tightness about his rugged face too and his eyes were lowered. Because of that and the fact that she remained discreetly back from the other mourners, he didn't see her until after the service was over and people had begun to drift slowly away.

Approaching him, she said, 'May I offer you my most sincere condolences?'

'No, you may not!' His words were quiet but vehement. 'My God, you're the limit! What bloody hypocrisy! You hound my father out of his shop. You leave him with nothing to live for. Then you've the gall to come to his funeral and . . .'

Rory watched in genuine distress as he struggled for control.

'Get to hell out of here,' he managed eventually. 'Get out of my sight!'

Biting her lip, she turned away and somehow found the right path to take her back to Cathedral Square. Perhaps she had been wrong in attending the funeral — not for the reasons Donovan gave, but simply because her appearance had upset him so much. She ought to have left him in peace to cope with his grief.

'Damn! Damn!' she kept repeating to herself as she returned to Stockwell Street. Looking along the wide expanse of window that fronted her business and the big gilt letters enblazoned above it, she tried to draw reassurance from its opulence. She had engaged some out-of-work painters to transform the dark peeling stonework of the building into startling white and the result was most handsome.

There was still a great deal of unemployment, although it was a few years now since the end of the war. The men had been only too glad of the job even at the rock-bottom price she paid them. She had learned a few lessons on her way out of Cowlairs Road and one important lesson was that the less you had the less you were given, and the more you had the more you could get.

She had recently found that she could get a large bank loan and she had her eye on the central hall in the Stockwell Street building. She'd heard that Messrs. Anderson, owners of the pottery and porcelain warehouse that occupied the premises, were retiring and she had already had dicussions with their lawyers.

To take over such an enormous addition to her business was extremely hazardous and took all the nerve she could muster. She was determined to do it, however, and had already discussed plans with Joe and Benny, with Joshua Cowan and his assistant cutter and fitter Mr Andrew Gordon, and Miss Elliot, the new first saleslady of the ladies' department. Rory believed in involving the senior staff in important decisions and had regular formal meetings with them, something she felt they appreciated and which to her made good business sense.

They had always been a bit shaken by her ideas about not confining herself to departments traditionally belonging only to a tailoring or drapery business. Her latest suggestion, however, had shocked them speechless. Not only did she talk of adding to the ordinary branches of that trade those of the hatter, the milliner, the glover and the shoemaker, but the tea-merchant, bookseller, jewellery and Uncle Tom Cobley and all.

'Why not?' she wanted to know.

Eventually the silence had been broken by Joshua. 'To be honest with you, Rory, I've never understood why a good tailoring establishment isn't enough. We've built up a first-class reputation with customers for our tailor-mades.'

Indeed, that side of the business had mushroomed faster than Rory had at first thought possible. Now in the huge basement of the shop brown paper patterns hung in dusty ranks like leaves of tobacco in a drying shed. Customers' measurements were always carefully checked and any alteration in the customer's size amended on the original pattern. 'This,' Joshua always insisted, 'is the difference between bespoke-cutting and "ready-make bespoke".'

Upstairs in the cutting-room the patterns were outlined with tailors chalk on the surface of the cloth as it lay stretched out across a long bench. There were, she had learned, eight main pieces for a straight coat, two for a waistcoat and four for a pair of trousers. The cloth was then cut with shears in a process known as 'striking'.

Later, Joshua and Andrew Gordon sat up crosslegged on the bench amongst a choppy ocean of cloth and often they sang as they worked:

Bill Smith was a tailor, a 'prentice he'd been
Whose work was as perfect as ever was seen.
He knew how to build up a front and to press a frock
coat, a morning coat, lounge or a dress.

For full forty years at the trade he had worked,
And during that period no job he had shirked. But one
fact his conscience continually mocked,
He'd not made a job yet that couldn't be cocked!
Fol-de-rol-liddle-lol; fol-de-rol-lay;
More collar-ology every day!

Benny said, 'The tea-merchants, booksellers and jewellers
and all the rest around here aren't going to like it.'

'Around here?' Andrew repeated worriedly. 'The whole
of Glasgow will be up in arms. First the wholesalers. Now
the retailers . . .'

'Forget about them,' Rory said. 'We mind our business.
Let them mind theirs.'

Joe drummed his fingers on the table. 'You think it'll pay
off?'

'Has anything I've attempted so far not paid off?'

It was Miss Elliot's turn to speak up. 'I shudder to think
what that awful newspaperman is going to write about this
when he finds out.'

'Nobody's going to find out for a while yet. I'll worry
about him when the time comes,' Rory answered.

But she was worried about him now as she returned from
his father's funeral. The suffering in his eyes haunted her.
The strength of the emotions she saw in them and the way
it jabbed out in barbs of hatred had shaken her. As soon
as she reached the privacy of her office at the back of the
shop, she lit a cigarette and poured herself a glass of
whisky. But nothing helped.

CHAPTER FORTY-NINE

Drummond sat on a stool outside the foreman's office at Eastfield depot, waiting until it was time to prepare the Perth engine. His diary lay unattended on his knee. The sun was shining on his face, warming him and causing an amber shimmer beneath his closed lids. Deep inside, however, he was weighed down by bleak depression. He kept telling himself there was no need for such desolation. Victoria was busy and cheerful; Jamie was a thriving child much admired by everyone; he himself was busy with work that he enjoyed — both as a railway fireman (now getting driving turns), as Union secretary and as a member of the Parish Council and active on several committees. He felt a sigh push up and heave at his chest. Why was he so low in spirits? It wasn't just the obvious reason that Victoria had been refusing to have any sexual contact with him since Jamie's birth. She had had a bad time and the stitches had left a tenderness long after they had been removed. The weight of the baby inside her had caused a painful haemorrhoid which had persisted for months after the birth and now lifting and laying such a hefty lad every day had caused her to suffer some lower back pain. She kept saying mysteriously, 'Something's not right down there.'

He had tried to persuade her to see Doctor Morton but she had rolled her eyes and scoffed at the mere idea.

'How can I afford to go to a doctor? It takes every penny to keep us in food every week.'

He paid the rent and bills like gas and rates. He gave her housekeeping money which was supposed to cover clothes as well as food. Recently, against his wishes, she had purchased articles on the instalment plan — expensive things like a big fancy pram. Not that he expected Victoria to go out with the baby tucked inside a shawl wrapped round her like most of the other women in Springburn, but he would have chosen a less expensive pram had he been given the chance for any say in the matter. However, the pram had been presented to him, standing in all its glory and dwarfing the kitchen, as a *fait accompli*.

Victoria was so happy with her purchase and greeted him with such an affectionate hug and kiss that he had not the heart to criticize her extravagance. Indeed, he volunteered to pay the instalments to save her any worry and had been rewarded by another enthusiastic kiss. He did point out, however, the difficulties there might be in getting the pram up and down the flight of stairs to and from their house every time she wanted to take Jamie out.

'I won't always be here to do it, Victoria. How will you manage with your bad back?'

Victoria impatiently brushed aside his objections, 'Och, there's always plenty of neighbours about.'

Having discovered the instalment method of purchasing, she had splashed out on some other things: a high-chair for the baby, a wooden barred swing that screwed to the lintel of the kitchen door, a set of silver spoon and pusher and a mug and plate of best china with paintings on it of rabbits and bluebirds. He was paying these up, too, but had warned her there must be no more. Twice he had been late with the rent as a result of struggling to meet these debts and there had been a terrible quarrel when she'd accused him of being selfish and mean and of being jealous of the baby. He had lost his temper and shouted abuse at her and as a result of the noise he made (Victoria never shouted), the baby had awakened and begun to scream.

'Now look what you've done, you wicked man!' she cried out in distress as she ran to comfort the child.

But it was not Victoria's extragavance with money which was depressing him. It was the way she never discussed

328

her purchases, or anything else, with him beforehand. It was the way she seemed to shut him out, especially since Jamie was born. He tried to tell himself that it was despicable for him to be jealous of their child just because it was now the centre of Victoria's love and concern. Wasn't it right and proper and perfectly natural for a good mother to be loving and attentive to her child, especially her first-born? But still he felt depressed. The only relationship that gave him any warmth at the moment — and indeed always had — was the one he enjoyed with Rory. He admired her enormously and felt flattered that she turned to him for help and advice in her troubles with the newspaper attacks on her. He had helped her to pen several letters to the papers. Then of couse there was her physical warmth. She was and always had been a passionate-natured person and he would not be human if he didn't feel a response to this in himself, especially now when his own deeply-felt passions were being denied.

Drummond opened his eyes and saw smoke from the engines at the outside pits blow across the rails and over the crane. He tried to concentrate his mind on the railway life going on around him. Charlie Thomas had got assistance with his 2758; he had waited on that engine coming through the lye. Number 2900 was waiting clear of the No 2 road to couple on. He could hear the raised voices of Millar the foreman and the office boys through the window behind him; Millar was accusing one of the boys of sitting in the bothy with the men.

An old driver nicknamed 'the Editor' came to peer at the spare diagrams, probably to size up those who had Sunday shifts. He passed in front of Drummond with a brief nod and a 'fine weather'. Then after scanning the sheets he marched back to the shed, folding his glasses, his greasy jacket blowing out from his sides as he went.

Next came Bob Fairfield, his wide blue trousers with many a fold on the way to his feet. He was best known as 'Toes' because of the way his toes turned sharply in as he walked. He disappeared into the bothy.

The 9498 went out, throwing thin black smoke up in the dry air; the 621 followed her. Then the Kilsyth came in for Queen's Street. Sam Parker stood for a minute with hands inside the front part of his overalls before stepping over the rails to the ballast siding and passing from view among the huts. Irvine coupled on to the 9035 — 'the Editor's' engine. Jimmy McKay spoke to him while they lifted off their lamps. Then a long and a short, a vast blowing from the cocks and off they went.

Soon it was his turn, but even as Drummond worked his shift the depression still clung like cobwebs in his mind. Interweaving with it, however, were his thoughts of Rory like colourful threads sweetening the trapped, hopeless feeling he had and making his physical need both painful and pleasurable.

The bothy was empty when he returned, save for one fireman who was stretched out on one of the benches snoring loudly. It was still a lovely summer's night when he left the shed and before moving away from the pit, he took a long look at the Balgray skyline; the fine big houses and the tall green trees in the Park. The slope down to the Bishopbriggs lines was light green and glittering in places as glass caught the soft sunlight. Tired now, he suddenly felt he couldn't face going home to Victoria's impatient kiss of greeting and her absent-minded attention as she pretended to listen to him while all the time listening for the baby. If only he could light some adoration in Victoria's eyes as Jamie could do, just by being Jamie. He would have been content with a small overflow from the love she lavished on the child, but every drop of affection was now conscientiously conserved for her son. He wondered if Victoria had ever loved him. But perhaps he was just being perverse. After all, it was not so long ago that he was raging at her for not allowing him a moment's privacy or peace to be his own man. She still interfered, but only if Jamie was sleeping and she had nothing better to do.

A longing to go and see Mrs Buchanan almost overcame him. Quite frequently he would drop in to see her on his way home from Eastfield. Sometimes he took her an ice-cream wafer from 'the Tallys'. She liked ice-cream and it gave him pleasure to watch her licking it and thoroughly enjoying it. She was fond of apples too, so he often took her an apple; she always cut it in half and scooped out the white flesh with a teaspoon. She was always very gentle and serious about everything, even eating ice-cream or an apple, but he only went to see her when he knew she would be alone. The last time they had been sitting opposite each other by the fire with the clock ticking quietly between them. She had been knitting and he had been thinking not about Victoria, but about Rory.

'Is there anything wrong, son?' she had asked suddenly.

He had gazed at her in silence for a long time, longing to unburden himself but knowing it was impossible. Eventually he had managed to smile. 'Nothing that need worry you, Mrs Buchanan. It's time I was off home now.'

She had followed him to the door as she always did and this time as well as her usual, 'Haste ye back' she added, 'Confide your troubles in the Lord, son. He is our help and comfort in every time of need.'

This did not annoy him as it would have done if Mrs Kipp had said it. To him, Mrs Buchanan was everything a good Christian ought to be. She sincerely believed in God and he only wished he could. This evening Mr Buchanan and Victoria's brothers would be in, so Drummond regretfully relinquished any thought of a visit.

Instead, he passed the Buchanan close and walked up the Balgray Hill, hoping a stroll through the Park might blow the cobwebs from his mind. As the tenement buildings gave way to the big villas he began to experience twinges of self-consciousness at still being in his greasy dungarees and railway cap. Normally he would not have worried — he was not ashamed of his railway uniform — but he did not wish to risk a meeting with Forbes-Cunningham while at any disadvantage. A soot-streaked face and sweating body would, he felt, put him at a distinct disadvantage.

331

At the first meeting of the Poor Law Committee, bathed, brushed and suitably attired in his best suit and stiff collar and well-polished boots, he had felt perfectly confident to meet the man eye-to-eye. For years he had hated him from a distance; now he had the chance to get to grips with him, be a thorn in his flesh, oppose him and defeat him. At that first meeting he had defeated him. The case arose of a man aged twenty-seven who had been born in the poorhouse but had been a hard-working employee in the local foundry until, through no fault of his own, he had been paid off. Since then he had been unable to find work to feed and support his wife (also twenty-seven) and three children aged five, three and two-and-a-half. Forbes-Cunningham had voted to refuse the man's application for relief, saying the man and wife should be sent to the poorhouse and the children 'boarded out'. The other members of the Committee were going along with this suggestion; Drummond very soon discovered in fact that they had a great respect for and deference to the area's wealthiest and most powerful man in the form of Forbes-Cunningham, and were only too ready to follow his lead in everything.

'I disagree,' Drummond had cut in calmly. 'The man has a perfectly good case for relief. Furthermore, I do not believe it is either right or proper to take his children away from him.'

At first there had been a shocked silence round the big mahogany table at which the meeting was taking place. Then Forbes-Cunningham had raised an eyebrow. 'Indeed?'

'In fact, gentlemen,' Drummond had continued, 'I believe it is totally reprehensible as well as irresponsible to make such peremptory judgements when we are dealing with human beings like ourselves.'

'Hardly like ourselves, Drummond,' Forbes-Cunningham said, and it infuriated Drummond to detect a glimmer of amusement in the older man's eyes.

'Is your contention then, sir,' he enquired coldly, 'that money and position make a man less human?'

There was a gasp around the table, but still Forbes-

Cunningham did not take the bait. He began arguing the case, but it was with as cool and sharp-witted a manner as Drummond himself. The argument centred around the relative cost to the Parish and the poorhouse, as well as the moral issues involved. Eventually, and again to Drummond's surprise, Forbes-Cunningham gave in. But it was astonishment he felt when Forbes-Cunningham stopped him as he was leaving and said, 'I've already made a few enquiries about you, Drummond.'

It was Drummond's turn to raise a brow. 'Oh? To what purpose, sir?'

'Never mind that just now. The point is, you're no run-of-the-mill railway worker. I could use a young fellow like you.'

'Indeed?' He'd stared in mock politeness at the older man. 'In what capacity? Digging coal?'

Anger flared in Forbes-Cunningham's eyes, but only for a second before his expression changed again. In a carefully controlled voice he said, 'No, in a managerial capacity. It would be to your advantage, I promise you.'

Drummond smiled. 'Well, that's one way to try getting rid of the opposition I suppose. Good afternoon, sir.'

He had been quite excited when he told Victoria afterwards about what had happened. To him, it was the measure of his worth as an opponent and he felt flattered.

'But what if he genuinely wanted to offer you a good collar-and-tie job?' Victoria too was excited. 'Oh, Matthew, it could change our whole lives! We'd be able to give Jamie a real chance to be somebody. He wouldn't say that if he didn't mean it. Next time you see him, tell him you've had time to consider his offer and—'

Drummond could hardly believe his ears.

'Don't be stupid, woman!' he interrupted. 'He wants me off that Committee, that's all.'

'So get off the Committee, then,' Victoria said. 'What does the Committee matter?'

'It matters a great deal to a great many people. For instance, one of the cases I fought for and won today was for financial help for a man and his wife and three young children. Winning that case meant that instead of the couple going to the Barnhill and having their children taken away from them, at least they will be able to survive and be together.'

He felt sorry for Victoria. He knew she was too kind-hearted and compassionate to say that people like the family he had described didn't matter. Yet nobody mattered to her except Jamie. She was in a distressing quandary; he could see it in her white face, large eyes and trembling lips.

'Darling . . .' He tried to take her in his arms, but she stiffened away from him. She was obviously fighting to contain her disappointment, her face and mouth hardening in the process. He could imagine the dream castles she'd built immediately he mentioned Forbes-Cunningham's offer. In a flash she had pictured herself living up the Balgray Hill and able to afford every comfort and luxury — especially for Jamie.

She had a habit of saying dreamily that she would get this, that or the other, 'when my ship comes in'. Forgiveness would not be easily found for the person responsible for sinking it.

Still, life went on and Victoria's innate cheerfulness and sociability got the better of her again. But as far as he was concerned, it was merely the icing on a frozen cake. She was happy and cheerful entertaining former Co-op customers and basking in their praise of her delicious home-baked fairy cakes and Empire biscuits, and her lovely home and beautiful child. But any praise he gave her was met only by tight travesties of smiles. She chatted to him about these social occasions, it was true, yet still she subtly distanced herself more and more from him. He felt the distance widen and his sadness increased.

Forbes-Cunningham's house was like a castle towering over Springburn, indeed with a view over the whole of Glasgow. Drummond was disturbed in a new way at the thought of the man. None of his old feelings or ideas about Forbes-Cunningham had changed, but they had taken on a strange new dimension. Having met him and spoken with him, he had the secret confusing suspicion that the man actually admired him and was genuine in his offer. He would have preferred it if Forbes-Cunningham had returned his hatred a thousandfold. That would have been more understandable and he would have known better how to cope with it. As far as his own feelings were concerned, he hated the man all the more for having intensified the strain in his relationship with Victoria.

Drummond passed 'The Towers' on his way into the deserted Park, his cap tugged down and his hands clenched inside the pockets of his jacket. He reached the sanctuary of the trees and breathed in the lush greenness and the earthy smell laced with the sweet perfume of flowers. The sun was beginning to fade and the still quiet of the evening reached his soul, but only to enlarge its burden of grief.

It was then that he saw Rory. She was sitting by herself on a wooden bench in a shadowy arbour.

Without a word, he went over and sat down beside her.

CHAPTER FIFTY

Victoria was happily dandling Jamie on her lap and hadn't noticed her mother's unhappy, strained expression and the two bright blobs of colour on her plump cheeks. She looked up in surprise when the older woman suddenly burst out, 'Are you doing your duty by your man, Victoria?'

'What on earth do you mean?'

Mrs Buchanan fiddled with her knitting and avoided her daughter's stare. She examined the grey wool of the sock she had on her needles, peering at it over the top of her spectacles, her lowered head accentuating the soft bulge of her plump cheeks. She cleared her throat. 'You're a married woman. You know very well what I mean.'

Victoria flushed a bright crimson. It was unbearable that she and her mother should be put under such a wretched strain of embarrassment. It was all Matthew's fault.

'Matthew's been talking to you about me!'

'No, he has not. But I haven't been married myself all these years, Victoria, without knowing a thing or two about men and about human nature.'

Victoria could have died with embarrassment and she felt sorry for the agony her mother was obviously suffering. The whole situation was unendurable. She didn't care how loyal her mother was to Matthew — it *was* his fault.

'Have you been doing your duty by your man, Victoria?' Mrs Buchanan repeated desperately.

'I don't know why you're so worried about him — you

of all people, mother. You said right from the start you didn't like him.'

Her mother now looked shocked as well as distressed and gazed up at her daughter wide-eyed like a child. 'May the good Lord forgive you, Victoria. I said no such thing.'

'You definitely liked Archie better.'

'I knew Archie better then. But I see now that although Matthew is not like Archie, or your father or your brothers, he is a good man in his own way. He means well, Victoria.'

'Och, I know that.'

'But bad or good,' Mrs Buchanan took to re-examining her knitting 'all men have certain needs.'

Victoria studied Jamie's hair and tidying it back managed eventually to blurt out, 'I don't like that . . . that side of marriage.'

'Liking has nothing to do with it, dear. Decent women don't like that sort of thing, but they do their duty and so must you. If you don't, you know what will happen.'

'No.' Victoria looked up, curiosity getting the better of her.

'He'll turn to someone else.'

'Oh, Matthew would never do that!' She had never felt more certain of anything in her life. 'He loves me.'

'Yes, I know he does, dear.' Her mother timidly raised her eyes as if frightened of what Victoria might see in them. 'But you mark my words, human nature being the powerful thing it is, he'll turn to someone else. I'm telling you, Victoria, unless you do your duty by him, it will be the end of your marriage. You'll lose your good man.'

It really was too upsetting for words and Victoria felt furious that she and her mother had been subjected to such an ordeal. After Mrs Buchanan left, Victoria felt at sixes and sevens and couldn't concentrate on anything. She had persuaded herself that her marriage was working very well. Jamie was such a joy and tending to him and loving him filled her days so delightfully. Certainly she and Matthew had their quarrels, but that was his fault and not hers. He

337

admitted himself that his bad temper was to blame; indeed, she had seen this confession in black and white in his diary. He had left it lying on his desk for a few minutes while going to the lavatory one day and she'd flicked through some of the pages. One entry had caught her eye. It said: 'Baby came with a cry. He did a lot of it afterwards . . .' She stiffened with resentment, thinking, 'How dare he say that Jamie cried a lot?' Although in fact he had. She read on: 'The first three months were bad ones. I take no credit from them. I was bad-tempered. Nights saw things at their worst. Me too. Baby nearly always howling. Victoria often crying too. I have a lot to make good for . . .'

Victoria wholeheartedly agreed. As far as she was concerned, she had been a good wife. She had been both patient and forgiving with him — at least until the occasion when Matthew had refused to follow up Mr Forbes-Cunningham's offer of a collar-and-tie job. She couldn't help admiring Matthew's strong principles, but it was unforgivable of him to turn down any opportunity of bettering himself and being able to provide his son with a good life. Matthew was lucky that she remained so conscientious. She doctored him when he had a cold or strained a muscle with doing his exercises; she fed him well and saw that his clothes were clean and respectable — not that she had to bother about his suit or his boots. He was so pernickety about his appearance that he preferred to sponge and press his suit and brush his boots himself. That and his habit of trying to slip away on his own had made her often accuse him of being a born bachelor.

She was a good wife. The trouble was, he wasn't a good husband! It was all very well for her mother to talk; she didn't know what it was like to be married to a man like Matthew. Her father was the most cheerful easygoing partner imaginable. She had never once seen him in any kind of bad mood, far less the black silent kind that Matthew inflicted on her. Living with Matthew was at times as bad as being alone. She didn't know how she would have survived her marriage had it not been for her oh so precious, adorable son. Jamie's love for her could never be tarnished in the way Matthew had tarnished his.

However, after her mother's talk she did resolve to try very hard to forgive Matthew. If she did, and if she continued to be a good wife to him, she was sure that he would be given the strength to overcome his baser animal instincts. He would keep his love for her as pure as her love was, and always would be, for him.

'How are you getting on?' Drummond said after they had both sat staring at the trees for a while in silence.

Rory shrugged deeper into her high-collared coat. 'Fine.'

'You don't seem too happy.'

'I was at a funeral. Mr Donovan — you know, him that used to have the hat-shop next door to me.'

'You've nothing to reproach yourself about, Rory.'

'Oh? What's made you change your tune?'

'Victoria told me how good you were to him and how you even gave him more money for his business than it was actually worth.'

Rory gave a wry smile. 'As usual, Victoria exaggerates.'

'I should never have doubted your integrity and certainly not your warm and loving nature,' Drummond said.

There was a silence again until Rory asked, 'What are you doing here?'

'I could ask you the same question.'

'I live across the road.'

'Even so.'

'I needed to think and the house can be noisy.'

It wasn't hard to guess why he was looking so miserable and sitting in the park instead of going straight home after his work.

He sighed. 'I wouldn't divulge this to anyone else, Rory, but . . . circumstances have become very strained in our house.'

'Can't you talk to her? Talk things out, I mean.'

'Yes, we can discuss some of our different attitudes and beliefs and feelings. Indeed, as you must know, Victoria likes to talk. Except on one taboo subject and unfortunately, that is the one we most need to discuss.'

'She's frigid.'

'No, I . . . I think it's just she's so innocent and naïve and . . . and perhaps frightened too. If only she could trust me.' He leaned his elbows down on his knees and wearily supported his head on his hands. 'If only she could understand what she's doing to me.'

'I've tried to talk to her,' Rory told him.

'Have you?' He straightened up in surprise.

'More than once. Not specifically about her relations with you; that's none of my business. Just her general attitude about men and sex. She needs to see a doctor.'

'I've tried to suggest that but she took it as an insult. She was furious and colder than ever and she informed me it was me who needed to see a doctor. A doctor in an asylum, she said. His mouth twisted with wretchedness. 'Maybe it is me.'

'No, it isn't,' Rory said. 'You're a good lover.'

His eyes met hers in anxious uncertainty. 'It was good between us, wasn't it?'

'Of course it was. Victoria doesn't know how lucky she is.'

'Oh, Rory . . .'

She looked away. 'One of the glove manufacturers is taking me to the next dinner-dance in the Trades House. A real posh affair. He's loaded with money.'

'I see,' he said quietly.

She couldn't bear to look round at the thin figure in the greasy dungarees and jacket. She didn't want to see the pale soot-streaked face and dark eyes bewildered with unhappiness.

'Still doing your bit for the Union?' she asked, lighting up a cigarette.

'Forbes-Cunningham is proposing not only wage reductions of from 12 to 15 shillings a week, but a longer working day for the miners.'

'Well, as long as he doesn't do it to the railwaymen, it's not your concern.'

340

'That's where you're wrong! Completely wrong. An injustice to one working man is an injustice to all. It's important for our very survival that we care about each other, Rory.'

She dragged at her cigarette, smiling to herself to think how easy it was to start the fire in him raging.

'Can you imagine the lack of caring, the heartlessness, the complete lack of compassion that is behind Forbes-Cunningham's decision?' He went on. 'Can you imagine the deprivation and even death that it will mean? Because it is the later hours of the shift worked that are the most dangerous — the time when men's vital energy is at its lowest and is impossible to replace. Do you know that while my father was working down the mine, between 1,000 and 1,500 men were killed each year? That makes an average of four miners killed every day in Britain, and for every four killed, a hundred or more were injured.'

She let him talk. It was one way of working out his passion.

'But do men like Forbes-Cunningham care? Not a bit! Now the government has stepped in and Stanley Baldwin has given a subsidy of twenty-four million pounds to offset the owners' wage cuts. But that's just going to last until the first of May 1926, which is only a few months away. Then what? They'll just be back where they started. And do you know what they're up to now?'

'Who?'

'Winston Churchill said they were just averting the crisis so that they could cope with it effectually when the time came, and that's exactly what they are doing. They're preparing, Rory. Now there's the OMS — the Organization for the Maintenance of Supplies. This is made up of people who would be prepared to volunteer to maintain supplies and vital services in the event of a general strike.'

'Surely there's no danger of a *general* strike?' Rory protested.

'That's what the triple industrial alliance is all about.

We'll come out in sympathy with the miners, and that's as it should be. But what infuriates me and what I think is dangerous to all the Unions, Rory, is the way Forbes-Cunningham and his crowd are organizing week-end courses to train people to drive railway engines and motor vehicles and other skills. No strike can succeed if other labour is used to replace the labour that has been withheld.'

All she was thinking about now as far as a potential strike was concerned was how it might affect her business. She glanced round at his thick shock of raven-black hair, his wild angry eyes. Let him worry about the whole human race if he liked; she had enough to do, worrying about herself.

She tossed her cigarette on to the path and ground it out with her heel. 'I'll have to go,' she announced, rising.

He rose too. 'I'll escort you home.'

'No. We've both a lot to think about. And thinking's better done alone.'

He looked so disappointed however, that she impulsively brushed his cheek with a kiss before walking away.

CHAPTER FIFTY-ONE

Rory wore a sleeveless evening dress of *chine d'or*, gold-embroidered, with a scooped-out neckline and an uneven hemline that hung in points below knee level. Round her neck glistened a gold and green art deco necklace. She was brushing her short hair into a side parting and taming it into soft, glossy waves in front of the sitting-room mirror.

'This must be him coming!' Scrap cried in excitement as he peered down from the sitting-room window, his cap squashing against the glass. 'My God, what a car! It's big enough to do a flitting. Ask him in when he comes up, hen.'

'He's not coming up. I'm going down.'

'Where's your manners?' Scrap protested. 'Ask the man in for a wee dram.'

'So's you can pick his pocket?' Rory replied. 'Not likely.'

'Do you hear that, Annie?' Scrap shouted in shocked indignation as if he had just arrived home from Holy Communion instead of Barlinnie prison. 'Do you hear what she said there?'

'She threw my good shawl in the bin,' Annie accused.

Rory groaned. 'Ma, will you never forget about that bloody shawl? I bought you a coat and hat instead, didn't I?'

'I had that good shawl for years. I carried all my weans in it.'

'A bloody disgrace,' Scrap sympathized and Henry, the dog, sensing the tragedy of the occasion, began to yelp and howl.

'Where will all this end?' Annie said, as if the new garments were yet another sign of approaching doom.

343

'Oh, shut up, Henry,' Rory said. 'Da, you'll have to do something about that dog.'

'There's nothing wrong with Henry.' Her Da sounded mortally aggrieved. 'There's nothing needs doing to him. You leave Henry alone.'

'He's too fat, too smelly and too old. He stinks the whole house. He needs to be put down.'

'*Put down!*' Scrap and Annie shouted in unison and Annie added, 'Is that not fuckin' terrible?'

'Hard-faced bitch!' Scrap said. He was flame-coloured with indignation. 'You'll be saying the same about me next.'

'Well . . .' Rory began in a contemplative tone, then burst out laughing. 'At least you're not fat, Da!'

'You watch that tongue to your Da,' Annie warned and then took such a bout of coughing she had to go and clutch herself down on to a chair.

'Are you all right, Ma?' Rory asked anxiously.

Annie hawked, spat into a piece a rag, then folded it and tucked it into the pocket of her apron. 'As right as I'll ever be!'

'Are you getting out for a walk in the park every day like I told you? The fresh air up here ought to be doing you good.'

'I try to get down to see Mrs Gilhooly and my other neighbours every day, but coming back up that hill's a killer.'

Rory sighed. 'Ma, why don't you make friends with the neighbours here? They're all very nice people, as far as I can see.'

It was Annie's turn to sigh. 'It's not the same. I'm used to my Cowlairs Road pals. Like I'm used to the Co-op. I've been a member of that Co-op in Cowlairs Road for a lifetime.'

'Och, Ma . . .'

'You can "Och Ma" me as often as you like. You can't teach an old dog new tricks and there's an end to it.'

A horn hooted impatiently outside. 'I've got to go.' Rory grabbed her coat and purse. The coat was black, hung in

344

loose straight lines and fastened with one large gold button over her left hip. Her purse had a gold chain. 'Cheerio!' she flung at Scrap and Annie over her shoulder.

Her escort for the evening at the Trades Hall dinner-dance was a Mr Duncan Wardrop, a bewhiskered gentleman of portly stature old enough to be her father. So great was his bulk, in fact, that she would not have had enough room beside him on the car seat had she not been so slim. He tapped his cane on the shoulder of his chauffeur and the car purred forward. A pleasant kindly man, Mr Wardrop enjoyed a social evening but didn't like to be the odd man out without a partner. This had happened to him on a few occasions since becoming a widower and it made him feel lonely. Even worse, sometimes his hosts invited another woman to partner him and she invariably turned out to be either a man-hunter bent on marriage, a crashing bore or both. He had confided this problem to Rory and when he subsequently invited her to partner him to the dinner-dance, she thought it good business to accept.

Her Da was not the only one impressed by Mr Wardrop's silver Rolls-Royce. Rory immediately saw it, felt it, savoured it as solid and unmistakable proof of success. Leaning back against the cushions, revelling in the luxury of them and the smell of expensive leather, she announced enthusiastically, 'Oh yes, this is for me! A car is definitely going to be my next purchase.'

'A Rolls?' Mr Wardrop laughed. 'My dear, you obviously don't know anything about either the purchase price or the running costs. It took me a lifetime to be able to afford this. Don't forget you'd need a chauffeur as well.'

'Well, perhaps not a Rolls to start with,' she conceded, 'but definitely a smart car.'

'Even so, the running costs would still . . .'

'To hell with a chauffeur! I'd want to be in charge. I'd want the thrill of handling it myself.'

Mr Wardrops's blank expression betrayed the fact that he didn't know what to make of this. 'But you're a woman!'

345

'So?'

'You know what I mean.'

'You mean that women are supposed to revert to the inferior position they had before the war, Mr Wardrop? Well, not this woman!'

'But . . .'

'Women drove tram-cars and buses and God-knows-all-what during the war. They proved once and for all that they can do anything men can do.'

Mr Wardrop's portly body began to heave with laughter and he shook his head as if enjoying a private joke.

'Damn it, they can!' Rory insisted. 'I'll get a car and I'll drive it myself, you'll see!'

Before they reached their destination, she had already purchased an automobile in her mind and ordered Joe to teach her to drive it. The sight of a woman at the wheel of a car in the streets of Glasgow would not just raise eyebrows but drop mouths open. She was really looking forward to the experience.

The Trades House was in Glassford Street, just across the other side of Argyle Street from Stockwell Street and her shop. She caught a glimpse of her imposing establishment before the Rolls swung into Glassford Street and the sight of it gave her a beautiful relaxed, safe feeling. Gone were the tense nightmare times in Cowlairs Road, when she had suffered not only poverty but physical violence. She was safe now. Safe even from the dangers of her own passions. This realization had come to her after being alone in Matthew's company a couple of times recently. Years ago, when she had first met him at the railway dance, she had felt sorry for him. After the pity had come the passion. Now there was only the pity again. Perhaps love too, but of a different and more tender kind.

The silver limousine glided to a halt at the Trades House in front of the cast-iron canopy with its lamps and four ornate columns which protruded over the central doorway and pavement. The chauffeur dashed round to assist both her and Mr Wardrop from the deep cushions of the car.

Rory swept into the building with her usual panache and cheeky tilt to the head, but was secretly impressed by the building's interior all the same. The entrance hall was of considerable length, with a marble floor and beautiful Adams ceiling in delicate pastel shades. Smiling and chatting to her escort as they ascended the main staircase that led to the banqueting hall, her eyes missed nothing — the portraits, the stained-glass windows depicting the coats of arms of the House and Crafts, the marble busts, the ornate doorway leading into the hall. It took all Rory's quick wits to prevent her from gasping out loud when they entered the hall itself. It could only be described as splendid; she had never seen anything so splendid in her life. She stared around at the sparkling gasoliers and equally radiant tables at which rainbow-clad and bejewelled ladies were comfortably seating themselves. She forced her eyes to photograph the scene and imprint it on the film of her mind, so that later she could give Victoria an accurate picture of the domed ceiling, the Spanish mahogany panelling and above the panelling the frieze on silk showing the crafts at work.

Still smiling and talking to her partner, she settled herself beside him in the places allotted to them and prepared to enjoy to the best of her ability the meal and later the dance.

Soon with the clatter of cutlery and voices, she was hard put to it to hear what Mr Wardrop was saying. It was not until she caught one familiar word that all the rest of the clattering, chattering noise seemed to recede into the distance.

'Who did you say?' she asked.

'Donovan, isn't it? The chap who's always having a dig at you. Very amusing with it though, don't you think?'

'Oh, hilarious!' She lit a cigarette with style and flung a puff of smoke skywards. 'Why do you mention Donovan?'

'That's him over there, isn't it? At the press table?'

'Press table?'

347

'Yes, there's always a table reserved for newspapermen at these functions. Over there, see?'

'Don't point, for God's sake! He's looking over and I don't want him to think I'm interested.'

Mr Wardrop's eyes twinkled. 'I see.'

'Because I'm *not*,' she said angrily.

It was maddening how the serene enjoyment of the occasion had suddenly evaporated. She felt agitated from the moment she was caught in Donovan's unwavering stare. Determined not to allow him to 'get at her' either in print or in person, after the meal she flung herself heart and soul into the spirit of the dance. With great verve she performed a side-kicking 'Charleston' and then 'The Black Bottom', a lively mixture of side turns, stamps, skating glides, skips and leaps. As it turned out, despite his bulk, Mr Wardrop was surprisingly light on his feet and a very good dancer. Soon she was flushed and laughing and whirling around with him and a merry confusion of other partners in a 'Paul Jones.'

Then, still laughing and out of breath, she found herself in Donovan's arms and her hilarity immediately died. Within seconds a weak, heart-pattering apprehension had taken its place. Then other nuances of emotion came to torment her caused by the hardness of his arm muscle against her fingers, his big fist enveloping her other hand, his arm like an iron band encircling her, the heat of his body brushing against her own. No one else in the room existed; even the music completely disappeared. The nuances were losing their painful delicacy — they were gathering strength like a storm when suddenly all was breathless confusion again and she was snatched and jostled away from him in the wild communal part of the dance.

Rory laughed with the others and was as gay and abandoned in her enjoyment as she had been before. But inside, her stomach was tightening with the realization that she was not safe after all.

CHAPTER FIFTY-TWO

'Don't pay any attention to him, I said,' Joe bawled at Rory in exasperation. 'Do you want to get us bloody killed?'

Rory was at the wheel of her newly acquired white Rover coupé. Joe was sitting by her side and had been for the past two hair-raising hours of jerking starts and stops, of mounting corners of pavements, of wild swerves to miss tram-cars by inches. Now, just when things were beginning to go more smoothly, Rory had seen Donovan's car draw alongside her.

'I'd give up if I were you!' Donovan shouted across to Joe. 'While you're still all in one piece!'

'Mind your own bloody business!' Joe bawled back. 'Rory, what the hell do you think you're doing now? This isn't a race-track! Rory, have you gone bloody mad? Take your foot off that pedal. Rory, for God's sake!'

The car was careering along Springburn Road like an aeroplane with a drunken pilot. It belted up the Balgray as if at any minute about to become airborne, swooped round into Broomfield Road and stopped with such a jerk at their close that both Rory and Joe were flung forward and banged their heads on the windscreen.

'You bloody maniac!' Joe howled as if about to burst into tears. 'From now on, you're on your own. That's the last lesson you're going to get from me.'

'I don't need any more,' Rory managed breathlessly, at the same time trying to straighten her hat. 'I know how to do it now.'

'Don't think he'll be impressed,' Joe sneered as they both walked rather unsteadily into the close and up the stairs.

349

'Who?'

'You know who. Either it will just have given him and that floozy he was with a good laugh. Or, more likely, it'll have given him something else to write about.'

'I don't care.'

'Well, you should bloody care. Why keep giving him ammunition to shoot at you? If you're not more careful, one of these days he'll bring you down.'

'Huh!' She gave a derisive laugh. 'Just let him try.'

'He *is* bloody trying!'

'Well, he's not going to succeed.'

Rory allowed Joe to use his key in case her own hand might betray a tremble. She could still see in her mind's eye Donovan's broad-shouldered figure, one hand resting easily on the steering wheel, the elbow of his other arm relaxing on the car's open window as he called across to Joe. Joe had used the right word to describe the woman Donovan was with: a floozy she certainly looked.

'Did you ever see such bleached hair?' She found herself giving voice to her thoughts. 'And so much flashy jewellery? She must have been jangling at least half-a-dozen bangles. Trust a man like Donovan to go for somebody like that.'

'Aw, shut up!' said Joe, entering the lobby and, hearing him, Annie called, 'Was it awful bad, son?'

'Diabolical, Ma! I've told her she's had all the driving instruction she's going to get from me.'

'Quite right, son. Come on through and have a wee nip out of my bottle. It'll steady your nerves.'

In the living-room Rory tossed her hat and coat on to the settee. The settee was part of a new three-piece-suite in bottle-green moquette that matched the new green velvet curtains.

'I don't know what all the fuss is about.' She went over and switched on the wireless, while Joe knocked back a large whisky. In between nonchalantly singing to the music — 'Toot, toot, tootsie, goodbye . . .' — she said, 'Anyway, I thought Joe wasn't supposed to have a nerve in his body.'

350

Joe's stocky body was still rigid with tension and she would have laughed at the state he was in had it not been for the state she was in herself.

'Selfish madam,' Annie said. 'You've never cared a damn about anybody but yourself.'

Rory lit up a cigarette. 'And just look where it's got me, Ma. What's for tea? I'm starving!'

Annie addressed Joe, 'It's no use talking to her. Are you all right now, son?'

Joe flexed his shoulders. 'I'm fine. Don't worry, Ma.'

'Right. I'll dish you a nice plate of broth. Do you want some as well, hen?'

'Fine, Ma!' Rory said, then continued with her cheery song. Later she would play some of her gramophone records and probably have a dance to herself. She was very fond of dancing. It not only gave expression and release to her store of lively energy, but also helped to divert her attention from any subject she did not want to dwell on . . . like Donovan. He was beginning to unnerve her. It wasn't his writing, she could cope with that. It was him — his aggressive self-confidence, his mocking eyes, his steely persistence. Not that she had any intention of giving in to her secret fears. She'd be damned if she would allow Donovan to get the better of her!

Amelia said, 'Darling, you haven't shown me yet where you were born and brought up.'

Donovan's fingers drummed impatiently on the steering wheel. 'The Gorbals isn't the most picturesque part of Glasgow.'

'Is it far from here?'

'No.'

'Then, why not? Darling, please.' Amelia smoothed her palm over Donovan's thigh.

'Naughty,' he said.

She purred close to him like a friendly cat. 'But nice!'

'All right. But after the Gorbals I'll have to dump you, sweetheart. I've work to do — and so have you.'

351

'Will you call for me after the show?'

'No.'

'You are a beast.'

'Terrible, isn't it?'

'But I adore you.'

He made no comment and she added, 'And I want to know everything about you. Absolutely everything! You've never told me anything about your family background. About your mother, for instance?'

'She's dead.'

'You have mentioned that, darling. I meant, what was she like?'

'Strong, determined, ambitious. Much more so than my father.'

'Did you get on well with her?'

'Yes.'

'And your father?'

'Yes.'

'You're still staying in his house, aren't you?'

'Yes, in Pollokshields.'

'My God!' Amelia's gaze was suddenly caught by the gloomy narrow streets into which the car was being swallowed. 'Look at all those horrible black buildings!'

'Tenements.'

'And those rough-looking people. I don't like it here, Donovan.'

'I didn't think you would.'

'This isn't . . . Donovan, this couldn't be where you came from?'

'Shocked, are you?'

She shivered. 'How could you have survived such a place?'

He grinned and brandished a clenched fist. 'This helped.'

'I don't know why you came back here.' Amelia hugged her fur around her.

'I've no nostalgic feelings about the place. They could knock it down tomorrow as far as I'm concerned. A trip into the past was your idea.'

'No, I meant Glasgow.'

'I had my reasons.'

Amelia shivered again. 'Take me back to my hotel, darling.'

'Don't worry, sweetheart,' Donovan said. 'We're on our way.'

CHAPTER FIFTY-THREE

'No wages?' Victoria echoed. 'But I need money to buy food. Strike or no strike, Jamie can't suffer.'

'I warned you weeks ago that this would happen. I told you we must save something in preparation. Instead you purchased a bed for Jamie on the instalment plan.'

'You bought a wireless — an unnecessary luxury.'

'That was months ago and it was for all of us.'

'What a wicked lie!' Victoria exclaimed. 'Nobody dare touch the thing when you're in.'

'You were allowing Jamie to play with the dials and try to poke things through the mesh at the front. He cannot be allowed to destroy property. He has to be told — for his own good.'

'A lot you care about his good. Now you're denying us money for the barest essentials of life and trying to make out it's my fault. What have you saved "in preparation" as you call it?'

'How can I save,' his voice rose in exasperation, 'when you keep burdening me with debt? Every penny I'm left with after I give you your money goes on paying up instalments. I've to work bloody overtime to pay the rent and rates and gas.'

'Don't you dare swear at me!' Victoria said coldly. 'You enjoy the comfort of anything I've ever bought for this house. As for things I've bought for Jamie, he's your child as well as mine, don't forget. You'd have a lot more reason to complain if I never bothered to get him anything, if I neglected him — if instead of cots and carpets, I bought furs and fripperies for myself.'

'Well, I'm on strike and there's no wages whether you like it or not!' And with that he stormed from the house.

Jamie was at his grandma's. Once a week her mother collected him so as to let Victoria get on with her washing and ironing. Then later she went to her mother's for high tea and to bring Jamie back home. Now she felt too worried to start ironing and instead began pacing about the small kitchen, kneading her hands together.

There was a strange silence outside and once she became aware of it she went over to stare down at the street below. Springburn Road, normally busy at this time of day, was empty of traffic. Not one tram-car or motor vehicle could be seen; it was as if 1926 was the last year of the world. Suddenly experiencing a frightening aloneness, she rushed to throw on her hat and coat and hurry from the house. Never before had she been so glad that she lived barely more than a hundred yards from her mother's close, so urgently did she need the older woman's calm and comforting presence.

'Oh, there you are, dear,' her mother greeted her. 'You're early.'

Jamie was sitting by the fire enjoying his customary treat of a biscuit from his granny's biscuit barrel.

'Hello, mummy,' he said. 'I had a fight with a big lion in Granny's back green and I punched its nose and it ran away.'

Victoria worriedly bit her lip. She wasn't too sure how to deal with Jamie's vivid imagination.

Her mother smiled. 'You were the very same yourself, Victoria. You were always telling stories of daring deeds.'

'You think I shouldn't try to stop him, then?'

'Don't worry about it. He's still just a baby.'

'I can't help worrying, mother. I hardly know what to do. How can I feed Jamie without any wages coming in?'

Mrs Buchanan sighed. 'The strike?'

'Yes. Will it affect father and the boys?'

Her mother nodded and picked up her knitting. 'It won't be the first time I've had to manage without and no doubt it won't be the last. You'll just have to learn to manage too, Victoria.'

'But how?'

'Have you not a copper or two put by?'

'Everything I've had has gone on Jamie. I've denied him nothing; he doesn't know what it is to do without.'

'Maybe it's time he learned, dear. Belonging to working folk means you've got to learn what life's all about. And it's mostly about hardship, I've found. Your father's had a lot of idle time in the past — through no fault of his own — and it hasn't been easy.'

Victoria was amazed at this revelation. She had no memories of suffering any hardship as a child, or being in the slightest degree aware — even as a young married woman — of her parents suffering.

But now she came to think of it, her father and indeed her brothers had all had periods when they were not earning. How on earth had her mother managed?

'Oh well,' she said, struggling to be brave, 'no doubt I'll manage somehow.'

'No doubt you will, dear. You're a good girl and I know you'll ask for God's help in your prayers tonight.' Her plump face creased with anxiety. 'You do still say your prayers every night, I hope?'

'Of course!' Victoria lied. She did try to remember her prayers, but often her mind was in such a turmoil of anger or resentment against Matthew that she forgot.

They had their usual high tea. Mrs Buchanan dished up ham and egg for her husband, Sam and Willie — Dave and Tommy having long since left to be married and set up house on their own — then she mashed boiled eggs with a little margarine for Jamie. But nothing for herself.

'Mother, aren't you having any?' Victoria asked.

'No dear, fries tend to give me indigestion.'

'A boiled egg, then?'

'No, one of my nice home-baked scones will do me fine.'

Later, when she was leaving, her mother drew her aside

and asked quietly, 'Have you anything in for your man's tea tonight, dear?'

Victoria felt defensive. Flushing, she said, 'I won't let him starve, don't worry.'

'I just thought two or three eggs might come in handy — just to tide you over, dear. Your father's friend Angus, him that works at a farm up by Balornock, brought us a dozen. You can work miracles with eggs if you put your mind to it, I always say.'

At first Victoria's pride nearly made her refuse, but just in time she remembered another saying of her mother's: 'Desperate straits need desperate measures.' 'I think I've a recipe somewhere for an egg and potato pie,' she said.

Her mother patted her arm. 'That's a good girl. Haste ye back now.'

The egg and potato pie turned out to be tasty and, what was equally if not more important, very filling. But now that the eggs and potatoes were used up, what then? Victoria examined the shelves in the kitchen cupboard. There was some custard powder, semolina, sugar, tea, a pot of her mother's home-made jam, oatmeal, salt, gravy browning, a few slices of bread, a little butter and a bag of flour . . . but no meat or vegetables and only one apple in the fruit bowl on the sideboard.

Of course, she had her store book. But she was already deeply in debt to the Co-op for the room carpet, to mention but only one item, and by rights no more credit would be allowed. She couldn't bear the thought of going to the grocery, begging for credit and being shamed by a refusal. Yet something would have to be done; she had only a few shillings in her purse. The milk was delivered by the Co-op — if she didn't pay her milk bill this week, would they stop sending it? Perhaps not right away, she thought.

She felt sick with worry and developed a headache with her thoughts jumbling round and round in mounting uncertainty. The milk came next day and they all had their usual breakfast of porridge. She bought some cheap mince and a few potatoes with the last of her money, and made a shepherd's pie and a custard pudding for the midday meal. In the evening they had bread and jam. The next day they could have the last of the oatmeal for breakfast. It seemed incredible that there would be nothing for dinner or tea except some custard or semolina pudding — perhaps not even that if the milk was stopped. Then there would soon be the even more awful business of no soap.

To add to her distress, she could see from her window that the OMS or volunteer strike breakers were beginning to man the trams and omnibuses, and angry strikers were surging about the streets hurling stones and breaking drivers' windows and anything else that could be smashed.

Strike breakers — who seemed in the main to be University students enjoying what they called 'a bit of a jape' — were also manning the railways. Already there had been several fatal accidents as a result. Trains and other vehicles had crashed and one man, acting as a passenger guard on an electric railway, had stepped on a live rail and been instantly killed.

The sound of tinkling glass and the threat of violence haunted Victoria's waking hours. At night she lay in a state of acute anxiety worrying about how to get something for her family to eat. Eventually she remembered that one of the railwaymen who had come to see Matthew on Union business had a plot; he had boasted about the vegetables he grew there. She didn't take time to argue with Matthew and make him go and ask the man for something, and anyway she had no faith in his ability to be tactful. Even if she succeeded in forcing him, at best he'd go with a scowl on his face. So she took Jamie and went straight to the plot, knowing that the man was also on strike and the chances were he would be tending his precious piece of ground and the food it could produce. Swallowing her pride and yet keeping her head held high, she had stopped to speak to him, admired his potatoes and carrots and leeks, tactfully reminded him how good Matthew had been to him in his hour of need, even spoke about the cup of tea and home-made baked scones she had given him.

'And welcome to them, Mr McGilvery,' she said with a smile. 'My husband and I are always ready to help anyone in need when we can.'

Then she stood with the smile still clinging resolutely to her face, not saying anything but just gazing at Mr McGilvery's vegetables. Jamie stood silently staring at the vegetables too, until at last the man was shamed into offering her a basketful although he had little enough left with which to feed his own large family.

Later, after Matthew and Jamie had enjoyed bowls of the vegetable soup she made, she told Matthew how she had got the vegetables. His face immediately darkened. 'I wish you'd just mind your own business.'

She laughed. At that moment nothing could lessen her feelings of pride and triumph at having succeeded in producing a meal. 'Don't be daft. It is my business to feed you and Jamie.'

'You took unfair advantage of McGilvery's Union business with me.'

'You enjoyed the soup, didn't you?'

'That's not the point at issue.'

'Och, you're not at a Union meeting now, Matthew. You and Jamie have got to be fed and I'll find a way, any way, to feed you. And that's that.'

She sailed away through to the scullery to wash the dishes and to ponder on how useless men were in a crisis.

CHAPTER FIFTY-FOUR

'I deeply regret,' Forbes-Cunningham said, 'the state taking over what has always been a Christian duty. State-provided welfare services undermine the characteristics of independence and hard work.'

'That may be your opinion, sir. It is not mine. The subject under discussion is Barnhill poorhouse and if anything is destined to undermine independence and the ability to work hard, it is the conditions in that place.'

'Nonsense, Drummond,' Bell, the banker, intervened. 'The paupers are well-housed and fed. They should think themselves lucky.'

'Well-housed?' Drummond raised a brow. 'Mr Bell, have you ever seen the outside of Barnhill? It looks more like a prison than Barlinnie. What is the point in the first place of having it surrounded by such a high, grim-looking wall? It has prison appearance enough with a water tower at the corner of each courtyard. It's common knowledge that the poorhouse is nicknamed "the Bastille"!'

'There's lunatics in there,' protested Bell, 'and vagrants and all sorts of riff-raff. The people who live nearby need to feel safe in their beds at night.'

'My concern at the moment is with the welfare and safety of the inmates of Barnhill, the vast majority of whom are decent, respectable people.'

'Decent, respectable people?' Forbes-Cunningham scoffed. 'Really, Drummond!'

'Let us take examples!' Drummond opened the file of papers in front of him. 'Here is a man and wife and four children. He's a carter by trade and he's had to accept admission to Barnhill following the death of his father and the ending of the family business in which he was employed. He tried but could find no other work. I saw him the other day, gentlemen — a broken man, in poor-house black moleskin suit, shuffling round the men's courtyard. In the separate courtyard for women, his wife was engaged in the same hopeless exercise. There are four identical courtyards: one for men, one for women, one for boys and one for girls. Inmates are confined to their own and are recognized by the colour of the tartan scarves they wear, which are different for each courtyard. But the couple's children are not just separated from them by the central corridor running the full length of the building. Their children have been boarded out many miles away.'

Forbes-Cunningham's portly body moved restlessly in his chair. 'He's a burden on this parish. He's an able-bodied man. If he had any gumption and if he wanted to, he'd have found work all right. There are far too many lay-abouts and scroungers these days. If I had my way, I'd do what they used to do back in the eighteenth century — just move 'em on, get rid of them.'

'I believe you Mr Forbes-Cunningham. We are, however, living in the twentieth century and we must deal with the running of Barnhill and the welfare of its inmates in a civilized manner and to the best of our ability.'

Just then one of the clerks entered and said in an agitated tone, 'Excuse me, sir. It's . . . I don't know how to . . . I'm very sorry it befalls me to . . .'

'For goodness sake, man,' Forbes-Cunningham burst out irritably, 'what is it? Say what you've come to say and get out. Can't you see we're having an important committee meeting?'

The clerk was wringing his hands now, so wretched was his agitation. 'It's your son, Mr Forbes-Cunningham. There's been an accident.'

The older man rose so suddenly that his chair fell back with a noise like an exploding gun. 'Where? What's happened?'

'Down Springburn Road, just at the corner of Vulcan Street. A car was coming out and hit his bike.'

'My God! Which hospital is he in?'

'I'm afraid it's too late for hospital, sir.'

But Forbes-Cunningham had already pushed the clerk aside and was striding from the room. The clerk sadly shook his head at Drummond and the remaining members of the committee before withdrawing and closing the door.

'Edgar killed!' Bell said under his breath. 'Forbes-Cunningham will never get over this. He lived for that boy, so did his wife. It'll kill her, mark my words.'

'I think it's appropriate in the circumstances to call the meeting to a close,' Drummond suggested.

He was as shaken as the rest by the unexpected tragedy. Death, especially violent death, was something he never took lightly, even when it happened to an enemy. It stirred up all the horror, the debasement of human dignity which death had meant in the trenches. Although the trenches had nothing to do with Edgar, Drummond would think of little else all day.

'Edgar Forbes-Cunningham killed?' Victoria was shocked when he told her the news. 'You'll be writing a letter of condolence to his father, of course?'

He stared at her in astonishment. 'Write to Forbes-Cunningham? Me?'

'It's the Christian thing to do, Matthew.'

'All my life I've hated the man's guts. I've hated everything he's stood for. If I write to him now as a friend, it would be sheer hypocrisy. I'm not a friend of his, nor is he a friend of mine.'

'He's a fellow human being and he's lost a son.'

'Victoria, he's the man who with the help of a titled Tory MP friend organized volunteers from England to come and "have a crack at those dirty Bolshies on the Clyde", to quote their favourite Tory paper. He meant men like your father and your brothers and your husband, Victoria. You talk about sons? Forbes-Cunningham's the man who sent

362

hundreds of mothers' sons to the trenches to rot. I heard him with my own ears say they died content; I can still hear the smug, self-satisfied way he said it. And how many sons do you think have died down his mines. Do you think he wrote to any of *their* fathers expressing sympathy?'

He had developed a blinding headache and a tightness in his chest with his struggle to prevent a build-up of emotion bursting out in red-hot rage.

Victoria tutted impatiently. 'He didn't send anybody to the trenches and you know it! He took the attitude that it was a glorious privilege to go and fight for King and Country; lots of people thought like that at the time. As for sending letters of sympathy to his employees — what employer does that? He didn't know any of them personally. But you know him personally and that's the difference. You're a colleague, a fellow Councillor, Matthew; you sit beside him round a table. You must write to him — it's the only decent thing to do.'

'Oh be quiet, woman!' he said. 'You don't know what you're talking about.'

'I will not be quiet. I do know what I'm talking about. And I'll tell you another thing — if you don't write, I will!'

His eyes flashed murder at her. 'Don't you dare,' he said quietly. 'Don't you dare interfere in Council business.'

'Don't *you* speak to me like that, or look at me like that.'

'You will not write to Councillor Forbes-Cunningham, Victoria. I forbid it.'

'Huh!' Victoria laughed and he had never been nearer to felling her with one violent blow. 'These aren't Victorian times, Matthew. You can't forbid me to do anything, I do what I like.'

He tried another tack. 'You talk about decency, Victoria. It is my opinion that the real motivation for you writing to Councillor Forbes-Cunningham goes beyond the bounds of decency.'

She was nonplussed for a second, then she said, 'What nonsense are you talking now?'

'You're a snob, Victoria. You'd do anything, take any opportunity to curry favour . . .'

Immediately she slapped his face. Her brown eyes were wide with distress and her skin had gone an unhealthy grey. 'That's a wicked lie! You're a wicked, evil man. You'd do anything to upset me and get me down. Well, you won't! God won't let you. God will protect me against you.'

'I'm sorry.' Drummond knew he had gone too far. Victoria never curried favours and his statement had been inaccurate. 'Darling, I didn't mean it. I've had a hellish day.'

'You've had a bad day!' she exclaimed. 'Oh, is that your excuse now? Well, I have bad days, plenty of them, but I don't take it out on you. I don't insult you . . .'

'I know, I know. I'm sorry.'

There was no use reaching out for her in an effort to make up — he knew that from plenty of previous experience. Once Victoria froze, only time and the requirements of normal everyday living — especially socializing with other people — could go any way towards unfreezing her. So he didn't even bother to tell her that an official letter of condolence had gone from the Parish Council, to which he had added his name.

Nothing he could do or say would narrow the cold distance between them, especially in bed. Lying in bed beside Victoria had become a torment. He longed with all the fire in him to make love to her, but each time he tried to caress her, the atmosphere changed. She stiffened. She complained about pains in her stomach, her prolapse, her weak back — anything and everything to keep him away from her.

He wanted to plead with her not to shut him out from her love. He knew in his heart, however, that no words of his, nothing he could do, could reach her.

Yet still he felt caught like a shipwrecked sailor mesmerized by the Lorelei.

CHAPTER FIFTY-FIVE

'A good idea,' Annie said. 'It's time you did something natural like other girls. Go to the dancing. I just hope to God you'll meet some fella that'll take you off our hands!'

'Married, you mean?' Rory raised a sarcastic brow. 'Why should I want to get married? I'm managing my life very well on my own, thank you very much. What could any man give me that I haven't got already?'

'Do you really want me to tell you, hen?'

Rory couldn't contain a peal of laughter. 'You're behind the times, Ma. You don't have to get married for that.'

'You're a disgrace, so you are,' Annie gasped. 'I blame you for our Alice having to get married.'

'Ma! How could I have anything to do with our Alice getting pregnant?'

'You and your flashy ideas! You've always been a bad influence on these girls.'

Rory rolled her eyes. 'God!'

'Away you go if you're going,' Annie said.

It was the first time Rory had gone to 'the dancing'. Previously she had attended or been invited to organized dances, railway dances, socials in the church hall, tennis club dances and dinner-dances like the one in the Trades House. 'The dancing' was an every-night-of-the-week activity, where you paid your money and took the floor with your partner — usually your girlfriend — or stood at the side and waited for a man to stroll over and ask, 'Are you dancing?' or maybe just give a perfunctory jerk of his head in the direction to the dancing area. Rory was no sooner in the hall when she regretted her impulsive decision to come. In the first place, she didn't see anyone she fancied. The dance-hall, despite being vibrant with music and movement, had a hollow, lonely feel to it. She wished she was in her shop; it was the only place where she really felt she belonged. There she could be herself, experience a sense of achievement and feel stimulated and 'challenged'. There was no stimulation, no challenge here and she simply wasn't interested. She was turning away with the intention of going back to the ladies' room to collect her coat when a hand gripped her elbow and steered her firmly towards the floor.

'What are you doing here?' Seeing it was Donovan, she tried to shake her arm free but without success.

He shrugged as he manoeuvred her among the dancers and then held her in such a steely grip that her feet were forced to follow his to the rhythm of the slow foxtrot.

'The same as you, I suppose,' he said. 'Sampling Glasgow's nightlife. Except that I'm never really off-duty and I'll probably end up writing a piece about it.'

'I thought you only wrote about me.'

'You flatter yourself, sweetheart.'

'So it's just coincidence you're here, in the same place and on the same night as I am?'

'You sound suspicious.'

'I am.'

'Come now, this is *the* dance hall and it's Saturday night. We're in little old Glasgow, not London. Relax.'

But Rory could not relax. Had he been in the shop talking to any of the female assistants? She had mentioned that she had taken a notion to go to 'the dancing'. Yet why should she worry? What did it matter if he hated her and planned to carry out a vendetta against her? Words couldn't hurt her; she didn't care what he wrote. However, she did care about how he was holding her and the havoc that the closeness of his body was wreaking on her senses.

As they were swallowed in amongst the dancers and the music had turned sweetly hypnotic, Rory began to feel drunk. To the melody of 'Moonlight and Roses' her mind reeled, her legs melted. She even staggered a little when the dance finished and he released his hold on her. Furious with herself, she struggled to gather enough wits together to take a dignified and scornful leave of him, but immediately the band started up again he caught hold of her.

'Do you always use bullying tactics like this with women?' she asked. 'Or is it just reserved for women you hate?' He made no reply and she added, 'I don't want to dance with you.'

The glimmering, mocking eyes stared down into hers. 'Don't you?'

'Even if you hadn't been rude to me on previous occasions and insulted me in one way or another in the past, I would still have said "No" if you'd had the politeness to ask me.'

Again he made no comment and again she became aware of his powerful sexuality. She couldn't understand it. It was not as if he was the type who had ever attracted her before. She had never really liked heavily-built men; right from the moment in her early teens when she first became aware of the male sex, she had admired slim, sensitive, artistic fellows like Matthew. When she had danced with Matthew she had been aware of the long bones of his legs brushing against hers. His legs had an almost delicate leanness but Donovan's thighs were all hard fleshy muscle, big hams that even the loose cut of his trousers could not disguise.

'How about a truce?' he said suddenly. 'At least for a few hours.'

'Why?'

'You *are* a suspicious type!'

'I've good reason to be suspicious of you.'

'You're the best-looking girl in the hall. And you're a good dancer.'

'Flattery will get you nowhere.'

'I don't flatter women. If you think I'm that type, you're not as astute as I thought you were.'

'All right, I believe you.'

367

'And we've both paid good money to come here and enjoy an evening's relaxation. So relax!'

She didn't trust Donovan. She didn't trust her own feelings and the physical longings he was awakening in her. Yet why should this be an anxiety? The physical longings indicated that she wanted sex. She had become hardened to taking what she wanted out of life and enjoying the taking, so why shouldn't she just enjoy what Donovan could give? To hell! In this day and age a woman didn't need to like everything about a man to enjoy sex with him. Sex was chemistry and her chemistry and Donovan's were an explosive mixture. Thinking of sex with Donovan began to take the form of an exciting challenge and she even toyed with the pleasurable prospect of reducing him to a helpless victim of his own passion; she could remember one occasion when Matthew had wept.

They didn't talk much during the rest of the evening — at least, not with words. But the way she hung round his neck as they moved about the floor, the way she pressed her body into his, the way his hands slid over the satin of her dress, the way his eyes held hers . . . said everything that needed to be said.

'How were you planning to get home?' he asked eventually.

'I have my car.'

'So have I. But I'll leave mine here. Don't worry,' he added, 'I enjoy exercise. There's no problem about walking down the hill and getting a tram-car in Springburn Road.'

She tossed a provocative, impudent look up at him. 'I wasn't worried. But I could go to the shop; I've a room upstairs I keep for staying overnight.'

'Have you got a set of keys with you?'

'Of course.'

'All right, sweetheart, the shop it will be.'

Immediately the unspoken invitation had been given and accepted, her nerve deserted her and she began to quake inside at the mere idea of her own audacity. Only by some miracle did she manage to maintain her jaunty sophisticated appearance. They each took their own car and she could hardly drive hers because she was shaking so much. On arrival at the shop, she had to use all her willpower to regain some remnants of nonchalance and steady herself sufficiently to find the keyhole of the door. The street-lamp gave only a grudging pool of light that did not reach the doorway and so was of little help. Donovan followed her silently through the dark central hall, recently acquired and even in darkness opulent and imposing. Luminous-faced dummies in top hats and tails or full Highland outfits, and stiff wax women in high-collared furs made a ghostly gauntlet. As they went along the back corridor and up the gaslit stairs, she could sense the swagger of Donovan without looking round; he had such an aura of easy self-confidence. She guessed she looked quite jaunty with self-confidence herself; at least she had a stylish appearance in her short dress with its layers of fringes that jerked and wiggled as she walked.

Her room was small and functional with only a single bed, bedside cupboard, wardrobe and chest of drawers. But leading off it was her pride and joy — her own private bathroom.

She fitted a cigarette into her holder and was about to light it when Donovan said, 'Put that away.' She raised a sarcastic brow; she was more used to giving orders now than taking them. He favoured her with a grin that made her conscious of the aggressiveness in his cleft chin. 'It cramps my style,' he told her.

Rory rolled her eyes in scorn at his conceit, but he took the holder from her and put it on the bedside table before drawing her into his arms.

As soon as he kissed her, she knew. It wasn't a case of being terribly sophisticated and modern and using him to get sex just because her body needed it and she wanted it. Enfolded in his arms, melted into his body, feeling the hard contours of it through his clothes, feeling his mouth opening and moving over hers, she knew that she had been fooling herself. She was in love with him;

she had been in love with him all along.

Rory sighed when he released her.

'Why the sigh?' he asked, staring quizzically down at her.

'Life's damnable,' she said. 'You think you've beaten it and suddenly it turns and belts you in the teeth again.' She sat down on the bed and kicked off her shoes. It was too late now to suddenly become virtuous; she was a tramp in his eyes and a tramp she must remain.

He jerked his tie loose and flung his jacket over a chair. 'That's an odd thing to say at a time like this.'

'You don't know me.'

'I know you well enough.'

He sat down beside her and began teasing her with his lips and exploring with his hands until they were lying side by side and she was in a frenzy of need for him to completely possess her. The fact that he seemed so much in control of the situation and of himself was driving her to distraction. No doubt he thought he was considering her needs and giving her time to enjoy the build-up to intercourse — the kisses, the more and more intimate caresses — but she didn't need time. She was ripe and ready and she tried to make him realize this by the hunger in her kisses and the desperation of her hands exploring his body.

'You're a very passionate woman,' he murmured against her ear. Her eager hands found the bulge of his manhood, but he immediately caught her wrist and jerked her hand away.

Incapable now of controlling them, her thoughts burst out in words: 'I want you.'

'I know,' he said in a chillingly calm voice, 'but you've got to learn that you can't get everything you want, honey.'

She could hardly credit it when he rose and shrugged into his jacket. Yet it was only too clear what had happened. This man believed she had ruined his father and eventually been the cause of his death. He had tried to ruin her in his column, but seen that she had beaten him at his

370

own game. She had turned everything to her advantage and gained more strength and more business, not less. He had to find her Achilles heel if he wanted to hurt her . . . and he had. He had said she was a passionate woman. And she was.

All she could hope for now was that he would accept this as revenge enough and leave her alone in future. She gazed at him with dull defeated eyes as he sauntered across the room. He turned and grinned at her and said, 'Sweet dreams,' before shutting the door behind him.

Rory rolled over on to her stomach and buried her face in the pillow. Why was it she always brought out the bastard in men? Bastard! Bastard! She tried to hold herself together with anger. But it was no use; a wave of grief surged towards her and carried her away on a wild sea of tears.

CHAPTER FIFTY-SIX

'Come on, Ma,' Rory pleaded. 'I'll take you down to visit your pals in Cowlairs Road and then call for you again and drive you back up the hill.'

She had become quite professional at driving the Rover, but her mother used every device to avoid putting a foot near the car.

Rory was getting worried about her mother. Annie didn't look well, and could not afford the weight she had lost recently; she complained that her 'bile' had got worse since coming to the new house. She was sure this was something to do with the draughts in the place, with it being so big, and she blamed the bathroom for making her cough worse.

'It's like an iceberg in there when I've to get up in the middle of the night. I was far better off with my pail; it was that nice and cosy in the cupboard in the front room.'

The bedrooms were too cold for her liking as well, and she abhorred the new free-standing bed Rory had bought. 'It used to be that cosy in our wee hole-in-the-wall bed next to the kitchen fire. Now it's like lying in the middle of the fuckin' park.'

Annie had no appreciation for the trees and lush greenery of the park that were framed in her bedroom window. 'I'd far rather see the men crushing along the road on their way to Cowlairs works or to the Calais. You can't even hear the works hooters away up here; I never know what time it is now.'

The new gas cooker was treated like an enemy which she had to defend herself against and the more labour-saving gadgets Rory bought for the house, the more confused and defensive her mother became.

Rory now filled her time when she wasn't working by going to the pictures or visiting Victoria. After her long working days when it was too late to go anywhere, she stayed home and listened to records on her gramophone. She collected records of cheerful, swinging songs like 'California Here I Come', 'Fascinating Rhythm', 'If You Knew Susie', 'Yes Sir, That's my Baby', and 'I'm Sitting on Top of the World'. She couldn't bear to listen to the kind of sad songs that Matthew played on his gramophone. His favourite was 'Greensleeves' and since early in their marriage, according to Victoria, they had romantically danced to this haunting refrain.

Rory couldn't bear anything that stirred up her emotions or made any cracks in her brittle cheerfulness. As usual, her obsessive devotion to her work helped. She had now managed to acquire most of the building in Stockwell Street where the central hall and balcony took pride of place. She still retained her reputation for well-cut clothes and avoided extremes of fashion — though dressing in extremes of fashion herself. She had long since found that in the tailoring side of the business it was most prudent to follow the lead of Savile Row. In Savile Row they were making suits at enormous prices and their customers didn't want these to be out of style next year. It was bad policy to lead fashion, especially in the hire business; it only led to mistakes. Her hire department now stocked a huge variety of items like peers' robes, minks and evening gowns, academic gowns, judges' and other legal robes, hunting coats and grey as well as black top-hats. Her catalogue service was thriving too, especially with customers from Edinburgh and further north.

She was having to employ more and more staff to cope with all the trade. No star in the business firmament in Scotland had risen so fast and so high. When Victoria or anyone else asked her what was her secret — how did she do it — she answered with a laugh and one word: 'Nerve!'

Rory firmly believed that apart from hard work, this was the truth of it. It had certainly taken nerve to open the hall and all the new departments off it, to stock the whole place with every different product she could think of. And let the rest of the shopkeepers in Glasgow be damned!

'Come on, Ma,' she repeated. 'Get your hat and coat on.'

'You'll be the death of me yet,' her mother said. But she went through to the bedroom and re-emerged in a few minutes an awkward unhappy figure in a wide-brimmed black hat from which protruded a giant hatpin with a large pearl on one end. The coat, also black, hung loose and long on her. She had of course refused anything resembling the new shorter lengths and looked as if she had wandered into the coat and under the hat by mistake and now longed to get away from them.

'You look great, Ma' Rory said, linking arms with her. 'All ready to go for a spin.'

'You know fine I'm terrified of that contraption,' Annie protested in exasperation. 'You're nothing but a torment to me, so you are.'

'Just relax and enjoy it,' Rory pleaded.

Annie allowed herself to be led out of the house and down the stairs, but she said as Rory helped her into the car, 'Why don't you buy a fuckin' shop in Australia and give your Da and me a bit of peace?'

Rory laughed, 'You never know your luck, Ma. I might well spread overseas one of these days.'

But for the moment the destination was Cowlairs Road, with Annie gripping the door-handle, poised for flight, and shouting things like, 'Are you trying to get up that police horse's bum?' 'Stop this bloody contraption.' 'I'll walk to Cowlairs Road. You can get arrested or killed or whatever the hell you like!'

'There you are!' Rory said when they reached the close. 'Safe and sound!'

'No thanks to you, m'lady.'

'I'll call back for you in a couple of hours.'

'Don't bother. You're not getting me in that contraption again.'

Laughing and shaking her head, Rory watched the tall figure enter the close and disappear into its shadows. Then she wondered where she should go. She had been in a fever of restlessness since the night at the dancing — fighting a desperate battle with herself not to think of Donovan. She had flung herself into the preparations for the new departments with such desperate energy that even Joe began to get rattled.

'What are you trying to do? What's all the bleedin' rush? Is the bank hounding you for money or something?'

'No, we're dong fine. Better than fine. In fact, Joe, "fine" is a real understatement!'

'You're going off your nut. Has that newspaperman got to you? He's going to have a field day over all this new stuff you're stocking. You do know that, do you? These guys are always looking for something to write about and you keep handing him stuff on a plate.'

'I don't care a damn what he writes.'

'There's a petition going round, by the way.'

'What petition?'

'The other shopkeepers, who do you think? Did you imagine Meikle's of Argyle Street for instance, *the* tea specialists,' he mimicked, 'were going to take the idea of you stocking tea without some sort of protest?'

She grinned and lit up a cigarette. 'And stocking it *cheaper*! Serves them right.'

'And Barker's Bookshop and—'

'They can all go to hell for all I care.'

Joe shrugged. 'You're the boss. But for God's sake ease up a bit or you will go off your nut.'

Sitting in the car desperately wondering where she could go or what she could do for two hours, Rory thought Joe could be right. It was becoming more and more difficult to relax and she couldn't even bear the thought of sitting talking to Victoria. Lighting up a cigarette, she was aware of the ragged snotty-nosed children crowding close and gawping at the Rover's sleek expensive appearance. They were staring at her too, at her eau-de-nil jumper suit, her long string of jet beads and jet drop earrings.

She stuck out her tongue and made a face at them before starting the engine. As she drove away they suddenly found courage and she could hear their raucous laughter and jeers.

At the next corner, she stopped again and bought an *Evening Citizen*. Then she found a quiet side-street further along where she could quickly leaf through the paper and find Donovan's column. Sure enough there he was in biting form, a regular crusader for the small struggling shop-keeper. She stubbed out her cigarette and lit another. She wanted to hate him. In a way she *did* hate him. All kinds of emotions were seething to boiling point and she didn't know how she was going to contain them.

CHAPTER FIFTY-SEVEN

Winston Churchill, editor of the government news-sheet, the *British Gazette*, lambasted the strikers, calling them 'the enemy' and their supporters 'Reds'. The way Victoria had gone on at Matthew, it was as if the strikers being tarred with a 'Red' brush was all his fault. Everything was his fault now. Anyone who heard the way she spoke to him would think that he was even to blame for the state of the buses, now windows had the holes boarded up to prevent further stones falling inside them. Drivers were protected from angry crowds of strikers by barbed wire — although Matthew had not been one of the violent men, always preferring reasoned argument to violent action. The barbed wire was fixed to the bonnets of buses to prevent strikers from getting at the engines. Policemen rode on the buses and trams as guards and as a result there were not enough policemen to go round. Again members of the public were recruited; they were supplied with steel helmets and truncheons and paid more than a miner's wage.

'Could you credit it?' Drummond said angrily at Rory, who had dropped into Victoria's while waiting to collect Annie from one of her visits to Cowlairs Road. 'Do you wonder that we are complaining? A pit labourer working like a damned slave gets £1.11s.7½d a week and not a halfpenny more. One of these so-called Special Constables gets £2.6s.3d per week, *plus* free accommodation, *plus* 2s.6d a day for food.'

'Don't swear in front of Jamie,' Victoria said.

'How long do you think it will last?' Rory wanted to know.

'I want it to last until the miners get a fair deal,' Drummond said, then added bitterly, 'but if Forbes-Cunningham has his way, he'll see them starve first.' Dour-faced, he went over to fiddle with the knobs on the wireless set, trying despite crackling noises to hear the news.

'How's the shop doing?' Victoria asked Rory.

'Fine.'

'Everything's so high-class.' Wistful dreaminess came to cloud Victoria's vision. 'Really superior. That sports department! I was intrigued when I saw these young people, so aristocratic-looking, sitting erect on that wooden horse wearing bowler hats.'

'They were trying out their new clothes for fit and comfort, especially the breeches, and the overall smartness of their appearance.'

Victoria shook her head. 'To think how you've got on from being a common rag-woman and now you've even got a motor car!' Her eyes focused again and hardened. 'Of course, you've got ambition. Not like some people.'

Suddenly Drummond burst out angrily. 'A sell-out, that's what it is!' He switched off the wireless in disgust. 'The TUC have ended the strike and left the miners to fight on alone and to starve.'

'Oh, thank God!' Victoria clasped her hands together in prayerful excitement. Then she hastily added, 'Of course, I'm terribly sorry for the poor miners and their wives and children. These past ten days have been more than long enough for me. I'll remember the miners and their families in my prayers tonight.'

'A lot of use that will be to a miner's wife and children! Prayers won't fill their bellies.'

Victoria turned to Rory. 'Isn't that awful? He's a wicked atheist, you know. He absolutely refuses to go to church with me. What a shocking example for his child.'

Rory lit a cigarette. 'He just gets upset about injustice.'

'He's wickedly contrary, that's all. If I said I didn't believe in God and refused to go to church — then he'd go.'

Drummond ran his fingers through his hair. 'Will you

two stop talking about me as if I wasn't here? And I'm not an atheist, Victoria. I'm an agnostic.'

'That's just typical of him,' Victoria continued to address Rory. 'He'd split any hair for the sake of an argument.'

'What has made the TUC suddenly give in, do you think, Matty?' Rory asked.

His eyes were beacons of anger. 'They say they've been given assurances by the Prime Minister that a settlement of the "mining problem", as the governemnt calls it, can be secured. Authur Cook, the president of the Miners' Federation, doesn't believe that and nor do I.'

Victoria said calmly, 'We'll just have to hope for the best. The poor wives — they're the ones I'm sorry for. It's they who'll starve first.'

'I'll put a collecting box in the shop,' offered Rory. 'It might raise enough to help somebody.'

Drummond suddenly came over and dropped a kiss on her head. 'Dear Rory — as practical as always. Hopefully other shopkeepers will follow your example and some worthwhile help can be given to local families.' His hands lingered warmly on her shoulders.

'Glad to be able to do something,' she said, stubbing out her cigarette. 'Now, it's time I was off. I really just meant to pop in with that basket of odds and ends and dash away again. I didn't mean to stay for a meal.'

Victoria rose with her. 'Goodness,' she said, 'as if I'd let you away without giving you something. Nobody's ever allowed to visit my house without at least having enjoyed a nice cup of tea.'

As the two friends made for the door, Drummond said, 'Goodbye, Rory.' She glanced round for a second and met his eyes and just for that second she saw such a dark hunger in them that she felt shocked.

'Thanks for all your help, Rory,' Victoria said. 'You're a true friend.' They kissed warmly.

Rory drove down Springburn Road and then turned off at the Cross into Cowlairs Road. This time her mother was visiting Mrs Docherty on the top flat — it was late, but Annie enjoyed a good long gossip with her cronies. The close swallowed Rory into its silent shadows and despite the bravely hissing gaslight she felt shivers of fear. Somehow she was more vulnerable to the stings of memory tonight. She remembered as a child braving these same shadows, racing through the damp urine smell, straining breathless and big-eyed up the stairs two at a time and shouting for someone to have the door open ready for her to dash into safety.

'O . . . pen! O . . . pen!'

It was a common enough cry in Glasgow closes at night.

She remembered too the horror of the rape. As she forced herself to walk and not run up the stairs, she heard again the sniggers, the grunts, the obscenities; she experienced again the anguish of shame. Her hand trembled as she lit a cigarette. Sucking in the smoke, she tried to reassure herself that such painful experiences were all in the past. She kept reaffirming to herself that she was safe. She belonged to a different world. She had money. She was a success. But still the arrows of fear kept shivering into her back, and the shadows sucked her in just the same as when she was poor. Somehow, tonight, she could not convince herself that she was safe.

'Oh hello, hen,' Mrs Docherty greeted her. 'Your Ma's not here. My Willie walked her up the hill and saw her safely into her house about an hour ago. But come in, you're welcome to a wee cup of tea.'

'No, thanks. It's late. And anyway, I had tea at Victoria's.'

'All right, hen, if you're sure.'

'Yes. Cheerio, Mrs Docherty.'

'Cheerio, hen.'

After the door shut she began walking daintily down the stairs, her heels clicking and echoing all around as if she was inside a drum. Nearing the foot, she could no longer bear to move slowly and sedately. The back close was a black mouth ready to suck her in. Not for years had she felt so vulnerable. She was in a terror of apprehension. She ran, she burst out on to the street like a thing possessed, fumbling frantically for the keys of her car. Then the car flew away like a white bird.

CHAPTER FIFTY-EIGHT

'Wait, Drummond,' Forbes-Cunningham said. 'I want to talk to you in private.'

Drummond felt uncomfortable. He sensed a social situation and experienced his usual urgency to escape and be safely by himself — although what kind of social situation, and why the need for one with Forbes-Cunningham, he could not imagine. The trouble and the danger lay in the fact that Forbes-Cunningham had not been himself since his son's death. He was obviously a broken man. More than that, though, he had been behaving most oddly, especially to Drummond. For one thing, he had stopped arguing with him. Oh, he still put up an opposing point of view, but it was mildness itself and almost deferential to Drummond's strongly held opinions. Drummond felt thrown off balance, confused and for some reason he couldn't fathom, secretly apprehensive. He began to actually long for the abrasive, self-centred, out-and-out Tory capitalist he had known and hated so much before.

Instead of a stimulating challenge to his brains and wits the Parish Council meetings and the committee meetings were becoming something of an ordeal. The other committee members were worried and uncomfortable, too; there were murmurings of, 'Poor chap, mind's become affected.'

Victoria could not help laughing when he told her. 'Just because he's being more friendly and agreeable to you? I can imagine how that's put the cat among the pigeons right enough. You should be glad.'

'Well, I'm not.'

'Oh, trust you!' Victoria rolled her eyes. 'Contrary as always.'

'I have another appointment, sir,' he told the older man.

'It's important,' Forbes-Cunningham said. 'Please sit down.'

The 'Please' unnerved Drummond and he sat down, silently cursing. Forbes-Cunningham's recent ridiculous behaviour towards him had only served to increase his bad feelings towards the man; he strongly resented being the focus of his pathetic attentions. Forbes-Cunningham would have been the first man to dismiss without a grain of sympathy the problems, mental or otherwise, of any poorhouse man who had suffered a bereavement. Drummond could quote actual cases to prove this. Only days before Edgar's death there had been a case where . . .

'It's important.' Forbes-Cunningham's repeated remark interrupted Drummond's thoughts. 'So important that I don't quite know how to begin. I want you to understand, you see.'

Drummond groaned inwardly. 'If it's about the McAulay case, Councillor Forbes-Cunningham, I understand perfectly . . .'

'No, no, it's not that. It's nothing to do with the Council work.'

'If that is so, Councillor, I certainly do not understand your reason for detaining me.' He made to rise. 'And as I said, I have another pressing engagement . . .'

'For God's sake.' To Drummond's horror, Forbes-Cunningham's voice broke. 'You've got to listen to me.'

'Councillor Forbes-Cunningham, you're not well. I strongly advise you to see a doctor.'

'Your mother used to work for my mother,' Forbes-Cunningham announced suddenly.

Drummond's voice went icy-cold. 'I am only too well aware of that fact.'

'I was young then and so was she. A fine-looking woman, your mother.'

'Not after she was worn down by working like a slave

for your family. My father was no great specimen of fine-looking, healthy manhood either, after working in the Forbes-Cunningham pit.'

'I am your father,' Forbes-Cunningham said.

The words dropped into a stunned silence. At first Drummond just stared incomprehendingly at the man. 'You're out of your mind!' he managed eventually. Yet a thousand small mysteries had clicked horrifyingly into place without him needing to remember them.

'I wanted to help her financially, but she wouldn't let me. A strange, independent woman, your mother. I see a lot of her in you. The worst of it was, I couldn't marry her. She was, after all, only a skivvy. My father would have . . .'

'I refuse to listen to another word of this.'

'Matthew!'

Drummond couldn't think, could hardly see for pains shooting through his head and across his eyes. The pain spread rapidly like a finger, gripping his chest and interfering with his breathing.

'Don't call me that!' he choked out.

Forbes-Cunningham's face was terrible to look at, a travesty of the man he had once been. 'Matthew, let me help you. It's the only thing that will make my life worth living now.'

Drummond couldn't stand being near the man a second longer. He would have died had Forbes-Cunningham reached out and touched him, as indeed he seemed about to do.

He turned and crashed from the room — not seeing where he was going and not caring as long as he got as far away as possible. Striding along the street at marathon pace, not heeding who he bumped into and was cursed by, his thoughts were racing far faster than his feet. He couldn't make sense of them and part of the time he believed they couldn't be true; Forbes-Cunningham had gone crazy, it was all a mistake. Those thoughts were little blessings of relief that soothed and relaxed him . . . But only for a second or two before the jumbled agonies would flood back. There could be no doubt that Forbes-Cunningham's revelation explained much that had puzzled him for a lifetime. John Drummond's words flew back to him: 'The lad's not going down the pit. I won't have it. I won't have you visiting the sins of the father on him . . .'

He had loved John Drummond and now he loved him even more. John Drummond had been a real father to him; he appreciated the man's true worth more than ever now and kept thinking 'If only he was alive so I could tell him.' He longed beyond all thought to touch him and with love enfold him in his arms.

Mixed with this anguish were poison darts of detestation of the man whose blood seeped like dirt through his veins. The knowledge made him an anathema to himself. The realization that his bad blood was something he could never escape from would drive him mad, he felt sure. It was impossible to come to terms with such an enormity.

Now, added to the repugnance he had always felt for Forbes-Cunningham and the abomination he had had for everything the man stood for, was the added rage against what he had done to his mother. Then he thought of all the years when John Drummond had slaved in the Forbes-Cunningham pit while so conscientiously and fairly caring for Forbes-Cunningham's son.

And Forbes-Cunningham knowing this and allowing him to slave . . .

Drummond just had time to stagger over to the gutter before being violently sick. Then, supporting himself against a lamp-post, he shivered and wiped his face and tried not to look at anyone in case he met their eyes and felt ashamed.

He began to think of having to go home. He felt ill. He thought of peace and the safety of familiar things; his front door bearing its brass nameplate and black letters saying 'Matthew Drummond'; his small welcoming lobby papered in sunshine yellow and very 'superior' as Victoria always said, with the oak hallstand, oval mirror, brass coat-hooks and brass stands for umbrellas. Then the front room, with the gold rayon curtains and matching bedspread and quilt on Jamie's bed; the kitchen with cheerful fireside, polished steel fender and fireside tools hanging on the gleaming stand which one of Victoria's brothers had given them as a wedding present. The cosy hole-in-the-wall bed high with patchwork quilt, and the bed-curtains and valance in the rose colour picked out from tones of the shades in the quilt. Their pride and joy, a ruby-red and fawn patterned carpet and two fireside chairs with loose floral covers. Not forgetting his gramophone. And his wireless.

He would go home now . . . listen to his wireless. If there was good music on he would lie back on his comfortable chair and close his eyes and forget everything.

Somehow he found his way through the jungle of Glasgow streets until eventually he reached Springburn Road. It never occurred to him to take a tram-car or a bus; it seemed so necessary to keep moving on his own volition, to keep physically occupied.

When he got home, he kept telling himself he would be all right. He'd rest. The pain would go. He'd forget. And he'd be all right.

But still his mother's face kept floating unbidden to his mind. He didn't want to understand her now and her attitude towards him. But he did. She had known about his bad blood. She had seen him only as part of Forbes-Cunningham; he had represented to her all that she resented and hated in her life. She had never loved him, he knew it. Yet, in his anguished heart, he loved her still.

CHAPTER FIFTY-NINE

Victoria clasped her hands ecstatically under her chin. She was almost airborne with joy.

'It's like a dream come true. A dream, a dream, a wonderful dream! I can't wait to tell Rory! She said she might drop in tonight too. Oh, fancy us being richer than her!'

'Don't be stupid, woman!' Drummond growled and lowered his brows in a desperate effort to hide his dangerously unbalanced emotions. He felt he couldn't stand any more; in his present state he believed he was only a hairs-breadth away from committing murder. 'As far as I'm concerned, it's a nightmare. Something I must try to forget.'

'Forget? Forget?' Victoria laughed. 'How can you forget that you're Forbes-Cunningham's son? Why should you want to forget it? He's one of the most powerful and wealthiest men in the whole country. Oh, think what he can do for Jamie. We need have no worries about his future.'

'Do you actually believe, Victoria, that I would accept one penny, one favour of any kind from that man?'

Nothing was going to spoil Victoria's finest hour. 'Don't be daft, he's not "that man". He's your father!'

Her eyes swam with dreamy delights; of fashionable furs and fabulous hats, of mansion houses and maids to do all the work, of pouring tea from a silver tea-pot and playing on a grand piano instead of the little old upright she had now. But most of all, she saw in her mind's eye her darling son growing up with every advantage life could offer. He could go to University now and train for any profession he had a mind to. He would never go hungry again. None of them would.

'He is *not* my father.'

'Och, don't be perverse, Matthew. You know fine he is.'

'As far as I'm concerned, the only man worthy of the name was the man who brought me up, John Drummond.'

'I know, I know. He was good to you and you thought a lot of him but . . .'

'Victoria, I loved him. *He* was my father.'

'Will you stay saying that?' Victoria's patience was beginning to fray at the edges; Matthew could be so irritating at times. She flipped a hand as if swatting him away. 'All right, you loved him. And I'm sure you did your best to be good to him when he was alive. But he's dead now, so let that be an end to it.'

'No, damn you! I will not let it be an end to it.'

'Oh, for goodness' sake, Matthew. You're just in one of your moods. This is so like you; you have every reason to rejoice, but you choose to do the opposite. There isn't another man in Springburn who wouldn't get down on his knees and thank his Maker for such a piece of luck.'

'Luck?' He couldn't understand how she could talk like this. The difference between them, the distance between them had never been more frightening.

'Yes, luck, luck!' Still clasping her hands under her chin, she began waltzing gaily around the kitchen.

He had to get away.

Blindly he made for the front door, then down the stairs and was soon swallowed up in the moving mass of Springburn humanity. He didn't know what to do, or where to go. But he seemed to naturally gravitate up to the Park. There on many previous occasions he had sought solace and privacy. Often he found a quiet corner to sit by himself and think, or commune with his diary.

The sun was shining, but an occasional sigh of wind rustled the leaves and gently lifted them. He found a secluded seat by the loch and gazed helplessly at a small bird, vigorous in its search for food, very upright between downward strikes of bill. Sometimes it almost danced as it chased some rapidly-moving prey in the shallows. Other birds came to splash and dip and wing-shake, giving a lively sparkle to the water.

He was reminded of the times when his father had brought him here as a child and helped him to view the natural world with wonder. He remembered one occasion when his mother had come too. She had brought bread spread with condensed milk and they had sat on the grass and eaten it. It was such a novelty to have his mother come with them that he could hardly take his eyes off her, her high smooth brow, her firm chin, the golden crown of her hair. Every second of her in such a setting had been precious to him. In his eyes she had always been beautiful, but her beauty was often drained and overshadowed by the drab poverty of her usual surroundings. Here, under the golden shimmer of the sun, leaning against the brown bark of a tree with its green shade rustling above her, he had never seen her look so relaxed and at peace.

They had stayed quite late and in the gathering dusk they made their way reluctantly home. His father had held his hand. His mother had walked a little in front, her long skirts swishing through the grass. He wished he could talk to her then and he wished he could talk to her now. But what was the use? The air became cooler as he sat; the sun had faded away and a cool breeze from the loch made him shiver. He felt calmer, however, and he rose and walked home taking deep cleansing breaths.

Jamie was in bed and asleep. Victoria was tidying away his clothes and toys, jauntily singing to herself as she worked: 'I'm Sitting on Top of the World . . .' Seeing him, she said, 'Oh, hallo, dear. Been for one of your wee walks, have you?'

It was a long time since she had called him 'dear'.

He nodded.

'Do you feel like your tea now?'

'I'm not hungry. But I'd enjoy a cup of tea.'

'The kettle's boiling, I'll make one in a jiffy. I feel like one myself. Where did you go? Up to the Park?'

'Yes.'

'You didn't call in to "The Towers" then?'

He made no comment.

'They say his wife's dying, poor soul. She had been ill of course — cancer, I think — but she was holding her own. Since Edgar's death she hasn't the will to live any more, they say. And who could blame her!'

She made the tea, poured out two cups and milked and sugared them. She seemed idyllically happy, as if she had never heard one word he said earlier. Sometimes Drummond thought she was quite incredible.

He drank his tea.

'When will you see your father?' she asked as she sipped daintily at hers.

'I told you. My father's dead.'

She sighed. 'Now, we're not going to start all that again, are we? All right, be awkward if you like. When will you next see Mr Forbes-Cunningham?'

'There's a meeting of the Parish Council tomorrow afternoon.'

'Good. I expect he'll want to invite both of us up to "The Towers", but I think first of all you should insist that he calls on us here. That way, he'll see our situation at first hand and without further delay.' She patted her hair. 'I'm not ashamed of this house and he'll be made welcome with a nice cup of tea and a home-baked scone as good if not better than any he's had at "The Towers". All the same, he's bound to see that this place is not good enough for his son and his grandson to live in — not good enough by a long chalk. He'll feel ashamed, I'm sure.'

'Victoria,' Drummond said quietly, 'will you please stop talking nonsense? I'm sorry, but as far as I'm concerned nothing has changed and nothing is going to change. I propose to ignore what Forbes-Cunningham said to me today as if he'd never said it. That means we'll never see the inside of "The Towers", nor will Forbes-Cunningham ever set foot inside this house. Even if he wanted to, I would not allow it. Now do you understand once and for all what I'm saying? Nothing has changed.'

'You can't mean that,' Victoria scoffed. 'You've had a bit of a shock, but you'll feel differently about it tomorrow.'

'No, I will not, Victoria.'

'But you can't!'

'I'm tired, I've been up to my eyes in Council and Union business all day. Now I'll have to get to bed and try to get some sleep.'

'Don't you dare go to bed until this is settled!' Victoria cried.

'It is settled,' he said wearily.

'No, it is not. You're not going to throw Jamie's future away for no reason at all. You're not going to ruin his life, I won't let you.'

'I have no intention of ruining Jamie's life.'

'That means you'll accept everything Forbes-Cunningham can offer you and more, then?'

'No, it does not, Victoria. It means that I continue to love Jamie as I've always done. It means that I continue to work as hard as I can to keep him until he can work himself.'

'Love him? You don't love him!'

'Victoria, please . . .'

'How can you when you're wanting to throw away his heritage? If you refuse Mr Forbes-Cunningham now, he could turn away from you again. He could disown you and not even leave you a penny piece in his will.'

'Victoria, I refuse to take part in this conversation any longer. I'm going to bed.'

'You can't be like this, Matthew, you just can't!'

Ignoring her, he tugged off his tie and began unbuttoning his shirt.

'If you don't see sense and see it now, I'll never forgive you. I've put up with your moods and your stupid perverse behaviour for years and I've forgiven you over and over again, but not this time, Matthew, I'm warning you.'

He stripped and climbed into the sanctuary of the bed, but even there he found no peace from Victoria's voice.

'You'll be nice to that man tomorrow, do you hear? You'll accept him as your real father and be grateful and thankful for all the help he offers. If you don't, Matthew . . . if you don't, you'll be sorry. Do you hear me, Matthew? You'll be sorry . . .'

CHAPTER SIXTY

Drummond was on his way to meet his new engine, something that normally would have delighted and excited him.
But at the moment his thoughts had no such sharpness,
his attention was dulled. He did not even see the Salvation
Army band, smartly turned out in their navy blue and
scarlet uniforms, coming marching along Springburn Road
towards the Wellfield corner and the foot of the steep
Avenue Road. They were watched by women leaning from
tenement windows, some elderly and smoking clay pipes.
At the corner the Band took their stance, made their circle,
blew their trumpets and banged their tambourines. A
crowd of people including barefoot children and women
in tartan shawls gathered around them. Men in caps and
mufflers lounging at the street corners perked up slightly,
as if grateful for the diversion. Matthew passed them
without stopping.

Despite having no peace from Victoria's bitterness and
hatred, he could remember the sweet days of their courting,
and with what hope and love and gratitude he had looked
forward to his wedding day. He remembered how, hand-
in-hand, with so much pride and happiness they had first
viewed the house in which they were going to spend the
rest of their lives together.

He remembered the first night of their marriage when
he had stumbled into the house and couldn't find any
matches to light the gas. And how, much later, they
laughed until the tears ran down their cheeks at the
incident. In the past, Victoria had always forgiven him
for his quick temper and all his other faults. Relating to

393

friends stories about his eccentricities, in a humorous way, had become one of her party pieces — almost as popular as her cheerful piano playing or earnest, high-bosomed singing.

Afterwards, if he had not been at the gathering, she would say, 'Matthew, I wish you'd been there! What a laugh we had. I was telling them about that time you . . .'

And then they would laugh together.

There was nothing funny, however, about his last 'outrage'. Or at least, what Victoria saw as an outrage. Victoria's sense of humour could not stretch that far. He didn't blame her; he understood how she felt. If only she would make some attempt to understand his feelings . . .

But she had become so consumed with hatred of him that he could not reach any closeness with her any more. Every time he opened his mouth, even to Jamie, Victoria's voice would scrape at him like a claw and try to draw blood. If he corrected Jamie for some wrongdoing, immediately Victoria would say, 'You're a fine one to talk! What right have you to criticize an innocent child? A child you've denied his birthright. You're not fit even to go near him.'

There was no way he could avoid Victoria's bitter, warped tongue. He sat at home buried in his Union books or Council work, glad now that he often had to take time off driving so as to attend Council meetings. But even his retreat into books did not save him from being a target for Victoria. Working about the room, she would keep passing his tense, hunched back and aiming daggers of words at it.

'Oh yes, you're very devoted and conscientious about your work! a pity you've never been able to give any of that conscientiousness and devotion to your family's welfare.' Or, 'Your Union members and the other strangers you help through your Council committees must think you're almost saintly. Such a help to everyone! If only they knew what your false pride has done to ruin your marriage and deny your son the kind of life he deserves.'

It was still summer, but he could feel a cold wind knifing through the thin material of his suit jacket as he walked. Suddenly John Drummond came unbidden to his mind and he saw a picture of him when they lived in the miners' row. It was winter and he had been watching at the window for his father coming home from night-shift at the pit. Usually he was still in bed and the big figure would burst into the room and shout, 'Come on, lazy-bones, up you get!'

He had thought his father was unique, larger than life. Somebody extra special who could put the world to rights. He had been quite a militant figure in the Miners' Union then. On this particular morning he had awakened early and run to press his face against the window and watch for his father coming. He remembered so vividly now what he had seen and felt.

Against the grey early morning sky was silhouetted a bedraggled band of weary black-faced humanity. His father was only one of many whose life's blood and joy of living was being callously exploited and drained away. He had wondered then as he wondered now at man's inhumanity to man. Not content with exploiting men in ordinary everyday living, the powers-that-be tossed them by the million into the cauldron of war.

Now a terrible depression swept over him as he remembered his father. How often had he seen him walking along as he was doing now, with cap pulled down, shoulders hunched against the cold wind and hands stuffed into trouser pockets. For a terrible moment, all his father's dreams and his own optimistic ambitions of reaching an apex of personal development and potential seemed only a mockery, a treadmill of working men's hopes that led nowhere. He saw millions of men like his father and himself moving along a giant conveyor belt of life and disappearing without trace as if they had never existed. Or had existed to no purpose except to feather the nests of men like Forbes-Cunningham whose faces never got dirty.

Victoria was right. It was his pride which had caused

him to refuse to be one of the Forbes-Cunninghams.

He was also too proud to admit defeat. He would go on fighting for his own class until the day he died. Victoria said he had a choice: his marriage, his wife and family — or his fellow workers. He had recently been put forward — in competition with several other men in Scotland — for a place on the Union's National Executive. The vote had gone in his favour. It meant being in London for three years as a full-time, paid Union official. He had known from the first time when the idea was mooted that this was the path that he must follow. It would be a lonely one, he realized that. In the first place, it would never even occur to Victoria to come with him. Indeed, he had seen in her eyes and bearing the first softening in his presence for many months when he had told her the result of the election. Not that the softening was directed *at* him; it was more a subtle relaxing of the tension needed to pursue her bitterness and hatred. It was a slight misting of the eyes as she visualized being free of him for long spells at a time and able to enjoy her home and child and friends without the irritant of his presence. It also gave her own pride a straw to catch on to; her cool but interested questions indicated this.

'Oh? Quite an important job, is it?'

'It's important to me.'

She didn't look as if she'd heard him, but answered herself: 'I suppose it must be if it's in London. None of my friends' husbands have ever worked in London.'

'I'll miss you and Jamie,' he said. 'I'll come home as often as I can, of course. I don't start until the autumn.'

'It will be a collar-and-tie job, won't it?'

'Oh yes.' He couldn't help sounding bitter, but she hadn't noticed.

'And what happens after the three years? Do you go back to working on engines? Surely not,' she answered herself.

But he said, 'I could eventually be elected to the post of District Organizer for the Union.'

Victoria's shoulders pushed back and her head tipped up. 'That sounds a very superior position and you're bound to get it.'

He sighed and tried to dismiss her from his mind and concentrate on thoughts of his present work. He had been on the Dock Pilot for a few shifts; it was an easy leisurely job — dodging about the dockside, looking at the coolies or any ladies who happened to pass; then sitting on the engine writing in his diary after the firemen went home. He was never in a hurry to go home to Victoria these days. Occasionally he would call in to see Rory, her shop being so near the river. He attempted to enter from round the back, not wanting to give her a showing up before any of her posh customers. In his greasy overalls and with soot-streaked face, he knew he looked very out of place in the plush sanctuary of the front shop. Rory, being Rory, would not hear of it, however.

'No friend of mine need feel he has to sneak in the back way. Walk through the front and to hell with them!'

Once she had been on her way out for a meal and invited him to accompany her. The idea horrified him, but Rory laughed. 'Wash yourself in my bathroom — I've a room upstairs I use when I'm working too late to go home. There's a bathroom next to it — and you can help yourself to a suit.'

It wasn't just his appearance which made him refuse — it was the idea of her paying for his meal. Again Rory had laughed at him, this time through a haze of cigarette smoke. 'You're so old-fashioned, Matty, but I could give you the money beforehand and you could pay the bill, so nobody would know.'

Her pert face had a hard look, but he realized it was just caused by the make-up she wore. Her eyebrows had been plucked and replaced by a pencilled arch; she wore mascara and a special powder to hide her freckles, and of course her usual bright challenge of a lipstick. On that occasion, after sticking stubbornly to his refusal, he had watched her slip into the driving seat of her white car, making a startling and expensive picture in her mauve cloche hat and matching crêpe dress with its froth of black feathers as a belt round her hips. With a cheery backward wave she was off. He was proud of her and their deepening friendship. Life was strange. Rory had her path to follow too — a very different one from his. Maybe there was a lesson to be learned here. He made a mental note to explore the general question of relationships in his journal the next time he had an opportunity.

However, there would be fewer opportunities now that he was off the Dock Pilot. He had to work the new engine until he was due to take up his London job.

On the Dock Pilot he had had time to think as he sat frying an egg or a bit of bacon on his shovel. It had been warm these past few shifts and sometimes a white haze from the River Clyde made it difficult to see the clock above the swing-bridge. Or black smoke from a Clan boat at the other side of the dock would rise in a fat, straight column. His lazy imagery soon evaporated when he reached Eastfield; he had plenty of time to get to know the new engine and settled down to treasure and savour every minute of it.

'Glasgow Lass', she was called and neglect cried out from every pore. Even the touch of the handrails as he climbed up to the cab told him they needed loving attention. Once in the cab, he wiped the driving seat clean of ash-dust and then settled down to have a good look around. He decided to work his way across the controls and write down everything that needed attention. He discovered that the vacuum brake application handle only required a touch to send it into 'full on'. A piece of string hanging from the governor casing was obviously used for tying up the handle to prevent it from shaking 'on' whenever the engine started to run. He cut the string, threw it away and made a careful note in his book.

The gauge column cocks needed all his strength to move; he noted this and the fact that the gauge glasses were showing a half-inch mourning ring at the bottom.

He shut and opened the throttle handle several times, positioned it at various openings and touched the handle lightly. Like the brake handle, it moved too easily to 'shut' and that also went into his book. Then he went round his engine from tender to engine-buffers and put down every single thing he could find which called for the attention he would make sure she received. Lastly, he stood over on the other road where he could appreciate the 'Glasgow Lass' from one end to the other. She was bedraggled, dirty, and dejected, but he didn't see the dirt; he saw what he could make of her and he vowed that as long as they ran together she would never again look neglected or dejected.

Soon she was shining from stem to stern, everything functioning to perfection; she was his pride and joy. He loved everything about trains. Often, before he was married, he would go into town to pass a pleasant hour in one of the big railway stations. Then he would saunter along admiring the giant, long-distance engines and their long line of carriages. He thrilled at the whole sense of adventure of the place: the station foreman blowing his whistle and causing passengers who had been gathering round tea-trolleys to hurry into the carriages; the metallic tap, tap, tap of the wheel-tapper; porters banging doors shut; the driver looking expectantly out of his window. Then the engine beginning to make its purring sound, impatient to be off, and the guard blowing his whistle and waving his green flag, followed by the shrill whistle of the engine as the train moved forward and the sight of the engine's chimney sending forth short, sharp beats of exhaust as the pace quickened. Rapidly the carriages passed away — the soft 'dit-dit, dit-dit' over the rail points becoming quicker as each carriage went by. The last coach and its tail-lamp disappeared, the merry 'chuff, chuff' of the engine getting fainter and faster. In a moment the train was out of sight and out of hearing, leaving him with the echo of excitement in his head and heart.

At times like these, it was good to be alive, good to be

a railwayman. The best time of all of course was when he was driving his own engine and feeling at one with it, singing along the steel highway. The thrill of speed, the glorious noise of roaring fire and rushing steel sent energy, pride and freedom surging through his veins. At such times his personal problems completely evaporated and he felt a lucky man. He felt it was possible to move mountains.

CHAPTER SIXTY-ONE

The gaslights glimmered fitfully through the wet curtain of fog drifting across Glasgow from the river. It alternately shrouded and exposed the four silhouettes which strode purposefully down the slab pavement of Stockwell Street. Foreshortened shadows gave them a solid neanderthal bulk, filling the pavement, overflowing into the gutter as they approached their destination.

They bunched close round the entrance to 'Rory's', condensation starring their heavy moustaches. One of the men pulled off his muffler, wrapped it tightly round his fist and rammed it through the glass panel. With a practised dexterity he reached in to unlock the shop door. Then as one, the four men were absorbed into the darkness. Open razors seemed to jump into every hand as they swept like a tidal wave of destruction down the length of the central hall of the shop, kicking displays, slashing cloth, breaking mirrors.

Rory and her brothers had been stocktaking and because they had been working until after midnight and were exhausted, they had decided to sleep on the premises. Joe, Benny and Coll crushed into the dormitory up in the attics used by the other male employees. Rory went to her own small room on the first floor. That was why she heard the noise first . . .

Since one of the staff had fallen down the stairs and broken a leg, the gaslights on the stairs and the back corridor were left on low during the night in case any of the employees had to get up and go to the lavatory. As a result, Rory was able to see her way. The noise seemed to have stopped by the time she reached the downstairs corridor. Still dazed with sleep, she tied her silk dressing-gown closer, and then turned up the gas so that she could check that everything was as it should be. Without think-ing, she opened the door that led to the main hall, but it was an action she instantly regretted. In a tomblike silence only broken by the all-pervading hiss of the lights at her back she saw the hunched figures. She started to slam the door, but they burst towards her.

Rory turned and raced screaming along the corridor, stumbling and bouncing from wall to wall in panic. It was her nightmare come true. Suddenly she was dragged back to all the horrors she had fought so hard to leave behind her. Somehow, in some shadowy nightmare corner of her mind, she had always known that she would never be free. Now shadows had caught up with her. Rough hands were tearing and clawing at her night-clothes; she felt the material give up the unequal struggle and abandon her with a harsh ripping sound.

Her brothers had slept through the racket of crashing display stands and breaking glass, but they heard the high-pitched screaming. Dressed only in the underpants they'd been sleeping in, they raced towards the sound, flying down the stairs, their bare feet only occasionally slapping against the wooden floor. Like hurricanes they swept along the corridor and the two men at the rear turned in surprise. Joe grabbed the lapels of the nearest and, his head tucked down in his chest, in one fluid motion he thrust forward. His forehead smashed into the man's nose, pulping it across his broad cheeks and making the man's head, still wearing his flat cap, jerk against the wall. As he slid down, blood and mucus was stringing from the lower part of his face. Benny had done much the same to the second man and was already grabbing the third. But young Coll, smaller and thinner and less practised than his brothers, had not been so successful with the fourth; a razor flashed with light before arcing down and sending a line of fire burning him from forehead to chin. Howling with rage at the bright carmine blood spraying in a fine mist from his young brother's face, Joe pounced on the assailant, knocking his arms back against the wall and at the same time crashing his knee into the man's groin.

The high-pitched shriek of a police-whistle galvanized the intruders into a desperate surge of action. They managed to break free and ran from the corridor, pursued by Joe and Benny, through the hall and out of the shop. The fog was on their side. They disappeared towards the river with gang slogans echoing in jeering defiance before the night silence of the city reasserted itself.

They came like vultures next morning. Reporters from the *Herald*, the *Record*, the *Express*, the *Bulletin*, the *Evening Times* . . . and Donovan.

Rory had managed to get the shattered windows and doors boarded up during the night, but had left the rest of the damage until first light of day. Then she had stood in silence surveying the hall. It looked like a battleground with stiff bodies in tattered clothing strewn haphazardly around. She felt physical pain at the sight of the desecrated clothes and anger boiled up and overflowed.

'Don't just stand there gawping!' she snapped at the staff. 'Strip off all the slashed clothes and replace them with new outfits. Get rid of all this broken glass; get new glass shelves out of store and — Johnny, come through to my office at once. I've some posters for you to do.'

Johnny Andrews, one of the assistants in 'gents' hire', had an artistic flair and had drawn posters for her before. In no time the boarded-up windows and doors were emblazoned with defiant notices to the effect that nothing and nobody was going to intimidate Rory and prevent her from continuing to give first-class service and supply the highest quality merchandize at the lowest possible prices. Nothing but the best was good enough for Rory's customers. She had just finished phoning in an advert to all the papers, couched in the same terms, when the reporters arrived.

'You never give up, do you?' she said to Donovan.

'Give up what?'

'But it's not going to work. I've a lot more spunk in me than you think.'

'Oh, I've never doubted you were spunky, sweetheart. I saw your posters outside — very typical I thought.'

'I'm going to do more than put up posters. I'm going to see my lawyers.'

'Good for you!'

'You're not going to get away with this.'

'Are you suggsting that the break-in was my fault?'

'You know it was. Your articles about the poor, hard-done-by-small shopkeepers have stirred up so much ill-feeling against me that this has been the result.'

'You're distorting the facts.'

'*I'm* distorting the facts?' she cried incredulously.

He shrugged. 'I've written a few light-hearted, amusing pieces about your business methods.'

'They may have been written in your usual facetious style,' she said, 'but they concerned how I was stocking everything which previously had been the sole livelihood of small individual shops.'

'Well, aren't you?'

'You're not going to get away with it,' she repeated. 'You'll be hearing from my solicitor.'

He grinned at her. 'Honey, I haven't worked on newspapers all these years without being very careful about the law of libel. All you'll end up with is legal fees.'

Even in the full heat of her anger, she suspected he was right and it made her angrier still. 'I despise you,' she said. 'You could have got my brother killed. His face was slashed with a razor.'

'Listen, you can't blame me if some crazy shopkeepers, or whoever hired a gang of thugs to break into your place and attack your brother. I've a job to do and I do it, that's all. You can't muzzle the press because there are some crazy or violent people around. And talking of violent people, sweetheart, your brothers are no strangers to violence. I'd play down that angle if I were you.'

'Get out of my shop!'

His hard knowledgeable eyes roamed around the place. 'I don't blame you for being mad at the break-in. You've obviously worked like a Trojan and stopped at nothing to get all this. I take my hat off to you; you've come a long way since Cowlairs Road.'

He had gone too far. Somehow it was the last straw, the idea of him going to Cowlairs Road, digging around her roots. It didn't upset her from a snobbish angle; she couldn't care a damn about that. Indeed, her background was one of the things she had used to her advantage, shocking people with it, using it to cock a snook at them, forcing admiration from them despite it . . . because of it. With him it made her feel strangely exposed and vulnerable. Maybe it was only delayed shock after the trauma of the break-in.

Whatever the reason she was horrified to feel in imminent danger of bursting into tears.

'Get out!' she repeated.

As she made her way blindly to her office at the back of the shop, she prayed that her hard bullets of words had betrayed none of the distress she felt. She barely reached the safety of the office when the tears came; she collapsed over her desk and sobbed wildly, helplessly.

CHAPTER SIXTY-TWO

It was disturbing how Donovan's presence lingered. For hours, indeed days after he had gone she still felt the force of his stare. The timbre of his deep voice still reverberated around her. She wandered about the shop.

She saw the tasteful drapings, the artfully displayed clothes and accessories, the myriad items of merchandize she had introduced. The trees of leather gloves, the rich rivers of material, the rainbows of ribbons. She saw the tea display with its cheerful painting of two ladies enjoying a pot of 'Rory's Famous Blend' — and the poem underneath which ran:

> A tea beneficial, a beautiful blend;
> A tea mild and mellow that none can mend;
> A tea strong and sunny, tasty and luscious;
> A National tea, tea quite nutritious;
> A capital tea, choice too and cheerful,
> The price of it, too, is not at all fearful.

She saw the greenery she had had put in the central well of the main hall and the fountain of water jetting gently up from it and then pattering gently down. She saw the brassbound trunks and tartan travelling rugs. She saw the colourful mountains of books.

But grafted across everything and more vividly demanding her attention was Donovan's rough tanned skin. Donovan's hard cleft chin, Donovan's slate-grey eyes. The easy fluid way his muscular body moved with its hint of swagger quickened all her senses; she kept having to retreat to her office to soothe herself with a cigarette. She kept challenging herself: was she going to allow a tough ex-Gorbals boy to get the better of her? Not bloody likely! She had not clawed her way up to this level to be dragged down by anybody, for any reason.

Rory stared at herself in the mirror. The woman who stared unblinkingly back at her was fashionably attired in a mastic yellow dress with an artificial posy of flowers pinned on one shoulder. She was slim and neat-featured, but not delicate looking. There was a wiry toughness about her which seemed to emanate from inside as much as from the exterior.

She was nobody's fool. She closed her eyes, urging herself, pleading with herself to remember that.

'He's been here?' Rory was horrified. 'Donovan?'

Victoria said, 'Actually he turned out to be quite a nice man. He stayed for tea and we all got on like a house on fire in the end.'

'He came to interview me,' Drummond explained, 'About my election to the national executive. I'm leaving for London soon. Quite a few of the reporters have been here.'

'It's all very exciting!' Victoria was flushed with pleasure and self-importance. 'One of the papers took photographs of Matthew and Jamie and me.'

Rory was shattered to the roots of her being. Donovan here? Trying to turn her best and dearest friends against her?

'Are you feeling all right, Rory?' Drummond asked. 'You look pale.'

'I hope . . .' She stared anxiously at them and both Matthew and Victoria stared back at her in sympathetic expectancy.

'You hope what, dear?' Victoria prompted.

'I hope he hasn't been trying to turn you against me.'

'As if anyone could!' Victoria scoffed. 'Fancy you thinking such a thing!'

Drummond leaned over and dropped a comforting kiss on her forehead. 'Victoria spent the whole time singing your praises — I couldn't get a word in. She told him how you'd been a really good friend to his father, always trying to help him and cheer him up. And how it was his father's depression after his wife's death that had been the ruination of his shop. He just didn't care about business any more — you did, that was all.'

'Matthew got his word in all right,' Victoria reassured her. 'He told him what a good friend you'd been to us too — helping us during the strike and everything. Of course I told him that I'd known you even longer than Matthew — ever since we were children in fact — and I'd always known you were special. A very superior type of girl.'

Rory couldn't help laughing. 'Oh, Victoria!'

Victoria's handsome head tipped up. 'Well, it's the truth.'

'He's a bit hard-nosed,' Drummond said. 'I suppose he has to be with his job. But apart from that I think our encounter went very well. I felt we had a lot in common.'

'What? You and Donovan?' Yet she supposed, thinking about it, that they were both crusaders in their own way. 'Oh well,' she added with a twist of bitterness in her voice, 'that's life!'

'I told him,' Victoria said, 'that he'd been very hard and unfair on you and had dreadfully upset you.'

'Damn it, Victoria!' Rory was angry now. 'You shouldn't have said that.'

'It was the truth,' Victoria protested indignantly. 'And I was only trying to help you.'

Drummond said, 'You always go too far, Victoria; that's your trouble. I keep telling you not to interfere so much in people's private business. You've never had any respect for other people's rights to privacy.'

'Oh, you mean allowing you to live like a selfish bachelor,' Victoria said bitterly, 'instead of forcing you to accept your responsibilities as a married man? Not to interfere in your life because you're a separate private person?'

'Yes, I am a separate person entitled to some privacy.'

'No, you are not! You're my husband and that means you're part of me — it said that in the marriage ceremony. God has joined us together whether you like it or not.'

Rory groaned. She had heard Victoria and Matthew battling often enough before, but it was more than she could bear at the moment. The thought of Victoria betraying her innermost feelings to Donovan — however unwittingly — terrified her. It flung her straight back into the painful vulnerability of her youth; she was right down in the pit again and this time not knowing how to claw her way up.

For Donovan to know her physical weakness and take cruel advantage of it was bad enough. But for him to become aware of other areas of vulnerability, to know her as a whole person, was to give him weapons to hurt the whole of her — to leave her without any defence. She had thought he had gone from her life, but now she was certain he would seek her out again; he wouldn't miss this chance. And of course she was right.

He was waiting outside the shop when she left next evening. Ignoring him, she unlocked her car and slid in to the driver's seat. Before she could start the engine, however, he had opened the other door and thumped his big body on to the seat beside her.

'You've a bloody nerve,' she said.

There was a glimmer of humour in his eyes as he looked round at her. 'I know.'

'Get out!'

'So have you. Maybe we're two of a kind?'

'Get out of my car, I said.'

He ignored her.

'I'm on my way home to Springburn. If you don't get out right now, then you'll have to find your way back from there.'

He shrugged. 'So be it.'

She started the car, distressingly aware of his nearness,

409

the aggressive male ambience of him. 'I don't see the point of this,' she said.

'Don't you?'

'Looking for more copy, are you?'

'Fair enough. I deserved that.'

'You deserve a lot more than that!'

'All right, we got off on the wrong foot and things have gone from bad to worse. I admit it.'

'Great!' she said sarcastically. 'That solves everything.' She could feel him staring at her in the silence that followed and his eyes, so coolly appraising, made it difficult to concentrate on the road.

At last he said, 'No, it doesn't solve everything but it's a start.'

Nothing more was said for the rest of the journey. The prolonged silence was an agony to her, yet she was afraid to break it.

Reaching Broomfield Road, she stopped the car and said abruptly, 'Right, this is it. Goodbye!'

'It's never goodbye with us, sweetheart.' Before she could latch on to any threatening nuances in his words, his arm was along the back of her seat, his fingers were digging into her shoulder, forcing her towards him. He tilted his head and found her lips.

It wasn't fair, she thought. Life wasn't fair. Why should she feel this deep stirring of passion, this awakening flame, this fever of need for a man like him? She could have wept at the unfairness of it.

'Darling!'

'Don't call me that. Just get out of my car!'

This was a man who had done nothing but hurt her; a man who had been responsible for plunging her back into a nightmare of violence; a ruthless man. A man, in fact, who had hurt her far more deeply than any other.

He hesitated, then suddenly opened the door and swung himself out. 'I'll be in touch,' he told her before slamming the door shut again.

'Don't bother.' She sat gripping the wheel, watching

410

...ll figure stride away before getting out herself.

The blancoed tenement stair in Broomfield Road had a superior smell of pine disinfectant. The walls were covered half-way up in sea-green tiles with blood-red designs on them. Victoria said they were very superior; it was her idea of heaven to live up a tiled close.

'When my ship comes in,' she often said to Rory, 'I'll move to a tiled close.'

Rory's thoughts clung desperately to her friend as she climbed the stone stairs. Victoria now seemed comparatively happy; her hopes had taken a tentative lift ever since hearing of Matthew's London job. She still nursed bitterness against him, but kept testing new ground with a cautious truce.

Rory was glad for Matty's sake, glad too of his London appointment. He would do a lot of good for the workers. She doubted, however, whether he would get much thanks for it all in the end. He was a strange man. She could understand only too well Victoria's anger and despair over his attitude to Forbes-Cunningham; it was just as well that it had been Victoria who married him and not her. All that money and the influence and security it could have given him! Maybe he would gain influence through his political work, of course, but she doubted if it would ever make him a fortune.

Thoughts of Matty only added to her distress and confusion. Once she had loved him with all the passion that was in her. She still remembered the anguish and hurt she had suffered as a result.

Now even deeper and stronger passions were rocking the very foundations of her life — just when she had felt safe and strong and unassailable.

She fumbled for the doorkey, willing the foolish tears not to spill over again — glad, yet sad at the fact that she'd packed Annie and Scrap and the girls off for a late holiday down the river to Rothesay. She needed the empty house in which to hide the shameful weakness of her tears. Yet the still silent void of the place penetrated any defence

411

she had left, suddenly releasing the trickle of tears in a torrent of violent sobbing. She ran to her bedroom and flung herself face-down on to the bed. There she punched the quilt with clenched fists until she exhausted herself. Then out of the exhaustion came resolve as her spunky spirit came swaggering back. She'd show him! She'd show them all! There could be no stopping her. She had the biggest shop in Glasgow now. Another site was going vacant at the posh end of town — in Sauchiehall Street. Why shouldn't she aim for that? If she could expand to different departments in one building, she could expand to different buildings in different locations.

Then another idea struck her as she moved restlessly about the house, smoking cigarettes and drinking coffee. Why shouldn't she also acquire one of the posh villas on the Balgray? By God, that would be a smack in the eye for all the snobby golfers and bridge-players who had had the place to themselves since it came into existence. An ex-ragwoman living in their hallowed midst. She couldn't help smiling, she even laughed out loud. She would do it!

The thought of positive impudent action cheered her up and kept her going for the next few days. It enabled her to be genuinely too busy to see Donovan to talk to him on the phone on the many occasions he tried to contact her — until, arriving at her usual table for lunch in Miss Buik's in Argyle Street, she was joined by him.

'This is a reserved table,' she informed him.

'I love your hat,' he said, taking off his own and putting it on the other vacant chair. 'The feathers curling round your face like that soften it.'

'You mean I'm hard-faced.'

'No.' She wished he wouldn't stare at her the way he did. He had such penetrating, knowledgeable eyes. 'You're a tough little devil, though,' he added.

'This is still a reserved table,' she reminded him.

'Honest too, in your own way.'

'Oh, thanks.'